THE WHITE PRINCESS

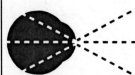 This Large Print Book carries the
Seal of Approval of N.A.V.H.

THE COUSINS' WAR

THE WHITE PRINCESS

PHILIPPA GREGORY

LARGE PRINT PRESS
A part of Gale, Cengage Learning

GALE
CENGAGE Learning·

Farmington Hills, Mich • San Francisco • New York • Waterville, Maine
Meriden, Conn • Mason, Ohio • Chicago

GALE
CENGAGE Learning·

Copyright © 2013 by Philippa Gregory.
Large Print Press, a part of Gale, Cengage Learning.

LIBRARY OF CONGRESS CATALOGING-IN-PUBLICATION DATA

Gregory, Philippa.
  The White Princess : The Cousins' War / by Philippa Gregory.
    pages cm. — (Thorndike Press Large Print Basic) (The Cousins' War ; 5)
    ISBN 978-1-4104-5978-7 (hardcover) — ISBN 1-4104-5978-0 (hardcover)
    1. Elizabeth, Queen, consort of Edward IV, King of England, 1437?–1492—Fiction. 2. Great Britain—History—Edward IV, 1461–1483—Fiction. 3. Historical fiction. 4. Large type books. I. Title.
PR6057.R386W53 2013
823'.914—dc23   2013023576

ISBN 13: 978-1-59413-727-3 (pbk. : alk. paper)
ISBN 10: 1-59413-727-7 (pbk. : alk. paper)

Published in 2014 by arrangement with Touchstone, a division of Simon & Schuster, Inc.

Printed in the United States of America
1 2 3 4 5   18 17 16 15 14

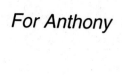

For Anthony

1485

SCOTLAND

IRELAND

Dublin
Sheriff
Hutton
Wexford
Stoke
Waterford
Bosworth
Northampton
London
Blackheath
Exeter
Portsmouth
Calais
Antwerp
FLANDERS
Malines
LOW COUNTRIES
Isle of Wight
Tournai

Paris

BURGUNDY

FRANCE

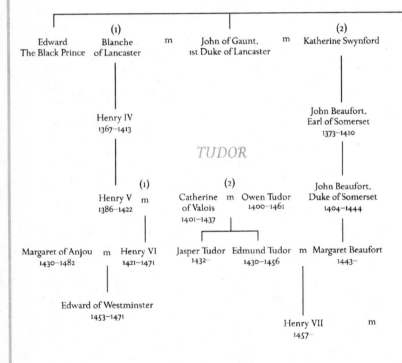

THE COUSINS AT WAR

The Houses of York, Lancaster
and Tudor in Spring 1485

 LANCASTER

| Edward
The Black Prince | (1)
Blanche
of Lancaster | m | John of Gaunt,
1st Duke of Lancaster | m | (2)
Katherine Swynford |

Henry IV
1367–1413

John Beaufort,
Earl of Somerset
1373–1410

TUDOR

| | (1) | | (2) | | |

Henry V m   Catherine m Owen Tudor   John Beaufort,
1386–1422   of Valois   1400–1461   Duke of Somerset
                  1401–1437   1404–1444

Margaret of Anjou m Henry VI   Jasper Tudor   Edmund Tudor m Margaret Beaufort
1430–1482   1421–1471   1432–   1430–1456   1443–

Edward of Westminster
1453–1471

Henry VII   m
1457–

Edward III
1312 – 1377

YORK

Edmund,   m   Isabelle
Duke of York   of Castille
1341–1402

Richard,
Earl of Cambridge
1385–1415

Richard,   m   Cecily Neville
Duke of York   1415–
1411–1460

Edward IV
1442–1483
m
Elizabeth Woodville
1437–

George,
Duke of Clarence
1449–1478
m
Isabelle Neville
1451–1476

Richard,
Duke of Gloucester
1452–1485
m
Anne Neville
1456–1485

Elizabeth
of York
1466–

Cecily 1469–
Richard 1473–
Anne 1476–
Catherine 1479–
Bridget 1480–

Margaret
1473–

Edward,
Earl of Warwick
1475–

SHERIFF HUTTON CASTLE, YORKSHIRE, AUTUMN 1485

I wish I could stop dreaming. I wish to God I could stop dreaming.

I am so tired; all I want to do is sleep. I want to sleep all the day, from dawn until twilight that every evening comes a little earlier and a little more drearily. In the daytime, all I think about is sleeping. But in the night all I do is try to stay awake.

I go to his quiet shuttered rooms to look at the candle as it gutters in the golden candlestick, burning slowly through the marked hours, though he will never see light again. The servants take a taper to a fresh candle every day at noon; each hour burns slowly away, although time means nothing to him now. Time is quite lost to him in his eternal darkness, in his eternal timelessness, though it leans so heavily on me. All day long I wait for the slow rolling in of the gray evening and the mournful tolling of the Compline bell, when I can go to the chapel and pray for his soul, though he will never again hear my

11

whispers, nor the quiet chanting of the priests.

Then I can go to bed. But when I get to bed I dare not sleep because I cannot bear the dreams that come. I dream of him. Over and over again I dream of him.

All day I keep my face smiling like a mask, smiling, smiling, my teeth bared, my eyes bright, my skin like strained parchment, paper-thin. I keep my voice clear and mellow, I speak words that have no meaning, and sometimes, when required, I even sing. At night I fall into my bed as if I were drowning in deep water, as if I were sinking below the depths, as if the water were possessing me, taking me like a mermaid, and for a moment I feel a deep relief as if, submerged in water, my grief can drain away, as if it were the river Lethe and the currents can bring forgetfulness and wash me into the cave of sleep; but then the dreams come.

I don't dream of his death — it would be the worst of nightmares to see him go down fighting. But I never dream of the battle, I don't see his final charge into the very heart of Henry Tudor's guard. I don't see him hacking his way through. I don't see Thomas Stanley's army sweep down and bury him under their hooves, as he is thrown from his horse, his sword arm failing, going down under a merciless cavalry charge, shouting: "Treason! Treason! Treason!" I don't see William Stanley raise his crown and put it on another man's head.

I don't dream any of this, and I thank God for that mercy at least. These are my constant daytime thoughts that I cannot escape. These are bloody daytime reveries that fill my mind while I walk and talk lightly of the unseasonal heat, of the dryness of the ground, of the poor harvest this year. But my dreams at night are more painful, far more painful than this, for then I dream that I am in his arms and he is waking me with a kiss. I dream that we are walking in a garden, planning our future. I dream that I am pregnant with his child, my rounded belly under his warm hand, and he is smiling, delighted, and I am promising him that we will have a son, the son that he needs, a son for York, a son for England, a son for the two of us. "We'll call him Arthur," he says. "We'll call him Arthur, like Arthur of Camelot, we'll call him Arthur for England."

The pain, when I wake to find that I have been dreaming again, seems to get worse every day. I wish to God I could stop dreaming.

My dearest daughter Elizabeth,
My heart and prayers are with you, dear child; but now, of all the times in your life, you must act the part of the queen that you were born to be.

13

The new king, Henry Tudor, commands you to come to me at the Palace of Westminster in London and you are to bring your sisters and cousins. Note this: he has not denied his betrothal to you. I expect it to go ahead.

I know this is not what you hoped for, my dear; but Richard is dead, and that part of your life is over. Henry is the victor and our task now is to make you his wife and Queen of England.

You will obey me in one other thing also: you will smile and look joyful as a bride coming to her betrothed. A princess does not share her grief with all the world. You were born a princess and you are the heir to a long line of courageous women. Lift up your chin and smile, my dear. I am waiting for you, and I will be smiling too.

Your loving mother
Elizabeth R
Dowager Queen of England

I read this letter with some care, for my mother has never been a straightforward woman and any word from her is always freighted with levels of meaning. I can imagine her thrilling at another chance at the throne of England. She is an indomitable woman; I have seen her brought very low, but never, even when she was widowed, even when nearly mad with grief, have I seen her humbled.

I understand at once her orders to look happy, to forget that the man I love is dead and tumbled into an unmarked grave, to forge the future of my family by hammering myself into marriage with his enemy. Henry Tudor has come to England, having spent his whole life in waiting, and he has won his battle, defeated the rightful king, my lover Richard, and now I am, like England itself, part of the spoils of war. If Richard had won at Bosworth — and who would ever have dreamed that he would not? — I would have been his queen and his loving wife. But he went down under the swords of traitors, the very men who mustered and swore to fight for him; and instead I am to marry Henry and the glorious sixteen months when I was Richard's lover, all but queen of his court, and he was the heart of my heart, will be forgotten. Indeed, I had better hope that they are forgotten. I have to forget them myself.

I read my mother's letter, standing under the archway of the gatehouse of the great castle of Sheriff Hutton, and I turn and walk into the hall, where a fire is burning in the central stone hearth, the air warm and hazy with woodsmoke. I crumple the single page into a ball and thrust it into the heart of the glowing logs, and watch it burn. Any mention of my love for Richard and his promises to me must be destroyed like this. And I must hide other secrets too, one especially. I was raised as a talkative princess in an open court rich with intellectual inquiry, where anything could be thought, said, and written; but in the years since my father's death, I have learned the secretive skills of a spy.

My eyes are filling with tears from the smoke of the fire, but I know that there is no point in weeping. I rub my face and go to find the children in the big chamber at the top of the west tower that serves as their schoolroom and playroom. My sixteen-year-old sister Cecily has been singing with them this morning, and I can hear their voices and the rhythmic thud of the tabor as I climb the stone stairs. When I push open the door, they break off and demand that I listen to a round they have composed. My ten-year-old sister Anne has been taught by the best masters since she was a baby, our twelve-year-old cousin Margaret can hold a tune, and her ten-year-old brother Edward has a clear soprano as sweet as a flute. I listen and then clap my hands in applause. "And now, I have news for you."

Edward Warwick, Margaret's little brother, lifts his heavy head from his slate. "Not for me?" he asks forlornly. "Not news for Teddy?"

"Yes, for you too, and for your sister Maggie, and Cecily and Anne. News for all of you. As you know, Henry Tudor has won the battle and is to be the new King of England."

These are royal children; their faces are glum, but they are too well trained to say one word of regret for their fallen uncle Richard. Instead, they wait for what will come next.

"The new King Henry is going to be a good king to his loyal people," I say, despising myself as I parrot the words that Sir Robert Willoughby said to me as he gave me my mother's letter. "And he has summoned all of us children of the House of York to London."

"But he'll be king," Cecily says flatly. "He's going to be king."

"Of course he'll be king! Who else?" I stumble over the question I have inadvertently posed. "Him, of course. Anyway, he has won the crown. And he will give us back our good name and recognize us as princesses of York."

Cecily makes a sulky face. In the last weeks before Richard the king rode out to battle, he ordered her to be married to Ralph Scrope, a next-to-nobody, to make sure that Henry Tudor could not claim her as a second choice of bride, after me. Cecily, like me, is a princess of York, and so marriage to either of us gives a man a claim to the throne. The shine was taken off me when gossip said that I was Richard's lover, and then Richard demeaned Cecily too by condemning her to a lowly marriage. She claims now that it was never consummated, now she says that she does not regard it, that Mother will have it annulled; but presumably she is Lady Scrope, the wife of a defeated Yorkist, and when we are restored to our royal titles and become princesses again, she will have to retain his name and her humiliation, even if no one knows where Ralph Scrope is today.

"You know, *I* should be king," ten-year-old Edward says, tugging at my sleeve. "I'm next, aren't I?"

I turn to him. "No, Teddy," I say gently. "You cannot be king. It's true that you are a boy of the House of York and Uncle Richard once named you as his heir; but he is dead now, and the new king will be Henry Tudor." I hear my voice quaver as I say "he is dead," and I take a breath and try again. "Richard is dead, Edward, you know that, don't you? You understand that King Richard is dead? And you will never be his heir now."

He looks at me so blankly that I think he has not understood anything at all, and then his big hazel eyes fill with tears, and he turns and goes back to copying his Greek alphabet on his slate. I stare at his brown head for a moment and think that his dumb animal grief is just like mine. Except that I am ordered to talk all the time, and to smile all the day.

"He can't understand," Cecily says to me, keeping her voice low so his sister Maggie cannot hear. "We've all told him, over and over again. He's too stupid to believe it."

I glance at Maggie, quietly seating herself beside her brother to help him to form his letters, and I think that I must be as stupid as Edward, for I cannot believe it either. One moment Richard was marching at the head of an invincible army of the great families of England; the next they brought us the news that he had been beaten, and that three of his trusted friends had sat on their horses and watched him lead a desperate charge to his death, as if it were a sunny day at the joust, as if they were spectators and he a daring rider, and the whole thing a game that could go either way and was worth long odds.

I shake my head. If I think of him, riding alone against his enemies, riding with my glove tucked inside his breastplate against his heart, then I will start to cry; and my mother has commanded me to smile.

"So we are going to London!" I say, as if I am delighted at the prospect. "To court! And we will live with our Lady Mother at Westminster Palace again, and be with our little sisters Catherine and Bridget again."

The two orphans of the Duke of Clarence look up at this. "But where will Teddy and me live?" Maggie asks.

"Perhaps you will live with us too," I say cheerfully. "I expect so."

"Hurrah!" Anne cheers, and Maggie tells Edward quietly that we will go to London, and that he can ride his pony all the way there from Yorkshire like a little knight at arms, as Cecily takes me by the elbow and draws me to one side, her fingers nipping my arm. "And what about you?" she asks. "Is the king going to marry you? Is he going to overlook what you did with Richard? Is it all to be forgotten?"

"I don't know," I say, pulling away. "And as far as we are concerned, nobody did anything with King Richard. You, of all people, my sister, would have seen nothing and will speak of nothing. As for Henry, I suppose whether he is going to marry me or not is the one thing that we all want to know. But only he knows the answer. Or perhaps two people: him — and that old crone, his mother, who thinks she can decide everything."

On the Great North Road, Autumn 1485

The journey south is easy in the mild September weather, and I tell our escort that there is no need to hurry. It is sunny and hot and we go by short stages as the younger children are on their ponies and cannot ride more than three hours without a rest. I sit astride my horse, the chestnut hunter that Richard gave me for my own, so that I could ride beside him, and I am glad to be on the move, leaving his castle of Sheriff Hutton, where we had planned a palace to rival Greenwich, abandoning the gardens where we walked together and the hall where we danced to the best musicians, and the chapel where he took my hand and promised that he would marry me as soon as he came back from the battle. Every day I am a little more distant from the place and hope to forget my memories of it. I try to outride my dreams but I can almost hear them, cantering like constant ghosts behind us.

Edward is excited by the journey, reveling

in the freedom of the Great North Road, and taking pleasure in the people who turn out all along the way to see what is left of the royal family of York. Every time our little procession halts, people come out to bless us, doffing their caps to Edward as the only remaining York heir, the only York boy, even though our house is defeated and people have heard that there is to be a new king on the throne — a Welshman that nobody knows, a stranger come in uninvited from Brittany or France or somewhere over the narrow seas. Teddy likes to pretend to be the rightful king, going to London to be crowned. He bows and waves his hand, pulls off his bonnet, and smiles when the people tumble out of their houses and shop doorways as we ride through the small towns. Although I tell him daily that we are going to the coronation of the new King Henry, he forgets it as soon as someone shouts, "À Warwick! À Warwick!"

Maggie, his sister, comes to me the night before we enter London. "Princess Elizabeth, may I speak with you?"

I smile at her. Poor little Maggie's mother died in childbirth and Maggie has been mother and father to her brother, and the mistress of his household, almost before she was out of short clothes. Maggie's father was George, Duke of Clarence, and he was executed in the Tower on the orders of my father, at the urging of my mother. Maggie never shows any sign of a grudge, though she wears a locket around her neck with her mother's hair in it, and on her wrist, a little charm bracelet with a silver barrel as a memorial for her father. It is always dangerous to be close to the throne; even at twelve, she knows this. The House of York eats its own young like a nervous cat.

"What is it, Maggie?"

Her little forehead is furrowed. "I am anxious about Teddy."

I wait. She is a devoted sister to the little boy.

"Anxious about his safety."

"What do you fear?"

"He is the only York boy, the only heir," she confides. "Of course there are other Yorks, the children of our aunt Elizabeth, Duchess of Suffolk; but Teddy is the only son left of the sons of York: your father King Edward, my father the Duke of Clarence, and our uncle King Richard. They're all dead now."

I register the familiar chord of pain that resonates in me at his name, as if I were a lute, strung achingly tight. "Yes," I say. "Yes, they are all dead now."

"From those three sons of York, there are no other sons anymore. Our Edward is the only boy left."

She glances at me, uncertainly. Nobody knows what happened to my brothers Edward and Richard, who were last seen playing on

23

the green before the Tower of London, waving from the window of the Garden Tower. Nobody knows for sure; but everyone thinks they are dead. What I know, I keep a close secret, and I don't know much.

"I'm sorry," she says awkwardly. "I didn't mean to distress you . . ."

"It's all right," I say, as if to speak of the disappearance of my brothers is not pain on pain. "Do you fear that Henry Tudor will take your brother into the Tower as King Richard took both of mine? And that he won't come out either?"

She twists her hand in her gown. "I don't even know if I should be taking him to London," she exclaims. "Should I try to get a ship and take him away to our aunt Margaret in Flanders? But I don't know how. I don't have any money to hire a ship. And I don't know who to ask. D'you think we should do that? Get Teddy away? Aunt Margaret would guard and keep him for love of the House of York. Should we do that? Would you know how to do it?"

"King Henry won't hurt him," I say. "Not right now, at any rate. He might later on, when he's established as king and secure on the throne, and people aren't watching him and wondering how he's going to act. But in the next few months he'll be seeking to make friends everywhere. He's won the battle, now he has to win the kingdom. It's not enough to kill the previous king, he has to be acclaimed by the people and crowned. He won't risk offending the House of York and everyone who loves us. Why, the poor man might even have to marry me to please them all!"

She smiles. "You'd make such a lovely queen! A really beautiful queen! And then I could be sure that Edward would be safe, for you could make him your ward, couldn't you? You'd guard him, wouldn't you? You know he's no danger to anyone. We'd both be faithful to the Tudor line. We'd both be faithful to you."

"If I'm ever made queen I will keep him safe," I promise her, thinking how many lives depend on me to make Henry honor his betrothal. "But in the meantime, I think you can come to London with us and we will be safe with my mother. She'll know what to do. She'll have a plan ready."

Maggie hesitates. There was bad blood between her mother Isabel and mine, and then she was raised by Richard's wife Anne, who hated my mother as a mortal enemy. "Will she care for us?" she asks very quietly. "Will your mother be kind to Teddy? They always said she was my family's enemy."

"She has no quarrel with either you or with Edward," I say reassuringly. "You are her niece and nephew. We're all of the House of York. She will protect you as she does us."

She is reassured, she trusts me, and I don't remind her that my mother had two boys of her own, Edward and Richard, that she loved more than life itself; but she couldn't keep them safe. And nobody knows where my little brothers are tonight.

WESTMINSTER PALACE, LONDON, AUTUMN 1485

There is no welcome party as we ride into London, and when one or two apprentices and market women catch sight of us in the narrow streets and cheer for the children of York, our escort closes up around us, to drive us as fast as they can into the courtyard of the royal Palace of Westminster, where the heavy wooden gates close behind us. Clearly, the new king Henry wants no rivals for the hearts of the city that he is calling his own. My mother is on the entrance steps, before the great doors, waiting for us with my little sisters, six-year-old Catherine and four-year-old Bridget, on either side of her. I tumble down from my horse and find myself in her arms, smelling her familiar perfume of rosewater and the scent of her hair, and as she holds me and pats my back, I find myself suddenly in tears, sobbing for the loss of the man I loved so passionately, and the future I had planned with him.

"Hush," my mother says firmly, and sends

me indoors while she greets my sisters and my cousins. She comes in after me, with Bridget on one hip and Catherine holding her hand, Anne and Cecily dancing around her. She is laughing, and looks happy and far younger than her forty-eight years. She is wearing a gown of dark blue, a blue leather belt around her slim waist, and her hair tied back into a blue velvet cap. All the children are shouting with excitement as she draws us into her private rooms, and sits down with Bridget on her knee. "Now tell me everything!" she says. "Did you really ride all the way, Anne? That was very good indeed. Edward, my dear boy, are you tired? Was your pony good?"

Everyone speaks at once, Bridget and Catherine are jumping and trying to interrupt. Cecily and I wait for the noise to die down, and my mother smiles at the two of us as she offers the children sugared plums and small ale, and they sit before the fire to enjoy their treats.

"And how are my two big girls?" she asks. "Cecily, you have grown again, I swear you are going to be as tall as me. Elizabeth, dear, you are pale and far too thin. Are you sleeping all right? Not fasting, are you?"

"Elizabeth says she can't be sure if Henry will marry her or not," Cecily bursts out at once. "And if he does not, what will happen to us all? What's going to happen to me?"

"Of course he will marry her," my mother says calmly. "He most certainly will. His mother has spoken to me already. They realize that we have too many friends in Parliament and in the country for him to risk insulting the House of York. He has to marry Elizabeth. He promised it nearly a year ago and he's not free to choose now. It was part of his plan of invasion and his agreement with his supporters from the very beginning."

"But isn't he angry about King Richard?" Cecily persists. "Richard and Elizabeth? And what she did?"

My mother turns a serene face to my spiteful sister. "I know nothing about the late usurper Richard," she says, just as I knew she would. "And no more do you. And King Henry knows even less."

Cecily opens her mouth as if she would argue, but one cool look from my mother silences her. "King Henry knows very little at all about his new kingdom as yet," my mother continues smoothly. "He has spent almost all his life overseas. But we will help him and tell him all that he needs to know."

"But Elizabeth and Richard . . ."

"That is one of the things he doesn't need to know."

"Oh, very well," Cecily says crossly. "But this is about all of us, not just Elizabeth. Elizabeth isn't the only one here, though she behaves as if nobody matters but her. And the Warwick children are always asking how they will be safe, and Maggie is afraid for Edward. And what about me? Am I married or not? What is going to happen to me?"

My mother frowns at this stream of demands. Cecily was married so quickly, just before the battle, and her bridegroom rode away before they were even bedded. Now, of course, he is missing, and the king who ordered the wedding is dead, and everything that everyone planned has failed. Cecily is perhaps a maid again, or perhaps a widow, or perhaps an abandoned wife. Nobody knows.

"Lady Margaret will make the Warwick children her wards. And she also has plans for you. She spoke most kindly of you and of all your sisters."

"Is Lady Margaret going to command the court?" I ask quietly.

"What plans?" Cecily demands.

"I'll tell you later, when I know more myself," my mother says to Cecily, and to me she remarks, "She's to be served on bended knee, she is to be called 'Your Grace,' she's to receive a royal bow."

I make a little face of disdain. "We didn't part the best of friends, she and I."

"When you're married and you are queen, she will curtsey to you, whatever name she goes by," my mother says simply. "It doesn't matter if she likes you or not, you're still going to marry her son." She turns to the younger children. "Now, I'll show you all your rooms."

"Aren't we in our usual rooms?" I ask thoughtlessly.

My mother's smile is slightly strained. "Of course we're not in the royal rooms anymore. Lady Margaret Stanley has reserved the queen's rooms as her own. And her husband's family, the Stanleys, have all the best apartments. We are in the second-best rooms. You are in Lady Margaret's old room. It seems that she and I have swapped places."

"Lady Margaret Stanley is to have the queen's rooms?" I ask. "Didn't she think that I would have them?"

"Not yet, at any rate," my mother says. "Not until the day that you marry and are crowned. Until then she is the first lady of Henry's court, and she is anxious that everyone knows it. Apparently, she has ordered everyone to call her My Lady the King's Mother."

"My Lady the King's Mother?" I repeat the strange title.

"Yes," my mother says with a wry smile. "Not bad for a woman who was my lady-in-waiting, and who has spent the last year estranged from her husband and under house arrest for treason, don't you think?"

We move into the second-best rooms in Westminster Palace and wait for King Henry to

31

command our presence. He does not. He holds his court at the palace of the Bishop of London, near St. Paul's Cathedral in the City, and every man who can pretend that he is of the House of Lancaster, or a longtime secret supporter of the Tudor cause, flocks to see him and claims a reward for his loyalty. We wait for an invitation to be presented at court, but none comes.

My mother orders new dresses for me, headdresses to make me look yet taller, new slippers to peep below the hem of the new gowns, and praises my looks. I am fair like she was, with gray eyes. She was the famously beautiful daughter of the best-looking couple in the kingdom and she says with quiet satisfaction that I have inherited the family looks.

She seems serene; but people are beginning to talk. Cecily says that we may be in the royal palace again, but it is as lonely and as quiet as being mewed up in sanctuary. I don't bother to disagree with her, but she's wrong. She's so very wrong. She can't remember sanctuary as I can; there is nothing, *nothing* worse than the darkness and the quiet, and knowing that you can't get out, and fearing that anyone can come in. Last time we were in sanctuary, we could not get out for nine months; it felt like nine years, and I thought I would fade and die without sunlight. Cecily says that she, as a married woman, should not even be with us, but she should be released to rejoin her husband.

"Except that you don't know where he is," I say. "He's probably run away to France."

"At least I was married," she says pointedly. "I didn't bed a man married to someone else. I was not a scarlet adulteress. And at least he's not dead."

"Ralph Scrope of Upsall," I reply scathingly. "Mr. Nobody of Nowhere. If you can find him, if he is still alive, you can live with him, for all I care. If he'll have you without being told to do so. If he'll be your husband without a royal command."

She hunches her shoulder and turns away from me. "My Lady the King's Mother will provide for me," she says defensively. "I am her goddaughter. It is she who matters, who commands everything now. She will remember me."

The weather is all wrong for the time of year, too sunny, too bright, too hot during the day and humid at night, so nobody can sleep. Nobody but me. Although I am cursed by dreams, I still cannot stop myself sleeping. I drop into darkness every night and dream that Richard has come to me, laughing. He tells me that the battle went his way and we are to be married. He holds my hands as I protest that they came and told me that Henry had won, and he kisses me and calls me a fool, a little darling fool. I wake believing it to be true, and feel a sudden sick realization when I look at the walls of the second-best bedroom, and Cecily sharing my bed, and remember that my love lies dead and cold in an unmarked grave, while his country sweats in the heat.

My maid, Jennie, who comes from a family of merchants in the City, tells me that there is terrible sickness in the crowded houses of the inner city. Then she tells me that two of her father's apprentices have fallen sick and died.

"The plague?" I ask. At once, I step back a little from her. There is no cure for the disease and I am afraid that she carries the illness with her and the hot plague wind will blow over me and my family.

"It's worse than the plague," she says. "It's not like anything anyone has seen before. Will, the first apprentice, said at breakfast that he was cold and that he ached as if he had been fighting with a singlestick all the night. My father said he could go back to his bed, and then he started to sweat; his shirt was wet with sweat, he was dripping with it. When my mother took him a pot of ale he said he was burning up and couldn't get cool. He said he would sleep and then he didn't waken. A young man of eighteen! Dead in an afternoon!"

"His skin?" I ask. "Did he have boils?"

"No boils, no rash," she insists. "As I say —

it's not the plague. It's this new illness. They call it the sweating sickness, a new plague that King Henry has brought upon us. Everyone says that his reign has started with death and won't last. He has brought death with him. We'll all die of his ambition. They say that he came in with sweat and will labor to keep his throne. It's a Tudor illness, he brought it in with him. He's cursed, everyone says so. It's autumn but it's as hot as midsummer, and we're all going to sweat to death."

"You can go home," I say nervously. "And, Jennie, stay at home until you can be sure you are well and everyone in your house is well. My mother won't want your service if there are sick people in your house. Don't come back to the palace until you are free of sickness. And go home without seeing my sisters or the Warwick children."

"But I'm well!" she protests. "And it's a fast disease. If I had it, I would be dead before I could even tell you about it. As long as I can walk to the palace from my home, I am well enough."

"Go home," I command. "I'll send for you when you can come again," and then I go to find my mother.

She is not in the palace, not in the shuttered shade of the empty queen's rooms, not even in the cool walks of the garden, but I find her seated on a stool at the far end of the landing stage that extends out into the river to catch the breeze that whispers along the water, listening to the lapping of the waves against the wood piling.

"Daughter mine," she greets me as I walk up to her. I kneel on the planks for her blessing, and then sit beside her with my feet dangling over the edge and my own reflection looking up at me as if I were a water goddess living under the river, waiting to be released from an enchantment, and not a spinster princess that nobody wants.

"Have you heard of this new illness in the City?" I ask her.

"Yes, for the king has decided he can't have his coronation and risk bringing together so many people who could be sick," she says. "Henry will have to be a conqueror and not a crowned king for a few more weeks until the sickness passes. His mother, Lady Margaret, is having special prayers said; she will be beside herself. She thinks that God has guided her son this far, but now sends a plague to try his fortitude."

Looking up at her, I have to squint against the bright western sky, where the sun is setting in a blaze of color, promising another unseasonably hot day tomorrow. "Mother, is this your doing?"

She laughs. "Are you accusing me of witchcraft?" she asks. "Cursing a nation with a plague wind? No, I couldn't make such a thing happen; and if I did have such a power, I wouldn't use it. This is a sickness that came with Henry because he hired the worst men in Christendom to invade this poor country, and they brought the disease from the darkest, dirtiest jails of France. It's not magic, it's men carrying illness with them as they march. That's why it started first in Wales and then came to London — it has followed his route, not by magic but by the dirt they left behind them and the women they raped on the way, poor souls. It is Henry's convict army which has brought the sickness, though everyone is taking it as a sign that God is against him."

"But could it be both?" I ask. "Both a sickness and a sign?"

"Without doubt it is both," she says. "They are saying that a king whose reign starts with sweat will have to labor to keep his throne. Henry's sickness is killing his friends and supporters as if the disease were a weapon against him and them. He is losing more allies now in his triumph than ever died on the battlefield. It would be funny if it weren't so bitter."

"What does it mean for us?" I ask.

She looks upstream, as if the very water of the river might float an answer to my dangling feet. "I don't know yet," she says thoughtfully. "I can't tell. But if he were to take the sickness himself and die, then people would be sure to say it was the judgment of God on a usurper, and would look for a York heir to the throne."

"And do we have one?" I ask, my voice barely audible above the lapping of the water. "A York heir?"

"Of course we do: Edward of Warwick."

I hesitate. "Do we have another? Even closer?"

Still looking away from me she nods, imperceptibly.

"My little brother Richard?"

Again she nods, as if she does not even trust the wind with her words.

I gasp. "You have him safe, Mother? You're sure of it? He's alive? In England?"

She shakes her head. "I have had no news. I can say nothing for certain, and certainly nothing to you. We have to pray for the two sons of York, Prince Edward and Prince Richard, as lost boys, until someone can tell us what has become of them." She smiles at me. "And better that I don't tell you what I hope," she says gently. "But who knows what the future will bring if Henry Tudor dies?"

"Can't you wish it on him?" I whisper. "Let him die of the illness that he has brought in with him?"

She turns her head away, as if to listen to the river. "If he killed my son, then my curse is already on him," she says flatly. "You cursed the murderer of our boys with me, remember? We asked Melusina, the goddess-ancestor of my mother's family, to take revenge for us. D'you remember what we said?"

"Not the exact words. I remember that night."

It was the night when my mother and I were distraught with grief and fear, imprisoned in sanctuary as my uncle Richard came and told her that both her sons, Edward and Richard, my beloved little brothers, had disappeared from their rooms in the Tower. That was the night that my mother and I wrote a curse on a piece of paper, folded it into a paper boat, lit it, and watched it flare as it floated downriver. "I don't remember exactly what we said."

She knows it word for word, the worst curse she has ever laid on anyone; she has it by heart. "We said: 'Know this: that there is no justice to be had for the wrong that someone has done to us, so we come to you, our Lady Mother, and we put into your dark depths this curse: that whoever took our firstborn son from us, that you take his firstborn son from him.' "

She turns her glance from the river to me, her pupils darkly dilated. "Do you remember now? As we sit here by the river? The very same river?"

I nod.

"We said: 'Our boy was taken when he was not yet a man, not yet king — though he was born to be both. So take his murderer's son while he is yet a boy, before he is a man, before he comes to his estate. And then take his grandson too and when you take him, we will know by these deaths that this is the working of our curse and this is payment for the loss of our son.' "

I give a shiver at the trance my mother is weaving around us as her quiet words fall on the river like rain. "We cursed his son and his grandson."

"He deserves it. And when his son and his grandson die and he has nothing left but girls, then we will know him for the murderer of our boy, Melusina's boy, and we will have had our revenge."

"That was an awful thing that we did," I say uncertainly. "A terrible curse on the innocent heirs. A terrible thing to wish the death of two innocent boys."

"Yes," my mother agrees calmly. "It was. And we did it because someone did it to us. And that someone will know my pain when his son dies, and when his grandson dies and he has no one but a girl left to inherit."

People have always whispered that my mother practices witchcraft, and indeed her own mother was tried and found guilty of the dark arts. Only she knows how much she believes, only she knows what she can do.

40

When I was a girl, I saw her call up a storm of rain, and I watched the river rise that washed away the Duke of Buckingham's army and his rebellion with it. I thought then that she had done it all with a whistle. She told me of a mist which she breathed out one cold night which hid my father's army, shrouding it so that he thundered out of a cloud on the hilltop and caught his enemy by surprise and destroyed them with sword and storm.

People believe that she has unearthly powers because her mother came from the royal house of Burgundy, and they can trace their ancestry back to the water witch Melusina. Certainly we can hear Melusina singing when one of her children dies. I have heard her myself, and it's a sound I won't forget. It was a cool, soft call, night after night, and then my brother was not playing on Tower Green anymore, his pale face was gone from the window, and we mourned for him as a dead boy.

What powers my mother has, and what luck runs her way that she claims as her doing, is unknown, perhaps even to her. Certainly she takes her good luck and calls it magic. When I was a girl, I thought her an enchanted being with the power to summon the rivers of England; but now, as I look at the defeat of our family, the loss of her son, and the mess we are in, I think that if she does conjure magic, then she can't do it very well.

So I am not surprised that Henry does not die, though the sickness he has brought to England takes first one Lord Mayor of London, and then his hastily elected successor, and then six aldermen die too, almost in the same month. They say that every home in the city has suffered a death, and the carts for the dead rattle down the streets every night, just as if it were a plague year, and a bad one at that.

When the illness dies out with the cold weather, Jennie my maid does not come back to work when I send for her, for she is dead too; her whole household took the sweat and died of it between Prime and Compline. No one has known such quick deaths before, and they whisper everywhere against the new king whose reign has started with a procession of death carts. It is not till the end of October that Henry decides that it is safe to call the lords and genty of the realm together to Westminster Abbey to his coronation.

Two heralds bearing the Beaufort standard, the portcullis, and a dozen guards wearing the Stanley colors, hammer on the great door of the palace to inform me that Lady Margaret Stanley of the Beaufort family, My Lady the King's Mother, is to honor me with a visit tomorrow. My mother inclines her head at the news and says softly — as if we are too nobly bred to ever raise our voices — that we will be delighted to see Her Grace.

As soon as they are gone and the door closed behind them, we fall into a frenzy about my dress. "Dark green," my mother says. "It has to be dark green."

It is our only safe color. Dark blue is the royal color of mourning, but I must not, for one moment, look as if I am grieving for my royal lover and the true king of England. Dark red is the color of martyrdom, but also sometimes, contradictorily, worn by whores to make their complexions appear flawlessly white. Neither association is one we want to inspire in the stern mind of the strict Lady Margaret. She must not think that marriage to her son is a torment for me, she must forget that everyone said that I was Richard's lover. Dark yellow would be all right — but who looks good in yellow? I don't like purple and anyway it is too imperial a color for a humbled girl whose only hope is to marry the king. Dark green it has to be and since it is the Tudor color, this can do nothing but good.

"But I don't have a dark green gown!" I exclaim. "There isn't time to get one."

"We had one made for Cecily," my mother replies. "You'll wear that."

"And what am I supposed to wear?" Cecily protests mutinously. "Am I to come in an old gown? Or will I not appear at all? Is Elizabeth going to be the only one who meets her? Are the rest of us to be in hiding? D'you want me to go to bed for the day?"

"Certainly, there's no need for you to be here," my mother says briskly. "But Lady Margaret is your godmother, so you will wear your blue and Elizabeth can wear your green, and you will make an effort — an exceptional effort — to be pleasant to your sister during the visit. Nobody likes a bad-tempered girl, and I have no use for one."

Cecily is furious at this, but she goes to the chest of clothes in silence and takes out her new green gown, shakes it out, and hands it to me.

"Put it on and come to my rooms," my mother says. "We'll have to let down the hem."

Dressed in the gown, now hemmed and trimmed with a new thin ribbon of cloth of gold, I wait in the presence chamber of my mother's rooms for the arrival of Lady Margaret. She comes by royal barge, now always laid on for her convenience, with the drummer beating to keep the time, and her standards fluttering brightly at prow and stern. I hear the crunching footsteps of her companions on the gravel of the garden paths, then beneath the window, and then the clatter of the metal heels of their boots on the stones of the courtyard. They throw open the double doors and she comes through the lobby and into the room.

My mother, my sisters, and I rise from our seats and curtsey to her as equals. The height of this curtsey has been difficult to decide. We offer a middling one and Lady Margaret ducks in a shallow bob. Though my mother is now known as mere Lady Grey, she was crowned Queen of England and this woman was her lady-in-waiting. Now, although Lady Margaret sails in the royal barge, her son has not yet been crowned king. Though she calls herself My Lady the King's Mother, he has not yet had the crown of England placed on his head. He just grabbed the circlet that Richard wore on his helmet and has to wait for his coronation.

I close my eyes quickly at the thought of the gold crown on the helmet, and Richard's smiling brown eyes looking at me through the visor.

"I would speak with Mistress Elizabeth alone," Lady Margaret says to my mother, not troubling with any word of greeting.

"Her Grace the Princess Elizabeth of York can take you to my privy chamber," my mother says smoothly.

I lead the way. I can feel my back under her scrutiny as I walk and at once I become conscious of myself. I fear that I am swinging my hips, or tossing my head. I open the door and go into my mother's private room and turn to face Lady Margaret, as she seats herself without invitation in the great chair.

"You may sit," she says, and I take a chair opposite to her and wait. My throat is dry. I swallow and hope that she does not notice.

She looks me up and down as if I am applying for a post in her household and then slowly she smiles. "You are lucky in your looks," she says. "Your mother was always a beauty and you are very like her: fair, slender, skin like a rose petal and that wonderful hair, gold and bronze all at once. Undoubtedly you will have beautiful children. I suppose you are still proud of your looks? I suppose you are still vain?"

I say nothing, and she clears her throat and remembers the reason for her visit.

"I have come to speak with you in private, as a friend," she says. "We parted on bad terms."

We parted like a pair of fishwives. But I was sure then that my lover would kill her son and make me Queen of England. Now, as it turns out, her son has killed my lover and my fate is entirely in her white, heavily ringed hands.

"I regret it," I say with simple insincerity.

"I too," she says, which surprises me. "I am to be your mother-in-law, Elizabeth. My son will marry you, despite everything."

There is no point in my sudden pulse of anger at the "despite everything." We are defeated, my hopes of happiness and being a beloved Queen of England went down under the hooves of the Stanley horsemen commanded by her husband.

I bow my head. "Thank you."

"I will be a good mother to you," she says earnestly. "You will find, when you come to know me, that I have great love to give, that I have a talent for loyalty. I am determined to do the will of God and I am certain that God has chosen you to be my daughter-in-law, the wife of my son, and" — her voice drops to an awed whisper at the thought of my destiny, at the divine promise of the Tudor line — "the mother of my grandson."

I bow my head again, and when I look up, I see that her face is shining; she is quite inspired.

"When I was a little girl, no more than a child myself, I was called on to give birth to Henry," she whispers, as if in prayer. "I thought I would die from the pain, I was certain it would kill me. I knew then that, if I survived, the child and I would have a great future, the greatest future that could be. He would be King of England and I would put him on the throne."

There is something very moving about her rapt expression, like a nun describing her vocation.

"I *knew*," she says. "I knew that he was to be king. And when I met you, I knew that you were destined to bear his son." She turns her intense gaze on me. "That is why I was hard on you, that is why I was so furious with you when I saw you straying from your path. That is why I couldn't *stand* it when I saw you falling from your position, from your destiny, from your calling."

"You think I have a calling?" I am whispering, she is so completely convincing.

"You will be the mother of the next King of England," she declares. "The red rose and the white, a rose without a thorn. You will have a son, and we will call him Arthur of England." She takes my hands. "This is your destiny, my daughter. I will help you."

"Arthur." Wonderingly, I repeat the name that Richard chose for the son he hoped to have with me.

"It is my dream," she says.

It was our dream too. I let her hold my hands and I don't pull away.

"God has brought us together," she tells me earnestly. "God has brought you to me, and you are going to give me a grandson. You are going to bring peace to England, you are going to be the peace which ends the Cousins' War. Elizabeth, you will be a peacemaker and God Himself will call you blessed."

Amazed at her vision, I let her hold my hands in her firm grip, and I don't disagree.

I never tell my mother what passed between

me and My Lady the King's Mother. She raises an eyebrow at my discretion but does not ask me more. "At any rate, she said nothing to make you think that she has changed her mind about the betrothal," she confirms.

"On the contrary, she assured me that we will marry. It will go ahead. She promised to be my friend."

My mother hides a smile. "How kind," is all she says. "Helpful of her."

So we wait, with some confidence, for our invitation to the coronation, expecting to be told to go to the royal wardrobe to be fitted for our gowns. Cecily, especially, is desperate for her new robes and for the chance for us all to be seen in the world as the five York princesses once more. Only when Henry has reversed the Act of Parliament that named us as bastards and our parents' marriage as a bigamous fraud can we wear our ermine and crowns once again. Henry's coronation will be our first chance since Richard's death to appear to the world in our true colors as princesses of York once again.

I am confident that we will all attend his coronation; yet, still, no word comes. I am certain that he must want his future wife to watch him take the crown on his head and the scepter in his hand. Even if he has no curiosity to see me, how can he not want to demonstrate his victory before us, the previous royal family? Surely he will want me to see him at his moment of greatest glory?

I feel more like a sleeping princess in a fairy story than the woman who is promised in marriage to the new King of England. I may live in the royal palace, and sleep in one of the best rooms, I may be served with courtesy though without the bended knee that people must show to the royal family. But I live here quietly, without a court, without the usual crowd of flatterers, friends, and petitioners, without sight of the king: a princess without a crown, a betrothed without a bridegroom, a bride with no date for her wedding.

God knows that once I was well enough known as Henry's betrothed. When he was an exiled pretender to the throne, he swore in Rennes Cathedral itself that he was King of England and I was his bride. But, of course, that was when he was mustering his army for his invasion, desperate for support from the House of York and all of our adherents. Now he has won the battle and sent his army away, perhaps he would like to be free of his promise too, as a weapon he needed then, but does not need now.

My mother has seen to it that we all have new gowns; all five of us princesses of York are exquisitely dressed. But we have nowhere to go, and no one ever sees us, and we are called not "Your Grace" as princesses, but "my lady" as if we were the bastard daughters of a bigamous marriage and my mother was not a dowager queen but the widow of a country squire. We are all no better off than Cecily, whose marriage has now been annulled but without a new husband on offer. She is not Lady Scrope but neither is she anything else. We are all girls without a name, without a family, without certainty. And girls like this have no future.

I had assumed that I would be restored as a princess, given my fortune, and married and crowned in one great ceremony at Henry's side; but the silence tells me that he is not an eager bridegroom.

No message comes from the royal wardrobe bidding us to come and pick out our gowns for the coronation procession. The Master of the Revels does not ask if he may come to the palace to teach us our dance for the coronation dinner. All the seamstresses and tirewomen in London are working day and night on gowns and headdresses: but not for us. Nobody is sent to us from the Lord Chamberlain's offices with instructions for the procession. We are not invited to stay in the Tower of London the night before the ceremony, as is the tradition. No horses are ordered for us to ride from the Tower to Westminster Abbey, no ruling comes as to the order of precedence on the day. Henry sends no gifts as a bridegroom should to his bride. Nothing at all comes from his mother. Where there should be bustle and business and a host of conflicting instructions from a new king and a new court anxious to look well, there is a silence that grows more and more noticeable as the days go on.

"We're not going to be invited to the coronation," I say flatly to my mother when I am alone with her, as she comes to say good night to me in the bedroom that I share with Cecily. "It's obvious, isn't it?"

She shakes her head. "I don't think we are."

"How can he not have me there at his side?"

Slowly, she goes to the window and looks out at the dark night sky and the silvery moon. "I think they don't want a host of Yorks beside the throne, so close to the crown," she says dryly.

"Why not?"

She takes the shutters and latches them, as if to shut out the silvery light that shines on her, giving her an unearthly radiance. "I don't know why for sure," she says. "But I suppose, if I was Henry's mother, I would not want my child, a pretender, a usurper, king only by right of battle, taking his crown alongside a princess, a true-bred princess of the royal family, beloved of the people, and a beauty. Apart from anything else I would not like how it looked."

"Why? What does he look like?" I demand.

"Ordinary." My mother condemns him in one damning word. "He's very, very ordinary."

Slowly it becomes clear to us all, even to Cecily, who is frantically hopeful almost up to the last day, that the new king will be crowned alone, and that he does not want me, distractingly beautiful, the only true royal, before the altar at his side. He will not even have us, the former royal family, as witnesses when he puts his hand on my lover's crown, the crown worn by the man I loved, and by my father before him.

No message comes from either Henry or from his mother, Lady Margaret Stanley, to confirm this decision one way or the other, and though my mother and I consider writing to Lady Margaret, neither of us can bear the humiliation of pleading with her for the chance to attend the coronation, nor to beg her to set a date for my wedding.

"Besides, if I were to attend his coronation as a dowager queen I would take precedence over her," my mother remarks waspishly. "Perhaps that's why we're not invited. She has seen nothing but my back at every great event for all of her life. She has never had a view that was not obscured by my headdress and veil. She has followed me into every single room in this palace, and then she followed Anne Neville when she was her lady-in-waiting, too. She walked behind Anne at her coronation, carrying the train. Perhaps Lady Margaret is feeling that it's her turn to be the first lady now, and she wants someone trailing along behind her."

"What about me?" Cecily says hopefully. "I'd carry her train. I'd be happy to carry her train."

"You will not," my mother says shortly.

Henry Tudor stays in Lambeth Palace until his coronation, and if he should choose to glance up from his breakfast, he would see my window in Westminster Palace, just across the river from him; but presumably he does not choose to look up, he does not wonder about his unknown bride, for still he sends no word. The nights before his coronation, he moves to the Tower of London, as is the tradition. There, he will stay in the royal rooms, and every day he will walk past the door where my brothers were last seen, every day he will walk across the green where my brother had an archery target and practiced shooting his bow. Can a man do such a thing without a chill going down his spine, without glimpsing the pale face of the imprisoned boy who should have been crowned king? Does his mother not see a slight shadow on the stair, or when she kneels in the royal stall in the chapel, does she not hear a faint echo of a boyish treble saying his prayers? How can the two Tudors go up the tightly curled stone stair in the Garden Tower and not listen at the wooden door for the voices of two little boys? And if they ever listen, are they not certain to hear Edward's quiet prayers?

"He'll be searching," my mother says grimly. "He'll be questioning everyone who ever guarded them. He'll want to know what became of the princes, and he'll be hoping to find something, someone who can be bribed to come forward and make an accusation, or someone who can be persuaded to confess, anything so that he can point the blame at Richard. If he can show that Richard killed our princes, then he can justify taking the throne because they are dead and he can name Richard as a tyrant and a regicide. If he can prove their death, then Henry's cause is won."

"Mother, I would swear on my life that Richard didn't hurt them," I say earnestly. "I know that Richard would have told me if he had done so. You know it. You were convinced on the night when he came to you to ask if it was you who had stolen them both away, weren't you? He didn't know where they were, or what had become of them. He thought you might have had them. I would swear that he never knew. Actually, it tormented him that he didn't know. At the very end, he didn't know who to name as his heir. He was desperate to be sure."

My mother's gaze is hard. "Oh, I believe

that Richard didn't kill the boys. Of course I know that. I would never have released you and your sisters into his care if I had thought he could bring himself to harm his own brother's children. But for sure, he kidnapped our Prince Edward on the road to London. He killed my brother Anthony who tried to defend him. He took Edward into the Tower and did all he could to take my younger boy Richard too. It wasn't him who killed them in secret, but he put them where a killer could find them. He defied your father's will and he took your brother's throne. He might not have killed them; but they should both have been left safe in my keeping. Richard of Gloucester took Edward from me, and he would have taken my son Richard too. He took the throne, and he killed my brother Anthony and my son Richard Grey. He was a usurper and a murderer, and I will never forgive him for those crimes. I don't need to lay others at Richard's door, he will go to hell for these, and I will never forgive him for these."

Miserably, I shake my head that my mother should say this of the man I love. I can't defend him, not to her, who lost her two boys and still does not know what has become of them. "I know," I whisper. "I know. I'm not denying that he had to act in terrible times, he did terrible things. He confessed them to his priest and he prayed for forgiveness for them. You have no idea how tortured he was by the things he had to do. But I'm certain that he didn't order the death of my brothers."

"Then Henry will find nothing in his search of the Tower," she observes. "If Richard did not kill them, there will be no bodies for Henry to bring out. Perhaps they are both alive, hidden somewhere in the Tower or in the houses nearby."

"And what would Henry do then? If he found them alive?" I am breathless at this speculation. "What would he do if someone came forward and said they had them hidden, safely hidden away, our boys, for all this long time?"

My mother's smile is as sad and as slow as a falling tear. "Why, he'd have to kill them," she says simply. "If he were to find my sons alive now, he would kill them at once, and blame it on Richard. If he found my sons alive, he would have to kill them, to take the throne, just as your father killed old King Henry to take the throne. Of course he would. We all know that."

"And would he do it, do you think? Could he do such a terrible thing?"

She shrugs. "I think he would make himself do it. He would have no choice. Otherwise, he would have risked his life and his army for nothing. His mother would have spent her life plotting and even marrying for nothing.

Yes, if Henry ever finds your brother Edward alive he would kill him in that moment. If he finds your brother Richard he would have to put him to death. It would be nothing more to him than continuing the work he did at Bosworth. He'd find some way of settling his conscience. He's a young man who has lived under the shadow of the sword from the moment when he fled England as a boy of fourteen to the day when he rode home to fight for his claim. Nobody knows better than he that any claimant to the throne has to be killed at once. A king cannot let a pretender live. No king can allow a pretender to live."

Henry's court goes with him to the Tower, and more and more men flock to the Tudor standard now that it is triumphant. We hear, through gossip from the city streets, of the round of rewards that comes from the Tudor throne as Henry hands out the spoils of Bosworth in the days before his coronation. His mother has all her lands and wealth returned to her; she enters a greatness that she always claimed but never enjoyed before now. Her husband, Thomas, Lord Stanley, is made Earl of Derby and High Constable of England, the greatest position in the realm, as reward for his great courage in looking both ways at once, the two-faced traitor that he is. I know, for I heard him swear the oath, that he promised his loyalty, his absolute fealty, to my Richard; I saw him go down on his knees and promise his love, even offering his son as a pledge of his loyalty. He swore that his brother, his whole family, were Richard's true men.

But that morning at Bosworth Field he and Sir William sat on their horses with their mighty armies behind him, and waited to see which way the battle would go. When they saw Richard charge into the heart of the fighting, on his own, aimed like a spear at Henry himself, the Stanleys, Lord William and Sir Thomas, acting as one, swept down on him from behind, with swords raised. They rescued Henry in that moment, and cut Richard down to the ground when he was just moments away from putting his sword through Henry Tudor's heart.

Sir William Stanley picked up my Richard's helmet from the mud, tore off the battle coronet, and handed the gold circlet to Henry: the most vile piece of work of a villainous day. Now, in puppyish gratitude, Henry makes Sir William his chamberlain, kisses him on both cheeks, declares that they are the new royal family. He surrounds himself with Stanleys, he cannot thank them enough. He has found his throne and his family in one triumph. He is inseparable from his mother, Margaret, and always, half a step behind her, is her devoted husband, Lord Thomas Stanley, and half a step behind him is his brother Sir William. Henry lolls in the lap of these newfound kinsmen who have put their boy on the throne and knows he is safe at last.

His uncle Jasper, who shared his exile and kept faith with the Tudor cause since Henry's birth, is there too, rewarded for a lifetime of loyalty with his share of the spoils. He gets his title back, and his lands returned; he will have his pick of the posts of government. And he gets even more than this. Henry writes to my aunt Katherine, the widow of the traitorous Duke of Buckingham, and tells her to prepare for remarriage. Jasper is to have her and the Buckingham fortune. It seems that all the Rivers women are part of the spoils of war. She brings the letter in her hand when she comes to see my mother as we are sitting in the second-best rooms at Westminster Palace.

"Is he mad?" she asks my mother. "Was it not enough that I was married to a boy, to the young duke who hated me, but I now have to marry another enemy of our family?"

"D'you get a fee?" my mother asks dryly, since she has her own letter to show her sister. "For see, here is our news. I am to be paid a pension. Cecily is to be married to Sir John Welles, and Elizabeth is to be betrothed to the king."

"Well, thank God for that at least!" my aunt Katherine exclaims. "You must have been anxious."

My mother nods. "Oh, he would have reneged on his vow if he could have done. He was looking for another bride, he was trying to get out of it."

I look up from my sewing at this, but my mother and her sister are intent on their letters, their heads together.

"When will it be? The wedding?"

"After the coronation." My mother points to the paragraph. "Of course, he won't want anyone to say that they are joint king and queen. He'll want to be seen to take the throne on his own merits. He won't want anyone saying she takes the queen's crown on her own account. He can't have anyone saying that he's got the crown through her."

"But we'll all go to his coronation?" my aunt Katherine asks. "They've left it very late but —"

"Not invited," my mother says shortly.

"It's an insult! He must have Elizabeth there!"

My mother shrugs her shoulders. "What if they cheered for her? What if they called for us?" she says quietly. "You know how people would cheer for her, if they saw her. You know how Londoners love the House of York. What if the people saw us and called for my nephew Edward of Warwick? What if they booed the House of Tudor and called for the House of

York? At his coronation? He's not going to risk it."

"There'll be York kinsmen there," Katherine points out. "Your sister-in-law Elizabeth has turned her coat, as her husband the Duke of Suffolk has changed sides again. Her son, John de la Pole, that King Richard named as his heir, has begged Henry's pardon and so they will be there."

My mother nods. "So they should be," she says. "And I am sure they will serve him loyally."

My aunt Katherine gives a short snort of laughter and my mother cannot stop her smile.

I go to find Cecily. "You're to be married," I say abruptly. "I heard Mother and Aunt Katherine talking."

She turns pale. "Who to?"

I understand at once that she is afraid that she is to be humiliated again by a marriage to some lowly supporter of the Tudor invasion. "You're all right," I say. "Lady Margaret is standing your friend. She's marrying you to her half brother, Sir John Welles."

She gives a shuddering sob and turns to me. "Oh, Lizzie, I was so afraid . . . I've been so afraid . . ."

I put my arm around her shoulders. "I know."

"And there was nothing I could do. And

when Father was alive, they all used to call me Princess of Scotland, as I was to marry the Scots king! Then to be pushed down to be Lady Scrope! And then to have no name at all! Oh, Lizzie, I've been vile to you."

"To everyone," I remind her.

"I know! I know!"

"But now you'll be a viscountess!" I say. "And no doubt better. Lady Margaret favors her family above everyone else, and Henry owes Sir John a debt of gratitude for his support. They'll give him another title and lands. You'll be rich, you'll be noble, you'll be allied to My Lady the King's Mother, you'll be — what? — her half sister-in-law, and kinswoman to the Stanley family."

"Anything for our sisters? What about our cousin Margaret?"

"Nothing yet. Thomas Grey, Mother's boy, is to come home later."

Cecily sighs. Our half brother has been like a father to us, fiercely loyal for all of our lives. He came into sanctuary with us, only breaking out to try to free our brothers in a secret attack on the Tower, serving at Henry's court in exile, trying to maintain our alliance with him, and spying for us all the while. When Mother became sure that Henry was an enemy to fear, she sent for Thomas to come home, but Henry captured him as he was leaving. Since then, he has been imprisoned in France. "He's pardoned? The king has forgiven him?"

"I think everyone knows he did nothing wrong. He was a hostage to ensure our alliance, Henry left him as a pledge with the French king, but now that Tudor sees that we're obedient, he can release Thomas and repay the French."

"And what about you?" Cecily demands.

"Apparently, Henry's going to marry me, because he can't get out of it. But he's in no sort of hurry. Apparently, everyone knows that he has been trying to renege."

She looks at me with sympathy. "It's an insult," she says.

"It is," I agree. "But I only want to be his queen; I don't want him as a man, so I don't care that he doesn't want me as his wife."

Westminster Palace, London, 30 October 1485

I watch from my bedroom window as the coronation barge goes down the river to the Tower, escorted by dozens of ships. I can hear the music ringing across the water. The royal barge has been regilded since we last sailed in it, and shines brightly golden on the cold water, while at prow and stern the flags of the Tudor red dragon and the Beaufort portcullis flap in triumph. Henry himself is a tiny figure. At this distance I can see only his long gown of purple velvet trimmed with ermine. He is standing so that everyone on the riverbanks can see him, arms akimbo, on the raised deck at the back of the barge. I shade my eyes and stare at him. This is the first time I have seen the man I am to marry, and at this distance he is no bigger than the tip of my little finger. The barge glides by, carrying my betrothed husband to his coronation without me, and he does not even know that I am watching him. He will not imagine that I put my little finger against the pane of thick glass to measure him, and then I snap my fingers with contempt.

The rowers are all in livery of green and white, the Tudor colors, the oars painted white with bright green blades. Henry Tudor has commanded springtime colors in autumn; it seems that nothing in England is good enough for this young invader. Though the leaves fall from the trees like brown tears, for him everything must be as green as fresh grass, as white as May blossom, as if to convince us all that the seasons are upside down and we are all Tudors now.

A second barge carries My Lady the King's Mother, seated in her triumph on a high chair, almost a throne, so that everyone can see Lady Margaret sailing into her own at last. Her husband stands beside her chair, one proprietorial hand on the gilded back, loyal to this king as he swore he was loyal to the previous one, and the one before that. His motto, his laughable motto, is *"Sans changer,"* which means "always unchanged," but the only way the Stanleys never change is their unending fidelity to themselves.

The next barge carries Jasper Tudor, the king's uncle, who will carry the crown at the coronation. My aunt Katherine, the prize for his victory, stands beside him, her hand resting lightly on his arm. She does not look up at our windows, though she will guess we are watching. She looks straight ahead, steady as

66

an archer, as she goes to witness the crowning of our enemy, her beautiful face quite impassive. She was married once before for the convenience of her family, to a young man who hated her; she is accustomed to grandeur abroad and humiliation at home. It has been the price she has paid for a lifetime of being one of the beautiful Rivers girls, always so close to the throne that it has bruised her like a wound.

My mother puts her arm around my waist, watching the procession with me. She says nothing, but I know that she is thinking of the day that we stood in sanctuary in the dark crypt below the abbey chapel, watching the royal barges go down the river, when they crowned my uncle Richard and passed over the true heir, my brother Edward. I thought then that we would all die in the darkness and solitude. I thought that an executioner would come for us silently one night. I thought I might wake briefly with the weight of a pillow on my face. I thought that I would never see sunshine again. I was a young woman then, and I thought that sorrow as deep as mine could only lead to death. I was grieving for my father and frightened by the absence of my brothers, and I thought that soon I would die too.

I realize that this is the third victorious coronation barge to sail past my mother. When I was just a little girl and my brother

Edward was not even born, she had to hide in sanctuary as my father the king was driven out of England. They brought back the old king and my mother stooped to look out of the low dirty window of the crypt under Westminster Abbey church to see Lady Margaret and her son Henry sail down the river in their pomp to celebrate the victory of the restored King Henry of Lancaster.

I was only a little girl then, and so I don't remember the ships sailing by nor the triumphant mother and her little son on a barge decked with red roses; but I do remember the pervasive scent of river water and damp. I do remember crying myself to sleep at night, utterly bewildered as to why we were suddenly living like poor people, hiding in a crypt under the chapel instead of enjoying the most beautiful palaces of the kingdom.

"This is the third time you have seen Lady Margaret sail by in triumph," I remark to my mother. "Once when King Henry was restored and she led the race to get to his court and introduce her son, once when her husband was high in Richard's favor and she carried Queen Anne's train at the coronation, and look, now she sails by you again."

"Yes," she acknowledges. I see her gray eyes narrow as she watches the gloriously gilded barge and the proud flap of the standards. "But I always find her so very . . . unconvincing, even in her greatest triumphs," she says.

"Unconvincing?" I repeat the odd word.

"She always looks to me like a woman who has been badly treated," my mother says, and she laughs joyously out loud, as if defeat is just a turn of the wheel of fortune and Lady Margaret is not on the rise and an instrument of the glorious will of God as she thinks, but has just been lucky on this turn, and is almost certain to fall on the next. "She always looks to me like a woman who has much to complain about," my mother explains. "And women like that are always badly treated."

She turns to look at me, and laughs aloud at my puzzled expression. "It doesn't matter," she says. "At any rate, we have her word that Henry will marry you, as soon as he is crowned, and then we'll have a York girl on the throne."

"He shows few signs of wanting to marry me," I say dryly. "I am hardly honored in the coronation procession. It's not us on the royal barge."

"Oh, he'll have to," she says confidently. "Whether he likes it or not. The Parliament will demand it of him. He won the battle, but they won't accept him as king without you at his side. He has had to promise. They've spoken to Thomas, Lord Stanley, and he, of all men, understands the way that power lies. Lord Stanley has spoken to his wife, she has spoken to her son. They all know that Henry has to marry you, like it or not."

"And what if I don't like it?" I turn to her and put my hands on her shoulders so she cannot glide away from my anger. "What if I don't want an unwilling bridegroom, a pretender to the crown, who won his throne through disloyalty and betrayal? What if I tell you that my heart is in an unmarked grave somewhere in Leicester?"

She does not flinch, but confronts my angry grief, her face serene. "Daughter mine, you have known for all your life that you would be married for the good of the country and the advancement of your family. You will do your duty like a princess, wherever your heart is buried, whoever you want or don't want, and I expect you to look happy as you do it."

"You'll marry me to a man that I wish were dead?"

Her smile does not waver. "Elizabeth, you know as well as I do that it is rare that a young woman can marry for love."

"You did," I accuse.

"I had the sense to fall in love with the King of England."

"So did I!" breaks from me like a cry.

She nods and puts her hand gently on the nape of my neck, and when I yield to her, she pulls my head to her shoulder. "I know, I know, my love. Richard was unlucky that day, and he had never been unlucky before. You would have thought he was certain to win. I

70

thought he was certain to win. I too staked my hopes and my happiness on his winning."

"Do I really have to marry Henry?"

"Yes, you do. You will be Queen of England and return our family to greatness. You will restore peace to England. These are great things to achieve. You should be glad. Or, at the very least, you can look glad."

WESTMINSTER PALACE, LONDON, NOVEMBER 1485

Henry's first Parliament is busy in their work, reversing the laws of Richard, pulling his signature from the statute books just as they pulled the coronet from his helmet. First they lift all the attainders of treason that were sworn against Tudor supporters, declaring themselves splendidly innocent and faithful only to their country's interest. My uncle the Duke of Suffolk and his sons John and Edmund de la Pole all become faithful Tudors and are no longer Yorkists, though their mother, Elizabeth, is a daughter of the House of York and sister to my Richard and to my late father. My half brother Thomas Grey, who was left in France as a hostage, is to be ransomed and brought home. The king is going to overlook the suspicions he felt as a pretender. Thomas writes a pleading letter saying that he never meant to appear as if he was trying to escape from Henry's ragbag pretender court, he was just returning to England at my mother's bidding. And Henry, confident in his new power, is prepared to forget the momentary betrayal.

They restore Henry's mother to her family fortune and properties; nothing is more important than building the wealth of this most powerful king's mother. Then they promise to pay my mother's pension as a dowager queen. They also agree that Richard's law that ruled my mother and father were never legally married must be dismissed as a slander. More than that, it must be forgotten, and nobody is ever to repeat it. At a stroke of the pen from the Tudor Parliament, we are restored to our family name and I and all my sisters are legitimate princesses of York once more. Cecily's first marriage is forgotten; it is as if it never was. She is Princess Cecily of York once again and free to be married to Lady Margaret's kinsman. In Westminster Palace, the servants now bend their knee to present a dish, and everyone calls each of us "Your Grace."

Cecily delights in our sudden restoration to our titles, all of us York princesses are glad to be ourselves once again; but I find my mother walking in silence by the cold river, her hood over her head, her cold hands clasped in her muff, her gray eyes on the gray water. "Lady Mother, what is it?" I go to take her hands and look into her pale face.

"He thinks my boys are dead," she whispers.

I look down and see the mud on her boots

and on the hem of her gown. She has been walking beside the river for an hour at least, whispering to the rippling water.

"Come inside, you're freezing," I say.

She lets me take her hand and lead her up the graveled path to the garden door, and help her up the stone stairs to her privy chamber.

"Henry must have certain proof that both my boys are dead."

I take off her cloak and press her into a chair beside the fire. My sisters are out, walking to the houses of the silk merchants, gold in their purses, servants to carry their purchases home, served on bended knee, laughing at their restoration. Only my mother and I struggle here, locked in grief. I kneel before her and feel the dry rushes under my knees release their cold perfume. I take her icy hands in mine. Our heads are so close together that no one, not even someone listening at the door, could hear our whispered conversation.

"Lady Mother," I say quietly. "How do you know?"

She bows her head as if she has been struck hard in the heart. "He must do. He must be absolutely sure that they are both dead."

"Were you still hoping for your son Edward, even now?"

A little gesture, like that of a wounded animal, tells me that she has never stopped hoping that her eldest York son had somehow escaped from the Tower and still lived, somewhere, against the odds.

"Really?"

"I thought I would know," she says very quietly. "In my heart. I thought that if my boy Edward had been killed I would have known in that moment. I thought that his spirit could not have left this world and not touched me as he went. You know, Elizabeth, I love him so much."

"But, Mother, we both heard the singing that night, the singing that comes when one of our house is dying."

She nods. "We did. But still I kept on hoping."

There is a little silence between us, as we observe the death of her hope.

"D'you think Henry has made a search and found the bodies?"

She shakes her head. She's certain of this. "No. For if he had the bodies, he would show them to the world and give them a great funeral for everyone to know they're gone. If he had the bodies, he would give them a royal burial. He'd have us all draped in darkest blue, in mourning for months. If he had any firm evidence, he would use it to blacken Richard's name. If he had anyone he could accuse of murder, he would put him on trial and publicly hang him. The best thing in the world for Henry would have been to find two

75

bodies. He will have been praying ever since he landed in England that he would find them dead and buried, so that his claim to the throne was secure, so that nobody could ever rise up and impersonate them. The only person in England who wants to know more urgently than me where my sons are tonight is Henry the new king.

"So he can't have found their bodies, but he must be certain that they are dead. Someone must have promised him that they were killed. Someone that he must trust. Because he would never have restored the royal title to our family if he thought we had a surviving boy. He would never have made you girls princesses of York if he thought that somewhere there was also a living prince."

"So he's been assured that both Edward and Richard are dead?"

"He must be sure. Otherwise, he would never have ruled that your father and I were married. The act that makes you a princess of York again makes your brothers princess of York. If our Edward is dead, then your younger brother is King Richard IV of England, and Henry is a usurper. Henry would never have restored a royal title to a live rival. He must be sure that both the boys are dead. Someone must have sworn to him that the murder was truly done. Someone must have told him, without doubt, that they killed two boys and saw them dead."

"Could it be his mother?" I whisper.

"She's the only one with reason to kill them, who was here when they disappeared, who is alive now," my mother says. "Henry was in exile, his uncle Jasper with him. Henry's ally the Duke of Buckingham might have done it; but he's dead, so we'll never know. If someone has reassured Henry, just now, that he is safe, then it must be his mother. The two of them must have convinced themselves that they are safe. They think both York princes are dead. Next, he will propose marriage to you."

"He has waited till he is certain that my two little brothers are dead before he names me princess and offers me marriage?" I ask. The taste in my mouth is as bitter as my question.

My mother shrugs. "Of course. What else could he do? This is the way of the world."

My mother is right. Early one wintry evening, a troop of the king's newly appointed yeomen of the guard, smart in their scarlet livery, march up to the door of Westminster Palace and a herald delivers the message that King Henry will have the pleasure of visiting me within the hour.

"Run," my mother says, taking in this letter with one swift glance. "Bess!" — to the new maid-in-waiting. "Go with Her Grace and fetch my new headdress, and her new green gown, and tell the boy to bring hot water to her room and the bath at once! Cecily! Anne! You get dressed too, and get your sisters dressed and get the Warwick children to go to the schoolroom and tell their schoolmaster to keep them there until I send for them. The Warwick children are not to come downstairs while the king is here. Make sure they understand that."

"I'll wear a hood, my black hood," I say stubbornly.

"My new headdress!" she exclaims. "My jeweled headdress! You are to be Queen of England, why look like his housekeeper? Why look like his mother? As dull as a nun?"

"Because that's what he must like," I say quickly. "Don't you see? He'll like girls who are as dull as nuns. He was never at our court, he never saw the fine dresses and the beautiful women. He never saw the dances and the gowns and the glamour of our court. He was stuck like a poor boy in Brittany with maidservants and housekeepers. He lived in one poor inn after another. And then he comes to England and spends all the time with his mother, who dresses like a nun and is as ugly as sin. I have to look modest, not grand."

My mother snaps her fingers in exasperation at herself. "Fool that I am! Quite right! Right! So go!" She gives me a little push in the back. "Go, and hurry!" I hear her laugh.

"Be as plain as you can! If you can manage not to be the most beautiful girl in England, that would be excellent!"

I run as she bids me, and the lad who brings the firewood rolls the great wooden bath into my bedroom and labors up the stairs with the heavy jugs of hot water to hand over at the door. I have to wash in a hurry as the maid brings in the jugs and fills up the bath, and then I dry and twist my damp hair up under my black gable hood, which sits heavily on my forehead, two great wings either side of my ears. I step into my linen and my green gown, and Bess darts around me threading the laces through the holes to fasten the bodice until I am trussed like a chicken, I slip on my shoes and turn to her, and she smiles at me and says: "Beautiful. You are so beautiful, Your Grace."

I take up the hand mirror and see my face reflected dimly in the beaten silver. I am flushed from the heat of the bath and I look well, my face oval, my eyes deep gray. I try a little smile and see my lips curve upwards, an empty expression without any glimmer of happiness. Richard told me I was the most beautiful girl that had ever been born, that one glance from me set him on fire with desire, that my skin was perfect, that my hair was his delight, that he never slept so well as with his face buried in my blond plait. I don't expect to hear such words of love ever again.

I don't expect to feel beautiful ever again. They buried my joy and my girl's vanity with my lover, and I don't expect to feel either ever again.

The bedroom door bursts open. "He's here," Anne says breathlessly. "Riding into the courtyard with about forty men. Mother says come at once."

"Are the Warwick children upstairs in the schoolroom?"

She nods. "They know not to come down."

And so I walk down the stairs, my head steady as if wearing a crown instead of the heavy hood, my green gown brushing aside the scented rushes, as they throw open the double doors and Henry Tudor, the conqueror of England, newly crowned king, the murderer of my happiness, walks into the great hall below me.

My first thought is relief; he is less of a man than I expected. All these years of knowing that there was a pretender to the throne waiting for his chance to invade turned him into a thing of terror, a beast, larger than life. They said that he was guarded by a giant of a man at Bosworth, and I had imagined him as a giant also. But the man who comes into the hall is slight of build, tall but spare, a man of nearly thirty, energy in his walk but strain in his face, brown hair, and narrow brown eyes. For the first time it strikes me that it must be hard to spend your life in exile and finally win your kingdom by a thread, by the action of a turncoat in battle, and to know that most of the country does not celebrate your luck, and the woman that you have to marry is in love with someone else: your dead enemy and the rightful king. I have been thinking of him as triumphant; but here I see a man burdened by an odd twist of fate, coming to victory by a sneaking disloyalty, on a hot day in August, uncertain even now, if God is with him.

I pause on the stairs, my hands on the cold marble balustrade, leaning over to look down on him. His reddish-brown hair is thinning slightly on the top of his head; I can see it from my vantage point as he takes off his hat and bows low over my mother's hand, and he comes up and smiles at her without warmth. His face is guarded, which is understandable, as he is coming to the home of a most unreliable ally. Sometimes my Lady Mother was supporting his plan against Richard, and sometimes she was against him. She sent her own son Thomas Grey to his court as his supporter but then called him home again, suspecting Henry of killing our prince. I imagine he never knew whether she was friend or enemy; of course he mistrusts her. He must mistrust all of us duplicitous princesses. He must fear my dishonesty, my infidelity, worst of all.

He kisses my mother's fingertips as lightly as he can, as if he expects nothing but sham appearances from her, perhaps from everyone. Then he straightens up and follows her upward glance, and sees me, standing above him, on the stairs.

He knows at once who I am, and my nod of acknowledgment tells him that I recognize in him the man that I am to marry. We look more like two strangers agreeing to undertake an uncomfortable expedition together than lovers greeting. Until four months ago I was the lover of his enemy and praying three times daily for Tudor's defeat. As recently as yesterday he was taking advice to see if he could avoid his betrothal to me. Last night, I was dreaming that he did not exist and woke wishing that it was the day before Bosworth and that he would invade only to face defeat and death. But he won at Bosworth, and now he cannot escape from his oath to marry me and I cannot escape from my mother's promise that I shall marry him.

I come slowly down the stairs as we take the measure of each other, as if to see the truth of a long-imagined enemy. It is extraordinary to me to think that whether I like it or not, I shall have to marry him, bed him, bear his children, and live with him for the rest of my life. I shall call him husband, he will be my master, I will be his wife and his chattel. I will never escape his power over me until his death. Coldly, I wonder if I will spend the rest of my life, daily wishing for his death.

"Good day, Your Grace," I say quietly, and I come down the last steps and curtsey and give him my hand.

He bows to kiss my fingers, and then draws me to him and kisses me on one cheek and then another, like a French courtier, pretty manners that mean nothing. His scent is clean, pleasant, I can smell the fresh winter countryside in his hair. He steps back, and I see his brown guarded eyes, and his tentative smile.

"Good day, Princess Elizabeth," he says. "I am glad to meet you at last."

"You will take a glass of wine?" my mother offers.

"Thank you," he says; but he does not shift his gaze from my face, as if he is judging me.

"This way," my mother says equably and leads the way to a private chamber off the great hall, where there is a decanter of Venetian glass and matching wine goblets for the three of us. The king seats himself on a chair but rudely gives no permission to us, and so we have to remain standing before him. My mother pours the wine and serves him first. He raises a glass to me and drinks as if he were in a taproom, but does not make a toast. He seems content to sit in silence, thoughtfully regarding me as I stand like a child before him.

"My other daughters." My mother introduces them serenely. It takes an awful lot to

83

shake my mother — this is a woman who has slept through a regicide — and she nods to the doorway. Cecily and Anne come in with Bridget and Catherine behind them. They all four curtsey very low. I can't stop myself smiling at Bridget's dignified sinking and rising. She is only a little girl, but she is no less than a duchess already in her grand manners. She looks at me reprovingly; she is a most serious five-year-old.

"I am glad to meet you all," the new king says generally, not bothering to get to his feet. "And you are comfortable here? You have everything you need?"

"I thank you, yes," my mother says, as if she did not once own all of England, and this was her favorite palace and run exactly as she commanded.

"Your allowance will be paid every quarter," he says to her. "My Lady Mother is making the arrangements."

"Please give my best wishes to Lady Margaret," my mother says. "Her friendship has sustained me recently, and her service was very dear to me in the past."

"Ah," he says, as if he doesn't much relish being reminded that his mother was my mother's lady-in-waiting. "And your son Thomas Grey will be released from France and can come home to you," he goes on, dispensing his goods.

"I thank you. And please tell your mother

that Cecily, her goddaughter, is well," my mother pursues. "And grateful to you and your mother for your care of her forthcoming marriage." Cecily drops a little extra curtsey to demonstrate to the king which one of us she is, and he gives a bored nod. She looks up as if she longs to remind him that she is only waiting for him to name her wedding day, and until he does so she is still neither widow nor maid. But he gives her no opportunity to speak.

"My advisors inform me that the people are eager to see Princess Elizabeth married," he says.

My mother inclines her head.

"I wanted to assure myself that you are well and happy," he says directly to me. "And that you consent."

Startled, I look up. I am not well, and I am far from happy; I am deep in grief for the man I love, the man killed by this new king and buried without honor. This man sitting before me now, asking so courteously that I consent, allowed his men to strip Richard of his armor, and then of his linen, and tie his naked body across the saddle of his horse and trot it home. They told me that they let Richard's dead lolling head knock, in passing, against the wooden beam of the Bow Bridge as they brought him in to Leicester. That clunk, the noise of dead skull against post, sounds through my days, echoes in my dreams. Then they exposed his naked broken body on the chancel steps of the church so that everyone knew he was completely and utterly dead, and that any chance of England's happiness under the House of York was completely and utterly over.

"My daughter is well and happy, and is your most obedient servant," my mother says pleasantly, in the little silence.

"And what motto shall you choose?" he asks. "When you are my wife?"

I begin to wonder if he has come only to torment me. I have not thought of this. Why on earth would I have thought of my wifely motto? "Oh, do you have a preference?" I ask him, my voice coldly uninterested. "For I have none."

"My Lady Mother suggested 'humble and penitent,'" he says.

Cecily snorts with laughter, turns it into a cough, and looks away, blushing. My mother and I exchange one horrified glance, but we both know we can say nothing.

"As you wish." I manage to sound indifferent, and I am glad of this. If nothing else, I can pretend that I don't care.

"Humble and penitent, then," he says, quietly to himself, as if he is pleased, and now I am sure that he is laughing at us.

Next day my mother comes to me, smiling. "Now I understand why we were honored with a royaal visit yesterday," she says. "The speaker of the House of Parliament himself stepped down from his chair and begged the king, in the name of the whole house, to marry you. The commons and the lords told him that they must have the issue resolved. The people will not stand for him as king without you at his side. They put such a petition to him that he could not deny them. They promised me this, but I wasn't sure they would dare to go through with it. Everyone is so afraid of him; but they want a York girl on the throne and the Cousins' War concluded by a marriage of the cousins more than anything in the world. Nobody can feel certain that peace has come with Henry Tudor unless you're on the throne too. They don't see him as anything more than a lucky pretender. They told him they want him to be a king grafted onto the Plantagenets, this sturdy vine."

"He can't have liked that."

"He was furious," she says gleefully. "But there was nothing he could do. He has to have you as his wife."

"Humble and penitent," I remind her sourly.

"Humble and penitent it is," my mother confirms cheerfully. She looks at my downcast face and laughs. "They're just words," she reminds me. "Words that he can force you to say now. But in return we make him marry you and we make you Queen of England, and then it really doesn't matter what your motto is."

WESTMINSTER PALACE, LONDON, DECEMBER 1485

Again the royal herald comes to the door with the news that the king proposes the pleasure of a visit with us. But this time he intends to dine, and about twenty of his court will come with him. My mother commands the groom of the servery, the groom of the kitchens, and the groom of the ewery to present themselves to her with a menu of dishes and wines that can be prepared and served this very day, and sets them to work. She has commanded banquets with scores of dishes served to hundreds of people when she was queen in this very palace and my father the most beloved King of England. She takes a pleasure in being able to show Henry, a man who spent fifteen years hanging on the fringes of the little court of Brittany, exiled from England and in fear of his life, how a truly great palace should be run.

The firewood boy toils up the stairs with another bath, and the Warwick children are banished to their rooms and told not to come downstairs, nor even to be seen at the windows.

"Why not?" Margaret asks me, slipping into my room behind the maids carrying an armful of warm linen and a bottle of rosewater for me to rinse my hair. "Does your lady mother think that Teddy is not quick enough to meet the king?" She flushes. "Is she ashamed of us?"

"Mother doesn't want the king distracted by the sight of a York boy," I say shortly. "It's nothing to do with you, or Edward. Henry knows about you both, of course, you can be sure that his mother, in her careful audit of everything that England holds, has not forgotten you. She has made you her wards; but you're safer out of sight."

She pales. "You don't think the king would take Teddy away?"

"No," I say. "But there's no need for them to dine together. It's better if we don't throw them together, surely. Besides, if Teddy tells Henry that he is expecting to be king, it would be awkward."

She gives a little laugh. "I wish no one had ever told him that he was next in line for the throne," she says. "He took it so much to heart."

"He's better out of the way until Henry is accustomed to everything," I say. "And Teddy is a darling, but he can't be trusted not to speak out."

She glances around at the preparations for my bath, and the laying out of my new gown, brought from the City this very day by the dressmaker, in Tudor green with love knots at the shoulders. "Do you mind very much, Elizabeth?"

I shrug my shoulders, denying my own pain. "I am a princess of York," I say. "I have to do this, I would always have had to marry someone to suit my father's plans. I was betrothed in the cradle. I have no choice; but I never expected to have a choice — except once, and that feels like an enchanted time now, like a dream. When your time comes, you will have to marry where you are ordered too."

"Does it make you sad?" she asks, she is such a dear serious girl.

I shake my head. "I feel nothing," I tell her the truth. "That's perhaps the worst thing. I don't feel anything at all."

Henry's court arrives on time, handsomely dressed, with shy half-hidden smiles. Half of his court is composed of old friends of ours; most of us are related by marriage if not by blood. There are many things left unsaid as the lords come in and greet us, just as they used to do when we were the royal family, entertaining them here, at the palace.

My cousin John de la Pole, who Richard named as his heir before Bosworth, is there with his mother, my aunt Elizabeth. She and all her family are now loyal Tudors and greet us with careful smiles.

My other aunt, Katherine, now carries the name of Tudor, and walks on the arm of the king's uncle Jasper; but she curtseys to my mother as low as she always did, and rises up to kiss her warmly.

My uncle Edward Woodville, my mother's own brother, is among the Tudor court, an honored and trusted friend of the new king. He has been with Henry since he went into exile, and he fought in his army at Bosworth. He bows low over my mother's hand, then kisses her on both cheeks as her brother, and I hear his whisper: "Good to see you back in your rightful place, Lizzie-Your-Grace!"

Mother has arranged an impressive feast with twenty-two courses, and after everyone has eaten and the plates and the trestle tables have been cleared away, my sisters Cecily and Anne dance before the court.

"Please, Princess Elizabeth, dance for us," the king says briefly to me.

I look to my mother; we had agreed that I would not dance. Last time I danced in these rooms it was the Christmas feast and I was wearing a dress of silk as rich as Queen Anne's own, made to the same pattern as the queen's, as if to force a comparison between her and me — her junior by ten years; and her husband the king, Richard, could not take his eyes off me. The whole court knew that he was falling in love with me and that he would leave his old sick wife to be with me. I danced with my sisters, but he saw only me. I danced before hundreds of people, but only for him.

"If you please," Henry says, and I meet his straight hazel gaze and see that I can make no excuse.

I rise from my seat and put out my hand to Cecily, who will have to be my partner, whether she likes it or not, and the musicians strike up a saltarello. Cecily has danced with me many times before King Richard, and I can see by the sharp twist of her mouth that she is thinking of that too. She may feel like a slave having to amuse a sultan but, in this instance, I am the one most humiliated — and this is a comfort to her. It's a fast dance, with a hop or a skip at the end of each step, and we are both quick-footed and graceful. We whirl round the room, partnering each other and then dance off to other partners and meet back again in the center. The musicians end with a flourish and we curtsey to the king and to each other and go back to stand beside my mother, a little rosy and damp and breathless, as the musicians take to the floor and play for the king.

He listens with attention, one hand tapping out the rhythm on the arm of his chair. Clearly he has a love of music and when they close with a flourish, he rewards them with a piece of gold, an adequate reward; but far from princely. Watching him, I understand that he is as careful with money as his mother — this is not a young man raised to think that the world owed him a throne. This is not a young man accustomed to a king's fortune who spends it gladly. Not a man like my Richard, who understood that a nobleman must live like a lord and spread his good fortune among his people. Then they play for general dancing and the king leans to my mother and says that he would like some time with me, alone.

"Of course, Your Grace." She is about to walk away from us and take the girls with her, leaving us on our own at the end of the great hall.

"Alone and undisturbed." He stops her with a gesture of his hand. "In a private room."

She hesitates, and I can almost see her calculating. Firstly, he is the king. Secondly, we are betrothed; and then finally her decision: he cannot, in any case, be refused. "You can be quite alone in the private chamber behind the great table," she says. "I will see that you are not disturbed."

He nods and rises to his feet. The musicians stop playing, the court sweeps down into a hundred bows and then rises up avidly to watch us as King Henry holds out his hand to me and, with my mother leading the way, escorts me from the raised dais and the great table where we took our dinner, through the arched doorway at the back of the great hall, into the private rooms. Everyone is rapt as we leave the court and the dancing. At the door to the chamber, my mother steps back and with a small shrug lets us go in, and it is as if we were playactors stepping off a stage into private life, into life without a playscript.

Once inside the room, he closes the door. Outside, I can hear the musicians start up again, the sound muffled through the thick wood. As if it were a matter of course, he turns the great key in the lock.

"What?" I say, startled from good manners. "What d'you think you are doing?"

He turns towards me and puts his hand firmly around my waist, locking me to his side with an irresistible grip. "We are going to become better acquainted," he says.

I don't shrink back from him like a fearful maid. I stand my ground. "I should like to go back to the hall."

He sits on a chair as big as a throne, and pulls me down so I am perched uncomfortably on his knee, as if he were a drunk and I a doxy in a tavern, and he had just paid for me. "No. I told you. We are going to become better acquainted."

I try to pull away from him, but he holds me firmly. If I struggle or fight with him I will be raising my hand against the King of England, and that is an act of treason. "Your Grace . . ." I say.

"It seems that we have to be married," he says, a harder note coming into his voice. "I am honored by the interest that Parliament takes in the matter. Your family still has many friends, it seems. Even among those who profess to be my friends. I understand from them that you are insisting on the wedding. I'm flattered, thank you for the attention. As we both know, we have been betrothed for two long years. So now we are going to consummate our betrothal."

"What?"

He sighs as if I am wearisomely stupid. "We are going to consummate our betrothal."

"I will not," I say flatly.

"You will have to do this on our wedding night. What is the difference now?"

"Because this is to dishonor me!" I exclaim. "You do this in my mother's rooms, with my sisters just a footstep through that door, in my mother's own palace, before our wedding, to dishonor me!"

His smile is cold. "I don't think you have much honor to defend, do you, Elizabeth? And please — don't be afraid that I will discover that you are not a virgin. I have lost count of the number of people who wrote to me, especially to tell me that you were King Richard's lover. And those who took the trouble to come all the way from England just to say that they saw you walking hand in hand with him in the gardens, that he came to your rooms every night, that you were his wife's lady-in-waiting but you spent all your time in his bed. And there were many who said that she died of poison and that it was you who passed her the physic in the glass. Your mother's Italian powders were courteously served to yet another victim. The Rivers flow sweetly over yet another obstacle."

I am so horrified I can hardly speak. "I never," I swear. "I never would have hurt Queen Anne."

He shrugs his shoulders as if it does not matter whether or not I am a murderess and a regicide. "Oh, who cares now? I daresay we have both done things we would rather not remember. She's dead, and he's dead, your brothers are dead, and you are betrothed to me."

"My brothers!" I exclaim, suddenly intent.

"Dead. There is no one left but us."

"How do you know this?"

"I know it. Here, lean closer."

"You speak of my dead brothers and you want to shame me?" I can hardly speak, I am choking with emotion.

He leans back and laughs as if he is genuinely amused. "Really! How could I shame a girl like you? Your reputation precedes you by miles. You are utterly shamed already. I have thought of you for this last year as little more than a murderous whore."

I am breathless as he insults me while his hard hands hold my waist, pinning me on his bony knees, like an unwilling child in a forced caress. "You cannot desire me. You know that I don't desire you."

"No indeed. Not at all. I'm not very fond of spoiled meats, I don't want another man's leavings. I particularly don't want a dead man's leavings. The thought of Richard the Usurper pawing you about and you fawning on him for the crown makes me quite sick."

"Then let me go!" I shout and pull away, but he holds me tightly down.

"No. For, as you see, I have to marry you; your witch of a mother has made sure of that. The Houses of Parliament have made sure of that. But I do insist on knowng that you're fertile. I want to know what I'm getting. Since I am forced to marry you, I must insist on a fertile wife. We have to have a Tudor prince. It would be a waste of everything if you turned out to be barren."

I struggle in earnest now, trying to stand, trying to pull away, trying to unwind his hard hands, pulling his fingers off my waist; but he is inescapable, his hands gripping me as if he would strangle me. "Now," he says, a little breathlessly, "am I to force you? Or will you lift that pretty gown for me and we can get the business done and return to your mother's dinner? Perhaps you will dance for us again? Like the slut that you are?"

For a moment I am quite frozen with horror, looking into his lean face, then, to my surprise, he suddenly snatches my wrist but releases my waist, and I jump up from his lap and stand before him. For one last moment I think of wrenching my hand free and dashing for the door and running away, but the skin on my arm is burning where he grips me, and the hardness of his expression tells me that there will be no escape, no chance of escape. I flush scarlet and the tears come to my eyes.

"Please," I say weakly. "Please don't make me do this."

He almost shrugs, as if there is nothing he can do but hold my wrist as if I were a prisoner, and with his free hand he makes a small lifting gesture to the hem of my gown, my Tudor green gown.

"I will come willingly to you tonight . . ." I offer. "I will come in secret, to your rooms."

He gives a hard condemning laugh. "Smuggled into the king's bed for old times' sake? So you are a whore, just as I thought. And I shall have you like a whore. Here and now."

"My father . . ." I whisper. "You're in his chair, my father's chair . . ."

"Your father is dead, and your uncle was no great protector of your honor," he says and gives a little snorting laugh as if he is genuinely amused. "Get on with it. Lift your dress and climb on me. Ride me. You're no virgin. You know how to do it."

He keeps tight hold of me as, slowly, I bend down and lift the hem of my gown. With his other hand, he unlaces his breeches and sits back on the chair, his legs spread, and I obey his gesture and the tug on my hand and step towards him.

One hand is still gripping my wrist as his other hand raises my daintily embroidered linen, and he makes me straddle him as if I were the whore he calls me. He pulls me down onto him, where he is sitting in the chair, and thrusts upwards no more than a dozen times. His hot breath on my face is spicy from dinner when he rears up towards me, and I close my eyes and turn my face to one side, holding my breath. I dare not think of Richard. If I think of Richard, who used to take me with such delight and whisper my name in his pleasure, then I will vomit. Mercifully, Henry groans in momentary pleasure, and I open my eyes and find that he is staring at me, his brown gaze quite blank. He has observed me like a prisoner on the rack of his desire, and he has got to his satisfaction without blinking.

"Don't cry," he says when I have climbed down and mopped myself with the hem on my fine linen shift. "How shall you walk out and face your mother and my court if you are crying?"

"You hurt me," I say resentfully. I show him the red weal on my wrist, and I bend and pull down my crumpled shift and my creased new gown in the merry Tudor green.

"I am sorry for that," he says indifferently. "I will try not to hurt you in the future. If you don't pull away, then I won't have to hold you so tightly."

"In the future?"

"Your maid-in-waiting or your charming sister, or even your agreeable mother, will admit me to your rooms. I shall come to you. You won't ever be in the king's bed again, so don't think of it. You can tell your sister, or whoever it is who sleeps with you, that she must bed elsewhere. I will come every night before midnight at a time of my choosing. Some nights I might be later. You'll have to wait up. You can tell your mother that this is your wish and mine."

"She'll never believe me," I say irritably, rubbing the tears from my face and nipping my lips to bring the color back to them. "She'll never think I have summoned you for love."

"She'll understand that I want a fertile bride," he says shrewdly. "She'll understand that you are to be carrying my child on your wedding day, or there will be no wedding. I won't be such a fool as to be forced to marry a barren bride. We have agreed on this."

"We?" I repeat. "We don't! I don't agree to this! I never said I agreed to this! And my mother would never believe that I consented to be shamed by you, that we have decided this together. She'll know at once that this is not my wish but yours, and that you forced me."

He smiles for the first time. "Ah no, you misunderstand me. I didn't say 'we' meaning you and I. I can't imagine speaking of you and me as 'we.' No; I meant me and my mother."

I stop fussing with my skirt and turn to face him, open-mouthed. "Your mother agreed that you should rape me?"

He nods. "Why not?"

I stammer: "Because she said she would be my friend, because she said that she saw my destiny! Because she said that she would pray for me!"

He is quite untroubled by this, seeing no contradiction in her tenderness to me and her command that I should be raped. "Of course she thinks it is your destiny," he says. "All this" — his gesture takes in my bruised wrist, my red eyes, my humiliation, the rawness in my groin, and the ache in my heart — "All this is God's will, as my lady mother sees it."

I am so horrified that I can do nothing but

stare at him.

He laughs, and stands to tuck his linen shirt back into his breeches and lace up the opening. "To make a prince for a Tudor throne is an act of God," he says. "My mother would regard it almost as a sacrament. However painful."

Roughly, I rub the tears from my face. "Then you serve a hard God and a harder mother," I spit at him.

He agrees. "I know. It is their determination which has brought me here. It is the only thing I can count on."

He is as good as his word and he visits me, like a man visiting the apothecary for leeches or medicine, without fail but without pleasure, every night. My mother, tight-lipped, changes my bedroom to one nearer the privy stairs that go down to the gardens and the pier for his barge. She tells Cecily that she is to sleep with her sisters, and I am now to sleep alone. Her white-faced fury prevents any comment or questions, even from Cecily, who is wild with curiosity. My lady mother herself admits Henry by the unbolted outer door, and escorts him in icy silence to my room. She never says one word of welcome to him; she walks him to and from the door as an enemy, her head held high in scorn. She waits for him in the privy hall with one candle burning and the fire banked low. She says not one word of farewell as he leaves, but opens the door for him and locks it behind him in a silent rage. He must have a determination of iron to walk in and out of my room past my speechlessly hating mother with her gray gaze burning like branding rods into his thin back.

In my room, I am silent too, but after the first few visits he becomes more assured, pausing for a glass of wine before he goes about his business, asking me what I have been doing during the day, telling me about his own work. He starts to sit in the chair by the fireside and eat some biscuits, cheese, and fruits before unlacing his breeches and taking me. While he is sitting, looking at the flames, he speaks to me as an equal, one who might have an interest in his day. He tells me the news of the court, the many men he is forgiving and hoping to bind to his rule, and his plans for the country. Despite myself, though I start the night in furious silence, I find that I volunteer what my father did in one county or another, or what Richard had planned to do in his reign. He listens with attention and sometimes says, "Good, thank you for telling me that, I didn't know that."

He is awkwardly conscious that he has spent his life in exile, speaks English with a foreign accent — part Breton, part French — and he knows nothing of the country that he calls his own except what he has been taught by his devoted uncle Jasper and the tutors that he hired. He has a vivid affectionate memory of Wales from when he was a little boy and the ward of William Herbert, one of my father's greatest friends; but everything else he knows from teachers, from his uncle Jasper, and from the confused and badly drawn maps of exiles.

He has one powerful memory that he relates like a fable, of going to the mad king's court, when my father was the king in exile, and my mother and my sisters and I were trapped in the dark cold of sanctuary for the first time. He remembers it as the pinnacle of his childhood, when his mother was sure that they would all be restored and would be the royal family forever, and he suddenly believed her, and knew that God was guiding her to the Beaufort destiny and that she was right.

"Oh, we watched you go by on your barge," I say, remembering. "I saw you on the sunlit river, sailing by to the court, while we were all locked up and sick of the darkness."

He says that he knelt and was blessed by Henry VI and felt, at that brush of the royal hand on his head, that he had been touched by a saint. "He was more of a holy man than a king," he says to me urgently, like a preacher who wants someone to believe. "You could feel it in him, he was a saint, he was like an angel." Then he suddenly falls silent, as if remembering that this is the man who was murdered in his sleep by my own father, when the mad king was as foolish as a little child trusting to the unreliable honor of the House of York. "A saint and a martyr," he says accusingly. "He died after he had said his prayers. He died in a state of grace. At the hand of those who were little more than heretics, traitors, regicides."

"I suppose so," I mutter.

Every time we speak we seem to remind each other of a conflict; our very touch smudges blood prints between us.

He is conscious that he has done a most vile thing by declaring his reign from the day before the battle that killed Richard. Everyone who fought on the side of the anointed king that day can now be named as a traitor and legally put to death. It is to set justice upside down and to start his reign as a tyrant.

"No one has ever done such a thing before," I remark. "Even the York and Lancaster kings accepted that it was a rivalry between two houses and that a man might choose one side or the other with honor. What you have done is to name men who have done nothing worse than suffer as traitors. You make them traitors for doing nothing worse than losing. You are saying that whoever wins is in the right."

"It looks harsh," he concedes.

"It looks like double-dealing. How can they be named traitors when they were defending the ordained king against an invasion? It's contrary to the law, and common sense. It must be against God's will too."

He smiles as if nothing matters more than that the Tudor reign is established, without question. "Oh no, it's certainly not against the will of God. My mother is a most holy woman, and she doesn't think so."

"And is she to be the only judge?" I ask sharply. "Of God's will? Of the law in England?"

"Certainly, hers is the only judgment I trust," he replies. He smiles. "Certainly I would take her advice before yours."

He takes a glass of wine and then he beckons me to the bed with a cheerful briskness that I begin to think hides his own discomfort at what he is doing. I lie on my back as still as a stone. I never remove my gown, I never even help him when he pulls it up out of his way. I allow him to take me without a word of protest, and I turn my face to the wall so that the first time, the very first time, that he leans down to kiss my cheek, it falls on my ear, and I ignore it as if it were the brush of a buzzing fly.

WESTMINSTER PALACE, LONDON, THE DAYS OF CHRISTMAS, 1485

After three long weeks of this, I go to my mother.

"I have missed my course," I say flatly. "I suppose that's a sign."

The delight in her face is answer enough. "Oh! My dear!"

"He has to marry me at once, I won't be publicly shamed by them."

"He'll have no reason to delay. This is what they wanted. Fancy you being so fertile! But I was just the same and my mother was too. We are women blessed with children."

"Yes," I say. I can't put any joy in my voice. "I don't feel blessed. It's not as if this is a baby conceived in love. Not even in wedlock."

She ignores the bleakness in my voice, and the strain in my pale face. She draws me to her and puts her hand on my belly, which is as slim and flat as ever. "It is a blessing," she assures me. "A new baby, perhaps a boy, perhaps a prince. It doesn't matter that he was conceived under duress; what matters is that he grows strong and tall and that we make him our own, a rose of York on the throne of England."

I stand quietly under her touch, like an obedient brood mare, and I know that she is right. "Will you tell him or shall I?"

At once she is planning: "You tell him," she says. "He will be happy hearing it from you. It will be the first good news that you can bring him." She smiles at me. "The first of many, I hope."

I can't smile back. "I suppose so."

That evening he comes early, and I serve him his wine and put up my hand to him in refusal as he goes to lead me to the bed.

"I have missed my course," I say quietly. "I may be with child."

There is no mistaking the joy in his face. His color flushes up, he takes my hands and draws me closer to him, almost as if he would wrap his arms around me, almost as if he wants to hold me with love. "Oh, I am glad," he says. "Very glad. Thank you for telling me, it makes my heart lighter. God bless you, Elizabeth. God bless you and the child you carry. This is great news. This is the best news." He takes a turn to the fire and comes back to me again. "This is such good news! And you so beautiful! And so fertile!"

I nod, my face like stone.

"And d'you know if it will be a boy?" he asks.

"It is too early to know anything," I say. "And a woman can miss her course from unhappiness or shock."

"Then I hope you are not unhappy or shocked," he says cheerfully, as if he wants to forget that I am heartbroken and raped. "And I hope that you have a Tudor boy in there." He pats my belly as if we were married already, a proprietorial touch. "This means everything," he says. "Have you told your mother?"

I shake my head, taking a small defiant pleasure in lying to him. "I saved the happy news for you first."

"I'll tell my mother when I get home tonight." He is quite deaf to my grim tone. "There's nothing I could say that would be better. She'll turn out the priest for a Te Deum."

"You'll be late home," I say. "It's after midnight now."

"She waits up for me," he says. "She never sleeps before I get in."

"Why ever not?" I say, diverted.

He has the grace to blush. "She likes to see me to my bed," he admits. "She likes to kiss me good night."

"She kisses you good night?" I query, thinking of the hard heart of the woman who could send her son to rape me and then wait up to kiss him good night.

"There were so many years when she couldn't kiss me before I slept," he says quietly. "There were so many years when she didn't know where I slept, or even if I was safely asleep at all. She likes to mark my forehead with the sign of a cross and kiss me good night. But tonight when she comes to bless me I will tell her that you are with child and I am hoping for a son!"

"I think I am with child," I say cautiously. "But it is early days. I can't be sure. Don't tell her that I said I was sure."

"I know, I know. And you will think I have been selfish, my mind only on the Tudor house. But if you have a boy, your family is of the royal house of England and your son will be king. You are in the position you were born to hold, and the wars of the cousins are ended forever, with a wedding and a baby. This is how it should be. This is the only happy ending that there can be, for this war and this country. You will have brought us all to peace." He looks at me as if he wants to take me in his arms and kiss me. "You have brought us to peace and a happy ending."

I hunch my shoulder against him. "I had thought of other endings," I say, remembering the king that I loved, who had wanted me to have his son, and who said that we would call him Arthur, in honor of Camelot, a royal heir who was not made in cold determination and bitterness, but with love in warm secret meetings.

"Even now there could be other endings," he says cautiously, taking my hand and holding it gently. He lowers his voice as if there could be eavesdroppers in this, our most private room. "We still have enemies. They are hidden but I know they are there. And if you have a girl it's no good to me, and all this will have been for nothing. But we will work and pray that it is a Tudor boy that you are carrying. And I will tell my mother that she can arrange our wedding. At least we know that you are fertile. Even if you fail and have a girl this time, we know that you can bear a child. And next time perhaps we'll get a boy."

"What would you have done if I had not conceived a child?" I ask curiously. "If you had taken me but no baby had come?" I begin to realize that this man and his mother have a plan for everything, they are always in readiness.

"Your sister," he says shortly. "I would have married Cecily."

I gasp in shock. "But you said she was to marry Sir John Welles?"

"Yes. But if you were barren I would still need to marry a woman who could give me a son from the House of York. It would have had to be her. I would have canceled her wedding to Sir John, and had her for my wife."

"And would you have raped her too?" I spit, pulling my hand away. "First me and then my sister?"

He raises his shoulders and spreads out his hands, a gesture entirely French, not like an Englishman at all. "Of course. I would have had no choice. I have to know that any wife can give me a son. Even you must see that I'm not taking the throne for myself, but to make a new royal family. I am not taking a wife for myself but to make a new royal family."

"Then we are like the poorest country people," I say bitterly. "They only marry when a baby is on the way. They always say you only buy a heifer in calf."

He chuckles, not at all abashed. "Do they? Then I'm an Englishman indeed." He ties the laces at his belt and laughs. "In the end I am an English peasant! I shall tell my Lady Mother tonight and she'll be sure to come and see you tomorrow. She has prayed for this every night that I have been doing my business here."

"She prayed while you were raping me?" I ask him.

"It isn't rape," he says. "Stop saying that. You're a fool to call it that. Since we're betrothed, it cannot be rape. As my wife you cannot refuse me. I have a right to you, as your betrothed husband. From now, till your death, you will never be able to refuse me.

There can be no rape between us, only my rights and your duty."

He looks at me and watches the protest die on my lips.

"Your side lost at Bosworth," he reminds me. "You are the spoils of war."

COLDHARBOUR PALACE, LONDON, CHRISTMAS FEAST, 1485

To celebrate the days of Christmas I am invited to visit my betrothed at his court and am taken to the finest rooms of the palace of Coldharbour, where his mother holds her court. As I enter, with my mother and two sisters walking behind me, a hush spreads through the room. A lady-in-waiting, reading from the Bible, looks up and sees me, trails off, and there is silence. Lady Margaret, seated on a chair under a canopy of state as if she were a queen crowned, looks up and calmly regards us as we come forwards.

I sweep her a curtsey; behind me I see my mother's carefully judged sinking down and rising up again. We have practiced this most difficult movement in my mother's rooms, trying to determine the exact level of deference. My mother has a steely dislike for Lady Margaret now, and I will never forgive her for telling her son to rape me before our wedding. Only Cecily and Anne curtsey with uncomplicated deference, as a pair of minor princesses to the king's all-powerful mother. Cecily even rises with an ingratiating smile, since she is Lady Margaret's goddaughter and counting on this most powerful woman's goodwill to make sure that her wedding goes ahead. My sister does not know, and I will never tell her, that they would have taken her, as coldly as they took me, if I had failed to conceive, and she would have been raped in my place while this flint-faced woman prayed for a baby.

"You are welcome to Coldharbour," Lady Margaret says, and I think it is well named, for it is a most miserable and unfriendly haven. "And to our capital city," she goes on, as if we girls had not been brought up here in London while she was stuck with a small and unimportant husband in the country, her son an exile and her house utterly defeated.

My mother looks around the rooms, and notes the second-rate cloth cushions on the plain window seat, and that the best tapestry has been replaced by an inferior copy. Lady Margaret Beaufort is a most careful house-keeper, not to say mean.

"Thank you," I say.

"I have the arrangements for the wedding all in hand," she says. "You can come to be fitted for your gown in the royal wardrobe next week. Your sisters and your mother also. I have decided that you will all attend."

"I am to attend my own wedding?" I ask

dryly, and see her flush with annoyance.

"All your family," she corrects me.

My mother gives her blandest smile. "And what about the York prince?" she asks.

There is a sudden silence as if a snap frost has just iced the room. "The York prince?" Lady Margaret repeats slowly, and I can hear a tremor in her hard voice. She looks at my mother in dawning horror, as if something terrible is about to be revealed. "What d'you mean? What York prince? What are you saying? What are you saying now?"

My mother blankly meets her gaze. "You have not forgotten the York prince?"

Lady Margaret has blanched white as white. I can see her grip the arms of her chair, and her fingernails are bleached with the pressure of her panic-stricken grip. I glance at my mother; she is enjoying this, like a bear leader teasing the bear with a long-handled prod.

"What d'you mean?" Lady Margaret says and her voice is sharp with fear. "You cannot be suggesting . . ." She breaks off with a little gasp, almost as if she is afraid of what she might say next. "You cannot be saying now . . ."

One of her ladies steps forwards. "Your Grace, are you unwell?"

My mother observes this with detached interest, as an alchemist might observe a transformation. The upstart king's mother is riven with terror at the very name of a York prince. My mother enjoys the sight for a moment, then she releases her from the spell. "I mean, Edward of Warwick, the son of George, Duke of Clarence," she says mildly.

Lady Margaret gives a shuddering sigh. "Oh, the Warwick boy," she says. "The Warwick boy. I had forgotten the Warwick boy."

"Who else?" my mother asks sweetly. "Who did you think I meant? Who else could I mean?"

"I had not forgotten the Warwick children." Lady Margaret grasps for her dignity. "I have ordered robes for them too. And gowns for your younger daughters also."

"I am so pleased," my mother says pleasantly. "And my daughter's coronation?"

"Will follow later," Lady Margaret says, trying to hide that she is gasping, still recovering from her shock, gulping for her words like a landed carp. "After the wedding. When I decide."

One of her ladies steps forwards with a glass of malmsey and she takes a sip and then another. The color comes back to her cheeks with the sweet wine. "After their wedding they will travel to show themselves to the people. A coronation will follow after the birth of an heir."

My mother nods, as if the matter is indifferent to her. "Of course, she's a princess born," she remarks, quietly pleased that being a princess born is far better than being a pretender king.

"I wish any child to be born at Winchester, at the heart of the old kingdom, Arthur's kingdom," Lady Margaret states, struggling to regain her authority. "My son is of the house of Arthur Pendragon."

"Really?" my mother exclaims, all sweetness. "I thought he was from a Tudor bastard out of a Valois dowager princess. And that, a secret wedding, never proved? How does that trace back to King Arthur?"

Lady Margaret pales with rage, and I want to tug my mother's sleeve to remind her not to torment this woman. She had Lady Margaret on the run at the mention of a York prince, but we are supplicants at this new court and there is no benefit in making its greatest woman angry.

"I don't need to explain my son's inheritance to you, whose own marriage and title was only restored by us, after you had been named as an adulteress," Lady Margaret says bluntly. "I have told you of the arrangements for the wedding, I will not delay you further."

My mother keeps her head up and smiles. "And I thank you," she says regally. "So much."

"My son will see Princess Elizabeth." Lady Margaret nods to a page. "Take the princess to the king's private rooms."

I have no choice but to go through the

interconnecting room, to the king's chambers. It seems the two of them are never more than a doorway apart. He is seated at a table that I recognize at once as one used in this palace by my lover Richard, made for my father, King Edward. It is so strange to see Henry seated in my father's chair, signing documents on Richard's table, as if he were king himself — until I remember that he is indeed the king himself, his pale, worried face the image that will be stamped on the coins of England.

He is dictating to a clerk with a portable writing desk slung around his neck, a quill in one hand, another tucked behind his ear, but when Henry sees me, he gives me a broad welcoming smile, waves the man away, and the guards close the door on him and we are alone.

"Are they spitting like cats on a barn roof?" He chuckles. "There's no great love lost between them, is there?"

I'm so relieved to have an ally that for a moment I nearly respond to his warmth, then I check myself. "Your mother is ordering everything, as usual," I say coldly.

The merry smile is wiped from his face. He frowns at the least hint of criticism of her. "You have to understand that she has waited for this moment all her life."

"I am sure we all know this. She does tell everyone."

"I owe her everything," he says frostily. "I can't hear a word against her."

I nod. "I know. She tells everyone that too."

He rises from his chair and comes around the table towards me. "Elizabeth, you will be her daughter-in-law. You will learn to respect her and love and value her. You know, in all the years when your father was on the throne, my mother never gave up her vision."

I grit my teeth. "I know," I say. "Everybody knows. She tells everyone that as well."

"You have to admire that in her."

I cannot bring myself to say that I admire her. "My mother too is a woman of great tenacity," I say carefully. Privately I think: But I don't worship her like a baby, she doesn't speak of nothing but me as if she had nothing in her life but one spoiled brat.

"I am sure they are filled with bile now, but before that they were friends and even allies," he reminds me. "When we are married, they will join together. They'll both have a grandson to love."

He pauses as if he hopes I will say something about their grandson.

Unhelpfully, I stay silent.

"You are well, Elizabeth?"

"Yes," I say shortly.

"And your course has not returned?"

I grit my teeth at having to discuss something so intimate with him. "No."

"That's good, that's so good," he says.

"That's the most important thing!" His pride and excitement would be such a pleasure from a loving husband, but from him it grates on me. I look at him in blank enmity and keep my silence.

"Now, Elizabeth, I just wanted to tell you that our wedding day is to be the feast of St. Margaret of Hungary. My mother has it all planned, you need do nothing."

"Except walk up the aisle and consent," I suggest. "I suppose even your mother will concede that I have to give my consent."

He nods. "Consent, and look happy," he adds. "England wants to see a joyful bride, and so do I. You will please me in this, Elizabeth. It is my wish."

St. Margaret of Hungary was a princess like me, but she lived in a convent in such poverty that she fasted to death. The choice of her day for my wedding by my mother-in-law does not escape me. "Humble and penitent." I remind him of the motto his mother chose for me. "Humble and penitent like St. Margaret."

He has the grace to chuckle. "You can be as humble and penitent as you like." He smiles and looks as if he would take my hand and kiss me. "You can't exceed in humility for us, my sweetheart."

WESTMINSTER PALACE, LONDON, 18 JANUARY 1486

I am a winter bride, and the morning of my wedding day is as bitterly cold as my heart. I wake to the flowers of frost on my windows, and Bess, coming into the room, begs me to stay in bed until she has the fire banked up and my linen laid out to warm before it.

I step out of my bed and she pulls my nightgown over my head and then offers me my undergarments, all new and trimmed with white silk embroidery on the white linen at the hem, then my red satin overgown slashed at the sleeves and opening at the front to show a black silk damask undergown. Fussing, she ties the laces under the arms while the two other maids-in-waiting tie those at the back. It is a little tighter than when it was first fitted on me. My breasts have grown fuller and my waist is thickening. I notice the changes, but nobody else does yet. I am losing the body that my lover adored, the girlish litheness that he used to wrap around his battle-hardened body. Instead I will be the shape that my husband's mother wants: a rounded fertile pear of a woman, a vessel for Tudor seed, a pot.

I stand like a child's doll, being dressed as if I were made of lumpy straw stuffed in a sock, limp in their hands. The gown is darkly magnificent, making my hair shine golden, and my skin gleams coldly white against the rich deep fabric. The door opens and my mother comes in. She is already in her gown of cream, trimmed with green and silver and ribbons, with her hair tied loosely at the back; later she will twist it under her heavy head-dress. For the first time, I notice that she has a fine scattering of gray hairs among the blond; she is a golden queen no more.

"You look lovely," she says, kissing me. "Does he know you are wearing red and black?"

"His mother watched them fit the gown," I say dully. "She chose the material. Of course he knows. She knows everything and she tells him."

"They didn't want green?"

"Lancaster red," I say bitterly. "Martyrdom red, whore's red, blood red."

"Hush," she commands. "This is your day of triumph."

At her touch, I find my throat is tightening, and the tears that have been blurring my view all morning spill down on my cheeks. Gently, she pushes them away with the heel of her hand, one cheek and then the other. "Now stop," she orders softly. "There is nothing that can be done but obey and smile. Sometimes we win; sometimes we lose. The main thing is that we always, we *always* go on."

"We, the House of York?" I ask her skeptically. "For this wedding dissolves York into Tudor. This is no victory for us, but our final defeat."

She smiles her secretive smile. "We, the daughters of Melusina," she corrects me. "Your grandmother was a daughter of the water goddess of the royal house of Burgundy and she never forgot that she was both royal and magical. When I was your age, I didn't know whether she could summon up a storm or whether it was all just luck and pretence to get her own way. But she taught me that there is nothing in the world more powerful than a woman who knows what she wants and walks a straight road towards it.

"It doesn't matter if you call it magic or determination. It doesn't matter if you make a spell or a plot. You have to make up your mind what you want, and have the courage to set your heart on it. You will be Queen of England, your husband is the king. Through you, the Yorks regain the throne of England that is their right. Walk through your sorrow, my daughter, it hardly matters as long as you walk to where you want to be."

"I have lost the man I love," I say bitterly.

"And this very day I am to marry the man who killed him. I don't think I will ever walk to where I want to be. I don't think that place exists in England anymore, I don't think that place exists in this world anymore."

She could almost laugh aloud in her easy confidence. "Of course you think that now! Today you are to marry a man that you despise; but who knows what will happen tomorrow? I can't foretell the future. You were born at the very heart of troubled times. Now you will marry one king, and perhaps you will see him challenged, and perhaps you will see him fall. Perhaps you will see Henry go down in the mud and die under the hooves of a traitor army. How can I know? No one can. But one thing I do know: today you can marry him and become Queen of England. You can make peace where he has made war. You can protect your friends and family and put a York boy on the throne. So go to your wedding with a smile."

He is standing at the chancel steps when I come in through the west door of Westminster Abbey to a sudden shout of silver trumpets. I walk alone; one of the ironies of this wedding is that if there was a man of my family to escort me, then Henry would not be King of England and waiting for me with a shy smile on his face. But my father the king is dead, my two York uncles are dead, my little brothers Edward and Richard are missing, presumed dead. The only York boy left for sure is little Edward of Warwick, who bobs his head to me in a funny regal gesture, as if granting his permission as I walk past the chairs of state where he stands, guarded by his sister, Margaret.

Ahead of me Henry is a blaze of gold. His mother has decided to sacrifice elegance for ostentation, and he is wearing a complete suit of cloth of gold as if he is a newly minted statue, a new Croesus. She had thought he would look regal, a gilded god, and that I would look dull and dark and modest. But against his tawdry brightness my dark black and red gown glows with quiet authority. I can see his mother looking crossly from him to me, and puzzling as to why I seem royal and he looks like a mountebank.

The gown is cut very full with a lot of material gathered at the front, and so nobody can yet see that my belly is bigger. I am a full month into my time, possibly more; but only the king, his mother, and my mother know. I render a silent prayer that they have told nobody.

The archbishop is waiting for us, his prayer book open, his old face smiling down as we walk towards him to the chancel steps. He is my kinsman, Thomas Bourchier, and his hands tremble as he takes my hand and places it in Henry's warm grip. He crowned my father nearly twenty-five years ago, and he crowned my mother, he crowned my darling Richard and his then-wife, Anne, and, if the baby I am carrying proves to be a son, then no doubt he will baptise the child Arthur and then crown me.

His round, lined face shines on me with simple goodwill as I stand before him. He would have performed my wedding service with Richard, and I would have stood here in a white gown trimmed with white roses and been married and crowned in one beautiful ceremony and been a beloved bride and a merry queen.

As his kind eyes fall on my face I can feel myself slipping into a reverie, almost fainting, as if I have entered one of my dreams, standing here at the chancel steps on my wedding day, just as I hoped I would be. In a daze, I take Henry's hand and repeat the words that I thought I would say to another man. "I, Elizabeth, take thee, H . . . H . . . H . . ." I stumble. It is as if I cannot speak this wrong name, I cannot wake to this awkward reality.

It is awful, I cannot say another word, I cannot catch my breath, the terrible fact that I am not pledging myself to Richard has stuck in my throat. I am starting to choke, in a moment I will retch. I can feel myself sweating, I can feel myself sway, my legs weakening under me. I cannot bring myself to say the name of the wrong man, I cannot make myself promise myself to anyone but Richard. I try again. I get as far as "I, Elizabeth, take thee . . ." before I choke into silence. It is hopeless, I cannot say it. I give a little whooping cough and raise my eyes to his face. I cannot help myself, I hate him like an enemy, I cannot stop myself dreaming of his enemy, I cannot say his name, I cannot possibly marry him.

But Henry, prosaic and real, understands exactly what is happening, and gives me a sharp corrective pinch with his fingers in the soft palm of my hand. He uses his nails, he digs into my flesh, I yelp at the pain, and his hard brown gaze emerges from the mist and I see his scowl. I snatch at a gasp of air.

"Say it!" he mutters furiously.

I master myself and say again, correctly this time, "I, Elizabeth, take thee, Henry . . ."

The wedding banquet is held at Westminster Palace and I am served on bended knee as if I were a queen, though My Lady the King's Mother mentions once or twice, as if in passing, that although I am the king's wife, I am not yet crowned. After the feast there is dancing and a little play put on by some skilled actors. There are tumblers, music from the choristers, the king's fool tells some bawdy jokes, and then my mother and sisters come to escort me to the bedroom.

It is warm with a long-established fire of

smoldering logs and scented pinecones in the hearth, and my mother gives me a drink of specially brewed wedding ale.

"Are you nervous?" Cecily asks, her tone as sweet as mead. We still don't have a date for her wedding day, and she is anxious that no one forget that she must come next. "I am sure that I will be nervous, on my wedding night. I shall be a nervous bride, I know, when it is my turn."

"No," I say shortly.

"Why don't you help your sister into bed?" my mother suggests to her, and Cecily turns back the covers and gives me an upward push into the high bed. I settle myself against the pillows and swallow down my apprehension.

We can hear the king and his friends approaching the door. The archbishop comes in first, to sprinkle holy water and pray over the marriage bed. Behind him comes Lady Margaret, a big ivory crucifix tightly in her hands, and behind her comes Henry, looking flushed and smiling among a band of men who slap him on the back and tell him that he has won the finest trophy in all of England.

One freezing look from Lady Margaret warns everyone that there are to be no bawdy jests. The page boy turns back the covers, the king's men in waiting take off his thick bejeweled robe, Henry in his beautifully embroidered white linen nightshirt slips between the sheets beside me, and we both sit up and sip our wedding ale like obedient children at bedtime while the archbishop finishes his prayers and steps back.

Reluctantly, the wedding guests go out, my mother gives me a quick farewell smile and shepherds my sisters away. Lady Margaret is the last to leave and as she goes to the door I see her look back at her son, as if she has to stop herself from coming back in to embrace him once more.

I remember that he told me of all the years when he went to sleep without her kiss or her blessing, and that she loves now to see him to his bed. I see her hesitating at the threshold as if she cannot bear to leave him, and I give her a smile, and I stretch out my hand and rest it lightly on her son's shoulder, a gentle proprietorial touch. "Good night, Lady Mother," I say. "Good night from us both." I let her see me take her son's fine linen collar in my fingers, the collar she embroidered herself in white-on-white embroidery, and I hold it as if it were the leash of a hunting dog who is wholly mine.

For a moment she stands watching us, her mouth a little open, drawing a breath, and as she stays there, I lean my head towards Henry as if I am going to rest it on his shoulder. He is smiling proudly, his face flushed, thinking that she is enjoying the sight of her son, her adored only son, in his wedding bed, a beautiful bride, a true princess, beside him.

Only I understand that the sight of me, with his shoulder under my cheek, smiling in his bed, is eating her up with jealousy as if a wolf had hold of her belly.

Her face is twisted as she closes the door on us, and as the lock clicks shut and we hear the guardsmen ground their pikes, we both breathe out, as if we have been waiting for this moment when we are finally alone. I raise my head and take my hand from his shoulder, but he catches it and presses my fingers to his collarbone. "Don't stop," he says.

Something in my face alerts him to the fact that it was not a caress but a false coin. "Oh, what were you doing? Some spiteful girlish trick?"

I take my hand back. "Nothing," I say stubbornly.

He looms towards me and for a moment I am afraid that I have angered him, and he is going to insist on confirming the marriage by bedding me, inspired by anger, wanting to give me pain for pain. But then he remembers the child that I carry, and that he may not touch me while I am pregnant, and he gets up bristling with offense, and throws his beautiful wedding robe around his shoulders and stirs the fire, draws a writing table to the chair and lights the candle. I realize that the whole day has been spoiled for him by this moment. He can declare a day ruined by the mishap of a minute and he will remember the minute and forget the day. He is always so anxious that he seeks disappointment — it confirms his pessimism. Now he will remember everything, the cathedral, the ceremony, the feasting, the moments that he enjoyed, through a veil of resentment, for the rest of his life.

"There was I, fool that I am, thinking that you were being loving to me," he says shortly. "I thought you were touching me tenderly. I thought that our marriage vows had moved your heart. I thought that you were resting your head on my shoulder for affection. Fool that I am."

I can make no reply. Of course I was not being loving to him. He is my enemy, the murderer of my betrothed lover. He is my rapist. How should he dream that there could ever be affection between us?

"You can sleep," he throws over his shoulder. "I am going to look at some requests. The world is filled with people who want something from me."

I care absolutely nothing for his ill temper. I will never allow myself to care for him, whether he is angry, or even — perhaps as now — hurt, and by me. He can comfort himself or sulk all night, just as he pleases. I pull the pillow down under my head, smooth out my nightgown across my rounded belly, and turn my back to him. Then I hear him say, "Oh! I forgot something." He comes back to the bed and I glance over my hunched shoulder and I see, to my horror, that he has a knife in his hand, unsheathed, the firelight glinting on the bare blade.

I freeze in fear. I think, dear God, I have angered him so badly that he is going to kill me now in revenge for making him a cuckold, and what a scandal there will be, and I did not say good-bye to my mother. Then I think irrelevantly that I lent a necklace to little Margaret of Warwick to wear on my wedding day, and I should like her to know that she can keep it if I am going to die, and then finally I think — oh God, if he cuts my throat now, then I will be able to sleep without dreaming of Richard. I think perhaps there will be a sudden terrible pain and then I will dream no more. Perhaps the stab of the dagger will thrust me into Richard's arms, and I will be with him in a sweet sleep of death together, and I will see his beloved smiling face and he will hold me and our eyes will close together. At the thought of Richard, of sharing death with Richard, I turn towards Henry and the knife in his hand.

"You're not afraid?" he asks curiously, staring at me as if he is seeing me for the very first time. "I'm standing over you with a dagger and yet you don't even flinch? Is it true then? What they say? That your heart is so broken that you wish for death?"

"I won't beg for my life, if that's what

you're hoping," I say bitterly. "I think I've had my best days and I never expect to be happy again. But no, you're wrong. I want to live. I would rather live than die and I would rather be queen than dead. But I'm not frightened of you or your knife. I've promised myself that I will never care for anything that you say or do. And if I were afraid, I would rather die than let you see it."

He laughs shortly and says, as if to himself, "Stubborn as a mule, just as I warned my Lady Mother . . ." Then he says out loud, "No, this is not to cut your pretty throat but only your foot. Give me your foot."

Unwillingly, I stretch out my foot, and he throws back the rich covers of the bed. "Seems a pity," he says to himself. "You do have the most exquisite skin, and the arch of your instep is just kissable — it's ridiculous that one should think of it, but any man would want to kiss just here . . ." and then he makes a quick painful slash that makes me flinch and cry out in pain.

"You hurt me!"

"Hold still," he says, and squeezes my foot over the sheets so that two, three drops of blood fall on the whiteness, then he hands me a linen cloth. "You can bind it up. It will hardly show in the morning, it was nothing more than a scratch, and anyway you will put on stockings."

I tie the cloth around my foot and look at

him. "There's no need to look so aggrieved," he says. "That has saved your reputation. They'll look at the sheets in the morning and there's the stain that shows that you bled like a virgin on your wedding night. When your belly shows, we will say that he was a wedding-night baby, and when he is born we will say that he is an eight-month baby, come early."

I put my hand to my belly where I can feel nothing more than a couple of handfuls of extra fat. "What would you know about an eight-month baby?" I ask. "What would you know about a show on the sheets?"

"My mother told me," he says. "She told me to cut your foot."

"I have so much to thank her for," I say bitterly.

"You should do. For she told me to do this to make him into a honeymoon baby," Henry says with grim humor. "A honeymoon baby, a blessing, and not a royal bastard."

Westminster Palace, London, February 1486

I am the wife of the King of England, but I don't have the queen's apartments in Westminster Palace. "Because you're not queen," Henry says simply.

Mouth downturned, eyes hostile, I just look at him.

"You're not! And besides, my mother works with me on the state papers and it is easier for us to share a private room. It's easy if our rooms are adjoining."

"You use the secret passage which goes from your bedroom to hers?"

He flushes. "It's hardly secret."

"Private, then. My father built it so that he could join my mother in her rooms without the whole court escorting him. He had it made so that he could bed her without the whole court knowing when he was going to her. They liked to be together in secret."

His quick flush rises to his cheeks. "Elizabeth — what's the matter with you? My mother and I often have supper together, we often talk together in the evening, we pray together," he says. "It's easier for us if she can come and see me or if I need to see her."

"You like to walk in and out of each other's rooms, night and day?" I ask again.

He pauses, irritated. I have learned to read his expressions and this tightening of his mouth and narrowing of his eyes shows me that I am embarrassing him. I love to set him on edge, it is one of the only pleasures of my marriage.

"Do I understand that you want to move into the queen's rooms so that I can walk in and out of your bedroom night and day, without notice? Have you developed a taste for my attention? Do you want me at your bedside? In your bed? Do you want me to come to you secretly for love? For love which is not for the procreation of children but for lust? Like your parents with their secret sinful meetings?"

I drop my eyes. "No," I say sulkily. "It's just that it looks odd that I don't have the queen's rooms."

"Is there anything wrong with the rooms you have? Are they not furnished to your liking? Are they too small?"

"No."

"Do you need better tapestries on the walls? Are you deficient in the matter of musicians? Or servants? Are you going hungry, shall the kitchens send you more little plates?"

"It's not that."

"Oh, do tell me if you are starving to death? If you are lonely or chilled?"

"My rooms are quite adequate," I say through my teeth.

"Then I suggest you let my mother stay in the apartments that she uses, which she needs as my principal advisor. And that you keep the rooms that she has allotted to you. And I will visit you every night, until I go on progress."

"You're going on progress?" This is the first I have heard of it.

He nods. "Not you. You're not coming. You're not to travel, Mother thinks it better that you should rest in London. She and I are going north. She thinks that I should be seen by as many people as possible, visit towns, spread loyalty. Confirm our supporters in their posts, befriend former enemies. The Tudors need to stamp their mark on this country."

"Oh, she definitely won't want me there then," I say spitefully. "Not if it's a Tudor progress. She won't want a York princess. What if people preferred me to you? What if they looked past her, past you, and cheered for me?"

He rises to his feet. "I believe she was thinking of nothing but your health, and the health of our baby — as was I," he says sharply. "And of course the kingdom has to be made loyal to the Tudor line. The child in your belly is a Tudor heir. We are doing this for you and for the child you carry. My mother is working for you and for her grandson. I wish you could find the grace to be grateful. You say you are a princess, I hear all the time that you are a princess by birth — I wish you would show it. I wish you would try to be queenly."

I lower my eyes. "Please tell her I am grateful," I say. "I am always, always grateful."

My mother comes to my rooms, her face pale, a letter in her hand.

"What d'you have there? Nothing good by the looks of it."

"It's a proposal from King Henry that I should marry."

I take the letter from her hands. "You?" I ask. "You? What does he mean?"

I start to scan the paper but I break off to look at her. Even her lips are white. She is nodding her head, as if she is lost for words, nodding and saying nothing.

"Marry who? Stop it, Mother. You're frightening me. What is he thinking of? Who is he thinking of?"

"James of Scotland." She gives a little gasp, almost a laugh. "There at the very bottom of the letter, after all the compliments and praising my youthful looks and good health. He says I am to marry the King of Scotland, and go far away to Edinburgh, and never come back."

I turn to the page again. It is a polite letter from my husband to my mother in which he says that she will oblige him very much by meeting with the Scottish ambassador and accepting his proposal of marriage from the King of Scotland, and agree to the date, which they will suggest, for a wedding this summer.

I look at her. "He's gone mad. He can't command this. He can't tell you to marry. He wouldn't dare. This will be his mother's plan. You can't possibly go."

She has a hand to her mouth to hide her trembling lips. "I imagine that I will have to go. They can make me go."

"Mother, I can't be here without you!"

"If he orders it?"

"I can't live here without you!"

"I can't bear to leave you. But if the king commands it, we'll have no choice."

"You can't marry again!" I am shocked at the very thought of it. "You shouldn't even think of it!"

She puts her hand over her eyes. "I can hardly imagine such a thing. Your father . . ." She breaks off. "Elizabeth, my dearest, I told you that you had to be a smiling bride, I told my sister Katherine that she of all people knows that women have to marry where they are bid, and I agreed to the betrothal of

Cecily to Henry's choice. I can't pretend that I am the only one of us who must be spared. Henry won the battle. He now commands England. If he orders that I marry, even that I marry the King of Scotland, I will have to go to Scotland."

"It'll be his mother," I burst out. "It'll be his mother who wants you out of the way, not him!"

"Yes," my mother says slowly. "It probably is her. But she has miscalculated. Not for the first time she has made a mistake in her dealings with me."

"Why?"

"Because they will want me in Edinburgh to make sure that the Scottish king holds to the new alliance with England. They'll want me to hold him in friendship with Henry. They'll think that if I am queen in Scotland then James will never invade my son-in-law's kingdom."

"And?" I whisper.

"They're wrong," she says vengefully. "They're so very wrong. The day that I am Queen of Scotland with an army to command and a husband to advise, I won't serve Henry Tudor. I won't persuade my husband to keep a peace treaty with Henry. If I were strong enough and could command the allies I would need, I would march against Henry Tudor myself, come south with an army of terror."

"You would invade with the Scots?" I whisper. It is the great terror of England — a Scots invasion, an army of barbarians sweeping down from the cold lands of the North, stealing everything. "Against Henry? To put a new king on the throne of England? A York pretender?"

She does not even nod, she just widens her gray eyes.

"But what about me?" I say simply. "What about me and my baby?"

We decide that I shall try to speak with Henry. In the weeks before he goes on his progress he comes to my room and sleeps in my bed every night. This is to give weight to the claim of a honeymoon baby. He does not touch me, since to do so would be to damage the child that is growing in my broadening belly, but he takes a little supper by the fireside, and he comes into bed beside me. Mostly he is restless, disturbed by dreams. Often he spends hours of the night on his knees, and I think then that he must be tormented by the knowledge that he made war on an ordained king, overturned the laws of God, and broke my heart. In the darkness of the night his conscience speaks louder than his mother's ambitions.

Some nights he comes in late from sitting with his mother, some nights he comes in a little drunk from laughing with his friends.

He has very few friends — only those from the years of exile, men he knows that he can trust for they were there when he was a pretender and they were as desperate as him. He admires only three men: his uncle Jasper, and his new kinsmen Lord Thomas Stanley and Sir William Stanley. They are his only advisors. This night he comes in early and thoughtful, a sheaf of papers in his hands, requests from men who supported him and now want a share in the wealth of England — the barefoot exiles queuing for dead men's shoes.

"Husband, I would talk with you." I am sitting at the fireside in my nightgown, a red robe over my shoulders, my hair brushed loose. I have some warmed ale for him and some small meat pies.

"It'll be about your mother," he guesses at once disagreeably, taking in my preparations in one quick glance. "Why else would you attempt to make me comfortable? Why else would you go to the trouble to look irresistible? You know you are more beautiful than any woman I have ever seen in my life before. Whenever you wear red and spread out your hair, I know that you hope to entrap me."

"It *is* about her," I say, not at all abashed. "I don't want her to be sent away from me. I don't want her to go to Scotland. And I don't want her to have to marry again. She loved my father. You never saw them together, but it was a marriage of true love, a deep love. I don't want her to have to wed and bed another man — a man fourteen years younger than her, and our enemy . . . it's . . . it's . . . ." I break off. "Truly, it is an awful thing to ask of her."

He sits in the chair facing the fire and says nothing for a moment, looking at the logs that are burning down to red embers.

"I understand that you don't want her to go," he says quietly. "And I'm sorry for that. But half of this country still supports the House of York. Nothing has changed for them. Sometimes I think that nothing will ever change them. Defeat does not alter them, it just makes them bitter and more dangerous. They supported Richard and they won't change sides for me. Some of them dream that your brothers are still alive, and whisper about a prince over the water. They see me as a newcomer, an invader. D'you know what they call me in the streets of York? My spies write to tell me. They call me Henry the Conqueror, as if I were William of Normandy — a foreign bastard come again. As if I am another foreign bastard. A pretender to the throne. And they hate me."

I stir, about to make up some reassuring lie; but he holds out his hand and I put my cold hand in his and he pulls me towards him, to stand before him.

"If anyone, any man at all, stood up with a

claim to the throne, and he came from the House of York, he would muster a thousand, perhaps many thousands of men," he says. "Think of it. You could put up a dog under the banner of the white rose and they would turn out and fight to the death for it. And I would be no further on. Dog or prince, I would have the whole battle to fight all over again. It would be like invading all over again. It would be like being sleepless before the battle of Bosworth again and dreaming of the day over and over again. Except for one thing — and it is all worse: this time I would have no French army, I would have no supporters from Brittany, I would have no foreign money to hire troops, I would have no well-trained mercenaries. I would have no foolish optimism of a lad in battle for the first time. This time, I would be on my own. This time, I would have no supporters but those men who have joined my court since I won the battle."

He sees the contempt for them in my face and he nods, agreeing with me. "I know: timeservers," he says. "Yes, I know. Men who join the winning side. D'you think I don't realize that they would have been Richard's greatest friends if he had won at Bosworth? D'you think I don't know that they would flock to whoever won a battle between me and a new pretender? D'you think I don't know that every one of them is my friend, my dearest friend, only because I won that single battle on that particular day? D'you think I don't count the very, very few who were with me in Brittany against the very, very many who are with me in London? D'you think I don't know that any new pretender who beat me would be just as I am, he would do just what I have done — change the law, distribute wealth, try to make and keep loyal friends."

"What new pretender?" I whisper, picking out the one word from his worries. At once I am frozen with fear that he has heard a rumor of a boy somewhere, hidden in Europe, perhaps writing to my mother. "What d'you mean, a new pretender?"

"Anyone," he says harshly. "Christ Himself can't know who is out there in hiding! I keep hearing of a boy, I keep getting whispers of a boy, but nobody can tell me where he is or what he claims to be. God knows what the people would do, if they heard just half of the stories that I have to listen to every day. John de la Pole, your cousin, may have sworn loyalty to me, but his mother is your father's sister, and he was named as Richard's heir — I don't know if I can trust him. Francis Lovell — Richard's greatest friend — is hidden away in sanctuary and nobody knows what he wants or what he plans, or who he is working with. God help me, I have moments when I even doubt your uncle Edward Woodville, and he has been in my household since Brittany. I am delaying the release of your half brother Thomas Grey because I fear that he won't come home to England a loyal subject but just be another recruit for them — whoever they are, whoever they are waiting for. Then there is Edward Earl of Warwick, in your mother's household, studying what exactly? Treason? I am surrounded by your family and I don't trust any of them."

"Edward is a child," I say quickly, breathless with relief that at least he has no news of a York prince, no knowledge of his whereabouts, no revealing detail of his looks, his education, his claim. "And completely loyal to you, as is my mother now. We gave you our word that Teddy would never challenge you. We promised him to you. He has sworn loyalty. Of all of us, above us all, you can trust him."

"I hope so," he says. "I hope so." He looks drained by his fears. "But even so — I have to do everything! I have to hold this country to peace, to secure the borders. I am trying to do a great thing here, Elizabeth. I am trying to do what your father did, to establish a new royal family, to set its stamp on the country, to lead the country to peace. Your father could never get an established peace with Scotland though he tried, just as I am trying. If your mother would go to Scotland for us, and hold them to an alliance, she would do you a service, and me a service, and her grandson would be in debt to her all his life for his safe inheritance of England. Think of that! Giving our son his kingdom with borders at peace! And she could do it!"

"I have to have her with me!" It is a wail like that of a child. "You wouldn't send your own mother away. She has to be with you all the time! You keep her close enough!"

"She serves our house," he says. "I am asking your mother to serve our house too. And she is a beautiful woman still, and she knows how to be queen. If she were Queen of Scotland, we would all be safer."

He stands. He puts his hands on either side of my thickening waist and looks down into my troubled face. "Ah, Elizabeth, I would do anything for you," he says gently. "Don't be troubled, not when you are carrying our son. Please don't cry. It's bad for you. It's bad for the baby. Please — don't cry."

"We don't even know if it is a son," I say resentfully. "You say it all the time, but it doesn't make it so."

He smiles. "Of course it is a boy. How could a beautiful girl like you make anything for me but a handsome firstborn son?"

"I have to have my mother with me," I stipulate. I look up into his face and catch a glimpse of an emotion I never expected to see. His hazel eyes are warm, his mouth is tender. He looks like a man in love.

"I need her in Scotland," he says, but his voice is soft.

"I cannot give birth without her here. She has to be with me. What if something goes wrong?"

It is my greatest card, a trump.

He hesitates. "If she is with you for the birth of our boy?"

Sulkily I nod my head. "She must be with me till he is christened. I will be happy in my confinement only if she is with me."

He drops a kiss on the top of my head. "Ah, then I promise," he says. "You have my word. You bend me to your will like the enchantress you are. And she can go to Scotland after the birth of your baby."

WESTMINSTER PALACE, LONDON, MARCH 1486

His mother is beside herself, planning and commanding the royal progress. My mother, veteran of progresses, pageants, and visitations, observes but says nothing as My Lady the King's Mother disappears into the royal wardrobe with tailors, seamstresses, shoemakers, and hatmakers for days at a time, trying to create a wardrobe of clothes for her son which will dazzle the Northerners into accepting him as a king. Like any usurping family, uncertain of their worth, she wants him to look every inch the part. He has to play the king; mere being is not enough. To the sly amusement of my mother and myself, Lady Margaret has only the example of my father to go on, and this leaves her utterly at a loss. My father was exceptionally tall and exceptionally handsome, and he only had to walk into a room to dominate the assembly of people. He revelled in the latest fashions and the most beautiful rich cloths and color. He was infallibly attractive to women, unable to help himself, greedy for their attention; and God knows they could not restrain their desires. A room full of women was always half in love with my father, and their husbands torn between admiration and envy. Best of all, he had my exceptionally beautiful mother always at his side and a quiverful of exquisite daughters trailing behind him. We were always a stained-glass window in motion, an icon of beauty and grace. My Lady the King's Mother knows that we were a royal family beyond compare: regal, fruitful, beautiful, rich. She was at our court as a lady-in-waiting and she saw for herself how the country saw us, as fairy-tale monarchs. She is driving herself quite mad trying to make her awkward, paler, quieter son match up.

She solves the problem by drowning him in jewels. He never goes out without a precious brooch in his hat, or a priceless pearl at his throat. He never rides without gloves encrusted with diamonds, or a saddle with stirrups of gold. She bedecks him in ermine as if she were decorating a relic for an Easter procession; and still he looks like a young man stretched beyond his abilities, living beyond his means, ambitious and anxious all at once, his face pale against purple velvet.

"I wish you could come with me," he says miserably one afternoon when we are in the stable yards of Westminster Palace, choosing the horses he will ride.

I am so surprised that I look twice at him to see if he is mocking me.

"You think I am joking? No. I really wish you could come with me. You've done this sort of thing all your life. Everyone says that you used to open the dancing at your father's court and talk to the ambassadors. And you have been all round the country, haven't you? You know most of the cities and towns?"

I nod. Both my father and Richard were well loved, especially in the northern counties. We rode out of London to visit the other cities of England every summer, and were greeted as if we were angels descending from heaven. Most of the great houses of every county celebrated our arrival with glorious pageants and feasts; most cities gave us purses of gold. I couldn't count how many mayors and councillors and sheriffs have kissed my hand from when I was a little girl on my mother's lap to when I could give a thank-you speech in faultless Latin on my own.

"I have to show myself everywhere," he says apprehensively. "I have to inspire loyalty. I have to convince people that I will bring them peace and wealth. And I have to do all this with nothing more than a smile and wave as I ride by?"

I can't help but laugh. "It does sound impossible," I say. "But it's not so bad. Remember, everyone on the roadside has come out just to see you. They want to see a great king, that's the show they've turned out for. They're expecting a smile and a wave. They are hoping for a happy lord. You just have to look the part and everyone is reassured. And remember that they have nothing else to look at — really, Henry, when you know England a little better you will see that almost nothing ever happens here. The crops fail, it rains too much in spring, it's too dry in summer. Offer the people a well-dressed and smiling young king and you will be the most wonderful thing they have seen in many years. These are poor people without entertainment. You will be the greatest show they have ever seen — especially since your mother is exhibiting you like a holy icon, wrapped in velvet and studded with jewels."

"It all takes so long," he grumbles. "We have to stop at practically every house and castle on the road, to hear a loyal address."

"Father used to say that while the speeches were going on he looked over their heads at the numbers in the crowd and worked out what they could afford to lend him," I volunteer. "He never listened to a word that anyone was saying, he counted the cows in the fields and the servants in the yard."

Henry is immediately interested. "Loans?"

"He always thought it was better to go straight to the people than go to Parliament for taxes, where they would argue with him as to how the country should be run, or whether he might go to war. He used to borrow from everyone that he visited. And the more passionate the speech and the more exaggerated the praise, the greater the sum of money he asked for, after dinner."

Henry laughs and puts an arm around my broad waist and draws me to him, in the stable yard, before everyone. "And did they always lend him money?"

"Almost always," I say. I don't pull away but neither do I lean towards him. I let him hold me, as he has a right to do, as a husband can hold his wife. And I feel the warmth of his hand as he spreads his fingers over my belly. It's comforting.

"I'll do that then," he says. "Because your father was right, it's an expensive business trying to rule this country. Everything that I am granted in taxes from Parliament I have to give away in gifts to keep the loyalty of the lords."

"Oh, don't they serve you for love?" I ask nastily. I cannot stop my sharp tongue.

At once, he releases me. "I think we both know that they don't." He pauses. "But I doubt they loved your father that much, either."

WESTMINSTER PALACE, LONDON, APRIL 1486

After weeks of preparation they are finally ready to leave. Lady Margaret is to ride out with her son for the first two days and then come back to London. If she dared, she would make the whole royal progress with him, but she is torn. She wants to be with him, she always wants to be with him, she can hardly bear to let him out of her sight; but at the same time, she cannot bear not to supervise my daily routine and keep me under constant control. She can trust no one else to order my food, to patrol my twice-daily walks, and provide me with uplifting books of sermons to read. No one but she can judge how much food or wine or ale should be served at my table, and only she can run the royal household as she wants it. It is unbearable to her that, in her absence, I might run it as I like. Or even worse — that the palace might be commanded once again by its former mistress: my mother.

Lady Margaret is so impressed with her

own rule making, by the quality of her advice, that she starts to write down the orders that she gives out in my household, so that everything will always be done exactly as she has devised, for years in the future, even after her death. I imagine her, beyond the grave, still ruling the world as my daughter and my granddaughters consult the great book of the royal household, and learn that they are not to eat fresh fruit, nor to sit too close to the fire. They are to avoid overheating and not to take a chill.

"Clearly, no one has ever had a baby before," says my mother, who had twelve.

Henry writes to his mother every other day and reports how he is greeted on the road as he makes his slow progress north, what families he meets, and what gifts he receives on the way. To me, he writes once a week, telling me where he is staying that evening, that he is in good health, and that he wishes me well. I reply with a formal note, and give my unsealed letter to his mother, who reads it before folding it in her own packet to him.

In Lent, the court fasts, eating no meat, but My Lady the King's Mother decides that this is not a rich enough diet for me. She sends a message to the Pope himself to request that I be allowed to eat meat throughout the season, to support the growth of the baby. Nothing is more important than a

Tudor son and heir, not even her famous piety.

On the death of Thomas Bourchier, Lady Margaret names her favorite and former conspirator John Morton for the post of Archbishop of Canterbury, and he is swiftly appointed. I am sorry that my old kinsman will not christen my son or put my crown on my head. But John Morton is like a well-bred hound, always with us, never a nuisance. He sits hogging the best place by the fire and makes me feel that he is my guardian and I am lucky to have him there. He is everywhere in the court, listening to everyone, befriending everyone, smoothing over difficulties and — without a doubt — reporting everything back to My Lady. Wherever I go, he is there, interested in all my doings, quick with sympathetic spiritual advice, constantly alert to my needs and my thoughts, chatting with my ladies. It does not take me long to realize that he knows everything that is going on at court, and I don't doubt that he reports it all to her. He has been My Lady's confessor and greatest friend for years, and he assures her that I should eat red meat, well cooked, and that he himself will answer for the papal permission. He pats my hand and tells me that nothing matters more than my health, nothing matters more to him than that I am well and strong, that the baby grows, and he assures me that God feels just the same.

Then, after Easter, while my mother and my two sisters are sewing baby clothes in My Lady the King's Mother's presence chamber, a messenger, covered with dust from the road, comes in all his dirt to the doorway, saying he has an urgent message from His Grace the King.

For once, she does not look down her long nose, insist on her own grandeur, and send him away to change his clothes. She takes one astounded look at his grave face and admits him at once into her private room, and goes in behind him, closing the door herself, so that no one can overhear the news that he brings.

My mother's needle is suspended over her sewing as she raises her head and watches the man go by. Then she gives a little sigh, as a woman quietly contented with her world, and goes back to her work. Cecily and I exchange one anxious look.

"What is it?" I ask my mother, as soft as a breath.

Her gray eyes are downcast, on her work. "How would I know?"

The door to My Lady's private room is closed for a long time. The messenger comes out, walks through all of us ladies as if he has been commanded to march by saying nothing, and still the door remains closed. Only at dinnertime does My Lady come out and take her seat on the great chair under the cloth of estate. Grim-faced, she waits in silence for the head of her household to tell her that dinner is served.

The archbishop, John Morton, comes and stands beside her as if ready to leap forwards with a benediction, but she sits, flinty-faced, saying nothing, not even when he leans down as if to catch the quietest whisper.

"Is everything well with His Grace the King?" my mother inquires, her voice light and pleasant.

My Lady looks as if she would rather keep her silence. "He has been troubled by some disloyalty," she says. "There are still traitors in the kingdom, I am sorry to say."

My mother raises her eyebrows, and makes a little tutting noise as if she is sorry too, and says nothing.

"I hope His Grace is safe?" I try.

"That fool and traitor Francis Lovell has abused the sanctuary he was allowed and come out and raised an army against my son!" Lady Margaret declares in a sudden, hideous outburst of rage. She is shaking all over, her face flushed scarlet. Now that she has allowed herself to speak, she cannot keep from shouting, spittle flying from her mouth, the words tumbling out, her headdress trembling in her fury as she clutches the arms of her chair as if to hold herself seated. "How could he? How dare he? He hid himself in sanctuary to avoid the punishment of defeat and now he is out of his earth like a fox."

"God forgive him!" the archbishop exclaims.

I gasp, I cannot help myself. Francis Lovell was Richard's boyhood friend and dearest companion. He rode out to battle at his side, and when Richard went down he fled to sanctuary. He can only have come out for a good reason. He is no fool, he would never ride out for a lost cause. Lovell would never have come out of sanctuary and raised his standard without knowing that he had support. There must be a ring of men, known only to one another, who have been waiting for the moment — perhaps as soon as Henry left the safety of London. They must be prepared and ready to challenge him. And they will not be coming against him alone, they must have an alternative king in mind. They must have someone to put in his place.

The king's mother glares at me as if I too might burst into the flames of rebellion, looking for signs of treason, as if she might see a mark of Cain on my forehead. "Like a dog," she says spitefully. "Isn't that what they called him? Lovell the dog? He has come out of his kennel like a cur and dares to challenge my son's peace. Henry will be distraught! And I not with him! He will be so shocked!"

"God bless him," the archbishop murmurs, touching the gold crucifix on the chain of pearls at his waist.

My mother is a portrait of concern. "Raised an army?" she repeats. "Francis Lovell?"

"He will regret it," My Lady swears. "Him and Thomas Stafford with him. They will regret challenging the peace and majesty of my son. God Himself brought Henry to England. An insurrection against my son is a rebellion against the will of God. They are heretics as well as traitors."

"Thomas Stafford too?" my mother coos. "A Stafford taking arms as well?"

"And his false-hearted brother! Two of them! Traitors! All of them!"

"Humphrey Stafford?" my mother exclaims softly. "Him too? And together the Staffords can call up so many men! Two sons of such a great name! And is His Grace the King marching against them? Is he mustering his troops?"

"No, no." Lady Margaret waves the question away with a flutter of her hand, as if no one will doubt the king's courage if she insists that he should hide in Lincoln and let someone else do the fighting. "Why should he go? There is no point in him going. I have written to him to bid him stay back. His uncle, Jasper Tudor, will lead his men. Henry has mustered thousands of men for Jasper's army. And promised forgiveness to everyone who surrenders. He wrote to me that they are chasing the rebels north, towards Middleham."

It was Richard's favorite castle, his boyhood home. In all the northern counties the men hurrying to join Francis Lovell, his dearest friend and boyhood companion, will be those who knew Richard and Francis when they were living there as children. Francis knows the country all around Middleham; he will know where to make ambushes and where to hide.

"Heavens," my mother says equably. "We must pray for the king."

The king's mother gasps with relief at the suggestion. "Of course, of course. The court will go to chapel after dinner. That's a very good suggestion of yours, Your Grace. I will order a special Mass." She nods at the archbishop, who bows and leaves, as if to alert God.

Maggie, my cousin, stirs slightly in her seat at this. She knows that a special Mass ordered by My Lady for the safety of her son is going to go on for two hours at least. At once, my Lady the King's Mother switches her hard gaze to my little cousin. "It seems that there are still some sinful fools who support the lost House of York," she says. "Even though the House of York is finished and all its heirs are dead."

Our cousin John de la Pole is a living heir, sworn to Henry's service; Maggie's brother Edward is an heir in direct line; but nobody is going to point this out to My Lady. Maggie's brother is safe in the nursery for now, and Maggie's gaze is pinned firmly on the floorboards beneath her slippered feet. She says nothing.

My mother rises and moves gracefully towards the door, pausing when she stands before Maggie, shielding her from the angry stare of My Lady. "I shall go and fetch my rosary and my prayer book," she says. "Would you want me to fetch your missal from your altar?"

My Lady the King's Mother is diverted at once. "Yes, yes, thank you. And summon the choir to the chapel as well. Everyone must fetch their rosaries," she says. "We'll go straight to chapel after dinner."

As we pray, I try to imagine what is happening, as if I had my mother's gift of sight and could see all the way up the Great North Road to Middleham Castle in Yorkshire. If Lovell can get behind those solid walls he can hold out for months, perhaps years. If the North rises up for him, then they will outnumber any Tudor army under the command of Jasper. The North has always been passionately for the House of York, Middleham loved Richard as their good lord, the altar in the Middleham chapel carries white roses, perhaps forever. I glance sideways at my mother, who is the picture of devotion, on her knees, her eyes closed, her face turned upwards, a shaft of light illuminating her serene loveliness, as beautiful as a timeless angel, meditating on the sins of the world.

"Did you know of this?" I whisper, bending my head over my working fingers as if I am telling my rosary beads.

She does not open her eyes or turn her head, while her lips move as if she is saying a prayer. "Some of it. Sir Francis sent me a message."

"Are they fighting for us?"

"Of course."

"D'you think they will win?"

A fleeting smile crosses her rapt face. "Perhaps. But I know one thing."

"What?"

"They have frightened the Tudors half to death. Did you see her face? Did you see her archbishop as he ran from the room?"

Westminster Palace, London, May 1486

The first I know of trouble in the streets is the great creak as the huge outer doors of Westminster Palace are hauled shut by dozens of men, and then the thunderous bang as they slam into place. Then I hear the heavy thud as the counterweighted beam is pulled into the struts to hold the gates shut. We are barricading ourselves inside the royal palace; the royal family of England is so afraid of Londoners that we are locking London out.

With my hand on my big belly, I go to my mother's rooms. She is at her window, looking over the walls to the streets beyond, my cousin Maggie on one side and my sister Anne on the other. She barely turns as I run in, but Maggie says over her shoulder, "They're doubling the guards on the palace walls. You can see them, dashing out of the guardhouse into place."

"What's happening?" I ask. "What's happening down there?"

"The people are rising against Henry

Tudor," my mother says calmly.

"What?"

"They're gathering outside the palace, mustering, in their hundreds."

I feel the baby move uneasily in my belly. I sit down, take a gasping breath. "What should we do?"

"Stay here," my mother says steadily. "Until we can see our way."

"What way?" I ask impatiently. "Where will we be safe?"

She looks back at my white face and smiles. "Be calm, my dear. I mean, we stay here till we know who's won."

"Do we even know who's fighting?"

She nods. "It is the English people who still love the House of York, against the new king," she says. "We're safe either way. If Lovell wins in Yorkshire, if the Stafford brothers win their battles in Worcestershire, if these London citizens take the Tower and then set siege here — then we come out."

"And do what?" I whisper. I am torn between a growing excitement and an absolute dread.

"Retake the throne," my mother says easily. "Henry Tudor is in a desperate fight to hold his kingdom, only nine months after winning it."

"Retake the throne!" My voice is a squeak of terror.

My mother shrugs. "It's not lost to us until

England is at peace and united behind Henry Tudor. This could be just another battle in the Cousins' War. Henry could be just an episode."

"The cousins are all gone!" I exclaim. "The brothers who were of the houses of Lancaster and York are all gone!"

She smiles. "Henry Tudor is a cousin of the House of Beaufort," she reminds me. "You are of the House of York. You have a cousin in John de la Pole, your aunt Elizabeth's son. You have a cousin in Edward Earl of Warwick, your uncle George's son. There is another generation of cousins — the question is only whether they want to go to war against the one who is now on the throne."

"He's ordained king! And my husband!" I raise my voice, but nothing perturbs her.

She shrugs. "So you win either way."

"D'you see what they're carrying?" Maggie squeaks with excitement. "Do you see the flag?"

I rise from my chair and look over her head. "I can't see it from here."

"It's my flag," she says, her voice trembling with joy. "It's the ragged staff of Warwick. And they're calling my name. They're calling À Warwick! À Warwick! They're calling for Teddy."

I look over her bobbing head to my mother. "They're calling for Edward, the heir of York," I say quietly. "They're calling for a

York boy."

"Yes," she says equably. "Of course they are."

We wait for news. It is hard for me to bear the wait, knowing that my friends and my family and my house are up in arms against my own husband. But it is harder on My Lady the King's Mother, who seems to have given up sleeping altogether but is every night on her knees before the little altar in her privy chamber, and all day in the chapel. She grows thin and gray with worry; the thought of her only son far away in this faithless country, with no protection but his uncle's army, makes her ill with fear. She accuses his friends of failing him, his supporters of fading away from him. She lists their names in her prayers to God, one after another, the men who flocked to the victor but will abandon a failure. She goes without food, fasting to draw down the blessing of God; but we can all see that she is sick with the growing fear that despite it all, her son is not blessed by God, that for some unknown reason, God has turned against the Tudors. He has given them the throne of England but not the power to hold it.

There are skirmishes between the London bands and the Tudor forces in the little villages in the countryside outside Westminster, as if every crossroads is calling out *À* Warwick! At Highbury there is a pitched battle with the rebels armed with stones, rakes, and scythes against the heavily armed royal guard. There are stories of Henry's soldiers throwing down the Tudor standard and running to join the rebels. There are whispers that the great merchants of London and even the City Fathers are supporting the mobs that roam the streets shouting for the return of the House of York.

Lady Margaret orders the shutters closed over all the windows that face the streets, so that we cannot see the running battles that are being fought below the very walls of the palace. Then she orders the shutters bolted on the other windows too so that we can't hear the mob shouting support for York, demanding that Edward of Warwick, my little cousin Teddy, come out and wave to them.

We keep him from the windows of the schoolroom, we forbid the servants to gossip, but still he knows that the people of England are calling for him to be king.

"Henry is the king," he volunteers to me as I listen to him read a story in the schoolroom.

"Henry is the king," I confirm.

Maggie glances over at the two of us, frowning with worry.

"So they shouldn't shout for me," he says. He seems quite resigned.

"No, they should not," I say. "They will soon stop shouting."

"But they don't want a Tudor king."

"Now, Teddy," Margaret interrupts. "You know you must say nothing."

I put my hand over his. "It doesn't matter what they want," I tell him. "Henry won the battle and was crowned Henry VII. He is King of England, whatever anyone says. And we would all be very, very wrong if we forgot that he is King of England."

He looks at me with his bright honest face. "I won't do that," he promises me. "I don't forget things. I know he's king. You'd better tell the boys in the streets."

I don't tell the boys in the streets. Lady Margaret does not allow anyone out of the great gates until slowly the excitement dies down. The walls of Westminster Palace are not breached, the thick gates cannot be forced. The ragged mobs are kept off, they are driven away, they flee the city or they go back into sullen hiding. The streets of London become quiet again, and we open the shutters at the windows and the heavy gates of the palace as if we were confident rulers and can welcome our people. But I notice that the mood in the capital is surly and every visit to market provokes a quarrel between the court servants and the traders. We keep double sentries on the walls and we still have no news from the North. We simply have no idea whether Henry has met the rebels in a battle, nor who

171

has won.

Finally at the end of May — when the court should be planning the sports of the summer, walking by the river, practicing jousting, rehearsing plays, making music, and courting — a letter comes from Henry for My Lady, with a note for me, and an open letter to the Parliament, carried by my uncle Edward Woodville with a smartly turned out party of yeomen of the guard, as if to show that the Tudor servants can wear their livery in safety all the way down the Great North Road from York to London.

"What does the king say?" my mother asks me.

"The rebellion is over," I say, reading rapidly. "He says that Jasper Tudor pursued the rebels far into the North and then came back. Francis Lovell has escaped, but the Stafford brothers have fled back into sanctuary. He's pulled them out of sanctuary." I pause and look at my mother over the top of the paper. "He's broken sanctuary," I remark. "He's broken the law of the Church. He says he'll execute them."

I hand her the letter, surprised at my own sense of relief. Of course I want the restoration of my house and the defeat of Richard's enemy — sometimes I feel a thrill of violent desire at the sudden vivid image of Henry falling from his horse and fighting for his life on the ground in the middle of a cavalry

charge as the hooves thunder by his head —
and yet, this letter brings me the good news
that my husband has survived. I am carrying
a Tudor in my belly. Despite myself, I can't
wish Henry Tudor dead, thrown naked and
bleeding across the back of his limping horse.
I married him, I gave him my word, he is the
father of my unborn child. I might have
buried my heart in an unmarked grave, but I
have promised my loyalty to the king. I was a
York princess, but I am a Tudor wife. My
future must be with Henry. "It's over," I
repeat. "Thank God it's over."

"It's not over at all," my mother quietly
disagrees. "It's just beginning."

PALACE OF SHEEN, RICHMOND, SUMMER 1486

Henry does not return to us for months, but continues his progress, enjoying the fruits of victory as the defeat of Lovell and the Staffords brings all the halfhearted supporters back to the Tudor side — some of them attracted by power, some of them afraid of defeat, all of them conscious that they failed to be prominent among the royal supporters when danger threatened. Humphrey Stafford is tried and executed for treason, but his younger brother Thomas is spared. Henry offers pardons as freely as he dares, terrified of driving supporters away by being too suspicious of them. He tells everyone that he will be a good king, a merciful king to all who accept his rule, and if they beg for forgiveness they will find him generous.

My Lady the King's Mother makes representation to the Holy Father through her cat's-paw John Morton, and the helpful word comes from Rome that the laws on sanctuary are to be changed to suit the Tudors. Traitors may not go into hiding behind the walls of the Church anymore. God is to be on the side of the king and to enforce the king's justice. My Lady wants her son to rule England inside sanctuary, right up to the altar, perhaps all the way to heaven, and the Pope is persuaded to her view. Nowhere on earth can be safe from Henry's yeomen of the guard. No door, not even one on holy ground, can be closed in their hard faces.

The might of English law is to favor the Tudors too. The judges obey the new king's commands, trying men who followed the Staffords or Francis Lovell, pardoning some, punishing others, according to their instructions from Henry. In my father's England the judges were supposed to make up their own minds, and a jury was supposed to be free of any influence but the truth. But now the judges wait to hear the preferences of the king before reaching their sentences. The statements of the accused men, even their pleas of guilt, are of less importance than what the king says they have done. Juries are not even consulted, not even sworn in. Henry, who stayed away from the fighting, rules at long distance through his spineless judges, and commands life and death.

Not until August does the king come home and at once he moves the court away from the city that threatened him, out of town to the beautiful newly restored Palace of Sheen by the river. My uncle Edward comes with him, and my cousin John de la Pole, riding easily in the royal train, smiling at comrades who do not wholly trust them, greeting my mother as a kinswoman in public and never, never talking with her in private, as if they have to demonstrate every day that there are no whispered secrets among the Yorks, that we are all reliably loyal to the House of Tudor.

There are many who are quick to say that the king does not dare to live in London, that he is afraid of the twisting streets and the dark ways of the city, of the sinuous secrets of the river and those who silently travel on it. There are many who say he is not sure of the loyalty of his own capital city and that he does not trust his safety within its walls. The trained bands of the city keep their own weapons to hand, and the apprentices are always ready to spring up and riot. If a king is well loved in London, then he has a wall of protection around him, a loyal army always at his doors guarding him. But a king with uncertain popularity is under threat every moment of the day, anything — hot weather, a play that goes wrong, an accident at a joust, the arrest of a popular youth — can trigger a riot which might unseat him.

Henry insists that we must move to Sheen as he loves the countryside in summer and exclaims at the beauty of the palace and the richness of the park. He congratulates me on the size of my belly and insists that I sit down all the time. When we walk together into dinner he demands that I lean heavily on his arm, as if my feet are likely to fail underneath me. He is tender and kind to me, and I am surprised to find that it is a relief to have him home. His mother's anguished vigilance is soothed by the sight of him, the constant uneasiness of being a new court in an uncertain country is eased, and the court feels more normal with Henry riding out to hunt every morning and coming home boasting of fresh venison and game every night. His looks have improved during his long summertime journey around England, his skin warmed by the sunshine, and his face more relaxed and smiling. He was afraid of the North of England before he went there, but once the worst of his fears did indeed happen, and he survived it, he felt victorious once again.

He comes to my room every evening, sometimes bringing a syllabub straight from the kitchen for me to drink while it is warm, as if we did not have a hundred servants to do my bidding. I laugh at him, carrying the little jug and the cup, neat as a groom of the servery.

"Well, you're used to having people do things for you," he says. "You were raised in a royal household with dozens of servants waiting around the room for something to do. But in Brittany I had to serve myself. Sometimes we had no house servants. Actually, sometimes we had no house, we were all but homeless."

I go to my chair by the fire, but that is not good enough for the mother of the next prince.

"Sit on the bed, sit on the bed, put your feet up," he urges, and helps me up, taking my shoes and pressing the cup in my hands. Like a pair of little merchants snug in their town house, we eat our supper alone together. Henry puts a poker into the heart of the fire and when it is hot, plunges it into a jug of small ale. The drink seethes and he pours it out while it is steaming and tastes it.

"I can tell you my heart turned to stone at York," he says to me frankly. "Freezing cold wind and a rain that could cut through you, and the faces of the women like stone itself. They looked at me as if I had personally murdered their only son. You know what they're like — they love Richard as dearly as if he rode out only yesterday. Why do they do that? Why do they cling to him still?"

I bury my face in the syllabub cup so that he cannot see my swift betraying flinch of grief.

"He had that York gift, didn't he?" he presses me. "Of making people love him? Like your father King Edward did? Like you have? It's a blessing, there's no real sense to it. It's just that some men have a charm, don't they? And then people follow them? People just follow them?"

I shrug. I can't trust my voice to speak of why everyone loved Richard, of the friends who would have laid down their lives for him and who, even now after his death, still fight his enemies for love of his memory. The common soldiers who will still brawl in taverns when someone says that he was a usurper. The fishwives who will draw a knife on anyone who says he was hunchbacked or weak.

"I don't have it, do I?" Henry asks me bluntly. "Whatever it is — a gift or a trick or a talent. I don't have it. Everywhere we went, I smiled and waved and did all that I could, all that I should. I acted the part of a king sure of his throne even though I sometimes felt like a penniless pretender with no one who believes in me but a besotted mother and a doting uncle, a pawn for the big players who are the kings of Europe. I've never been someone deeply beloved by a city, I've never had an army roar my name. I'm not a man who is followed for love."

"You won the battle," I say dryly. "You had enough men follow you on the day. That's all that matters, that one day. As you tell everyone: you're king. You're king by right of conquest."

"I won with hired troops, paid by the King

of France. I won with an army loaned to me from Brittany. One half of them were mercenaries and the other half were murderous criminals pulled out of the jails. I didn't have men that served me for love. I'm not beloved," he says quietly. "I don't think I ever will be. I don't have the knack of it."

I lower the cup and for a moment our eyes meet. In that one accidental exchange I can see that he is thinking that he is not even loved by his own wife. He is — simply — loveless. He spent his youth waiting for the throne of England, he risked his life fighting for the throne of England, and now he finds it is a hollow crown indeed; there is no heart at the center. It is empty.

I can think of nothing to fill the awkward silence. "You have adherents," I offer.

He gives a short bitter laugh. "Oh yes, I have bought some: the Courtenays and the Howards. And I have the friends that my mother has made for me. I can count on a few friends from the old days, my uncle, the Earl of Oxford. I can trust the Stanleys, and my mother's kin." He pauses. "It's an odd question for a husband to ask his wife, but I could think of nothing else when they told me that Lovell had come against me. I know that he was Richard's friend. I see that Francis Lovell loves Richard so much that he fights on even when Richard is dead. It made me wonder: can I count on you?"

"Why would you even ask?"

"Because they all tell me that you loved Richard too. And I know you well enough now to be sure that you were not guided by ambition to be his queen, you were driven by love. So that's why I ask you. Do you love him still? Like Lord Lovell? Like the women of York? Do you love him despite his death? Like York does, like Lord Lovell does? Or can I count on you?"

I shift slightly as if I am uncomfortable on the soft bed, sipping my drink. I gesture to my belly. "As you say, I am your wife. You can count on that. I am about to have your child. You can count on that."

He nods. "We both know how that came about. It was done to breed a child; it was not an act of love. You would have refused me if you could have done, and every night you turned your face away. But I have been wondering, while I was gone, facing such unfriendliness, facing a rebellion, whether loyalty might grow, whether trust can grow between us?"

He does not even mention love.

I glance away. I cannot meet his steady gaze, and I cannot answer his question. "All this I have already promised," I say inadequately. "I said my marriage vows."

He hears the refusal in my voice. Gently he leans over and takes the empty cup from me.

"I'll leave it at that, then," he says, and goes from my room.

St. Swithin's Priory, Winchester, September 1486

A rosy sun in saffron clouds is sinking below the sill of my window in the September evening as I wake from my afternoon nap and lie, enjoying the warmth on my face, knowing that this is my last day of sunshine. This evening I have to dress up, take the compliments of the court, receive their gifts, and go into confinement to await the birth of my baby. My confinement rooms will be darkened by shutters, my windows closed, even the feeble light of the candles will be shaded until the baby is born.

If My Lady the King's Mother was able publicly to declare when the baby was conceived — a full month before our wedding — she would have had me locked up four weeks ago. She has already written in her Royal Book that a queen must be confined a full six weeks before the expected date of a birth. She must give a farewell dinner and the court must escort her to the door of the confinement chamber. She must go in, and not come out again (God willing, writes the pious lady at this point) until six weeks after the birth of a healthy child, when the babe is brought out to be christened, and she emerges to be churched and can take her place at court once more. A stay in silence and darkness of a long three months' duration. I read this, in her elegant black-ink handwriting, and I study her opinions about the quality of the tapestries on the walls and the hangings on the bed, and I think that only a barren woman would compose such a regime.

My Lady the King's Mother had only one child, her precious son Henry, and she has been barren since his birth. I think that if there were any chance that she would be put away from the world for three months every year, the orders on confinement would be very different. These rules are not to secure my privacy and rest, they are to keep me out of the way of the court so that she can take my place for three glorious long months every time her son gets me with child. It is as simple as that.

But this time, wonderfully, the joke is on her, for since we have, all three of us, loudly and publicly declared that the baby is a honeymoon baby, the blessedly quick result of a January wedding, it should be born in the middle of October, and so by her own rules, I don't have to go into confinement until now, the first week in September. If she had put me into darkness at seven and a half months, I should have missed all of August, but I have been free — big-bellied but gloriously free — and I have laughed up my sleeve for a month as I have seen this deception eat away at her.

Now I expect to spend only a week or so before the birth in this gloomy twilight, banned from the outside world, seeing no man but a priest through a shaded screen. Then I will have six long weeks of isolation after the birth. In my absence I know that My Lady will relish ruling the court, receiving congratulations on the birth of her grandchild, supervising the christening and ordering the feast, while I am locked in my rooms and no man — not even my husband, her son — can see me.

My maid is bringing a green gown from the wardrobe for my official farewell. I wave it away, I am so very tired of wearing Tudor green, when the door bursts open and Maggie comes running into the room and flings herself on her knees before me. "Elizabeth, I mean Your Grace! Elizabeth! Oh, Elizabeth, save Teddy!"

The baby seems to jump in alarm in my belly as I leap off the bed and catch at the hangings as the room swings dizzily around me. "Teddy?"

"They're taking him! They're taking him away!"

185

"Careful!" my sister Cecily warns at once, hurrying to my side and steadying me on my feet. I don't even hear her.

"Taking him where?"

"To the Tower!" Maggie cries out. "To the Tower! Oh! Come quick and stop them. Please!"

"Go to the king," I throw at Cecily over my shoulder as I quickly head to the door. "Give him my compliments and ask if I may come to see him at once." I grab my cousin Maggie's arm and say, "Come on, I'll come with you and stop them."

Hurriedly, I go barefoot down the long stone corridors, the herbs brushed by my trailing nightgown, then Maggie sprints ahead of me up the circular stone staircase to the nursery floor, where she and Edward and my little sisters Catherine and Bridget have their rooms with their tutors and their maids. But then I see her fall back, and I hear the noise of half a dozen heavy boots coming down the stairs. "You can't take him!" I hear her say. "I have the queen here! You can't take him."

As they come down the curve of the stair I see first the booted feet of the leading man, then his deep scarlet leggings, and then his bright scarlet tunic trimmed and quartered with gold lace: the uniform of the yeomen of the guard, Henry's newly created personal troop. Behind him comes another, and another; they have sent a corps of ten men to collect a pale and shaking little boy of eleven. Edward is so afraid that the last man is holding him under the armpits so that he does not fall down the stairs; his feet are dangling, his skinny legs kicking as they half-carry him to where I am standing at the foot of the stairs. He looks like a doll with brown tousled curls and wide frightened eyes.

"Maggie!" he cries, on seeing his sister. "Maggie, tell them to put me down!"

I step forwards. "I am Elizabeth of York," I say to the man at the front. "Wife of the king. This is my cousin, the Earl of Warwick. You shouldn't even touch him. What d'you think you are doing?"

"Elizabeth, tell them to put me down!" Teddy insists. "Put me down! Put me down!"

"Release him," I say to the man who is holding him.

Abruptly the guard drops him, but as soon as Teddy's feet touch the floor he collapses into a heap, weeping with frustration. Maggie is down beside him in a moment, hugging him to her shoulder, smoothing his hair, stroking his cheeks, petting him into quietness. He pulls back from her shoulder to look earnestly into her eyes. "They lifted me from my desk in the schoolroom," he exclaims in his piping little-boy voice. He is shocked that anyone should touch him without his permission; he has been an earl all his life, he has only ever been gently raised and carefully served. For a moment, looking at his tearstained face I think of the two boys in the Tower who were lifted from their beds, and there was no one there to stop the men who came for them.

"Orders of the king," the commander of the yeomen says briefly to me. "He won't be harmed."

"There has been a mistake. He has to stay here, with us, his family," I reply. "Wait here, while I go to speak to His Grace the King, my husband."

"My orders are clear," the man starts to argue, as the door opens and Henry appears in the doorway, dressed for riding, a whip in one hand, his expensive leather gloves in the other. My sister Cecily peeps around him to see Maggie and me, with young Edward struggling to his feet.

"What's this?" Henry demands, without a word of greeting.

"There's been some mistake," I say. I am so relieved to see him that I forget to curtsey, but go quickly towards him and take his warm hand. "The yeomen thought they had to take Edward to the Tower."

"They do," Henry says shortly.

I am startled at his tone. "But my lord . . ."

He nods at the yeoman. "Carry on. Take the boy."

Maggie gives a little yelp of dismay and

flings her arm around Teddy's neck.

"My lord," I say urgently. "Edward is my cousin. He has done nothing. He is studying in the nursery here with my sisters and his sister. He loves you as his king."

"I do," Teddy says clearly. "I have promised. They told me to say that I promise, and so I did."

The yeomen have closed up around him again, but they are waiting for Henry to speak.

"Please," I say. "Please let Teddy stay here with all of us. You know he would never harm anyone. Certainly not you."

Henry takes me gently by the shoulder and leads me away from the rest of them. "You should be resting," he says. "You should not have been disturbed by this. You should not be upset. You should be going into confinement. This was all supposed to happen after you had gone in."

"I'm very near to my time," I whisper urgently to him. "As you know. Very near. Your mother says that I must stay calm, it might hurt the baby if I'm not calm. But I won't be able to be calm if Teddy is taken from us. Please let him stay with us. I am feeling unhappy." I take a swift glance at his piercing brown eyes which are scanning my face. "Very unhappy, Henry. I feel distressed. I am troubled. Please tell me that it'll be all right."

"Go and lie down in your room," he says. "I'll sort this out. You shouldn't have been troubled. You shouldn't have been told."

"I'll go to my room," I promise. "But I must have your word that Teddy stays with us. I'll go, as soon as I know that Teddy can stay here."

With a sudden sense of dread I see My Lady the King's Mother step into the room. "I will take you back to your bedchamber," she offers. Some of her ladies-in-waiting come in behind her. "Come."

I hesitate. "Go on," Henry says. "Go with my mother. I'll settle things here and then come and see you."

"But Teddy stays with us," I stipulate.

Henry hesitates and as he does so, his mother steps quietly around me to stand behind me. She wraps me in her arms, holding me close. For a moment I think it is a loving embrace, then I feel the strength in her grip. Two of her ladies-in-waiting come up on either side of her and hold my arms. I am captured, to my absolute amazement, I am held. One of the ladies scoops up Maggie and two of them hold her as the yeomen of the guard lift Teddy bodily and carry him from the room.

"No!" I scream.

Maggie is struggling and kicking, lashing out to get to her brother.

"No! You can't take Teddy, he's done nothing! Not the Tower! Not Teddy!"

Henry throws one horrified glance at me, held by his mother, struggling to be free, and then turns and goes out of the room, following his guard.

"Henry!" I scream after him.

My Lady the King's Mother puts a hard hand over my mouth to silence me and we hear the tramp of the guards' feet going down the gallery and then down the stairs at the end. Then we hear the outer door bang. When there is silence, My Lady takes her hand from my mouth.

"How dare you! How dare you hold me? Let me go!"

"I will take you to your room," she says steadily. "You must not be upset."

"I am upset!" I scream at her. "I am upset! Teddy can't go to the Tower."

She does not even answer me but nods at her ladies to follow her and they guide me firmly from the room. Behind me, Maggie has collapsed into tears, and the women who were holding her lower her gently to the ground and wipe her face and whisper to her that everything will be well. My sister Cecily is aghast at the sudden, smooth violence of the scene. I want her to go and fetch our mother, but she is stupid with shock, staring, from me to My Lady, as if the king's mother had grown fangs and wings and was holding me prisoner.

"Come," My Lady says. "You should lie down."

She leads the way and the women release me to follow her. I walk behind her, struggling to regain my temper. "My Lady, I must ask you to intercede for my little cousin Edward," I say to her stiff back, her white wimple, her rigid shoulders. "I beg you to speak to your son and ask him to release Teddy. You know Teddy is a young boy innocent of any bad thought. You made him your ward, any accusation of him is a reflection on you."

She says nothing, leading the way past the closed doors. I am following her blindly, searching for words that will make her stop, turn, agree, as she opens the double doors of a darkened room.

"He is your ward," I say. "He should be in your keeping."

She does not answer me. "Here. Come in. Rest."

I step inside. "Lady Margaret, I beg of you . . ." I start, and then I see that her ladies have followed us into the shadowy room and one of them has turned the key in the lock of the door and given it quietly to My Lady.

"What are you doing?" I demand.

"This is your confinement chamber," she answers.

Now, for the first time, I realize where she has led me. It is a long, beautiful room with tall arched windows, blocked with tapestries so that no light creeps in. One of the ladies-in-waiting is lighting the candles, their yellow flickering light illuminating the bare stone walls and the high arched ceiling. The far end of the room is sheltered by a screen, and I can see an altar and the candles burning before a monstrance, a crucifix, a picture of Our Lady. Before the screen are prayer stools and before them the fireplace and a grand chair and lesser stools arranged in a conversational circle. Chillingly, I see that my sewing is on the table by the grand chair, and the book that I was reading before I lay down for my nap has been taken from my bedchamber and is open beside it.

Next is a dining table and six chairs, wine and water in beautiful Venetian glass jugs on the table, gold plates ready for serving dinner, a box with pastries in case of hunger.

Nearest to us is a grand bed, with thick oak posts and rich curtains and tester. On an impulse I open the chest at the foot of the bed and there, neatly folded and interspersed with dried lavender flowers, are my favorite gowns and my best linen, ready for me to wear when they fit me again. There is a day bed, next to the chest, and a beautifully carved and engraved royal cradle, all ready with linen beside the bed.

"What is this?" I ask as if I don't know. "What is this? What is this?"

"You are in confinement," Lady Margaret says patiently, as if speaking to an idiot. "For your health and for the health of your child."

"What about Teddy?"

"He has been taken to the Tower for his own safety. He was in danger here. He needs to be carefully guarded. But I will speak to the king about your cousin. I will tell you what he says. Without question, he will judge rightly."

"I want to see the king now!"

She pauses. "Now, daughter, you know that you cannot see him, or any man, until you come out of confinement," she says reasonably. "But I will give him any message or take him any letter you wish to write."

"When I have given birth you will have to let me out," I say breathlessly. It is as if the room is airless and I am struggling to breathe. "Then I will see the king and tell him that I have been imprisoned in here."

She sighs as if I am very foolish. "Really, Your Grace! You must be calm. We all agreed you were entering your confinement this evening, you knew full well that you were doing this today."

"What about the dinner and bidding farewell to the court?"

"Your health was not strong enough. You said so yourself."

I am so amazed by her lie that I gape at her. "When did I say that?"

"You said you were distressed. You said you were troubled. Here there is neither distress nor trouble. You will stay here, under my guidance, until you have safely given birth to the child."

"I will see my mother, I will see her at once!" I say. I am furious to hear my voice tremble. But I am afraid of My Lady in this darkened room, and I feel powerless. My earliest memory is of being confined, in sanctuary, in a damp warren of cold rooms under the chapel at Westminster Abbey. I have a horror of confined spaces and dark places, and now I am trembling with anger and fear. "I will see my mother. The king said that I should see her. The king promised me that she would be with me in here."

"She will come into confinement with you," she concedes. "Of course." She pauses. "And she will stay with you until you come out. When the baby is born. She will share your confinement."

I just gape at her. She has all the power and I have none. I have been as good as imprisoned by her and by the convention of royal births which she has codified and to which I agreed. Now I am locked in one shadowy room for weeks, and she has the key.

"I am free," I say boldly. "I'm not a prisoner. I am here to give birth. I chose to come in here. I am not held against my will. I am free. If I want to walk out, I can just walk out. Nobody can stop me, I am the wife of the King of England."

"Of course you are," she says, and then she goes out through the door and turns the key in the lock from the outside, and leaves me. I am locked in.

My mother comes in at dinnertime, holding Maggie's hand. "We've come to join you," she says.

Maggie is white as if she were deathly sick, her eyes red-rimmed from crying.

"What about Teddy?"

My mother shakes her head. "They took him to the Tower."

"Why would they do that?"

"They shouted À Warwick when they fought Jasper Tudor in the North. They carried the standard of the ragged staff in London," my mother says, as if this is reason enough.

"They were fighting for Teddy," Maggie tells me. "Even though he didn't ask them to — even though he would never ask them to. He knows not to say such things. I've taught him. He knows that King Henry is the king. He knows to say nothing about the House of York."

"There's no charge against him," my mother says briefly. "He's not charged with treason. Not charged with anything. The king says he is only acting to protect Teddy. He says that Teddy might be seized by rebels and used by them as a figurehead. He says that

Teddy is safer in the Tower for now."

My laughter at this extraordinary lie turns into a sob. "Safer in the Tower! Were my brothers safer in the Tower?"

My mother grimaces.

"I'm sorry," I say at once. "Forgive me, I'm sorry. Did the king say how long he will keep Teddy there?"

Maggie goes quietly to the fireside and sinks down onto a footstool, her head turned away. "Poor child," my mother says. To me she replies, "He didn't say. I didn't ask. They took Teddy's clothes and his books. I think we have to assume that His Grace will keep him there until he feels safe from rebellion."

I look at her, the only one of us who may know how many rebels are biding their time, waiting for a call to rise for York, seeing the last skirmish as a stepping-stone to another, and from that to another — not as a defeat. She is a woman who never sees defeat. I wonder if she is their leader, if it is her determined optimism that drives them on. "Is something going to happen?"

She shakes her head. "I don't know."

Prior's Great Hall, Winchester, 19 September 1486

I have to endure my confinement in a state of frightened misery. It is so like the long months in the darkness of the crypt below the chapel at Westminster that I wake every morning gasping for air and clinging to the carved headboard to stop myself jumping out of bed and screaming for help. I still have nightmares about darkness and the crowded rooms. My mother was pregnant, my father had fled overseas, our enemy was on the throne, I was four years old and Mary, my darling little sister now in heaven, and Cecily cried all the time for their toys, for their pets, for their father, not really knowing what they were crying for, only that our whole life was plunged into darkness, cold, and want. I used to look at my mother's bleak white face and wonder if she would ever smile at me again. I knew that we were in terrible danger, but I was only four, I didn't know what the danger was, or how this damp prison could keep us safe. Half a year we spent inside the walls of the crypt, half a year and we never saw the sun, never walked outside, never took a breath of fresh air. We became accustomed to a life in prison, as convicts become accustomed to the limits of their cell. Mother gave birth to Edward inside those damp walls, and we were filled with joy that at last we had a boy, an heir; but we knew we had no way of getting him to the throne — not even of getting him into the sun and air of his own country. Six months is a long, long time for a little girl of only four years old. I thought that we would never get out, I thought I would grow up taller and taller like a thin pale weed and die blanched like asparagus by the darkness. I had a dream that we were all turning into white-faced worms and that we would live underground forever. That was when I grew to hate confined spaces, hate the smell of damp, even hate the sound of the river lapping against the walls at nighttime, as I feared the waters would rise and rise and seep into my bed and drown me.

When my father came home, won two battles one after the other, saved us, rescued us like a knight in a storybook, we emerged from the crypt, out of the darkness like the risen Lord Himself coming into light. Then I swore to myself a childish oath that I would never be confined again.

This is fortune's wheel — as my grandmother Jacquetta would say. Fortune's wheel that takes you very high and then throws you very low, and there is nothing you can do but face the turn of it with courage. I remember clearly enough that as a little girl I could not find that courage.

When I was seventeen and the favorite of my father's court, the most beautiful princess in England with everything before me, my father died and we fled back into sanctuary, for fear of his brother, my uncle Richard. Nine long months we waited in sanctuary, squabbling with one another, furious at our own failure, until my mother came to terms with Richard and I was freed into the light, to the court, to love. For the second time I came out of the dark like a ghost returning to life. Once again I blinked in the warm light of freedom like a hooded hawk suddenly set free to fly, and I swore I would never again be imprisoned. Once again, I am proved wrong.

My pains start at midnight. "It's too early," one of my women breathes in fear. "It's at least a month too early." I see a swift glance between those habitual conspirators, my mother and My Lady the King's Mother. "It is a month too early," My Lady confirms loudly for anyone who is counting. "We will have to pray."

"My Lady, would you go to your own

chapel and pray for our daughter?" my mother asks quickly and cleverly. "An early baby needs intercession with the saints. If you would be so good as to pray for her in her time of travail?"

My Lady hesitates, torn between God and curiosity. "I had thought to help her here. I thought I should witness . . ."

My mother shrugs at the room, the midwives, my sisters, the ladies-in-waiting. "Earthly tasks," she says simply. "But who can pray like you?"

"I'll get the priest, and the choir," My Lady says. "Send me news throughout the night. I'll get them to wake the archbishop. Our Lady will hear my prayers."

They open the door for her and she goes out, excited by her mission. My mother does not even smile as she turns back to me and says, "Now, let's get you walking."

While My Lady labors on her knees, I labor all the night, until at dawn I turn my sweating face to my mother and say, "I feel strange, Lady Mother. I feel strange, like nothing I have felt before. I feel as if something terrible is about to happen. I'm afraid, Mama."

She has laid aside her headdress, her hair is in a plait down her back, she has walked all the night beside me and now her tired face beams. "Lean on the women," is all she says.

I had thought it would be a struggle, having heard all the terrible stories that women tell each other about screaming pain and babies that have to be turned, or babies that cannot be born and sometimes, fatally, have to be cut out; but my mother orders two of the midwives to stand on either side of me to bear me up, and she takes my face in her cool hands and looks into my eyes with her gray gaze and says quietly, "I am going to count for you. Be very still, beloved, and listen to my voice. I am going to count from one to ten and as I count you will find your limbs get heavier and your breathing gets deeper and all you can hear is my voice. You will feel as if you are floating, as if you are Melusina on the water, and you are floating down a river of sweet water and you will feel no pain, only a deep restfulness like sleep."

I am watching her eyes and then I can see nothing but her steady expression and hear nothing but her quiet counting. The pains come and go in my belly, but it feels like a long way away and I float, as she promised that I would, as if on a current of sweet water.

I can see the steadiness of her gaze, and the illumination of her face, and I feel that we are in a time of unreality, as if she is making magic around us with her reliable quiet count which seemed to go slowly and take an eternity.

"There is nothing to fear," she says to me softly. "There is never anything to fear. The worst fear is of fear itself, and you can conquer that."

"How?" I murmur. It feels as if I am talking in my sleep, floating down a stream of sleep. "How can I conquer the worst fear?"

"You just decide," she says simply. "Just decide that you are not going to be a fearful woman and when you come to something that makes you apprehensive, you face it and walk towards it. Remember — anything you fear, you walk slowly and steadily towards it. And smile."

Her certainty and the description of her own courage make me smile even though my pains are coming and then easing, faster now, every few minutes or so, and I see her beloved beam in reply as her eyes crinkle.

"Choose to be brave," she urges me. "All the women of your family are as brave as lions. We don't whimper and we don't regret."

My stomach seems to grip and turn. "I think the baby is coming," I say, and I breathe deeply.

"I think so too," she says, and turns to the midwives who hold me up, one under each arm, while the third kneels before me and listens with her ear against my straining belly.

"Now," she says.

My mother says to me: "Your baby is ready, let him come into the world."

"She needs to push," one of the midwives says sharply. "She needs to struggle. He has to be born in travail and pain."

My mother overrules her. "You don't need to struggle," she says. "Your baby is coming. Help him come to us, open your body and let him come into the world. You give birth, you don't force birth or besiege it. It's not a battle, it's an act of love. You give birth to your child and you can do it gently."

I can feel the sinews of my body opening and stretching. "It's coming!" I say, suddenly alert. "I can feel . . ."

And then there is a rush and a thrust and an inescapable sense of movement, and then the sharp crying noise of a child and my mother smiling, though her eyes are filled with tears, and she says to me: "You have a baby. Well done, Elizabeth. Your father would be proud of your courage."

They release me from the grip they have taken on my arms, and I lie down on the day bed and turn to where the woman is wrapping a little wriggling bloody bundle and I hold out my arms, saying impatiently: "Give me my baby!" I take it, with a sense of wonder that it is a baby, so perfectly formed, with brown hair and a rosy mouth open to bellow, and a cross flushed face. But my mother pulls back the linen that they have wrapped it in, and shows me the perfect little body.

"A boy," she says, and there is neither triumph nor joy in her voice, just a deep wonder, though her voice is hoarse with weariness. "God has answered Lady Margaret's prayers again. His ways are mysterious indeed. You have given the Tudors what they need: a boy."

The king himself has been waiting all night outside the door for the news, like a loving husband who cannot wait for a messenger. My mother throws her robe over her stained linen shift and goes out to tell him of our triumph, her head high with pride. They send word to My Lady the King's Mother in the chapel that her prayers have been answered and God has secured the Tudor line. She comes in as the women are helping me into the great state bed to rest, and washing and swaddling the baby. His wet nurse curtseys and shows him to My Lady, who reaches for him greedily, as if he were a crown in a hawthorn bush. She snatches him up and holds him to her heart.

"A boy," she says like a miser might breathe "God." "God has answered my prayers."

I nod. I am too tired to speak to her. My mother holds a cup of spiced hot ale to my lips and I smell the sugar and the brandy and drink deep. I feel as if I am floating, dreamy with exhaustion and the ending of pain, drunk on the birthing ale, triumphant at a successful birth, and dizzy with the thought that I have a baby, a son, and that he is perfect.

"Bring him here," I command.

She does as I tell her and hands him to me. He is tiny, small as a doll, but every detail of him is perfect as if he has been handcrafted with endless care. He has hands like plump little starfish and tiny fingernails like the smallest of shells. As I hold him he opens his eyes of the most surprising dark blue, like a sea at midnight. He looks at me gravely, as if he too is surprised. He looks at me as if he understands all that is to be, as if he knows that he has been born to a great destiny and must fulfill it.

"Give him to the wet nurse," My Lady prompts.

"In a moment." I don't care what she tells me to do. She may have command of her son, but I shall have command of mine. This is my baby, not hers, this is my son, not hers; he is an heir to the Tudors but he is my beloved.

He is the Tudor heir that makes the throne safe, that will start a dynasty that will last forever. "We will call him Arthur," My Lady declares. I knew this was coming. They dragged me to Winchester for the birth so that we could claim the legacy of Arthur, so the baby could be born all but on the famous Round Table of the knights of Camelot, so the Tudors could claim to be the heirs of that miraculous kingdom, the greatness of England revived, and the beautiful chivalry of the country springing again from their noble line.

"I know," I say. I have no objection. How can I? It was the very name that Richard had chosen for a son with me. He too dreamed of Camelot and chivalry, but unlike the Tudors he really tried to make a court of noble knights; unlike the Tudors he lived his life by the precepts of being a perfect gentle knight. I close my eyes at the ridiculous thought that Richard would have loved this baby, that he chose his name, that he wished him into being with me, that this is our child.

"Prince Arthur," My Lady rules.

"I know," I say again. It is as if everything I do with my husband, Henry, is a sad parody of the dreams I had with my lover, Richard.

"Why are you crying?" she demands impatiently.

I lift the sheet of my bed and wipe my eyes. "I'm not," I say.

Prior's Great Hall, Winchester, 24 September 1486

The christening of the flower of England, the rose of chivalry, is as grand and exaggerated as a regime newly come to power can devise. My Lady has been planning it for the past nine months, everything is done as ostentatiously as possible.

"I think they are going to dip him in gold and serve him on a platter," my mother says sarcastically with a hidden smile at me, as she lifts the baby from his cradle early in the morning of his grand christening day. The rockers stand obediently behind her, watching her every move with the suspicion of professionals. The wet nurse is unlacing her bodice, impatient to feed the baby. My mother holds her grandson to her face and kisses his warm little body. He is sleepy, making a little snuffling noise. I hold out my arms, yearning for him, and she gives him to me and hugs us both.

As we watch, he opens his mouth in a little yawn, compresses his tiny face, flaps his arms like a fledgling, and then wails to be fed. "My lord prince," my mother says lovingly. "Impatient as a king. Here, I'll give him to Meg."

The wet nurse is ready for him, but he cries and fusses and cannot latch on.

"Should I feed him?" I ask eagerly. "Would he feed from me?"

The rockers, the wet nurse, even my mother, all shake their heads in absolute unison.

"No," my mother says regretfully. "That's the price you pay for being a great lady, a queen. You can't nurse your own child. You have won him a golden spoon and the best food in the world for all his life, but he cannot have his mother's milk. You can't mother him as you might wish. You're not a poor woman. You're not free. You have to be back in the king's bed as soon as you are able and give us another baby boy."

Jealously, I watch as he nuzzles at another woman's breast and finally starts to feed. The wet nurse gives me a reassuring smile. "He'll do well on my milk," she says quietly. "You need not fear for him."

"How many boys do you need?" I demand irritably of my mother. "Before I can stop bearing them? Before I can feed one?"

My mother, who gave birth to three royal boys and has none of them today, shrugs her shoulders. "It's a dangerous world," is all she says.

The door opens without a knock and My Lady comes in. "Is he ready?" she asks without preamble.

"He's feeding." My mother rises to her feet. "He'll be ready in a little while. Are you waiting for him?"

Lady Margaret inhales the sweet, clean smell of the room as if she is greedy for him. "It's all ready," she says. "I have ordered it to the last detail. They are lining up in the Great Hall, waiting only for the Earl of Oxford." She looks around for Anne and Cecily, and nods approval at their ornate gowns. "You are honored," she says. "I have allowed you two the most important positions: carrying the chrism, carrying the prince himself." She turns to my mother. "And you, named as godmother to a prince, a Tudor prince! Nobody can say that we have not united the families. Nobody can declare for York anymore. We are all one. I have planned today to prove it." She looks at the wet nurse as if she would snatch the baby from her. "Will he be ready soon?"

My mother hides a smile. It is very clear that My Lady may know everything about christening princes but nothing about babies. "He will be as long as he needs," she rules. "Probably less than an hour."

"And what is he to wear?"

My mother gestures to the beautiful gown that she has made for him from the finest

French lace. It has a train that sweeps to the floor and a tiny pleated ruff. Only she and I know that she cut it too large, so that this baby who was a full nine months in the womb will look small, as if he had come a month before his time.

"It will be the greatest ceremony in this reign," My Lady the King's Mother says. "Everyone is here. Everyone will see the future King of England, my grandson."

They wait and wait. It makes no difference to me, bidden to rest in bed whatever takes place. The tradition is that the mother shall not be present at the christening and My Lady is not likely to break such a custom in order to bring me forwards. Besides, I am exhausted, torn between a sort of wild joy and a desperate fatigue. The baby feeds, they change his clout, they put him into my arms, and we sleep together, my arms around his tiny form, my nose sniffing his soft head.

The Earl of Oxford, hastily summoned, rides to Winchester as fast as he can, but My Lady the King's Mother rules that they have waited long enough and will go on without him. They take the baby and off they all go. My mother is godmother, my sister Cecily carries the baby, my cousin Margaret leads the procession of women, Lord Neville goes before them carrying a lit taper. Thomas, Lord Stanley, and his son, and his brother

Sir William — all heroes of Bosworth who stood on the hillside and watched Richard their king lead a charge without them, and then rode him down to his death — all walk together behind my son, as if he can count on their support, as if their word is worth anything, and present him to the altar.

While they are christening my boy, I wash and they dress me in a fine new gown of crimson lace and cloth of gold, they put the best sheets on my great bed, and help me back onto the pillows, so that I can be arranged, like a triumphant Madonna, for congratulations. I hear the trumpets outside my room, and the tramp of many feet. They throw open the double doors to my chamber and Cecily comes in, beaming, and puts my baby Arthur into my arms. My mother gives me a beautiful cup of gold for him, the Earl of Oxford has sent a pair of gilt basins, the Earl of Derby a saltcellar of gold. Everyone comes piling into my bedchamber with gifts, kneeling to me as the mother of the next king, kneeling to him to show their loyalty. I hold him and I smile and thank people for their kindness, as I look at men who loved Richard and promised loyalty to him, and who are now smiling at me and kissing my hand and agreeing, without words, that we shall never mention those long seasons ever again. That time shall be as if it never was. We will never speak of it, though they were the happiest days of my life, and maybe the happiest days of theirs, too.

The men swear their loyalty, and pay compliments, and then my mother says quietly: "Her Grace the Queen should rest now," and My Lady the King's Mother says at once, so that it shall not be my mother who gives an order: "Prince Arthur must be taken to his nursery. I have everything prepared for him."

This day marks his entry into royal life, as a Tudor prince. In a few weeks' time he will have his own nursery palace; we will not even sleep under the same roof. I shall reenter the court as soon as I am churched and Henry will come back to my bed to make another prince for the Tudors. I look at my little son, the tiny baby that he is, in his nursemaid's arms, and know that they are taking him from me, and that he is prince and I am queen and we are mother and child alone together no more.

Even before I am churched and out of confinement, Henry rewards us Yorks with the marriage of my sister. The timing of the announcement is a compliment to me, a reward for giving him a son; but I understand by their waiting so long that if I had died in childbed, he would have had to marry another princess of York to secure the throne. He and his mother kept Cecily unmarried in case of my death. I went into the danger of childbed with my sister marked out for my widower. Truly, My Lady plans for everything.

Cecily comes to me breathless with excitement, her face flushed as if she is in love. I am tired, my breasts hurt, my privates hurt, everything hurts as my sister dances into my rooms and declares: "He has favored me! The king has favored me! My Lady has spoken for me, and the wedding is to happen at last! I am her goddaughter, but now I am to be even closer!"

"They have set your wedding day?"

"My betrothed came to tell me himself. Sir John. I shall be Lady Welles. And he is so handsome! And so rich!"

I look at her, a hundred harsh words on the tip of my tongue. This is a man who was raised to hate our family, whose father died under our arrows at the battle of Towton when his own artillery could not fire in the snow, whose half brother Sir Richard Welles and his son Robert were executed by our father on the battlefield for treachery. Cecily's betrothed is Lady Margaret's half brother, a Lancastrian by birth, by inclination, and by lifelong enmity to us. He is thirty-six years old to my sister's seventeen, he has been our enemy all his life. He must hate her. "And this makes you happy?" I ask.

She does not even hear the skepticism in my tone. "Lady Margaret herself made this wedding," she says. "She told him that though I am a princess of York I am charming. She said that: charming. She said that I am utterly suited to be the wife of a nobleman of the Tudor court. She said I am most likely to be fertile, she even praised you for having a boy. She said I am not puffed up with false pride."

"Did she say legitimate?" I ask dryly. "For I can never remember whether we are princesses or not at the moment."

Finally she hears the bitterness in my voice and she pauses in her jig, takes hold of my bedpost, and swings around to look at me. "Are you jealous of me for making a marriage for love, to a nobleman, and that I come to him untouched? With the favor of My Lady?" she taunts me. "That my reputation is as good as any maid's in the world? With no secrets behind me? No scandals that might be unearthed? Nobody can say one word against me?"

"No," I say wearily. I could weep for the aches and pains, the seep of blood, the matching seep of tears. I am missing my baby, and I am mourning for Richard. "I am glad for you, really. I am just tired."

"Shall I send for your mother?" Our cousin Maggie steps forwards, frowning at Cecily. "Her Grace is still recovering!" she says quietly. "She shouldn't be disturbed."

"I only came to tell you I am to be married, I thought you would be happy for me,"

Cecily says, aggrieved. "It is you who is being so unpleasant . . ."

"I know." I force myself to change my tone. "And I should have said that I am glad for you, and that he is a lucky man to have such a princess."

"Father had greater plans for me than this," she points out. "I was raised for better than this. If you don't congratulate me, you should pity me."

"Yes," I reply. "But all my pity is used up on myself. It doesn't matter, Cecily, you can't understand how I feel. You should be happy, I am glad for you. He's a lucky man and, as you say, handsome and wealthy, and any one of My Lady the King's Mother's family is always going to be a favorite."

"We'll marry before Christmas," she says. "When you are churched and back at court, we'll marry and you can give me the royal wedding gift."

"I shall so look forward to that," I say, and little Maggie hears the sarcasm in my voice and shoots me a hidden smile.

"Good," Cecily says. "I think I'll wear scarlet like you did."

"You can have my gown," I promise her. "You can remake it to your size."

"I can?" She flies to my chest of gowns and flings open the top. "And the wedding linen too?"

"Not the linen," I stipulate. "But you can

216

have the gown and the headdress."

She gathers it up in her arms. "Everyone will compare us," she warns me, her face bright with excitement. "How shall you like it if they say I look better than you in scarlet and black? How shall you like it if they say I am a prettier bride?"

I lie back on the pillows. "D'you know? I shan't mind at all."

WESTMINSTER PALACE, LONDON, CHRISTMAS 1486

Churched, dressed, wearing a little crown, I come out of my confinement to attend my sister's wedding, and Henry greets me at the door with a kiss on my cheek and conducts me to the royal seats in the chapel at Westminster. It is to be a family affair. Lady Margaret is there, beaming at her half brother. My mother is in attendance on my sister. Anne is behind her, my cousin Maggie stands with me. Henry and I are side by side, and I can see him glance over at me, as if wanting to begin a conversation, but not knowing quite where to start.

Of course there is an unbearable awkwardness between us. When he last saw me, I was imploring him to let Teddy stay with us; he last saw me held by his mother and pushed into confinement. He did not do as I begged, and Teddy is still imprisoned in the Tower. He is afraid that I am angry with him. I see him glance sideways at me throughout the long prayers of the Wedding Mass, trying to guess at my mood.

"Will you come with me to the nursery when this is over?" he finally says, as the couple say their vows and the bishop raises their hands wrapped in his stole and tells us all that those whom God has joined together, no man can put asunder.

I turn a warm face to him. "Yes," I say. "Of course. I go every day. Isn't he perfect?"

"Such a handsome boy! And so strong!" he whispers eagerly. "And how do you feel? Are you . . ." He breaks off, embarrassed. "I hope you are fully recovered? I hope it was not too . . . painful?"

I try to look queenly and dignified, but his genuine expression of anxiety and concern prompt me to honesty: "I had no idea it would go on for so long! But my mother was a great comfort to me."

"I hope you will forgive him for causing you pain?"

"I love him," I say simply. "I've never seen a more beautiful baby. I have them bring him to me all day, every day, till they tell me I will spoil him."

"I have been going to his nursery in the nighttime, before I go to bed," he confesses. "I just sit by his crib and watch him sleeping. I can hardly believe that we have him. I keep fearing that he is not breathing and I tell his nurse to lift him and she swears he is all right, and then I see him give a little sigh and know that he is well. She must think I am a complete fool."

Cecily and Sir John turn towards us all and start to walk, hand in hand, down the short aisle. Cecily is radiant in my red and black gown, her fair hair spread on her shoulders like a golden veil. She is shorter than me and they have taken up the hem. A maid, as I was not on my wedding day, she can lace it tightly, and they have tailored the sleeves so that her husband can see an enticing glimpse of wrist and arm. Beside her, Sir John looks weary, his face lined, grooves under his eyes like an old hound. But he pats her hand on his arm and inclines his head to listen to her.

Henry and I smile on the newly wedded couple. "I have provided a good husband for your sister," he says to remind me that I am beholden to him, that I should be grateful. They pause when they reach us and Cecily sweeps a triumphant curtsey. I go forwards and kiss her on both cheeks, and I give my hand to her husband. "Sir John and Lady Welles," I say, speaking the name that was once a byword for treachery. "I hope you will both be very happy."

We give them the honor of the day and let them go first, before us all, and we follow them out of the chapel. As Henry takes my hand I say: "About Teddy . . ."

The face he turns to me is stern. "Don't ask," he says. "I am doing all that I dare for you by allowing your mother to stay at court. I should not even be doing that."

"My mother? What is my mother to do with this?"

"God alone knows," he says angrily. "Teddy's part in the rebellion is nothing to what I hear about her. The rumors I hear and the news that my spies bring me are very bad. I can't tell you how bad. It makes me sick to my belly to hear what they say. I have done all that I can for you and yours, Elizabeth. Don't ask me to do more. Not just now."

"What do they say against her?" I persist.

His face is bleak. "She is at the center of every whisper of disloyalty, she is almost certainly faithless to me, plotting against me, betraying us both, destroying the inheritance of her grandson. If she has spoken to even half the people who have been seen talking to her servants, then she is false, Elizabeth, false in her heart and false in her doings. She gives every sign of putting together rings of people who would rise against us. If I had any sense I would put her on trial for treason and know the truth. It is only for you and for your sake that I tell all the men who come to me with reports that they are all, every one of them, mistaken, all liars, all fools, and that she is true to me and to you."

I can feel my knees start to buckle, as I look over to where my mother is laughing with her nephew John de la Pole. "My mother is innocent of everything!"

Henry shakes his head. "That's too great a claim; for I know that she is not. All it shows me is that you are lying too. You have just shown me that you will lie for her, and to me."

They are bringing in the yule log to burn in the great hearth of the hall of Westminster Palace. It is the trunk of a great tree, a gray-barked ash, many times broader than my arms' span. It will burn without being extinguished for all the days of Christmas. The jester is dressed all in green, riding astride on it as they drag it in, standing up and trying to balance, falling from it, bounding up again like a deer, pretending to lie before it and rolling away before someone drags it over him. Both the servants and the court are singing carols that have words of the birth of Christ set to a tune and the rhythmic beat of a drum that is older by far. This is not just the Christmas story but a celebration of the return of the sun to the earth, and that is a story as ancient as the earth itself.

My Lady smilingly watches the scene, ready as ever to frown at bawdiness or point a finger at someone who uses the revels as an excuse for bad behavior. I am surprised she has allowed this pagan bringing-in of the green, but she is always anxious to adopt the habits of the former kings of England as if to show that her rule is not that much different from those others — the real kings who went before. She hopes to pass herself and her son off as royal by mimicking our ways.

My newly married sister, Cecily, my cousin Maggie, and my younger sister Anne are among my ladies watching with me, applauding as they wrestle the great tree trunk into the wide hearth. My mother is nearby with Catherine and Bridget at her side. Bridget is clapping her hands and laughing so loudly she can hardly stand. The servants are straining at the ropes that they have tied around the massive trunk, and now the jester has torn off a piece of ivy and is pretending to beat them. Bridget's knees give way beneath her in her delight and she is nearly crying with laughter. My Lady looks over with a slight frown. The jester's inventions are supposed to be amusing but not excessively so. My mother exchanges a rueful look with me, but she does not restrain Bridget's exuberant joy.

As we watch, they finally get the yule log dragged into the fireplace and rolled over into the hot embers, and then the fire boys shovel the red-hot coals around it. The ivy that is binding the trunk crisps, smokes, and flares, and then the whole thing settles into the ashes and starts to glow. A little flicker of flame licks around the bark. The yule log is alight, the Christmas celebrations can begin.

The musicians start to play and I nod to my ladies that they can dance. I take pleasure in a court of beautiful, well-behaved ladies-in-waiting, just as my mother did when she was queen. I am watching them as they go through their paces, when I see my uncle Edward Woodville, my mother's brother, stroll into the room from a side door, and come over to my mother with a little smile. They exchange a kiss on each cheek, and then they turn together, as if they would speak privately. It's nothing, no one but me would notice it, but I watch as he speaks briefly but intently to her, as she nods as if in agreement. He bows over her hand, and comes across to me.

"I must bid you farewell, my niece, and wish you a happy Christmas and good health for you and the prince."

"Surely you are staying at court for Christmas?"

He shakes his head. "I am going on a journey. I'm going on a great crusade as I have long promised I would."

"Leaving court? But where are you going, my lord uncle?"

"To Lisbon. I'm taking a ship out of Greenwich tonight, and from there to Granada. I will serve under the most Christian kings and help them drive the Moors from Granada."

"Lisbon! And then Granada?"

At once I glance towards My Lady the

King's Mother.

"She knows," he reassures me. "The king knows. Indeed, I am going at his bidding. She is delighted at the thought of an Englishman on crusade against the heretic, and he has a few little tasks for me on the way."

"What tasks?" I cannot stop myself lowering my voice to a whisper. My uncle Edward is one of the few members of our family trusted by the king and his mother. He was in exile with Henry, a sworn friend when Henry had few sworn friends. He escaped from my uncle Richard with two ships of his fleet, and was among the first to join Henry in Brittany. My uncle's constant, reliable presence at the exiled little court assured Henry that we, the fallen royal family scuffling in sanctuary, were his allies. As Richard took the throne and made himself king, Henry, the pretender, was encouraged to trust us by the steady presence of my uncle Edward, fiercely loyal to his sister, the former queen.

He was not the only York loyalist who made his way to Henry's court of turncoats and exiles. My half brother Thomas Grey was there too, keeping our claim before Henry, reminding him of his promises to marry me. I can only imagine Henry's horror when he woke one morning and his scant servants at his tiny court told him that Thomas Grey's horse was gone from the stables and his bed was untouched and he realized that we had changed sides and were for Richard. Henry and Jasper sent riders after Thomas Grey and they captured him. They held him as a prisoner for my mother's goodwill — fearing that nothing could guarantee her goodwill — and they still hold him in France, a guest of honor with a promise to return but still without a horse to ride home.

My uncle Edward played a longer game, a deeper game. He stayed with Henry and invaded with him at Bosworth, and served beside him at the battle. He serves him still. Henry never forgets his friends, nor does he forget those who changed their minds during his time of exile. I think he will never again trust my brother Thomas, but he loves my uncle Edward and calls him his friend.

"He is sending me on a diplomatic mission," my uncle says.

"To the King of Portugal? Surely Lisbon is not on the way to Granada?"

He spreads his hand and smiles at me, as if I might share a joke, or a secret. "Not directly to the King of Portugal. He wants me to see something that has arisen, appeared at the Portuguese court."

"What sort of thing?"

He drops on his knee and kisses my hand. "A secret thing, a precious thing," he says gleefully, then he rises up and goes. I look around for my mother and see her smiling at him as he works his way through the laughing, dancing, celebrating court. She watches his swift bow to Henry and the king's discreet acknowledgment, and then my uncle slips through the great doors of the hall, as quiet as any spy.

That night Henry comes to my bed. He will come every single night only excepting the week of my course, or the nights of holy fasts or saints' days. We have to conceive another child, we have to have another son. One is not enough to ensure the safety of the line. One is not enough to keep a new king steady on his throne. One son does not demonstrate powerfully enough the blessing of God on the new family.

It is an act without desire for me, from which I get no pleasure, part of my work as wife to the king. I face it with a sort of resigned weariness. He takes care not to hurt me, he keeps his weight off me, he does not kiss or caress me, which I would hate; he is as quick and as gentle as he can be. He takes care not to disgust me, washing before he comes to me, wearing clean linen. I don't ask for any more.

But I find that I enjoy his company, the quiet peaceful time alone with him at the end of a day that is always crowded with people. He and I sit before the fire and we talk about the baby, how he is feeding today, how he is starting to smile when he sees me. I am certain that he knows me from all others, and knows Henry too, and that this proves his remarkable intelligence and promise. I can speak of our baby like this to no one else. Who but his father would linger over the exact width of his gummy little smile or the blueness of his eyes, or the sweetness of his little lick of tawny hair on his forehead? Who but his father would speculate with me as to whether he will be a scholar prince, or a warrior prince, or a prince like my father, who loved learning and was a commander of men above all others?

The servants leave us with mulled wine, bread and cheese, nuts and candied fruits, and we have a supper, cozy in our night robes, side by side in our chairs, my feet tucked under me for warmth, his bare feet proffered to the glowing fire. We look like a happy couple in easy companionship. Sometimes I forget myself, and think this is what we are.

"You said good-bye to your uncle?"

"Yes, I did," I say cautiously. "He said he was going on crusade, and to serve you."

"Did your mother tell you what he is doing for me?"

I shake my head.

"You're a discreet family." Henry smiles. "Anyone would think you had been raised to be spies."

I shake my head at once. "You know we were not. We were raised as royals."

"I know. But now that I am a king it sometimes seems to me that it's the same thing. There's a rumor reached me that there is some page boy in Portugal pretending to be a bastard son of your father, saying that he should be recognized as a royal duke of England."

I am watching the flames and I keep facing the fire and only slowly turn to my husband. I meet an intense brown glare. He is watching me closely, and I have a sense of an unexpected interrogation, something keen and unfriendly in the warmth of the evening room. I am aware of my expression, of keeping my face absolutely impassive. I am suddenly aware of everything. "Oh, really? Who is he?"

"Of course your father had more bastards than anyone could count," he says carelessly. "I suppose we should expect to find one or two every year."

"Yes he did," I say. "And I hope that God forgives him, for my mother never did."

He laughs at that, but it only diverts him for a moment. "Did she not? How did he dare to defy her?"

I smile. "He would laugh at her and kiss her and buy her earrings. And besides, she was almost always with child, and he was king. Who could say no to him?"

"It's inconvenient. It leaves a scattering of bastard half brothers and sisters," Henry points out. "More Yorks than any man needs."

"Especially if he's not York himself," I observe. "But we know most of them. Grace, in my mother's service, is one of my father's bastard daughters. She could not love Mother more if she were her own daughter, and we treat her as a half sister. She is absolutely loyal to you."

"Well, this lad is claiming royal blood like her, but I don't expect to bring him to court. I thought your uncle might go and take a look at him. Speak to his master, say that we don't want the embarrassment of a bastard twig making much of himself, another little shoot on the Plantagenet vine. Tell him that we don't need a new royal duke, that we have Yorks enough. Quietly remind him who is king now in England. Point out that connections to the earlier king are no advantage, not to the page boy nor to his master."

"Who's his master? A Portuguese?"

"Oh, I don't know," he says vaguely, but his gaze on my face never wavers. "I can't remember. Is it Edward Brampton? D'you know of him? Ever heard of him?"

I frown as if I am trying to recall, though his name strikes a chord in my mind so loud that I think Henry must hear it like a tolling bell. Slowly, I shake my head. I swallow, but my throat is dry and I take a sip of wine.

"Edward Brampton?" I query. "I recognize the name. I think he served my father? I'm not sure. Is he an Englishman?"

"A Jew," Henry says contemptuously. "A Jew that was in England, converted to serve your father, indeed your father stood as his sponsor into the Church. So you must have heard of him, though you've forgotten him. He must have come to court. He's not been in England since I came to the throne, and now he lives everywhere and nowhere, so he's probably still a heretic Jew, reverted to his heresy. He has this lad in his keeping, making claims, causing trouble for no reason. Your uncle will speak to him, I don't doubt. Your uncle will prevail upon him to silence the lad. Your uncle Edward is very eager to serve me."

"He is," I agree. "We all want you to know that we are loyal to you."

He smiles. "Well, here's a little claimant whose loyalty I don't want. Your uncle will no doubt silence him one way or another."

I nod as if I am not much interested.

"You don't want to see the lad?" he asks idly, as if offering me a treat. "This imposter? What if he is a bastard child of your father's? Your half brother? Don't you want to see him? Shall I tell Edward to bring the lad to court? You could take him into your household? Or shall I say he must be silenced where he is, overseas, far away?"

I shake my head. I imagine that the boy's

life depends upon what I say. I gamble that Henry is keenly watching me, expecting me to ask for the boy to be brought home. I think his little life may depend upon my appearance of indifference. "He's of no interest to me," I say, shrugging. "And it would irritate my mother. But you do what you think best."

There is a little silence, in which I sip my wine. I offer to pour him another cup. The chink of silver jug against silver cup makes a noise like the counting of coins, of thirty pieces of silver.

The boy may be of no interest to me; but it seems he is of interest to others. In London there are the wildest rumors that both my brothers Edward and Richard escaped from imprisonment in the Tower years ago, almost as soon as our uncle Richard was crowned, and are making their way home from their hiding place, to claim the throne. The sons of York will walk in the garden of England again, this bitterly cold winter will turn to spring with their coming, the white roses will bloom, and everyone will be happy.

Someone pins a ballad on my saddle when I am about to ride. I scan the lines; it is predicting the sun of York shining on England again and everyone being happy. At once I rip it from the pommel and take it to the king, leaving my horse waiting in the stable yard.

"I thought you should see this. What does it mean?" I ask Henry.

"It means that there are people who are prepared to print treason as well as tell lies," he says grimly. He twitches it out of my hand. "It means there are people wasting their time setting treason to music."

"What are you going to do with it?"

"Find the man that printed it and slit his ears," he says bleakly. "Cut out his tongue. What are you going to do?"

I shrug as if I am quite indifferent to the poet who sang of the House of York, or the printer who published his poem. "Shall I go riding?" I ask him.

"You don't care about this —" he gestures to the ballad in his hand "— this dross?"

I shake my head, my eyes wide. "No. Why should I? Does it matter at all?"

He smiles. "Not to you, it seems."

I turn away. "People will always talk nonsense," I say indifferently.

He catches my hand and kisses it. "You were right to bring it to me," he says. "Always tell me whatever nonsense you hear, however unimportant it seems to you."

"Of course," I say.

He walks with me to the stable yard. "At least it reassures me about you."

Then my own maid whispers to me that there was a great stir in the meat market of Smithfield when someone said that Edward, my little cousin Teddy, was escaped from the Tower and was planting his standard in Warwick Castle, and the House of York was rallying to his cause.

"Half the butcher apprentices said they should take their meat cleavers and march to serve him," she says. "The others said they should march on the Tower and free him."

I dare not even ask Henry about this, his face is so grim. We are all trapped inside the palace by the icy winds and sleet and snow that fall every day. Henry rides out on frozen roads in a quiet fury, while his mother spends all her time on her knees on the cold stone floors of the chapel. Every day brings more and more stories of stars that have been seen to dance in the cold skies, prophesying a white rose. Someone sees a white rose made from the frost on the grass at Bosworth at dawn. There are poems nailed to the door of Westminster Abbey. A gang of wherry boys sings carols under the windows of the Tower, and Edward of Warwick swings open his window and waves to them, and calls out "Merry Christmas!" The king and his mother walk stiffly as if they are frozen with horror.

"Well, they *are* frozen with horror," my mother confirms cheerfully. "Their great fear is that the battle of Bosworth turns out not to be the end of the war but just another battle, just one of the many, many battles that have been. So many battles that people are forgetting their names. Their great fear is that the Cousins' War goes on, only now with the House of Beaufort against York instead of Lancaster against York."

"But who would fight for York?"

"Thousands," my mother says shortly. "Tens of thousands. Nobody knows how many. Your husband has not made himself very beloved in the country, though God knows that he has tried. Those people who served him and had their rewards are looking for more than he can bring himself to give. Those that he has pardoned find they have to pay fees to him for their good behavior, and then more fines as surety. This king's pardon is more like a punishment for life than a true forgiveness. People resent it. Those who opposed him have seen no reason to change their minds. He's not a York king like your father. He's not beloved. He does not have a way with people."

"He has to establish his rule," I protest. He spends half his time looking behind him to see if his allies are still with him."

She gives me a funny sideways smile. "You defend him?" she asks incredulously. "To me?"

"I don't blame him for being anxious," I say. "I don't blame him for not being the sweet herb of March. I don't blame him for not having a white rose made of snow or three suns in the sky shining on him. He can't help that."

At once her face softens. "Truly, a king like Edward comes perhaps once in a century," she says. "Everyone loved him."

I grit my teeth. "Charm is not a measure of a king," I say irritably. "He can't be king based on whether he's charming or not."

"No," she says. "And Master Tudor is certainly not that."

"What did you call him?"

She claps her hand over her mouth and her gray eyes dance. "Little Master Tudor, and his mother, Madonna Margaret of the Unending Self-Congratulation."

I cannot help but laugh but then I wave my hand to still her. "No, hush. He can't help how he is," I say. "He was raised in hiding, he was brought up to be a pretender to the throne. People can only be charming when they're confident. He can't be confident."

"Exactly," she says. "So no one has any confidence in him."

"But who would lead the rebels?" I ask. "There's no one of age, there are no York commanders. We don't have an heir." At her silence I press her. "We don't have an heir. Do we?"

Her eyes slide away from my question. "Edward of Warwick is the heir, of course, and if you're looking for another heir to the House of York, there is your cousin John de la Pole. There's his younger brother Edmund. They are both Edward's nephews just as much as Edward of Warwick."

"Descended from my aunt Elizabeth," I point out. "The female line. Not the son of a royal duke, but the son of a duchess. And John has sworn loyalty and he serves in the privy council. Edmund too. And Edward, poor Teddy, has sworn loyalty and is in the Tower. We have all promised that he would not turn against Henry and we have all taught him to be loyal. In truth, there are no sons of York who would lead a rebellion against Henry Tudor — are there?"

She shrugs. "I'm sure I don't know. All the people speak of a hero like a ghost or a sleeping saint, or a pretender. It would almost make you believe that there is an heir of York hidden out in the hills, a king waiting for the call to battle, sleeping like the true Arthur of England, ready to rise. People love to dream, so how should anyone contradict them?"

I take her hands. "Mother, please, let's have the truth between us for once. I don't forget that night, long ago, when we sent a page boy into the Tower instead of my brother Richard."

She looks at me as if I am dreaming, like the people who hope for King Arthur to rise again; but I have a very clear memory of the poor boy from the streets of the City, whose parents sold him to us, assured that we needed him for nothing more than a little playacting, that we would send him back safely to them. I put the cap on his little head myself, and I drew up the scarf around his face, and warned him to say nothing. We told the men who came for my brother Richard that the little boy was the prince himself, we said he was ill with a sore throat and had lost his voice. Nobody could imagine that we would dare to create such an imposter. Of course, they wanted to believe us, and the old archbishop himself, Thomas Bourchier, took him away and told everyone that Prince Richard was in the Tower with his brother.

She does not glance to right or left; she knows that no one is nearby. But even alone with me, speaking in a whisper, she does not confirm or deny it either.

"You sent a page boy into the Tower, and you sent my little brother away," I whisper. "You told me to say nothing about it. Not to ask you, not to speak to anyone, not even to tell my sisters, and I never have. Only once you told me that he was safe. Once you told me that Sir Edward Brampton had brought him to you. I've never asked for more than that."

"He is hidden in silence," is all she says.

"Is he still alive?" I ask urgently. "Is he alive and is he going to come back to England for his throne?"

"He is safe in silence."

"Is he the boy in Portugal?" I demand. "The boy that Uncle Edward has gone to see? Sir Edward Brampton's page boy?"

She looks at me as if she would tell me the truth if she could. "How would I know?" she asks. "How do I know who is claiming to be a prince of York? In Lisbon, so far away? I'll know him when I see him, I can tell you that. I will tell you when I see him, I can promise you that. But perhaps I'll never see him."

THE TOWER OF LONDON, SPRING 1487

We move the court to the City that is buzzing like a beehive waking to spring. It feels as if everyone is talking about princes and dukes and the House of York rising up again like a climbing plant bursting into leaf. Everyone has heard for certain from someone that the Yorks have a boy, an heir, that he is on a ship coming into Greenwich, that he has been hiding in a secret chamber in the Tower under a stone stair, that he is marching from Scotland, that he is going to be put on the throne by his own brother-in-law, Henry, that his sister the queen has him at court and is only waiting to reveal him to her astounded husband. That he is a page boy with an Englishman in Portugal, a boatman's son in Flanders, hidden by his aunt the Dowager Duchess of Burgundy, asleep on a distant island, living off apples in the loft of his mother's old house at Grafton, hidden in the Tower with his cousin Edward of Warwick. Suddenly, like butterflies in springtime, there are a thousand pretend boys, dancing about like motes in the sunlight, waiting for the word to come together into an army. The Tudors who thought they had taken the crown on a muddy field in the middle of England, who thought they had secured their line by trudging up the road to London, find themselves besieged by will-o'-the-wisps, defied by faeries. Everyone talks of a York heir, everyone knows someone who has seen him and swears it is true. Everywhere Henry goes, people fall silent so that no whisper reaches his ears; but before and behind him there is a patter of sound like a warning drizzle before a storm of rain. The people of England are waiting for a new king to present himself, for a prince to rise like the spring tide and flood the world with white roses.

We move to the Tower as if Henry no longer loves his country palace in springtime, as he swore that he did, only last year. This year, he feels the need of a castle that is easily defended, as if he wants his home to dominate the skyline, as if he wants to be in the heart of the city, unmistakably its lord; though everyone talks of another, from the drovers coming into Smithfield discussing a priceless white ram glimpsed on a dawn hillside, to the fisherwomen on the quay, who swear that one dark night, two years ago, they saw the watergate of the Tower slide up in silence and a little wherry come out under the dripping

241

gate which carried a boy, a single boy, the flower of York, and it went swiftly downstream to freedom.

Henry and I are lodged in the royal rooms in the White Tower, overlooking the lower building that housed the two boys: my brother Edward awaiting his coronation but expecting death, and the page boy that my mother and I sent in place of Richard. Henry sees my pallor as we enter the royal rooms that are bright with wood fires, and hung with rich tapestries, and presses my hand, saying nothing. The baby comes in behind me, in the arms of his nursemaid, and I say flatly: "Prince Arthur is to sleep next door, in my privy chamber."

"My Lady Mother put your crucifix and prie-dieu in there," he says. "She has made a pretty privy chamber for you, and prepared his nursery on the next floor."

I don't waste time arguing. "I'm not staying in this place unless our baby sleeps next door to me."

"Elizabeth . . ." he says gently. "You know we are safe here, safer here than anywhere else."

"My son sleeps beside me."

He nods. He doesn't argue or even ask me what I fear. We have been married little more than a year and already there is a terrible silence around some subjects. We never speak of the disappearance of my brothers — a stranger listening to us would think it was a secret between us, a guilty secret. We never speak of my year at Richard's court. We never speak of the conception of Arthur and that he was not, as My Lady so loudly celebrates, a honeymoon child conceived in sanctified love on the very night of a happy wedding. Together we hold so many secrets in silence, after only a year. What lies will we tell each other in ten years?

"It looks odd," is all he says. "People will talk."

"Why are we even here and not in the country?"

He shifts his feet, looking away from me. "We're going in procession to Mass next Sunday," he says. "All of us."

"What d'you mean, all of us?"

His discomfort increases. "The royal family . . ."

I wait.

"Your cousin Edward is going to walk with us."

"What has Teddy to do with this?"

He takes my arm and leads me away from my ladies-in-waiting, who are entering the rooms and remarking on the tapestries, unpacking their sewing and packs of cards. Someone is tuning a lute, the twanging chords echoing loudly. I am the only one who hates this bleak castle; to everyone else it is a familiar home. Henry and I go out into the

243

long gallery, where the scent of the fresh strewing herbs is heady in the narrow room.

"People are saying that Edward has escaped from the Tower and is raising an army in Warwickshire."

"Edward?" I repeat stupidly.

"Edward of Warwick, your cousin Teddy. So he's going to process in state with us to St. Paul's so that everyone can see him and know that he lives with us as a valued member of the family."

I nod. "He walks with us. You show him."

"Yes."

"And when everyone has seen him, they know that he is not raising his standard in Warwickshire."

"Yes."

"They know that he is alive."

"Yes."

"And these rumors die down . . ."

Henry waits.

"Then after that he can live with us as a member of our family," I rule. "He can be as he seems to be. We can show him as our beloved cousin and he can be our beloved cousin. We show him going to Mass with us freely, he can live with us freely. We can turn the show into the reality. That's what you want to do, as king. You show yourself as king and then you hope to be accepted as king. If I take part in this play, in this masque of Teddy being beloved and living with us, then you will make it true."

He hesitates.

"It is my condition," I say simply. "If you want me to act as if Teddy is our beloved cousin freely living with us, then you have to make the act into reality. I'll walk with you in procession on Sunday to show that Teddy and all the Yorks are loyal supporters. And you will treat me, and all my family, as if you trust us."

He hesitates for a moment and then, "Yes," he says. "If our procession persuades everyone, and the rumors die down and everyone accepts that Teddy lives at court, as a loyal member of the family, he can come out of the Tower and live freely at court."

"Free and trusted like my mother," I insist. "Despite what anyone says."

"Like your mother," he agrees. "If the rumors die down."

Maggie is at my side before dinner, rosy with joy at having spent all afternoon with her brother. "He has grown! He is taller than me! Oh! I have missed him so much!"

"Does he understand what he has to do?"

She nods. "I have told him carefully, and we practiced, so that he should make no mistake. He knows that he is to walk behind you and the king, he knows that he has to kneel to pray at Mass. I can walk beside him, can't I? And then I can make sure he does it right?"

"Yes, yes, that would be best," I say. "And if anyone cheers for him, he's not to wave or shout a reply, or anything."

"He knows," she says. "He understands. I have explained to him why they want him to be seen."

"Maggie, if he shows that he is a loyal member of the family, I believe that he can come back to live with us. It is essential that he does this right."

Her mouth, her whole face trembles. "Could he?"

I take her in my arms and find that she is shaking with hope. "Oh, Maggie, I will try my best for him."

Her tearstained face looks up at me. "He has to come out of here, Your Grace, it's destroying him. He's not doing his lessons in here, he sees no one."

"Surely the king has provided tutors for him?"

She shakes her head. "They don't come to him anymore. He spends his day lying in his bed reading the books that I send him, or staring at the ceiling, and looking out of the window. He is allowed out once a day to walk in the gardens. But he's only eleven, he's twelve this month. He should be at court, doing his lessons, playing games, learning how to ride. He should be growing into a man, with boys of his own age. But he is here, quite alone, seeing no one but the guards when they bring him his meals. He tells me that he thinks he is forgetting how to speak. He said that one day he spent all day trying to remember my face. He says that a whole day goes by and he cannot remember it has passed. So now he makes a mark on the wall for every day, like a prisoner. But then he fears he has lost count of the months.

"And he knows our father was executed in here, and he knows your brothers disappeared from here — boys just like him. He is bored and afraid at the same time, and he has no one to talk to. His guards are rough men, they play cards with him and win his few shillings off him, they swear in front of him and drink. He can't stay here. I have to get him out."

"I am horrified. "Oh, Maggie . . ."

"How is he to grow up as a royal duke if he is treated as a child traitor?" she demands. "This is destroying him, and I swore to my father that I would take care of him!"

I nod. "I'll speak with the king again, Maggie. I will do what I can. And once people stop talking about him all the time, then I'm sure Henry will let him out." I pause. "It's as if our name is both our greatest pride and our curse," I say. "If he were Edward of nowhere and not Edward of Warwick he would be living with us now."

"I wish we were all no one of nowhere," she says bitterly. "If I could choose I would have the name of Nobody and never come to court at all."

My husband calls a meeting of the privy council to ask them for their advice on how to silence the rumors of the coming of a prince of York. They all know, they have all heard of a duke of York, even a bastard of York, coming to England to take the throne. John de la Pole, the son of my aunt Elizabeth of York, advises the king to keep a steady nerve, that the whispers will stop. His father, the Duke of Suffolk, tells Henry to be assured that there is no division between York and Tudor. Once the people see Edward walking with his family, they will be quiet again. John asks that Teddy might be released from the Tower — so that everyone can see that the Houses of York and Tudor are united. "We should show that we have nothing to fear," he says, smiling at the king. "That's the best way to scotch the rumors: show that we fear nothing."

"That we are as one," Henry says.

John reaches out to him and the king warmly clasps his hand. "We are as one," he assures him.

The king sends for Edward, and Maggie and I bustle him into a new jerkin and comb down his hair. He is pale, with the terrible pallor of a child who never gets outside, and his arms and legs are thin though he should be growing strong. He has the York charm and good looks in his little-boy face but he is nervous, as my brothers never were. He reads so much and talks so little that he stammers when he has to speak, and will break off in the middle of a sentence to try to recall what he means to say. Living alone among rough men, he is desperately shy; he smiles only at Maggie and only with her can he talk fluently and without hesitation.

Maggie and I walk with him to the closed door of the privy council chamber, where the yeomen of the guard stand with their pikes crossed, shutting everyone out. He stops, like a young colt refusing a jump.

"They don't want me to go in," he says anxiously, looking at the big blank-faced men who stare past the three of us. "You have to do what they say. You always have to do what they say."

The quaver of fear in his voice reminds me of the day that the men in this very livery carried him down the stairs and I could not save him.

"The king himself wants to see you," I tell him. "They will open the door as you walk towards them. The doors will open as you get close."

He glances up at me, his shy smile lighting up his face with sudden hope. "Because I'm an earl?"

"You are an earl," I say quietly. "But they will open the door because it is the king's wish. It is the king who matters, not us. What you must remember to say is that you are loyal to the king."

He nods emphatically. "I promised," he says. "I promised just as Maggie said I should."

The procession from the Tower of London to St. Paul's Cathedral is deliberately informal, as if the royal family strolled to church in their capital city every day. The yeomen of the guard walk with us, beside, behind, and in front, but more as if they were members of the household, leading the way to church, than guards. Henry goes in front with my mother, to signal to everyone the unity of this king with the former queen, and My Lady chooses to go hand in hand with me, showing everyone that the Princess of York is embedded in the House of Tudor. Behind us come my sisters, Cecily with her new husband, so that everyone can see that there is no princess of York of marrying age to form the focus of dissent, and behind her comes Edward our cousin, walking alone so that people waiting both on the right and left can see him clearly. He is well dressed, but he looks awkward and stumbles once as he starts to walk. Maggie walks behind him with my sisters Anne, Catherine, and Bridget, and she has to hold herself back from her little brother and not take his hand, as she used to do. This is a walk he has to do alone, this is a walk where he has to show himself alone, without any supporter, without any coercion, freely following in the train of the Tudor king.

When we get into the deep vaulted gloom of the church we all stand at the chancel steps for the Mass, and sense the crowds of London in the vast space behind us. Henry puts a hand on Edward's shoulder and whispers in his ear and the boy obediently falls to his knees on the prie-dieu, rests his elbows on the velvet shelf, and raises his eyes to the altar. All the rest of us step back a little, as if to leave him in prayer, but in truth to make sure that everyone sees Edward of Warwick is devout, loyal, and, above everything else, in our keeping. He is not at Warwick Castle raising his standard, he is not in Ireland raising an army, he is not with his aunt the Duchess of Burgundy in Flanders creating a conspiracy. He is where he ought to be, with his loving royal family, on his knees to God.

After the service we dine with the clergy of St. Paul's and then start to walk down to the river. Edward makes better progress and smiles and talks to my sisters. Then Henry orders him to walk beside John de la Pole, the two York cousins together. John de la Pole has been loyal to Henry since the first day of his reign, is constantly in his company, and serves him on the privy council, the inner circle of advisors. He is well known for his loyalty to the king and it sends a strong message to the crowds who line our way, and who lean out of the windows above our heads. Everyone can see that this is the real Edward of Warwick, beside the real John de la Pole, everyone can see that they are talking together and strolling home from church, as cousins do. Everyone can see that they are happy with their Tudor family; as I am, as Cecily is, as my mother is.

Henry waves to the citizens of London who are massing on the riverbank to see us all, and he summons me to stand beside him, and Edward beside me, so that everyone can see that we are as one, that Henry Tudor has done what some people swore was impossible: brought peace to England and an end to the wars of the cousins.

Then some fool in the crowd shouts loudly, *"À Warwick!"* the old rallying cry, and I flinch and look to my husband, expecting to see him furious. But his smile never falters, his hand raised in a lordly wave does not tremble. I look back at the crowd, and I see a small scuffle at the rear, as if the man who shouted has been knocked to the ground and is being pinned down. "What's happening?" I ask Henry nervously.

"Nothing," he says. "Nothing at all," and

turns and goes to his great throne in the stern of the boat, beckons us all on board, and sits down, kingly in every way, and gives the signal to cast off.

PALACE OF SHEEN, RICHMOND, SPRING 1487

But not even the evidence of their own eyes convinces people who are determined to believe the opposite. Only days after our walk through the streets of London, with the boy smiling in our midst, there are people swearing that Edward of Warwick escaped from the Tower while walking to church and is hiding in York, biding his time to come against the tyrant of the red dragon, the pretender to the throne, Henry the usurper, the false claimant.

We move out of the city to the Palace of Sheen, but Edward cannot be released from his rooms in the Tower to come too. "How can I take him with us?" Henry demands of me. "Can you doubt for a moment that if he was outside the safety of those walls then someone would get hold of him and next thing we would hear of him would be at the head of an army?"

"He would not!" I say despairingly. I begin to think that my husband will hold my little cousin in prison for life, he is so overly cautious. "You know Edward would not run away from us to lead an army! All he wants is to be in the schoolroom doing his lessons again. All he wants is to be allowed to ride out. All he wants is to be with his sister."

But Henry looks at me with hard eyes as dark as Welsh coal, and says: "Of course he would lead an army. Anybody would. And besides, they might not give him any choice."

"He's twelve!" I exclaim. "He's a child!"

"He's old enough to sit on a horse while an army fights for him."

"This is my cousin," I say. "This is my own cousin, the son of my father's brother. Please, be kingly, and release him."

"You think he should be released because he is the son of your father's brother? You think your family were so kindly when they had power? Elizabeth, your father held his own brother, Edward's father, in the Tower and then executed him for treason! Your cousin Edward is the son of a traitor and a rebel, and the traitors shout his name when they muster against me. He won't come out of the Tower until I know that we are safe, all four of us, my mother, you and me, and the true heir: Prince Arthur."

He stamps to the door and turns to glower at me. "Don't ask me again," he orders. "Don't dare to ask me again. You don't know how much I do for love of you, already. More than I should. Far more than I should."

He slams the door behind him and I hear the rattle as the guards hastily present arms as he marches by.

"How much do you do?" I ask the polished wood panels of the door. "And for love?"

Henry does not come to my room for all of Lent. It is traditional that a devout man would not touch his wife in the weeks before Easter, though the daffodils flood into gold alongside the riverbanks, the blackbirds sing love songs in a penetrating trill every dawn, the swans set about building huge bulky nests on the river path, and every other living thing is filled with joy and seeking a mate; but not us. Henry observes the fast of Lent as an obedient son of his mother and the Church, and so Maggie is my bedfellow and I become accustomed to her kneeling for hours in prayer and whispering her brother's name over and over again.

One day I realize that she is praying to St. Anthony for her brother, and I quietly turn away. St. Anthony is the saint for missing things, for forlorn hopes and lost causes; she must feel that her brother is near to disappearing — an invisible boy like my own brothers, all three of them lost to their sisters, gone forever.

The court fasts throughout Lent, eating no meat, and there is no dancing or playing. My

Lady wears black all the time, as if the ordeal of Christ has a special message for her, as if she alone understands His suffering. She and Henry pray together in private every evening as if they have been called to endure the coldness of the hearts of Englishmen to the Tudors, just as Jesus had to endure the loneliness of the desert and the failure of his disciples. The two of them are as martyrs together; nobody understands what they suffer but themselves.

Around My Lady and her son is a tight little world: the only advisor that she trusts, John Morton, her friend and confessor; Jasper Tudor, Henry's uncle who raised him in exile; the friend who stood by him, John de Vere, the Earl of Oxford, and the Stanleys, Lord Thomas and his brother Sir William. There are very, very few of them, isolated in such a great court, and they are so afraid of everyone else, it is as if they are always under siege in their own safe home.

I really begin to think that they experience a different world from the rest of us. One day, My Lady and I are walking together by the dazzling river, sun on our faces, white blossom on the hawthorn bushes, and the sweet light scent of nectar on the air, when she remarks that England is indeed a benighted desert of sin. My mother, light-footed on the spring grass, a bunch of dripping-stemmed daffodils sticky in her hand, hears this and cannot stop herself laughing out loud.

I fall back among my ladies to walk beside my mother. "I have to talk to you," I say. "I have to know what you know."

Her smile is serene and lovely as always. "A lifetime of learning," she teases me. "An understanding of four languages, a love of music and appreciation of art, a great interest in printing and in writing in English as well as Latin. I am glad to see that at last you apply yourself to my wisdom."

"My Lady the King's Mother is ill with fear," I point out to her. "She thinks the English springtime is a benighted desert. Her son is all but dumb. They trust no one but their own circle and every day there are more rumors in the outside world. It's coming, isn't it? A new rebellion? You know the plans and you know who will lead them." I pause and lower my voice to a whisper. "He's on the way, isn't he?"

My mother says nothing for a moment but walks beside me in silence, graceful as ever. She pauses and turns to me, takes a daffodil bud, and tucks it gently into my hat. "Do you think I have said nothing to you ever since your marriage about these matters because it slipped my mind?" she asks quietly.

"No, of course not."

"Because I thought you had no interest?"

I shake my head.

"Elizabeth, on your wedding day you promised to love, honor, and obey the king. On the day of your coronation you will have to promise, before God in the most solemn and binding of vows, to be his loyal subject, the first of his loyal subjects. You will take the crown on your head, you will take the holy oil on your breast. You cannot be forsworn then. You cannot know anything that you would have to keep from him. You cannot have secrets from him."

"He doesn't trust me!" I burst out. "Without you ever telling me a word he already suspects me of knowing a whole conspiracy and keeping it secret. Over and over again he asks me what I know, over and over again he warns me that he is making allowances for us. His mother is certain that I am a traitor to him, and I believe that he thinks so too."

"He will come to trust you, perhaps," she says. "If you have years together. You may grow to be a loving husband and wife, if you have long enough. And if I never tell you anything, then there will never be a moment where you have to lie to him. Or worse — never a moment when you have to choose where your loyalties lie. I wouldn't want you to have to choose between your father's family and your husband's. I wouldn't want you to have to choose between the claims of your little son and another."

I am horrified at the thought of having to

choose between Tudor and York. "But if I know nothing, then I am like a leaf on the water, I go wherever the current takes me. I don't act, I do nothing."

She smiles. "Yes. Why don't you let the river take you? And we'll see what she says."

We turn in silence and head back along the riverbank to Sheen, the beautiful palace of many towers which dominates the curve of the river. As we walk towards the palace I see half a dozen horses gallop up to the king's private door. The men dismount, and one pulls off his hat and goes inside.

My mother leads the ladies past the men-at-arms, and graciously acknowledges their salute. "You look weary," she says pleasantly. "Come far?"

"Without stopping for sleep, all the way from Flanders," one boasts. "We rode as if the devil was behind us."

"Did you?"

"But he's not behind us, he's before us," he confides quietly. "Ahead of us, and ahead of His Grace, and out and about raising an army while the rest of us are amazed."

"That's enough," another man says. He pulls off his hat to me and to my mother. "I apologize, Your Grace. He's been breathless for so long he has to talk now."

My mother smiles on the man and on his captain. "Oh, that's all right," she says.

■ ■ ■ ■

Within an hour the king has called a meeting of his inner council, the men he turns to when he is in danger. Jasper Tudor is there, his red head bowed, his grizzled eyebrows knitting together with worry at the threat to his nephew, to his line. The Earl of Oxford walks arm in arm with Henry, discussing mustering men, and which counties can be trusted and which must not be alarmed. John de la Pole comes into the council chamber on the heels of his fiercely loyal father, and the other friends and family follow: the Stanleys, the Courtenays, John Morton the archbishop, Reginald Bray, who is My Lady's steward — all the men who put Henry Tudor on the throne and now find it is hard to keep him there.

I go to the nursery. I find My Lady the King's Mother sitting in the big chair in the corner, watching the nurse changing the baby's clout and wrapping him tight in his swaddling clothes. It is unusual for her to come here, but I see from her strained face and the beads in her hand that she is praying for his safety.

"Is it bad news?" I ask quietly.

She looks at me reproachfully, as if it is all my fault. "They say that the Duchess of Burgundy, your aunt, has found a general

261

who will take her pay and do her bidding," she says. "They say he is all but unbeatable."

"A general?"

"And he is recruiting an army."

"Will they come here?" I whisper. I look out of the window to the river and the quiet fields beyond.

"No," she says determinedly. "For Jasper will stop them, Henry will stop them, and God Himself will stop them."

On my way to my mother's chambers, I hurry past the king's rooms, but the door to the great presence chamber is still closed. He has most of the lords gathered together, and they will be frantically trying to judge what new threat this presents to the Tudor throne, how much they should fear, what they should do.

I find I am quickening my pace, my hand to my mouth. I am afraid of what is threatening us, and I am also afraid of the defense that Henry will mount against his own people that might be more violent and deadly than an actual invasion.

My mother's rooms are closed too, the doors tightly shut, and there is no servant waiting outside to swing open the doors for me. The place is quiet — too quiet. I push open the door myself, and look at the empty room spread out in front of me like a tableau in a pageant before the actors arrive. None of her ladies is here, her musicians are absent, a lute leaning against a wall. All her things are untouched: her chairs, her tapestries, her book on a table, her sewing in a box; but she is missing. It seems as if she has gone.

Like a child, I can't believe it. I say, "Mother? Lady Mother?" and I step into the quiet sunny presence chamber and look all around me.

I open the door to her privy chamber and it is empty too. There is a scrap of sewing left on one of the chairs, and a ribbon on the window seat, but nothing else. Helplessly, I pick up the ribbon as if it might be a sign, I twist it in my fingers. I cannot believe how quiet it is. The corner of a tapestry stirs in the draft from the door, the only movement in the room. Outside a wood pigeon coos, but that is the only sound. I say again: "Mama? Lady Mother?"

I tap on the door to her bedroom and swing it open, but I don't expect to find her there. Her bed is stripped of her linen, the mattress lies bare. The wooden posts are stripped of her bed curtains. Wherever she has gone, she has taken her bedding with her. I open the chest at the foot of her bed, and find her clothes have gone too. I turn to the table where she sits while her maid combs her hair; her silvered mirror has gone, her ivory combs, her golden hairpins, her cut-glass phial of oil of lilies.

Her rooms are empty. It is like an enchantment; she has silently disappeared, in the space of a morning, and all in a moment.

I turn on my heel at once and go to the best rooms, the queen's rooms, where My Lady the King's Mother spends her days among her women, running her great estates, maintaining her power while her women sew shirts for the poor and listen to readings from the Bible. Her rooms are busy with people coming and going; I can hear the buzz of happy noise through the doors as I walk towards them, and when they are swung open and I am announced, I enter to see My Lady, seated under a cloth of gold like a queen, while around her are her own ladies and among them my mother's companions, merged into one great court. My mother's ladies look at me wide-eyed, as if they would whisper secrets to me; but whoever has taken my mother has made sure that they are silent.

"My Lady," I say, sweeping her the smallest of curtseys due to my mother-in-law and mother to the king. She rises and executes the tiniest of bobs, and then we kiss each other's cold cheeks. Her lips barely touch me, as I hold my breath as if I don't want to inhale the smoky smell of incense that always hangs in her veiled headdress. We step back and take the measure of the other.

"Where is my mother?" I ask flatly.

She looks grave as if she were not ready to dance for joy. "Perhaps you should speak with my son the king."

"He is in his chambers with his council. I don't want to disturb him. But I shall do so and tell him that you sent me, if that is what you wish. Or can you tell me where my mother is. Or don't you know? Are you just pretending to knowledge?"

"Of course I know!" she says, instantly affronted. She looks around at the avid faces and gestures to me that we should go through to an inner chamber, where we can talk alone. I follow her. As I go by my mother's ladies I see that some of them are missing; my half sister Grace, my father's bastard, is not here. I hope she has gone with my mother, wherever she is.

My Lady the King's Mother closes the door herself, and gestures that I should sit. Careful of protocol, even now, we sit simultaneously.

"Where is my mother?" I say again.

"She was responsible for the rebellion," My Lady says quietly. "She sent money and servants to Francis Lovell, she had messages from him. She knew what he was doing and she advised and supported him. She told him which households would hide him and give him men and arms outside York. While I was planning the king's royal progress, she was planning a rebellion against him, planning to ambush him on his very route. She is the enemy of your husband and your son. I am

265

very sorry for you, Elizabeth."

I bristle, hardly hearing her. "I don't need your pity!"

"You do," she presses on. "For it is you and your husband that your own mother is plotting against. It is your death and downfall she is planning. She worked for Lovell's rebellion and now she writes secretly to her sister-in-law in Flanders urging her to invade."

"No. She would not."

"We have proof," she says. "There's no doubt. I am sorry for it. This is a great shame to fall on you and your family. A disgrace to your family name."

"Where is she?" I ask. My greatest fear is that they have taken her to the Tower, that she will be kept where her sons were held, and that she won't come out either.

"She has retired from the world," Lady Margaret says solemnly.

"What?"

"She has seen the error of her ways and gone to confess her sins and live with the good sisters at Bermondsey Abbey. She has chosen to live there. When my son put the evidence of her conspiracy before her, she accepted that she had sinned and that she would have to go."

"I want to see her."

"Certainly, you can go to see her," Lady Margaret says quietly. "Of course." I see a little hope flare in her veiled eyes. "You could stay with her."

"Of course I'm not going to stay in Bermondsey Abbey. I shall visit her, and I shall speak with Henry, as she must come back to court."

"She cannot have wealth and influence," Lady Margaret says. "She would use it against your husband and your son. I know that you love her dearly, but, Elizabeth — she has become your enemy. She is no mother to you and your sisters anymore. She was providing funds to the men who hope to throw down the Tudor throne; she was giving them advice, sending them messages. She was plotting with Duchess Margaret, who is mustering an army. She was living with us, playing with your child, our precious prince, seeing you daily, and yet working for our destruction."

I rise from my chair and go to the window. Outside the first swallows of summer are skimming along the surface of the river, twisting and turning in flight, their bellies a flash of cream as if they are glad to be dipping their beaks into their own reflections, playing with the sweet water of the Thames. I turn back. "Lady Margaret, my mother is not dishonorable. And she would never do anything to hurt me."

Slowly she shakes her head. "She insisted that you marry my son," she says. "She demanded it, as the price of her loyalty. She was present at the birth of the prince. She was honored at his christening, she is his godmother. We have honored her and housed her and paid her. But now she plots against her own grandson's inheritance and strives to put another on his throne. This is dishonorable, Elizabeth. You cannot deny that she is playing a double game, a shameful game."

I put my hands over my face, so that I can shut out her expression. If she looked triumphant I would simply hate her, but she looks horrified, as if she feels, like me, that everything we have been trying to do is going to be pulled apart.

"She and I have not always agreed." She appeals to me. "But I did not see her leave court with any pleasure. This is a disaster for us as well as for her. I hoped we would make one family, one royal family standing together. But she was always pretending. She has been untrue to us."

I can't defend her; I bow my head and a little moan of horror escapes through my gritted teeth.

"She's not at peace," Lady Margaret concludes. "She is going on and on fighting the war that you Yorks have lost. She's not made peace with us, and now she's at war with you, her own daughter."

I give a little wail and sink down in the window seat, my hands hiding my face. There is a silence as Lady Margaret crosses the room and seats herself heavily beside me.

"It's for her son, isn't it?" she asks wearily. "That's the only claim she would fight for in preference to yours. That's the only pretender that she would put against her grandson. She loves Arthur as well as we do, I know that. The only claim she would favor over his would be that of her own son. She must think that one of her boys, Richard or Edward, is still alive and she hopes to put him on the throne."

"I don't know, I don't know!" I am crying now, I can hardly speak. I can hardly hear her through my sobs.

"Well, who is it?" she suddenly shouts, flashing out into rage. "Who else could it be? Who could she put above her own grandson? Who can she prefer to our Prince Arthur? Arthur that was born at Winchester, Arthur of Camelot? Who can she prefer to him?"

Dumbly, I shake my head. I can feel the hot tears pooling in my icy hands and making my face wet.

"She would throw you down for no one else," Lady Margaret whispers. "Of course it is one of the boys. Tell me, Elizabeth. Tell me all that you know so that we can make your son, Arthur, safe in his inheritance. Does your mother have one of her boys hidden somewhere? Is he with your aunt in Flanders?"

"I don't know," I say helplessly. "She would never tell me anything. I said I don't know, and truly, I don't know. She made sure that there was never anything that I could tell you. She did not want me ever to have an inquisition like this. She tried to protect me from it, so I don't know."

Henry comes to my rooms with his court before dinner, a tight, unconvincing smile on his face, playing the part of a king, trying to hide his fear that he is losing everything.

"I'll talk with you later," he says in a hard undertone. "When I come to your room tonight."

"My lord . . ." I whisper.

"Not now," he says firmly. "Everyone needs to see that we are united, that we are as one."

"My mother cannot be held against her will," I stipulate. I think of my cousin in the Tower, my mother in Bermondsey Abbey. "I cannot tolerate my family being held. Whatever you suspect. I will not bear it."

"Tonight," he says. "When I come to your rooms. I'll explain."

My cousin Maggie gives me one single aghast look and then comes behind me, picks up my train, and straightens it out as my husband takes my hand and leads me into dinner before the court, and I smile, as I must do, to the left and to the right, and wonder what my mother will have for her dinner tonight, while the court, that once was her court, is merry.

■ ■ ■ ■

At least Henry comes to me promptly, straight after chapel, dressed for bed, and the lords who escort him to my bedroom quickly withdraw to leave us alone, and my cousin Maggie waits only to see if there is anything that we need, and then she goes too, with one wide-eyed glance at me, as if she fears that next morning I will have disappeared as well.

"I don't mean your mother to be enclosed," Henry says briskly. "And I won't put her on trial if I can avoid it."

"What has she done?" I demand. I cannot maintain the pretence that she is innocent of everything.

"Do you mean that?" he shoots back at me. "Or are you trying to discover how much I know?"

I give a little exclamation, and turn away from him.

"Sit down, sit down," he says. He comes after me and takes my hand and leads me to the fireside chair where we used to sit so comfortably. He presses me down into the seat and pats my flushed cheek. For a moment I long to throw myself into his arms and cry on his chest and tell him that I know nothing for sure, but that I fear everything just as he does. That I am torn between love

271

for my mother and my lost brothers, and love for my son. That I cannot be expected to choose the next King of England and finally, most puzzling of all for me, I would give anything in the world to see my beloved brother again and know that he is safe. I would give anything but the throne of England, anything but Henry's crown.

"I don't know all of it," he says, sitting heavily opposite me, his chin on his fist, looking at the flames. "That's the worst thing: I don't know all of it. But she has been writing to your aunt Margaret in Flanders, and Margaret is mustering an army against us. Your mother has been in contact with all the old York families, those of her household, those who remember your father or your uncle, calling them to be ready for when Margaret's army lands. She has been writing to men in exile, to men in hiding. She has been whispering with her sister-in-law, Elizabeth — John de la Pole's mother. She's even been visiting your grandmother Duchess Cecily, her mother-in-law. They were at daggers drawn for all of her marriage but now they are in alliance against a greater enemy: me. I know that she was writing to Francis Lovell. I have seen the letters. She was behind his rebellion, I have evidence for that now. I even know how much she sent him to equip his army. It was the money I gave her, the allowance that I granted her. All this I know, I have seen it with my own eyes. I have held her letters in my own hands. There is no doubt."

He exhales wearily and takes a sip of his drink. I look at him in horror. This evidence is enough to have my mother locked up for the rest of her life. If she were a man, they would behead her for treason.

"That's not the worst of it," he goes on grimly. "There is probably more; but I don't know what else she's been doing. I don't know all her allies, I don't know her most secret plans. I don't dare to think."

"Henry, what do you fear?" I whisper. "What do you fear that she has been doing, when you look like this?"

He looks as if he is being harried beyond bearing. "I don't know what to fear," he says. "Your aunt the Dowager Duchess of Burgundy is raising an army, a great army against me, I know that much."

"She is?"

He nods. "And your mother was raising rebels at home. Today I had my council here. I'm in command of the lords, I'm sure of that. At any rate . . . they all swore fealty. But who can I trust if your mother and your aunt put an army in the field, and at the head of it is —" He breaks off.

"Is who?" I ask. "Who do you fear might lead such an invasion?"

He looks away from me. "I think you know."

I cross the room and take his hand, horrified. "Truly, I don't know."

He holds my hand very tightly and stares into my eyes as if trying to read my thoughts, as if he wants more than anything else in the world to know he can trust me, his wife and the mother of his child.

"Do you think John de la Pole would turn his coat and lead the army against you?" I ask, naming my own cousin, Richard's heir. "Is it him you fear?"

"Do you know anything against him?"

I shake my head. "Nothing, I swear."

"Worse than him," he says shortly.

I stand before him in silence, wondering if he will name the enemy that he fears the most: the figurehead who would be more potent than a York cousin.

"Who?" I whisper.

But it is as if the ghost has entered our private room, the ghost that everyone speaks of, but no one dares to name. Superstitiously, Henry will not name him either.

"I'm ready for him," is all he says. "Whoever it is that she has to head her army. You can tell everyone that I am ready for him."

"Who?" I dare him to speak.

But Henry just shakes his head.

And then, the very next morning, John de la Pole is missing from the chapel at the service of Lauds. I glance down from my raised seat in the gallery and notice that his usual place is empty. He is missing at dinnertime too.

"Where is my cousin John?" I ask My Lady the King's Mother as we wait after dinner for the priest to finish the long reading that she has commanded for all the days of Lent.

She looks at me as if I have insulted her. "You ask me?" she says.

"I ask you where is my cousin John?" I repeat, thinking that she has not heard me. "He was not at chapel this morning, and I haven't seen him all day."

"You should perhaps ask your mother, rather than me," she says bitterly. "She may know. You should perhaps ask your aunt Elizabeth of York, his mother — she may know. You should ask your aunt Margaret of York, the false Dowager Duchess of Burgundy: she certainly knows, for he is on his way to her."

I gasp and put my hand over my mouth. "Are you saying that John de la Pole is going to Flanders? How can you think such a thing?"

"I don't think it, I know it," she says. "I would be ashamed to say such a thing if there was any doubt. He is false, as I always said he was. He is false and he sat in our councils and heard our plans for our defense, and heard our fears of rebellion, and now he runs overseas to his aunt to tell her everything we know and everything we fear, and he asks her to put him on our throne, because she is of York, and now he says he is wholly for York, he was always wholly for York — just like you and all your family."

"John is false?" I repeat. I cannot believe what she is saying. If it is true, then perhaps everything else that they fear is true: perhaps there is an earl, a duke, perhaps even a prince of York somewhere out there, biding his time, planning his campaign. "My cousin John has gone to Flanders?"

"False as a Yorkist," she says, insulting me to my face. "As false as only a white rose can be, as a white rose always is."

My Lady the King's Mother tells me that we will go to Norwich, in the early summer since the king wants to be seen by his people, and take his justice to them. I can tell at once from the strained look in her eyes that this is a lie; but I don't challenge her. Instead I wait for her to become absorbed in the planning of her son's progress, and one day at the end of April I announce that I am feeling unwell and will rest in bed. I leave Maggie to guard the door to my bedroom, and to tell people that I am sleeping, and I put on my plainest gown, wrap myself in a dark cloak, and slip down to the pier outside the palace and hail a wherry boat to take me downriver.

It's cold on the water with a biting wind that gives me an excuse to pull up my hood and wrap a scarf around my face. My groom travels with me, not knowing what we are doing but anxious because he guesses that it is forbidden. The boat goes swiftly with the tide downstream. It will be slower coming back, but I have timed my visit so that the tide will be running inland when we start for Sheen.

The wherry takes me to the abbey's water stairs and Wes the groom jumps ashore and holds out his hands for me. The boatman promises he will wait to take me back to Sheen, the twinkle in his eyes making it clear that he thinks I am a maid of the court creeping out to meet my lover. I go up the wet steps to the little bridge that spans the watercourse and walk round the walls of the abbey till I come to the main gate and the gatehouse. I pull on the bell and wait for the porter, leaning back against the dark flint and red-brick wall.

A little door inside the great gate opens. "I want to see . . ." I break off. I don't know what they call my mother now that she is no longer queen, now that she is under suspicion of treason. I don't even know if she is here under her true name.

"Her Grace the Dowager Queen," the woman says gruffly, as if Bosworth had never happened, as if Plantagenets still grew green and fresh in the garden of England. She swings open the door for me and lets me in, gesturing that the lad must wait for me outside.

"How did you know I meant her?" I ask.

She smiles at me. "You're not the first that has come for her, and I doubt you'll be the last," she says, and leads me across smooth scythed turf to the cells on the west of the building. "She is a great lady; people will always be loyal to her. She's at chapel now." She nods at the church with the graveyard before it. "But you can wait in her cell and she will come in a moment."

She shows me into a clean whitewashed room, with a bookshelf for my mother's best-loved volumes, both bound manuscripts and the new print books. There is a crucifix of ivory and gold hanging on the wall, and the little nightgown that she is sewing for Arthur in a box by a chair by the fireside. It is nothing like I had imagined, and for a moment I hesitate on the threshold, weak with relief that my mother is not imprisoned in a cold tower or held in some poor nunnery, but is making her surroundings suit her — as she always does.

Through an inner door I can see her privy chamber and beyond that her curtained bed with her fine embroidered sheets. This is not a woman starving in solitary confinement; my mother is living like a queen in retirement and obviously has the whole nunnery running to her beck and call.

I sink down on a stool at the fireside until I hear a quick step on the paving stone outside and the door opens, and there is my mother, and I am in her arms and I am crying and she is hushing and soothing me and then we are seated by the fireside, and my hands are in hers and she is smiling at me, as she always does, and assuring me that everything will be well.

"But you're not free to leave?" I confirm.

"No," she says. "Did you ask Henry for my freedom?"

"Of course, the moment you disappeared. He said no."

"I thought he would. I have to stay here. For now, at least. How are your sisters?"

"They're well," I say. "Catherine and Bridget are in the schoolroom, and I've told them that you have gone on a retreat. Bridget wants to join you, of course. She says the vanity of the world is too much for her."

My mother smiles. "We meant her for the Church," she says. "She's always taken it very seriously. And my nephews? John de la Pole?"

"Disappeared," I say bluntly. Her hands grip me a little tighter.

"Arrested?" she asks.

I shake my head. "Run away," I say shortly. "I don't even know if you are telling me the truth when you seem not to know."

She does not trouble herself to answer me.

"Henry says he has evidence that you are working against us."

"Us?" she repeats.

"Against the Tudors," I say, flushing.

"Ah," she says. " 'Us Tudors.' Do you know what exactly he knows?"

"He knows that you were writing to my aunt Margaret, and calling up York friends. He mentioned my aunt Elizabeth and even my grandmother Duchess Cecily."

She nods. "Nothing more?"

"Mother, that is more than enough!"

"I know. But you see, Elizabeth, he might know more than this."

"There is more than this?" I am horrified.

She shrugs. "It's a conspiracy. Of course there is more than this."

"Well, that's all that he told me. Neither he nor his mother trusts me."

She laughs out loud at that. "They hardly trust their own shadows, why would they trust you?"

"Because I am his wife and queen?"

She nods as if it hardly matters. "And where does he think John de la Pole has gone?"

"Perhaps to My Lady Aunt Margaret in Flanders?"

Clearly, this is no surprise to her. "He got safely away?"

"As far as I know. But Lady Mother —"

She softens at once at the fear in my voice. "Yes, my dear. Of course you are anxious, you will be frightened. But I think that everything is going to change."

"What about my son?"

"Arthur was born a prince, nobody can take

that from him. Nobody would want to."

"My husband?"

Almost she laughs out loud. "Ah well, Henry was born a commoner," she says. "Maybe he will die as one."

"Mother, I cannot have you making war against my husband. We agreed to a peace, you wanted me to marry him. Now we have a son, and he should be the next King of England."

She rises up and goes in three paces across the small room to look out of the window set high in the wall, to the quiet lawns and little convent church. "Perhaps so. Perhaps he will be king. I have never had a sense of it. I can't see it myself, but it might happen."

"Can't you tell me?" I ask her. "Can't you tell what's going to happen?"

She turns and I see that her eyes are veiled and she is smiling. "As a seer, as my mother would have done? Or as a plotter? As a treasonous rebel?"

"As either!" I exclaim. "As anything! Can't you, can't *someone* tell me what is happening?"

She shakes her head. "I can't be sure," is all she will say.

"I have to go," I say irritably. "I have to catch the tide back to Sheen. And then we're going on progress."

"Where to?" she asks.

I realize, as I tell her, that she will use this

281

information. She will write to rebels as they muster, to enemies in England and overseas. As soon as I tell her so much as one word, that means I am working for York; I am spying for York against my own husband.

"Norwich," I say tightly. "We're going for Corpus Christi. Should I expect an attack now I've told you that?"

"Ah, so he thinks we're invading the east coast," she says gleefully. "So that's what he's expecting."

"What?"

"He's not going to Norwich for the pleasure of the feast. He's going so that he can prepare the east coast for invasion."

"They will invade? From Flanders?"

She puts a kiss on my forehead, completely ignoring my fearful questions. "Now don't you worry about it," she says. "You don't need to know."

She walks with me to the gatehouse, and then round the outside walls to where the pier runs out into the Neckinger River and my boat is waiting, bobbing on the rising tide. She kisses me and I kneel for her blessing and feel her warm hand rest gently on my hood. "God bless you," she says sweetly. "Come and see me when you return from Norwich, if you are able to come, if you are allowed."

"I'm going to be alone at court without you," I remind her. "I have Cecily and I have

Anne, and Maggie, but I feel alone without you. My little sisters miss you too. And My Lady the King's Mother thinks I am plotting with you and my husband doubts me. And I have to live there, with them, all of them, being watched by them all the time, without you."

"Not for long," she says, her buoyant confidence unchanged. "And very soon you will come to me or — who knows — I will find a way to come to you."

We get back to Richmond on the inflowing tide and as soon as we round the bend in the river I can see a tall slight figure waiting on the landing stage. It is the king. It is Henry. I recognize him from far away, and I don't know whether to tell the wherry to just turn around and row away, or to go on. I should have known that he would know where I was. My uncle Edward warned me that this is a king who knows everything. I should have known that he would not accept the lie of illness without questioning my cousin Margaret, and demanding to see me.

His mother is not at his side, nor any of his court. He is standing alone like an anxious husband, not like a suspicious king. As the little boat nudges up against the wooden pilings and my groom jumps ashore, Henry puts him to one side and helps me out of the boat himself. He throws a coin to the boatman, who rings it against his teeth as if surprised to find that it is good, and then disappears into the mist of the twilight river.

"You should have told me you wanted to go and I would have sent you more comfortably on the barge," Henry says shortly.

"I am sorry. I thought you would not want me to visit."

"And so you thought you would get out and back without my knowing?"

I nod. There is no point denying it. Obviously I had hoped that he would not know. "Because you don't trust me," he says flatly. "Because you don't think that I would let you visit her, if it was safe for you to do so. You prefer to deceive me and creep out like a spy to meet my enemy in secret."

I say nothing. He tucks my hand into the crook of his elbow as if we were a loving husband and wife, and he makes me walk, stride by stride, with him.

"And did you find your mother comfortably housed? And well?"

I nod. "Yes. I thank you."

"And did she tell you what she has been doing?"

"No." I hesitate. "She tells me nothing. I told her that we were going to Norwich, I hope that wasn't wrong?"

For a moment his hard gaze at me is softened, as if he is sorry for the tearing apart of my loyalties; but then he speaks bitterly. "No.

It doesn't matter. She will have other spies set around me as well as you. She probably knew already. What did she ask you?"

It is like a nightmare, reviewing my conversation with my mother and wondering what will incriminate her, or even incriminate me. "Almost nothing," I answer. "She asked me if John de la Pole had left court, and I said yes."

"Did she hazard a guess as to why he had gone? Did she know where he had gone?"

I shake my head. "I told her that it was thought that he has gone to Flanders," I confess.

"Did she not know already?"

I shrug. "I don't know."

"Was he expected?"

"I don't know."

"Will his family follow him, do you think? His brother Edmund? His mother, Elizabeth, your aunt? His father? Are they all faithless, though I have trusted them and taken them into my court and listened to their counsels? Will they just take note of everything I said and take it to their kinsmen, my enemies?"

I shake my head again. "I don't know."

He releases my hand to step back and look at me, his dark eyes unsmiling and suspicious, his face hard. "When I think of the fortune that was spent on your education, Elizabeth, I am really amazed at how little you know."

St. Mary's in the Fields, Norwich, Summer 1487

The court travels east on muddy roads and we celebrate the feast of Corpus Christi at Norwich, and we stay at the chapel of the college of St. Mary's in the Fields and go into the wealthy town to observe the procession of the guilds to the cathedral.

The town is the richest in the kingdom, and every guild based on the wool business dresses up in the finest robes and pays for costumes, scenery, and horses to make a massive procession with merchants, masters, and apprentices in solemn order to celebrate the feast of the church and their own importance.

I stand beside Henry, both in our best robes as we watch the long procession, each guild headed by a gorgeously embroidered banner and a litter carrying a display to celebrate their work or show their patron saint. Now and then I can see Henry glance sideways at me. He is watching me as the guilds go by. "You smile at someone when he catches your eye," he says suddenly.

I am surprised. "Just out of courtesy," I say defensively. "It means nothing."

"No, I know. It's just that you look at them as if you wish them well; you smile in a friendly way."

I cannot understand what he is saying. "Yes, of course, my lord. I'm enjoying the procession."

"Enjoying it?" he queries as if this explains everything. "You like this?"

I nod, though he makes me feel almost guilty to have a moment of pleasure. "Who would not? It's so rich and varied, and the tableaux so well made, and the singing! I don't think I've ever heard such music."

He shakes his head in impatience at himself, and then remembers everyone is watching us and raises a hand to a passing litter with a splendid castle built out of gold-painted wood. "I can't just enjoy it," he says. "I keep thinking that these people put on this show, but what are they thinking in their hearts? They might smile and wave at us and doff their hats, but do they truly accept my rule?"

A little child, dressed as a cherub, waves at me from a pillow of white on blue, representing a cloud. I smile and blow him a kiss, which makes him wriggle with delight.

"But you just enjoy it," Henry says, as if pleasure was a puzzle to him.

I laugh. "Ah well," I say. "I was raised in a happy court and my father loved nothing better than a joust or a play or a celebration. We were always making music and dancing. I can't help but enjoy a spectacle, and this is as fine as anything I have ever seen."

"You forget your worries?" he asks me.

I consider. "For a moment I do. D'you think that makes me very foolish?"

Ruefully, he smiles. "No. I think you were born and raised to be a merry woman. It is a pity that so much sorrow has come into your life."

There is a roar of cannon, in salute from the castle, and I see Henry flinch at the noise, and then grit his teeth and master himself.

"Are you well, my lord husband?" I ask him quietly. "Clearly you're not easily amused like me."

The face he turns to me is pale. "Troubled," he says shortly, and I remember with a sudden pulse of dread that my mother said that the court was at Norwich because Henry expects an invasion on the east coast, and that I have been smiling and waving like a fool while my husband fears for his life.

We follow the procession into the great cathedral for the solemn mass of Corpus Christi, where My Lady the King's Mother drops to her knees the moment that we enter, and spends the entire two-hour service bent low. Her more devout ladies-in-waiting kneel behind her, as if they were all part of an order of exceptional devotion. I think of my mother naming My Lady as Madonna Margaret of the Unending Self-Congratulation, and have to compose my face into a serious expression as I sit beside my husband on a pair of great matching chairs and listen to the long service in Latin and watch the service of the Mass.

Today, as it is such an important feast day, we will take communion and Henry and I go side by side up to the altar, my ladies following me, his court following him. At the moment that he is offered the sacred bread I see him hesitate, for one revealing second, before he opens his mouth and takes it, and I realize this is the only time that he does not have a taster to make sure his food is not poisoned. The thought that he might close his lips to the Host, to the sacred bread of the Mass, the body of Christ Himself, makes me shut my eyes in horror. When it is my turn, the wafer is dry in my mouth at that thought. How can Henry be so afraid that he thinks he is in danger before the altar of a cathedral?

The chancel rail is cold beneath my forehead as I kneel to pray and I remember that the church is no longer a place of holy safety. Henry has pulled his enemies out of sanctuary and put them to death; why should he not be poisoned at the altar?

I walk back to my throne, past My Lady the King's Mother, who is still on her knees, and know that her anguished expression is because she is praying earnestly for her son's safety in this country that he has won, but cannot trust.

When the service is over we go to a great banquet in the castle, and there are mummers and dancers, a pageant and a choir. Henry sits on his great chair at the head of the hall and smiles, and eats well. But I see his brown gaze raking the room, and the way that his hand is always clenched on the arm of his chair.

We stay on in Norwich after Corpus Christi and the court makes merry in the sunny weather; but I soon realize that Henry is planning something. He has men at every port along the coast appointed to warn him of foreign shipping. He organizes a series of beacons that are to be lit if a fleet is sighted. Every morning he has men brought into his room by a private covered way directly leading from the stable yard to the big plain room he has taken for his councils. Nobody knows who they are, but we all see sweat-stained horses in the stables, and men who will not stop to dine in the great hall, who have no time for singing or drinking but say that they will get their meat on the road. When the stable lads ask them, "Which road?" they won't say.

Suddenly, Henry announces that he is going on a pilgrimage to the shrine of Our Lady of Walsingham, a full day's ride north. He will go without me to this holy shrine.

"Is there something wrong?" I ask him. "Don't you want me to come with you?"

"No," he says shortly. "I'll go alone."

Our Lady of Walsingham is famous for helping barren women. I cannot think why Henry would suddenly want to make a pilgrimage there.

"Will you take your mother? I can't understand why you would want to go."

"Why shouldn't I go to a holy shrine?" he asks irritably. "I'm always observing saints' days. We're a devout family."

"I know, I know," I placate him. "I just thought it was odd. Will you go quite alone?"

"I'll take only a few men. I'll ride with the Duke of Suffolk."

The duke is my uncle, married to my father's sister Elizabeth, and the father of my missing cousin John de la Pole. This only makes me more uneasy.

"As a companion? You choose the Duke of Suffolk as your principal companion to go on pilgrimage?"

Henry shows me a wolfish smile. "What else but as my companion? He has always been so faithful and loyal to me. Why would I not want to ride with him?"

I have no answer to this question. Henry's expression is sly.

"Is it to speak to him about his son?" I venture. "Are you going to question him?" I cannot help but be anxious for my uncle. He is a quiet, steady man who fought for Richard at Bosworth but sought and obtained a pardon from Henry. His father was a famous Lancastrian, but he has always been devoted to the House of York, married to a York duchess. "I am certain, I am absolutely certain that he knows nothing about his son John's running away."

"And what does John de la Pole's mother know? And what does your mother know?" Henry demands.

When I am silent he laughs shortly. "You are right to be anxious. I feel that I can trust none of the York cousins. Do you think I am taking your uncle as a hostage for the good behavior of his son? D'you think I'm going to take him away from everyone and remind him that he has another son and that the whole family might easily go on from Walsingham to the Tower? And from there to the block?"

I look at my husband and fear this icy fury of his. "Don't speak of the Tower and the block," I say quietly. "Please don't speak of such things to me."

"Don't give me cause."

St. Mary's in the Fields, Norwich, Summer 1487

Henry and my uncle Suffolk go on their pilgrimage and come home again, no worse for wear but certainly not visibly spiritually blessed. Henry says nothing about the journey and my uncle is similarly silent. I have to assume that my husband questioned and perhaps threatened my uncle, and he — a man accustomed to living in dangerous proximity to the throne — answered well enough to keep himself and his wife and other children safe. Where his eldest son, John de la Pole, has gone, what my handsome cousin is doing in exile, nobody knows for sure.

Then, one evening, Henry comes to my room, not dressed for bed but in his day clothes, his lean face compressed and dark. "The Irish have run mad," he says shortly.

I am at the window, looking out over the darkening garden to the river. Somewhere out in the darkness I can hear the loving call of a barn owl, and I am looking for the flash of a white wing. His mate hoots in reply as I turn and take in the strain in my husband's hunched shoulders, the grayness of his face. "You look so tired," I say. "Can't you rest at all?"

"Tired? I am driven half to my grave by these people. What d'you think they have done now?"

I shake my head, close the shutters on the peace of the garden, and turn to him. For a moment I feel a whisper of irritation that he cannot be at peace, that we are always under siege from his fears. "Who? Who now?"

He looks at the paper in his hand. "Those I mistrusted — rightly as it turns out — and those that I had not even known about. My kingdom is cursed with English traitors. I hadn't even thought about the Irish. I haven't even had time to go among them and meet them; but already they are gone to the bad."

"Who is treacherous?" I try to ask with a light voice, but I can feel my throat tightening with fear. My family have always been well loved in Ireland; it will be our friends and allies who are frightening Henry. "Who is treacherous and what are they doing?"

"Your cousin John de la Pole is false as I thought he was, though his father swore he was not. As we rode together he looked me straight in the eye and lied like a tinker. John de la Pole has done what his father swore he would not do. He went straight to the court of Margaret of York in Flanders and she is supporting him. Now he's gone to Dublin."

"Dublin?"

"With Francis Lovell."

I gasp. "Francis Lovell again?"

Henry nods grimly. "They met at the court of your aunt. All of Europe knows she will support any enemy of mine. She is determined to see York back on the throne of England and she has the command of her stepdaughter's fortune and the friendship of half of the crowned heads of Europe. She is the most powerful woman in Christendom, a terrible enemy for me. And she has no reason! No reason to persecute me . . ."

"John *did* go to her, then?"

"I knew at once," Henry said. "I have a spy in every port in England. Nobody can come or go without me knowing it within two days. I knew that his father was lying when he said he had probably run to France. I knew that your mother was lying when she said that she could not say. I knew that you were lying when you said you did not know."

"But I didn't know!"

He does not even hear me. "But there is worse. The duchess has put a great army at their disposal and someone has made them a pretender."

"Made them?" I repeat.

"Like a mummer's dummy. They've made a boy." He looks at my aghast face. "She's got herself a boy."

"A boy?"

"A boy of the right age, and the right looks. A boy that can serve."

"Serve as what?"

"A York heir."

I can feel myself grow weak at the knees. I steady myself on the stone windowsill and feel the chill under the palm of my sweating hand. "Who? What boy?"

He comes behind me as if he wants to hold me with love. He wraps his arms around my waist and holds me close, my back pressed to him, bending his head to whisper against my hair as if he would inhale the smell of treason on my breath. "A boy who calls himself Richard. A boy who says he is your missing brother: Richard of York."

My knees give way and he holds me up for a moment and then lifts me like a lover, but dumps me, ungently, on the bed. "It's not possible," I stammer, struggling to sit upright. "How is it possible?"

"Don't tell me you didn't know, you little traitor!" He explodes into one of his sudden rages. "Don't look at me with your beautiful innocent face and tell me you knew nothing of this. Don't look at me with those clear eyes and lie to me from that pretty mouth. When I look at you I think that you must be an honorable woman, I think that no one as beautiful as a saint could be such a spy.

D'you really expect me to believe that your mother didn't tell you? That you don't know?"

"Know what? I don't know anything," I say urgently. "I swear that I know nothing."

"Anyway, he's changed his tune." Henry abruptly drops into a chair by the fireside and puts his hand to shade his eyes. He looks exhausted by his own outburst. "He was your brother Richard only for a few days. Now he says he's Edward. It's like being challenged by a shape-shifter. Who is he anyway?"

I have a sudden pang of wild hope. "Edward? Edward, my brother? Edward, Prince of Wales?"

"No. Edward of Warwick, your cousin. It's a pity you have such a big family."

My head swims, and for a moment I close my eyes and take a breath. When I look up I see he is watching me, as if he would read every secret that I know, by staring at my face.

"You think that Edward your brother is alive!" he accuses me, his voice hard with suspicion. "All this time you have been hoping that he will come. When I spoke of a pretender then, you thought it might be him!"

I fold my lips together, shaking my head. "How could he be?"

He is horrified. "I was asking you."

I draw a breath. "Surely, no one can think that this boy is my cousin, Edward of Warwick. Everyone knows that Edward of Warwick is in the Tower. We showed him to everyone. You made sure that he was seen by all of London."

He smiles grimly. "Yes. I had him walk side by side with John de la Pole, my friend and ally. But now John de la Pole who knelt at Mass beside the real Edward has taken a boy he claims is Edward to Ireland. The very show that we put on to tell everyone that Edward of Warwick was in London they are repeating, to tell everyone that he is in Ireland, summoning an army. John de la Pole walked with this boy to Dublin Cathedral, Elizabeth. They took him to the cathedral and they crowned him king of Ireland, England, and France. They have taken a boy and made him king. They put the crown on his head. They have set up a rival king to me and they have touched him with the sacred oil. They have crowned a new King of England. A York king. What d'you think of that?"

I grip the embroidered cover on the bed as if to hold myself in the real world and not drift away into this illusion laid upon illusion. "Who is he? In real life? This boy?"

"It's not your brother Edward. And it's not your brother Richard, if that's what you're hoping," he says spitefully. "I have spies all over this country. I found the true birth of this boy ten days ago. He's a nothing, a common lad that some priest has coached for the part, for spite. The priest will be some sort of malevolent old trickster who longs for the old days again, who wants the Yorks back. Your mother must see ten of them a day and give half of them the pension that I pay to her. But this one matters. He's not acting alone. Someone has paid him to put this lad up as a pretend prince so that the people will rise for him. When he wins, they bring out the real prince, and he takes the throne."

"When he wins?" I repeat the betraying words.

"If he wins." He shakes his head as if to resist the dangerous vision of defeat. "It'll be close. He has a good-sized army paid for by your aunt the duchess and by others of your family: your mother of course, your aunt Elizabeth I suspect, your grandmother for certain. He has mustered the Irish clans and my uncle Jasper tells me they are wild fighters. And, we shall see: he may have the support of the people of England. Who knows? When he raises the standard of the ragged staff they may turn out for him. When he cries, À Warwick, they may answer for old times' sake. They may be all for him. Perhaps they have tried me and find me wanting; now they want a return to the familiar, like a dog eating its vomit." He looks at me, as I sit in a heap on the bed. "What d'you think? What would your mother say? Can a York pretender command England still? Will they all turn out for a counterfeit prince under the standard of the white rose?"

"They will bring out the real prince?" It is what he said. It is what he himself said. "The real prince?"

He doesn't even answer me, his mouth twisted in a sort of snarl, as if he has no means to explain what he has just said.

We fall silent for a moment.

"What will you do?" It comes out as a whisper.

"I shall have to muster all the troops I can, and get ready for another battle," he says bitterly. "I thought I had won this country but — rather like being married to you, perhaps — a man can never be quite sure that the job is done. I won a great battle and was crowned king here, and now they have crowned another and I have to fight again. It seems I can be sure of nothing in this country of mists and cousins."

"And what will they do?" I whisper.

He looks at me as if he hates me, me and all of my unreliable family. "When they win, they'll change boys."

"Change boys?"

"This pretender will slip away, and a real boy will take his place, step up to the throne. A boy who is safe in hiding now, biding his time, waiting to be embodied."

"Embodied?"

"Out of thin air. Back from the dead."

"Who?"

Spitefully, he mimicks my horrified whisper, "Who?" and goes to the door of my room. "Who d'you think? Or should that be, who do you know?" When I say nothing he laughs shortly, with no humor. "So I will bid you farewell now, my beautiful wife, and hope that I will return to your warm bed as King of England."

"What else?" I ask stupidly. "What else could you be?"

"Dead, I suppose," he says bleakly.

I slide off the bed and step towards him, stretching out my hands. He takes them but does not draw me close. He holds me at arm's length and scrutinizes my face for deceit.

"D'you think the duchess has your brother Richard in hiding?" he asks me, matter-of-factly, as if it is a question of mild interest. "The trophy of a long plot between her and your mother? D'you think your mother sent him to her the moment that he was in danger, and sent a pretend prince into the Tower? D'you think he has been there for these four years? A pretender waiting for the battle to be fought for him, before he springs out, triumphant? Like Jesus from the tomb? Naked but for his winding sheet and his vanquished wounds? Triumphing over death and then me?"

I can't meet his eyes. "I don't know," I say.

"I don't know anything. Before God, Henry —"

He checks me. "Don't be forsworn," he says. "I have men swearing lies to me ten times a day. All I wanted from you was the simple truth."

I stand before him in silence, and he nods as if he knows there can never be a simple truth between us, and he goes out.

COVENTRY CASTLE, SUMMER 1487

Henry tells his mother and me that we are to act in his absence as if we are on a royal progress, enjoying the early summer weather, free of worries. We order musicians and plays, dancing and pageants. There is to be a joust, the lords are to gather with us at Coventry as if for revels. But they are to bring their men, clothed, booted, and armed for war, ready for an invasion from Ireland. We are to demonstrate confidence while secretly preparing for war.

My Lady the King's Mother cannot do it. She cannot act as queen of a happy court when every day another rider comes from Ireland with more bad news. John de la Pole and Francis Lovell have landed in Ireland with a massive trained force of two thousand men. My Lady walks everywhere with her rosary in her hands, telling her beads and whispering prayers for the safe deliverance of her son from danger.

We learn that, just as Henry told me privately, they have crowned a boy king in Dublin and declared that he is Edward of Warwick and the true king of England, Ireland, and France.

My Lady stops speaking to me; she can hardly bear to be in the same room as me. I may be her daughter-in-law, but she can only see me as the daughter of the house that has raised up this threat, whose aunt Margaret is pouring money and weapons into Ireland, whose aunt Elizabeth provided the commander, whose mother is masterminding the plot from behind the high walls of Bermondsey Abbey. She will not speak to me, she cannot bear to look at me. Only once in this difficult time she stops me as I walk past her rooms with my sisters and my cousin on my way to the stables for our horses. She puts her hand on my arm as I walk by, and I drop a curtsey to her and wait for what she has to say.

"You know, don't you?" she demands. "You know where he is. You know he is alive."

I cannot answer her white-faced fears. "I don't know what you mean."

"You know very well what I mean!" she spits furiously. "You know he's alive. You know where he is. You know what they plan for him!"

"Shall I call your ladies?" I ask her. The hand that grips my arm is shaking, I really fear that she is going to fall down in a fit.

Her gaze, always intense, is fixed on my face, as if she would force her way into my mind. "My Lady, shall I call your ladies and help you to your rooms?"

"You've fooled my son, but you don't fool me!" she hisses. "And you will see that I command here, and that everyone who has treasonous thoughts, high or low, will be punished. Treasonous heads will be cut from their corrupt bodies. High and low, nobody will be spared at Judgment Day. The sheep will be parted from the goats, and the unclean will go down to hell."

Cecily is staring at her godmother, quite horrified. She steps forwards, and then she shrinks back from the woman's anguished dark glare.

"Ah," I say coldly. "I misunderstood you. You are speaking of this pretender in Ireland? And whether you command here, or whether you have to flee from here in terror, we will know very soon, I am sure."

At the very word "flee," she tightens her grip and sways on her feet. "Are you my enemy? Tell me, let us have honesty between us. Are you my enemy? Are you the enemy of my beloved son?"

"I am your daughter-in-law and the mother of your grandchild," I say as quietly as her. "This is what you wanted and this is what you have. Whether I love him or hate him, that is between ourselves. Whether I love you or hate you, that was your doing too. And I think you know the answer."

She flings my hand away as if my touch is repellent. "I will see you destroyed the day that you raise him up against us," she warns me.

"Raise him up?" I repeat furiously. "Raise him up? It sounds like you think we would raise the dead! What can you mean? Who do you fear, My Lady?"

She gives a racking sob and she gulps down an answer. I sweep her the smallest curtsey, and I go on my way to the stables. I duck into my horse's stall and slam the stable door behind me to rest my head against his warm neck. I take a shuddering breath and realize that she has told me that they believe my brother is alive.

Kenilworth Castle, Warwickshire, June 1487

The court gives up the pretence that we are enjoying the summer, staying in the midlands of England for the beauty of the forests and the quality of the hunting. The news comes that the Irish army has landed and is sweeping across the country. The Irish troops travel light, like savage marauders. The German mercenaries who have been paid to win England back for York march at speed, earning their bounty. Duchess Margaret has hired the very best, commanded by a brilliant soldier. Every day another spy, another lookout, comes riding into court and says that they have gone past like an unstoppable wave. They are disciplined, they march with scouts before them and no baggage train trailing behind. There are hundreds of them, thousands, and at the head is a boy, a child, Edward of Warwick, and he marches under the royal standard and the ragged staff. They have crowned him King of England and Ireland. They call him king and he is served on bended knee and everywhere he goes people come out into the streets and shout, "À Warwick!"

I hardly see Henry, who is closeted with his uncle Jasper and John de Vere, the Earl of Oxford, forever sending messages to the lords, trying their loyalty, asking them to come to him. Many, very many, take their time in replying. Nobody wants to declare as a rebel too soon; but equally, nobody wants to be on the losing side with a new king. Everyone remembers that Richard looked unbeatable when he rode out from Leicester, and yet a small paid army confronted him, and a traitor cut him down. The lords who promised their support to that king, and yet sat on their horses and watched for the outcome on the day of battle, may decide to be bystanders once again and intervene only on the winning side.

Henry comes to my rooms only once during this anxious time, with a letter in his hand. "I will tell you this myself so that you don't hear it from a York traitor," he says unpleasantly.

I rise to my feet and my ladies melt away from my husband's temper. They have learned, we have all learned, to keep out of the way of the Tudors, mother and son, when they are pale with fear. "Your Grace?" I say steadily.

"The King of France has chosen this moment, this *very* moment, to release your brother Thomas Grey."

"Thomas!"

"He writes that he will come to support me," Henry says bitterly. "You know, I don't think we'll risk that. When Thomas was last supporting me on the road to Bosworth, he changed his mind and turned his coat before we even left France. Who knows what he would have done on the battlefield? But they're releasing him now. Just in time for another battle. What d'you think I should do?"

I hold on to the back of a chair so that my hands don't tremble. "If he gives you his word . . ." I begin.

He laughs at me. "His word!" he says scathingly. "The York word! Would that be as binding as your mother's word of honor? Or your cousin John's? Your marriage vows?"

I start to stammer a reply but he puts up his hand for silence. "I'll hold him in the Tower. I don't want his help, and I don't trust him free. I don't want him talking to his mother, and I don't want him seeing you."

"He could . . ."

"No, he couldn't."

I take a breath. "May I at least write and tell my mother that her son, my half brother, is coming home?"

He laughs, a jeering unconvincing laugh. "D'you think she won't know already? D'you think she has not paid his ransom and commanded his return?"

I write to my mother at Bermondsey Abbey. I leave the letter unsealed for I know that Henry or his mother or his spies will open it and read it anyway.

My dear Lady Mother,
I greet you well.
    I write to tell you that your son Thomas Grey has been released from France and has offered his service to the king, who has decided, in his wisdom, to hold my half brother in safekeeping in the Tower of London for the time being.
    I am in good health, as is your grandson.
Elizabeth

P.S. Arthur is crawling everywhere and pulling himself up on chairs so that he can stand. He's very strong and proud of himself, but he can't walk yet.

Henry says he must leave me and the ladies of the court, our son Arthur with his own yeomen of the guard in his nursery, and his frantically anxious mother behind the strong walls of Kenilworth Castle, muster his army, and march out. I walk with him to the great entrance gate of the castle, where his army is drawn up in battle array, behind their two great commanders: his uncle Jasper Tudor and his most reliable friend and ally, the Earl of Oxford. Henry looks tall and powerful in his armor, reminding me of my father, who always rode out to battle in the absolute certainty that he would win.

"If it goes against us, you should withdraw to London," Henry says tightly. I can hear the fear in his voice. "Get yourself into sanctuary. Whoever they put on the throne will be your kinsman. They won't hurt you. But guard our son. He'll be half a Tudor. And please . . ." He breaks off. "Be merciful to my mother, see that they spare her."

"I'm never going into sanctuary again," I say flatly. "I'm not raising my son inside four dark rooms."

He takes my hand. "Save yourself at any rate," he says. "Go to the Tower. Whether they put Edward of Warwick on the throne or whether they have someone else . . ."

I don't even ask him who else they might have to serve as a prince for York.

He shakes his head. "Nobody can tell me who might be in hiding, waiting for this moment. I have enemies but I don't even know if they are alive or dead. I feel that I am looking for ghosts, that an army of ghosts is coming for me." He pauses and composes himself. "At any rate, whoever they are, they are of the House of York and you will be safe with them. Our son will be safe with you. And you will give me your word that you will protect my mother?"

"You are preparing to lose?" I ask incredulously. I take his hands and I can feel the tight sinews in his fingers; he is rigid with anxiety from head to toe.

"I don't know," he says. "Nobody can know. If the country rises up for them then we will be outnumbered. The Irish will fight to the death and the mercenaries are well paid and have pledged themselves to this. All I have now is the men who will stand by me. My army at Bosworth has been paid off and gone home. And I can't inspire a new army with the promise of fresh gains, or rewards. If the rebels have a true prince to put at their head, then I am probably lost."

"A true prince?" I repeat.

We step out of the shadow of the great arch of the portcullis gate and his army raises a deep cheer as they see him. Henry waves at them and then turns to me.

"I shall kiss you," he warns me, to ensure that we make an encouraging picture for his men. He puts his arms around me and he draws me to him. His light battle armor is hard against me; it is like hugging a man of metal. I look up into his scowling face and he brings his head down and kisses me. For a moment, uncomfortably pinioned in his arms, I am overwhelmed with pity for him.

"God bless you, my husband, and bring you

safe home to me," I say shakily.

There is a roar of pleasure from the army at the kiss, but he does not even hear it. His attention is all on me. "You mean it? I go with your blessing?"

"You do," I say in sudden earnestness. "You do. And I shall pray that you come safely home to me. And I shall guard our son, and I shall protect your mother."

For a moment he looks as if he would stay and speak with me. As if he wants to speak gently and truthfully to me, for the first time ever. "I have to go," he says unwillingly.

"You go," I say. "Send me news as soon as you can. I shall be looking for news from you, and praying that it is good."

They bring his great warhorse, and they help him into the saddle, his standard bearer riding up beside him so the white and green flag with the Tudor red dragon ripples out over his head. The other flag is unfurled: the royal standard. Last time I saw that above an army, the man I loved, Richard, rode beneath it; and I put my hand to my heart to ease the sudden thud of pain.

"God bless you, my wife," Henry says, but I have no smile for him anymore. He is riding the warhorse he rode at Bosworth when he stood on a hill and Richard rode to his death. He is under the Tudor flag he unfurled there, that Richard cut down in his last fatal charge.

I raise my hand to say farewell, but I am

choked, and can't repeat my blessing, and Henry wheels his horse around and leads his army out, east to where his spies tell him the great York army has taken up their position, just beyond Newark.

KENILWORTH CASTLE, WARWICKSHIRE, 17 JUNE 1487

The ladies gather in my chamber to wait for news without the king's mother, who is on her knees in the beautiful Kenilworth chapel. We can hear a horseman on the road, and then the grinding noise of the portcullis going up and the drawbridge coming down to admit him. Cecily flies to the window and cranes her neck to look out. "A messenger," she says. "The king's messenger."

I rise to my feet to wait for him, then I realize that My Lady will intercept him before he gets to me, so I say, "Wait here!" to my ladies and slip from the room and down the stairs to the stable yard. Just as I thought, My Lady is there in her black gown striding across the yard, as the messenger swings down from the saddle.

"I was told to report to you and to Her Grace the Queen," he is saying.

"The king's wife," she corrects him. "She is not yet crowned. You can tell me everything, I will pass on the news to her."

"I'm here," I say quickly. "I'll hear him myself. What's the news?"

He turns to me. "It started badly," he says. "They recruited as they marched. They marched fast, faster than we thought they could have gone. The Irishmen are lightly armed, they carry almost nothing, the German soldiers are unstoppable."

My Lady the King's Mother blanches white and totters slightly, as if she will faint. But I have received messengers from battles before. "Never mind all that," I say sharply. "Tell me the end of the message, not the beginning. Is the king alive or dead?"

"Alive," he says.

"Did he win?"

"His commanders won."

I disregard this too. "Are the Irish and the German mercenaries defeated?"

He nods.

"John de la Pole?"

"Dead."

I take a breath at the death of my cousin.

"And Francis Lovell?" My Lady interrupts eagerly.

"Run away. Probably drowned in the river."

"Now, you can tell me how it was," I say.

This is the speech he has prepared. "They marched fast," he says. "Past York, had a few running battles, but drew up at a village called East Stoke, outside Newark. People came out to support them, and they were recruiting right up to the last moment before the battle."

"How many were they?" My Lady demands.

"We thought about eight thousand."

"How many men did the king have by then?"

"We were twice their number. We should have felt safe. But we did not." He shakes his head at the memory of their fear. "We did not.

"Anyway, they charged early, down from the hill, almost as soon as the battle began, and so all of them came against the Earl of Oxford who was commanding about six thousand men. He took the brunt of the fighting and his men held firm. They pushed back, and forced the Irish into a valley, and they couldn't get out."

"They were trapped?" I ask.

"We think they decided to fight to the death. They call the valley the Red Gutter now. It was very bad."

I turn my head from the thought of it. "Where was the king during this massacre?"

"Safely in the rear of his army." The messenger nods to his mother, who sees no shame in this. "But they brought the pretender to him when it was over."

"He's safe?" My Lady confirms. "You are certain that the king is safe?"

"Safe as ever."

I swallow an exclamation. "And who is the pretender?" I ask as calmly as possible.

The man looks at me curiously. I realize I am gritting my teeth, and I try to breathe normally. "Is he a poor imposter as my lord thought?"

"Lambert Simnel: a lad trained to do the bidding of others, a schoolboy from Oxford, a handsome boy. His Grace has him under arrest, and the schoolmaster who taught him, and many of the other leaders."

"And Francis Lovell?" My Lady demands, her voice hard. "Did anyone see him drown?"

He shakes his head. "His horse plunged into the river with him and they were swept away together."

I cross myself. My Lady Mother makes the sign but her face is dark. "We had to capture him," she says. "We had to take him and John de la Pole alive. We had to know what they planned. It was essential. We had to have them so that we could know what they know."

"The heat of the battle . . ." The man shrugs. "It's harder to capture a man than to kill him. It was a close thing. Even though we outnumbered them by so many, it was a very close thing. They fought like men possessed. They were ready to die for their cause and we were —"

"You were what?" I ask curiously.

"We did as we were ordered," he says carefully. "We did enough. We did the job."

I pause at that. I have heard reports from many battles, though none in which the victory was described so calmly. But then I have never heard a report from a battle where the chief commander, the king himself, sat at the rear of his army, an army twice the size of his enemy, and refused to parlay with defeated men but let them be slaughtered like dumb cattle.

"But they're dead," My Lady says to comfort herself. "And my son is alive."

"He's well. Not a scratch on him. How could they touch him? He was so far back they couldn't see him!"

"You can dine in the hall," My Lady rules, "and this is for you." I see a piece of gold pass from her hand to his. She must be grateful for the good news to pay so highly for it. She turns to me. "So it is over."

"Praise be to God," I say devoutly.

She nods. "His will be done," she says, and I know that this victory will make her more certain than ever that her son was born to be king.

LINCOLN CASTLE, LINCOLN, JULY 1487

The king commands that we meet him at Lincoln and he and I go hand in hand into the great cathedral for a service of thanksgiving. Behind us, half a step behind, wearing a coronal, like a queen herself, comes My Lady the King's Mother and either side of her are the king's commanders, his uncle Jasper Tudor, who planned the battle, and his most loyal friend, John de Vere, Earl of Oxford, whose men took the brunt of the fighting.

The archbishop, John Morton, is trembling at the nearness of the escape, his face flushed, his hands shaking as he distributes the Host. My Lady is in floods of tears of joy. Henry himself is profoundly moved, as if this is his first victory, fought all over again. Winning this means more to him than winning at Bosworth; it doubles his confidence.

"I am relieved," he says to me when we are in our private room at the end of the day. "I cannot easily say how deeply I am relieved."

"Because you won?" I ask. I am sitting at the window, looking east where the high spires of the cathedral pierce the low cloudy skies, but as he comes in my room I turn and look at his flushed complexion.

"Not just that," he says. "Once I knew that we outnumbered them I thought we were almost certain to win, and the Irish were practically unarmed — when they turned and faced us they were all but naked. I knew they couldn't stand against archery — they had no shields, they had no padded jackets, nobody had chain mail, poor fools — no, what made it so wonderful was capturing the boy."

"The boy they said was my cousin Teddy?"

"Yes, because now I can show him. Now everyone can see that he is no heir to York. He's a schoolboy, a lad of ten years old, name of Lambert Simnel, nothing special about him but his looks . . ." He glances at me. "Handsome, charming, like all the Yorks."

I nod as if this is a reasonable complaint against us.

"And better than that." He smiles to himself, he is all but hugging himself with joy. "No one else landed, no one else came. Even though they marched all the way across England, there was no one anchored off the east coast, there was no one waiting for them at Newark."

"What d'you mean?"

He gets to his feet and stretches himself as if he would spread his arms to hug all of the kingdom. "If they had a pretender, a better likeness than the little schoolboy, they would have had him nearby, waiting. So that when they claimed victory they could produce him, exchange him for the little lad, and take him to London for a second coronation."

I wait.

"Like with players!" He is almost laughing with joy. "When they make a switch in a play. Like the Easter play — there's the body in the tomb, someone flicks a cape and there's the risen Lord. You have to have your switch ready, you have to have your player in the wings. But when they didn't have a boy waiting to take the place of the Simnel lad — that's when I knew that they were defeated. They don't have anyone!" He cracks into a laugh. "See? They don't have anyone. Nobody was landed to meet them at Newark. Nobody came in from Flanders, nobody sailed up the Thames and arrived in London to wait for the triumphant procession. Nobody arrived in Wales, nobody came down from Scotland. Don't you see?" He laughs in my face. "All they have is an impersonator, the schoolboy. They don't have the real thing."

"The real thing?"

In his relief he speaks his fear clearly for the first time. "They don't have one of your brothers. They don't have Edward Prince of

322

Wales, they don't have Richard Duke of York, his brother and heir. If they had either one of them, they would have had him ready, standing by to take the throne as soon as the battle was won. If either one of your brothers was alive they would have had him, ready to claim the throne, as soon as I was dead. But they don't! They don't!

"It's all been gossip, and rumors, and false sightings and lying reports. They did all this for a bluff. They fooled me — I don't mind telling you that they frightened me — but it was a May game, a nothing. They made rumors about a boy in Portugal, they whispered about a boy who got out of the Tower alive; but it was all nothing. I have had men hunting all over Christendom for a boy and now I see he is nothing more than a dream. I am content now, that it was all nothing."

I register the color in his cheeks and the brightness of his eyes and realize that I am seeing my husband for the first time without his constant burden of fear. I smile at him; his relief is so powerful that I feel it myself. "We're safe," I say.

"We Tudors are safe at last," he responds. He puts out his hand to me and I understand that he will stay in my bed tonight. I rise to my feet but I am not eager, I feel no desire. I am not unwilling, I am a faithful wife and my husband is safe home from a terrible battle, happier than I have ever seen him, and I cannot help but be glad that he is safe. I welcome him home, I even welcome him to my bed.

Gently, he unties the laces under my chin and takes off my nightcap. He turns me around and pulls my hair from the plait, unties the belt at my waist and the little ties at my shoulders, and drops my gown to the ground, so that I am naked before him, my hair tumbling down. He sighs and put his lips to my bare shoulder. "I shall crown you as Queen of England," he says simply, and takes me into his arms.

We go on a progress to celebrate the king's great victory. My Lady the King's Mother rides a great warhorse, as if she were caparisoned for battle. I ride the horse that Richard gave me; I feel as if he and I have been through many journeys together, and always riding away from Richard, and never with him as he promised. Henry rides often at my side. I know that he wants to demonstrate to the people who come out to see us that he is married to the York princess, that he has unified the houses and defeated the rebels. But now there is more than this: I know that he likes to be with me. We even laugh together as we ride through the small villages of Lincolnshire and the people come tumbling out of their houses and run across their fields to see us go by.

"Smiling," Henry says to me, beaming at

half a dozen peasants whose opinions — surely — matter not at all, one way or the other.

"Waving," I coach him, and take my hand from the reins and make a little gesture.

"How do you do it?" He stops his rictus grin at the crowd and turns to me. "That little wave, you look as if it's easy. You don't look practiced at all."

I think for a moment. "My father used to say that you must remember they have turned out to see you, they want to feel that you are their friend. You are among friends and loyal supporters. A smile or a wave is a greeting to people who have only come to admire you. You might not know them — but they think they know you. They deserve to be greeted as friends."

"But did he never think that they would turn out just as eagerly to greet his enemy? Did he not think that these are false smiles and hollow cheers?"

I consider this for a moment, and then I giggle. "To tell you the truth, I think it never occurred to him at all," I say. "He was terribly vain, you know. He always thought that everybody adored him. And mostly, they did. He rode around thinking everyone loved him. He claimed the throne on his merits as a true heir. He always thought he was the finest man in England, he never doubted it."

He shakes his head, and forgets to wave to

someone who calls, *À* Tudor! It is only one voice, no one else takes up the call, and the cry just sounds wrong, strangely unconvincing. "He can't have been told more often than I that he was born to be king," he says. "Nobody in the world could be more sure than my mother that her son should be king."

"He was fighting from boyhood," I say. "At the age that you were in hiding, he was recruiting men and demanding their allegiance. It was very different for him. He was claiming the throne and drawing on the will of the people. He was the claimant: not his mother. Three suns appeared in the sky over his army. He was certain that he was chosen by God to be king. He was visible, he showed himself, at the same age, you were in hiding. He was fighting, you were running away."

He nods. I think, but I don't say, and he was blessed with bravery, he had a great natural courage and you are naturally fearful. And he had a wife that adored him, who married him for irresistible love, and her family embraced him, and his cause was their cause, and all of us — his daughters, his sons, his brothers-in-law, his sisters-in-law — we were all utterly loyal to him. He was at the center of a loving family and every one of them would have laid down their life for him. But you only have your mother and your uncle Jasper, and they are both cold of heart.

Someone ahead of us shouts "Hurrah!" and the yeomen of the guard raise their pikes and shout "Hurrah!" in full-throated reply, and I think that my father would never have created yeomen of the guard to lead the cheers for he always believed that everyone loved him, and he never had need of guarding.

Westminster Palace, London, August 1487

We go back to London to prepare for my coronation. Henry makes a royal entry into the city, and attends a service of thanksgiving for his victory in St. Paul's. He rewards the faithful, even those who had little choice but to be faithful since they were locked up in the Tower, releasing Thomas Howard the Earl of Surrey and my half brother Thomas Grey from their imprisonment.

Archbishop John Morton is made Lord Chancellor, which only makes me and others wonder what assistance a Father of the Church could provide for a king that should lead to so great a reward.

"Spying," Thomas Grey tells me. "Morton and My Lady the King's Mother together run the greatest spy network that the world has ever seen, and not a man moves in and out of England but their son and protégé know of it."

My half brother is seated with me in my presence chamber, and the music for dancing covers our words as my ladies practice new steps in one corner of the room and we talk in another. I hold up my sewing to cover my face so that no one can see my lips. I am so pleased to see him after so long that I cannot keep myself from beaming.

"Have you seen our Lady Mother?" I ask.

He nods.

"Is she well? Does she know I am to be crowned?"

"She's well, quite happy at the abbey. She sent you her love and best wishes for your coronation."

"I can't get him to release her to court," I admit. "But he knows he can't hold her there forever. He has no cause."

"Yes but he *does* have cause," my half brother says with a wry smile. "He knows that she sent money to Francis Lovell and John de la Pole. He knows that she has united all of the Yorkists who plot against him. Under Henry's nose, under your nose, she was running a spy network of her own, from Scotland to Flanders. He knows that she has been linking all of them, in turn, to Duchess Margaret in Flanders. But what drives him quite mad is that he can't say that out loud. He can't accuse her, because to do so would be to admit that there was a plot against him, inspired by our mother, funded by your aunt, and assisted by your grandmother, Duchess Cecily. He can't admit to England that the surviving House of York is completely united against him. By exposing the conspiracy, he shows the threat they are. It looks far too much like a conspiracy of women in favor of a child of their household. It is overwhelming evidence for the one thing that Henry wants to deny."

"What is that?" I ask.

Thomas leans his chin on his hand so his fingers cover his mouth. No one can read his lips as he whispers, "It looks as though those women are working together for a York prince."

"But Henry says that since no York prince came to England, ready for the victory, he cannot exist."

"Such a boy would be a precious boy," Thomas objects. "You wouldn't bring him to England until the victory was won and the coast secure."

"A precious boy?" I echo. "You mean a pretend prince, a false token. A counterfeit."

He smiles at me. Thomas has been under arrest in one place or another for two long years: in France since before the battle of Bosworth, and more recently in the Tower of London. He's not going to say anything that will put him back behind bars again.

"A pretender. Of course, that is all that he could possibly be."

Henry stays in London only long enough to

assure everyone that his victory over the rebels was total, that he was never in any danger, and that the crowned king that they paraded in Dublin is now a frightened boy in prison; then he takes his most trusted lords and goes north again, to one great house after another where he holds inquiries and learns which lords failed to secure the roads, who whispered to someone else that there was no need to support the king, those who looked the other way while the rebel army stormed by, and those who saddled up, sharpened their swords, and treasonously went out to join them. Relentlessly, dealing in details and whispers, gatepost gossip and alehouse insults, Henry tracks down every single man whose loyalty wavered when the cry went up for York. He is determined that those men who joined the rebels should be punished, some put to death as traitors but most fined to the point of ruin, and the profit paid to the royal treasury. He ventures as far north as Newcastle, deep into the York heartlands, and sends ambassadors to the court of James III of Scotland with proposals for a peace treaty and for marriages to make the treaties hold firm. Then he turns and rides home to London, a conquering hero, leaving the North reeling with death and debt.

He summons the boy Lambert Simnel to his presence chamber and commands the attendance of his whole court: My Lady the

King's Mother, an eager spectator of her son's doings; myself with my ladies headed by my two sisters, my cousin Maggie at my side; my aunt Katherine, smilingly accompanying her victorious husband, Jasper Tudor; all the faithful lords and those who have managed to pass as faithful. The double doors slam open, and the yeomen guard ground their pikes with a bang and shout the name, "John Lambert Simnel!" and everyone turns to see a skinny boy, frozen in the doorway until someone pushes him inwards and he takes a few steps into the room and then sinks on his knees to the king.

My first thought is that he does indeed look very like my brother looked, when I last saw him. This is a blond, pretty boy of about ten years old, and when my mother and I smuggled my brother out of sanctuary that dark evening, he was as bright and as slender as this. Now, if he is alive somewhere, he would be about fourteen, he would be growing into a young man. This child could never have passed for him.

"Does he remind you of anybody?" The king takes my hand and leads me from my chair beside his to walk down the long room to where the boy is kneeling, his head bowed, the nape of his neck exposed, as if he expects to be beheaded here and now. Everyone is silent. There are about a hundred people in the privy chamber and everyone turns to look at the boy as Henry approaches him, and the child droops lower and his ears burn.

"Anyone think he looks familiar?" Henry's hard gaze rakes my family, my sisters with their heads down as if they are guilty, my cousin Maggie with her eyes on the little boy who looks so like her brother, my half brother Thomas who is gazing around indifferently, determined that no one shall see him flinch.

"No," I say shortly. He is slight like my brother Richard and has cropped blond hair like his. I can't see his face but I caught a glimpse of hazel eyes like my brother's, and at the back of his head there are a few child-ish curls on the nape of the neck, just like Richard's. When he used to sit at my mother's feet, she would twist his curls around her fingers as if they were bright golden rings, and she would read to him until he was sleepy and ready for bed. The sight of the little boy, on his knees, makes me think once more of my brother Richard, and of the page that we sent into the Tower to take his place, of my missing brother Prince Edward, and of my cousin Edward of Warwick — Maggie's brother — in the Tower alone. It is as if there is a succession of boys, York boys, all bright, all charming, all filled with promise; but nobody can be sure where they are tonight, or even if they are alive or dead, or if they are unreal, flights of fancy and pretenders like this one.

"Does he not remind you of your cousin Edward of Warwick?" Henry asks me, speaking clearly so that the whole court can hear.

"No, not at all."

"Would you ever have mistaken him for your dead brother Richard?"

"No."

He turns from me, now that this masque has been played out and everyone can say that the boy knelt before us and I looked at him and denied him. "So anyone who thought that he was a son of York was either deceived or a deceiver," Henry rules. "Either a fool or a liar."

He waits for everyone to understand that John de la Pole, Francis Lovell, and my own mother were fools and liars, and then he goes on: "So, boy, you are not who you said you were. My wife, a princess of York, does not recognize you. She would say if you were her kinsman as you claim. But she says you are not. So who are you?"

For a moment I think the child is so afraid that he has lost the power of speech. But then, keeping his head down and his eyes on the ground, he whispers: "John Lambert Simnel, if it please Your Grace. Sorry," he adds awkwardly.

"John Lambert Simnel." Henry rolls the name around his tongue like a bullying schoolmaster. "John. Lambert. Simnel. And how ever have you got from your nursery,

John, to here? For it has been a long journey for you, and a costly and time-consuming trouble for me."

"I know, Sire. I'm very sorry, Sire," the child says.

Someone smiles in sympathy at the little treble voice, and then catches Henry's furious look and glances away. I see Maggie's face is white and strained and Anne is shaking and slips her hand into Cecily's arm.

"Did you take the crown on your head though you knew you had no right to it?"

"Yes, Sire."

"You took it under a false name. It was put on your head but you knew your lowborn head did not deserve it."

"Yes, Sire."

"The boy whose name you took, Edward of Warwick, is loyal to me, recognizing me as his king. As does everyone in England."

The child has lost his voice; only I am close enough to hear a little sob.

"What d'you say?" Henry shouts at him.

"Yes, Sire," the child quavers.

"So it meant nothing. You are not a crowned king?"

Obviously, the child is not a crowned king. He is a lost little boy in a dangerous world. I nip my lower lip to stop myself from crying. I step forwards and I gently put my hand in Henry's arm. But nothing will restrain him.

"You took the holy oil on your breast but

you are not a king, nor did you have any right to the oil, the sacred oil."

"Sorry," comes a little gulp from the child.

"And then you marched into my country, at the head of an army of paid men and wicked rebels, and were completely, utterly defeated by the power of my army and the will of God!"

At the mention of God, My Lady the King's Mother steps forwards a little, as if she too wants to scold the child. But he stays kneeling, his head sinks lower, he almost has his forehead on the rushes on the floor. He has nothing to say to either power or God.

"What shall I do with you?" Henry asks rhetorically. At the startled look on the faces of the court, I realize that they have suddenly understood, like me, that this is a hanging matter. It is a matter for hanging, drawing, and quartering. If Henry hands this child over to the judge, then he will be hanged by his neck until he is faint with pain, then the executioner will cut him down, slide a knife from his little genitals to his breastbone, pull out his heart, his lungs, and his belly, set light to them before his goggling eyes, and then cut off his legs and his arms, one by one.

I press Henry's arm. "Please," I whisper. "Mercy."

I meet Maggie's aghast gaze and see that she too has realized that Henry may take this tableau through to a deathly conclusion. Unless we play another scene altogether. Maggie knows that I can perform one great piece of theater and that I may have to do this. As the wife of the king, I can kneel to him publicly and ask for clemency for a criminal. Maggie will come forwards and take off my hood, and my hair will tumble down around my shoulders, and then she will kneel, all my ladies will kneel behind me.

We in the House of York have never done such a thing, as my father liked to deal out punishment or mercy on his own account, having no time for the theater of cruelty. We in the House of York never had to intercede for a little boy against a vindictive king. They did it in the House of Lancaster: Margaret of Anjou on her knees for misled commoners before her sainted husband. It is a royal tradition, it is a recognized ceremony. I may have to do it to save this little boy from unbearable pain. "Henry," I whisper. "Do you want me to kneel for him?"

He shakes his head. And at once, I am so afraid that he does not want me to intercede for mercy because he is determined to order the child to be executed. I grip his hand again. "Henry!"

The boy looks up. He has bright hazel eyes just like my little brother. "Will you forgive me, Sire?" he asks. "Out of your mercy? Because I'm only ten years old? And I know that I shouldn't have done it?"

There is a terrible silence. Henry turns from the boy and conducts me back to the dais. He takes his seat and I sit beside him. I am conscious of a sudden deep throbbing in my temples as I rack my brains as to what I can do to save this child.

Henry points at him. "You can work in the kitchens," he says. "Spit lad. You look like you could be lively in my kitchens. Will you do it?"

The boy flushes with relief and the tears fill his eyes and spill down his rosy cheeks. "Oh, yes, Sire!" he says. "You are very good. Very merciful!"

"Do as you are bid and perhaps you will work your way up to be a cook," Henry commends him. "Now go to work." He snaps his fingers to a waiting servant. "Take Master Simnel to the kitchen with my compliments and tell them to set him to work."

There is a rustle of applause and then suddenly a gale of laughter sweeps the court. I take Henry's hand, and I am laughing too, the relief at his decision is so great. He is smiling, he is smiling at me. "You never thought that I would make war on such a child?"

I shake my head, and there are tears in my own eyes from laughter and relief. "I was so afraid for him."

"He did nothing, he was their little standard. It is the ones behind him that I must punish. It is the ones who set him up that deserve the scaffold." His eyes rove down the court as they talk among themselves and share their relief. He looks at my aunt, Elizabeth de la Pole, who has lost her son, who has tight hold of Maggie's hands and they are both crying. "The real traitors will not get off so lightly," he says ominously. "Whoever they are."

GREENWICH PALACE, LONDON, NOVEMBER 1487

I dress for my coronation and reflect that it is a different task preparing to be queen than it was preparing to be a bride. This time, laced into a gown of white and gold, with lacings of gold trimmed with royal ermine, I am not shivering with unhappiness. I know what to expect from my husband and we have found a way to be together which skirts the secrets of the past and shields our gaze from the uncertainty in our future. I have given him a son for us to love, he is giving me a crown. His mother's preference for him above all other and her fierce enmity to my family is a feature of my life that I have come to accept. The mystery of my absent brother and Henry's fear of my family is something that we live with daily.

I have learned to recognize his temper, his sudden rush into rage; I have learned that it is always caused by his fear that despite the victory, despite the support of his mother, despite her declaration that God Himself is on the side of the Tudors, he will fail her and God and be cut from the throne as cruelly and as unjustly as the king he saw killed at his feet.

But I have also learned his tenderness, his love of his son, his dutiful powerful obedient submission to his mother, and — growing every day — his warmth towards me. When I disappoint him, when he suspects me, it is as if his whole world is uncertain once again. More and more he wants to love and trust me; and more and more I find that I want him to.

There is much to give me joy today. I have a son in the nursery and a husband who is secure on his throne. My sisters are safe and I am no longer haunted by dreams or ill with grief. But still, I have much to regret. Although it is my coronation day, my family are defeated. My mother is missing, enclosed in Bermondsey Abbey, my cousin John de la Pole is dead. My uncle Edward is high in the king's trust, but is far away in Granada on crusade against the Moors, and my half brother Thomas is so careful around the king that every day he performs a sort of relentless dance on tiptoe to ensure that he doesn't alert Henry's suspicions. Cecily is a girl of York no longer, married to a Tudor supporter, never speaking a word without her husband's sanction, and all my other sisters will be earmarked by My Lady the King's

Mother for Tudor loyalists; she won't risk any one of them being made a focus for rebellion. Worst of all, worse than everything, is that Teddy is still held in the Tower and the surge of confidence that Henry felt after the battle of East Stoke has not led him to release the boy, though I have asked for it, even asked for Teddy's freedom as a coronation day gift. His sister Maggie's white face among my ladies is a constant reproach to me. I said that she and Teddy could come to London and that they would be safe. I said that my mother could keep them safe. I said that I would be Teddy's guardian but I was powerless, my mother herself is enclosed, My Lady the King's Mother has Teddy as her ward and has taken his fortune into her keeping. I did not allow for Henry's secret terror. I did not think that a king would persecute a boy.

There have been triumphs for the House of York. Henry may have won at the battle of East Stoke but it was not a heroic campaign; and though most of his lords brought their men, very few of them actually joined the battle. A troubling number of them did not even attend. Henry has the crown on his head and an heir in his nursery but one of his kingdoms offered their crown to someone else — an unknown boy — in preference to him; and there is a constant continuing whisper about another heir, another heir somewhere in hiding, waiting his turn.

It is not my mother but Maggie who brushes out my hair and straightens it over my shoulders where it falls down my back, almost to my waist. Cecily puts the gold net over my head, and on top of that I will wear a gold circlet with diamonds and rubies. There are a lot of rubies, they signify a virtuous woman, and this will be my principal role for the rest of my life — a virtuous woman and a Tudor queen whose motto is "humble and penitent." It does not matter that in my heart I am passionate and independent. My true self will be hidden and history will never speak of me except as the daughter of one king, the wife of another, and the mother of a third.

The royal barge is to take me upriver to Westminster and the Mayor of London and all the guilds will come in their liveried ships with music and singing to escort me. Yet again my mother will look from her window and see a royal procession going along the river to a coronation; but this time it will be her daughter in the barge that rows past her prison. I know that she will look out of the abbey windows to see me go by, and I hope she will take a pleasure in knowing that this plan of hers, at least, has come to fruition. She has put me on the throne of England and though the gilded barge is being rowed upstream past her without acknowledgment — and it is the fourth coronation procession without her on board — this time at least she has put her daughter on the golden throne and the people lining the riverbank will call À York.

I walk down to the pier with my ladies holding my train high to stop it sweeping on the damp carpet, and they help me on board the ship. It is magnificent, decked out for the day with flags and flowers, escorted by decorated barges and vessels of all sorts. They play music as I come on board, and a choir sings an anthem to my virtues. I take my place in the stern, a cloth of gold over my head, the gold throne cushioned with velvet. My ladies gather around me. We are a famously beautiful court and today every woman is dressed in her very best. The rowers take the beat from the drum, the other barges assemble before and behind us. I pin a smile on my face as the oars dig deep in the water and we set off.

One of the accompanying barges has a figurehead in the shape of a dragon's head, and a coiled tail fixed on the stern. It is a Tudor dragon and every so often they light a flame in its mouth and it breathes fire over the water, so that the people on the riverbank scream and cheer. They call À York to me, in defiance of all the evidence that this is a Tudor celebration. I cannot help but smile at the faithful love that people have for my house, even as the pennants flutter white and green and the Tudor dragon gives his little sputtering roar.

The royal barge is mid-river, moving easily on the inward tide, but as we get to Bermondsey and I see the brick and flint gatehouse of the abbey, the steersman sets a course for the opposite bank so that we are as far away as possible from my mother's prison. I can see the people waiting by the sheltering perimeter walls of the abbey, but I cannot make out the figures. I raise my hand to shield my eyes and the gold crown scratches my fingers. I cannot see my mother among the crowd, we are too far out on the river and there are too many people for me to spot her. I want to see her, I *so* want to see her. I want her to know that I am looking for her. For a moment I wonder if she has been ordered to stay in her cell as the barge goes by. I wonder if she will be seated in her chair, in the cool whitewashed cell, listening to the music bawled across the water, smiling at the noisy roar of the dragon vomiting fire, but not knowing that I am looking for her.

And then, suddenly, as if by magic, I see her. There is a standard, uncurling and flapping in the breeze from the river. It is Tudor green, the new color of loyalty, Tudor green background embroidered with the Tudor rose of white and red, as every sensible person would show today. But this flag is different: it's a white rose on the Tudor green and if there is a red center to the rose, it is stitched so small that it cannot be seen. At first glance, at closer glance, this is the white rose of York. And there, of course, is my mother standing under the standard of the husband she adored, and as I look towards her and raise my hand, she gives a girlish jump of joy that I have seen her and she waves both her hands above her head, shouting my name, exuberant, laughing, rebellious as ever. She starts to run along the riverbank, keeping pace with my distant barge, shouting, "Elizabeth! Elizabeth! Hurrah!" so clearly that I can hear her over the noise across the water. I rise up from my solemn throne, rush to the side of the boat, and lean out to wave back at her, quite without any dignity, and shout, "Lady Mother! Here I am!" and laugh aloud in delight that I have seen her, and that she has seen me, and that I am going to my coronation with her laughing, easy blessing.

My coronation is the signal for a rash of betrothals, as Henry, in his methodical way, exploits my sisters one by one as players for the House of Tudor, and makes political matches to his own advantage. Even my mother is brought into play again. He allows me to visit her at Bermondsey with my sisters, and take her the news that she is so far forgiven by the Tudors that they have revived the idea of her marriage, and she is to go to James III of Scotland.

I am afraid that the abbey will be cold and unwelcoming but I find my mother before a roaring fire of applewood, which gives a smoky scent to her presence chamber, my half sister, Grace, seated beside her, and two ladies-in-waiting working on their sewing.

My mother rises up as I come in with my sisters and kisses us all. "How lovely to see you." She curtseys to me. "I should have said "Your Grace.' " She steps back to see me. "You look very well."

She holds open her arms for Bridget and Catherine, who rush to hug her, and she smiles at Anne over their bobbing heads. "And you, Cecily, what a pretty gown, and what a fine brooch in your bonnet. Your husband is kind to you?"

"He is," Cecily says stiffly, well aware of the suspicions against my mother. "And he is very highly regarded by His Grace the King and My Lady the King's Mother. He is famous for his loyalty, and so am I."

My mother smiles as if it does not matter much to her either way, and sits back down again, drawing my little sisters, seven-year-old Bridget and eight-year-old Catherine, onto her knee. Anne takes a footstool beside them and my mother rests her hand on her shoulder and looks expectantly at me.

"We're to be married!" Catherine bursts out, unable to wait any longer. "All of us but

Bridget."

"Because I am a bride of Christ," Bridget says, solemn as a moppet can be.

"Of course you are." My mother gives her a hug. "And who are the lucky men to be? Staunch Tudors, I expect?"

Cecily bristles at the reference to her husband. "You're betrothed as well," she says spitefully.

My mother is completely unmoved. "James of Scotland again?" she asks me, smiling.

I realize that she knows of this already. Her spy network must still be in place and serving her as well here, where she is supposed to be isolated and secluded, as it did in the royal court where she was supposed to be surrounded by loyalists.

"You knew?"

"I knew the king had sent ambassadors to Scotland and was forging a peace with them," she says smoothly. "Of course he would make it binding with a wedding. And since he had thought of me earlier, I imagined he would return to the plan."

"Do you mind?" I ask urgently. "Because if you want to refuse, I could perhaps . . ."

Gently she reaches forwards and takes my hand. "I don't think you could," she says. "If you can't prevent him from keeping your cousin Edward in the Tower, nor persuade him that I need not be behind these walls, then I doubt you can influence his policy with

Scotland. He has made you queen, but though you carry the scepter, you have no power."

"That's what I always say," Cecily adds. "She can't do anything."

"Then I am sure you are right." My mother smiles at her. To me she says quietly: "And you should not reproach yourself. I know you do the best that you can. A woman always has only as much power as she can win, and you are not married into a family which trusts you with authority."

"But I am to be married to a Scottish prince!" Catherine squeaks, unable to hold back the news any longer. "The younger one. So I shall go to Scotland with you, Lady Mother, and I can be in your rooms, I can be your lady-in-waiting."

"Ah, how glad I shall be to have you with me." My mother leans forward and drops a kiss on Catherine's white-lace-capped head. "It will be so much easier if we are together. And we can make great state visits to your sister. We can ride to London in a procession and she can put on a banquet for us royal ladies of Scotland."

"And I am to marry the heir, the next King of Scotland," Anne says quietly. She is less exuberant than Catherine. At twelve she knows well enough that to marry your country's enemy in an attempt to hold him to an alliance is no great treat.

My mother looks at her with silent compassion. "Well, we will all be together, that's one good thing," she says. "And I can advise you, and help you. And to be a queen of Scotland is no small part to play, Anne."

"What about me?" Bridget asks.

My mother's gaze flicks to my face. "Perhaps you will be allowed to come with me to Scotland," she says. "I would think the king would grant that."

"And if not, I'll come here," Bridget says with satisfaction, looking round at my mother's beautiful rooms.

"I thought you wanted to be a nun," Cecily says crushingly. "Not live like a pope."

My mother giggles. "Oh Cecily, d'you really think I live like a pope? How quite wonderful. Do you think I have rooms full of hidden cardinals who serve me? And eat off gold plates?"

She gets to her feet and puts out her hands to the two little ones. "Come, Cecily reminds me that we must go and dine. You can say grace for the Sisters, Bridget."

As we go out she draws me close to her. "Don't fret," she says quietly. "There are many slips between a betrothal and a wedding, and holding the Scots to a peace treaty is a miracle that I have yet to witness. Nobody is riding up the Great North Road just yet."

PALACE OF SHEEN, RICHMOND, SPRING 1488

My uncle Edward comes home from the crusades as brown as a Moor himself, but missing all his front teeth. He's cheerful about this and says that God can now see more clearly into his heart, but it gives him a lisp that I cannot help but find comical. I am so pleased to see him that I fall into his arms and hear him sweetly lisp over my head, "Bleth you, bleth you!" and this makes me laugh and cry at once.

I expect him to be appalled at the news that his sister is enclosed at Bermondsey, but his shrug and smile tell me that he sees this as a temporary setback in a life which has been filled with defeats and victories. "Is she comfortable?" he asks, as if it is the only question.

"Yes, she has lovely rooms and she's well served. Clearly, they all adore her," I reply. "Grace is with her, and the porteress calls her 'the queen' as if nothing had changed."

"Then she will no doubt organize her life

just as she wants," he says. "She usually does."

He is full of news of the crusade in Granada, of the beauty and elegance of the Moorish empire, of the determination of the Christian kings to drive the Moors completely from Spain. And he tells me stories about the Portuguese court, and their adventures. They are exploring far south down the coast of Afric, and he says there are mines of gold there, and markets full of spices, and a treasure house of ivory to be picked up by anyone who dares to go far enough as the sky gets hotter and the seas more stormy. There is a kingdom where the fields are made of gold and any man can have a fortune if he picks up the pebbles. There are strange animals and rare beasts — he has seen the hides, spotted and striped and gold as a noble — and perhaps there is a place ruled by a white Christian in the very heart of the great land, perhaps there is a kingdom of black men, devoted to a white Christian hero called Prester John.

Henry has no interest in news of magical kingdoms, but he takes Uncle Edward into his privy chamber the minute he arrives and they are locked together for half a day before Edward comes out with his toothless grin and Henry's arm around his shoulders and I know that whatever he has reported, it has set Henry's anxious mind at rest.

Henry trusts him so much that he is to lead a defense of Brittany. "When will you go?" I ask him.

"Almost at once," he says. "There's no time to lose and —" he grins his toothless smile "— I like to be busy."

I take him immediately to the nursery at Eltham Palace to show him how much Arthur has grown. He can stand up now and walk alongside a chair or a stool. His greatest pleasure is to hold my fingers and take wavering steps across the room, turn around with his little feet pigeon-toed, and forge back again. He beams when he sees me and reaches out for me. He is starting to speak, singing like a little bird, though he has no words yet, but he says "Ma," which I take to mean me, and "Boh," which means anything that pleases him. But he giggles when I tickle him and drops anything that he is given in the hope that someone will pick it up and return it to him, so that he can drop it again. His greatest joy is when Bridget gives him a ball to drop, and flies after it as if they were playing tennis and she has to recover it before it bounces too often; it makes him gurgle and crow to see her run. "Is he not the most beautiful boy you have ever seen?" I ask Uncle Edward, and am rewarded by his toothless beam.

"And the boy you went to see?" I ask quietly, taking Arthur against my shoulder and gently patting his back. He is heavy on my shoulder and warm against my cheek. I have a sudden fierce desire that nothing shall ever threaten his peace or his safety. "Henry told me that he sent you to look at a boy in Portugal? I have heard nothing of him since you left."

"Then the king will tell you that I saw a page boy in the service of Sir Edward Brampton," my uncle says, his lisp endearing. "Some mischief-maker thought that he looked like my poor lost nephew Richard. People will make trouble over nothing. Alas, that they have nothing better to do."

"And does he look like him?" I press.

Edward shakes his head. "No, not particularly."

I glance around. There is no one near but the baby's wet nurse and she has no interest in anything but eating enormous meals and drinking ale. "My lord uncle, are you sure? Can you speak to my Lady Mother about him?"

"I won't speak to her of this lad because it would distress her," he says firmly. "It was a boy who looked nothing like your brother, her son. I am sure of it."

"And Edward Brampton?" I persist.

"Sir Edward is to come on a visit to England as soon as he can leave his business in Portugal," he says. "He is letting his handsome page go out of his service. He does not want to cause any embarrassment to us or to the king with such a forward boy."

There is more here than I can understand. "If the boy is nothing, a braggart, then how could such a nothing make such a loud noise in Lisbon that we can hear him in London? If he is a nothing, why did you go all the way to Portugal to see him? It's nowhere near Granada. And why is Sir Edward coming to England? To meet with the king? Why would he be so honored, when he was known to be loyal to York and he loved my father? And why is he dismissing his page if the boy is a nobody?"

"I think the king would prefer it," Edward says lightly.

I look at him for a moment. "There is something here that I don't understand," I say. "There is a secret here."

My uncle pats my hand as I hold the baby's warm body to my heart. "You know, there are always secrets everywhere; but it is better sometimes that you don't know what they are. Don't trouble yourself, Your Grace," he says. "This new world is filled with mysteries. The things they told me in Portugal!"

"Did they speak of a boy returned from the dead?" I challenge him. "Did they speak of a boy who was hidden from unknown killers, smuggled abroad, and waiting for his time?"

He does not flinch. "They did. But I reminded them that the King of England has no interest in miracles."

There is a little silence. "At least the king

trusts you," I say as I hand Arthur back to his wet nurse and watch him settle on her broad lap. "At least he is sure of you. Perhaps you can speak to him of my Lady Mother and she can come back to court. If there is no boy, then he has nothing to fear."

"He's not naturally a very trusting man," my uncle observes with a smile. "I was followed all the way to Lisbon and my hooded companion noted everyone that I met. Another man followed me home again too, to make sure that I did not call on your aunt in Flanders on my way."

"Henry spied on you? His own messenger? His spy? He spied on his spy?"

He nods. "And there will be a woman in your household who tells him what you say in your most private moments. Your own private confessor is bound to report to his Father in God, the Archbishop of Canterbury, John Morton. John Morton is the greatest friend of My Lady the King's Mother. They plotted together against King Richard, together they destroyed the Duke of Buckingham. They meet every day and he tells her everything. Don't ever dream that the king trusts any of us. Don't ever think that you're not watched. You are watched all the time. We all are."

"But we're doing nothing!" I exclaim. I lower my voice. "Aren't we, Uncle? We are doing nothing?"

He pats my hand. "We're doing nothing," he assures me.

WINDSOR CASTLE, SUMMER 1488

But my aunt Margaret is not doing nothing. Her Grace the Dowager Duchess of Flanders, sister to my father, is certainly not idle. Constantly, she writes to James III of Scotland, even sending him an envoy of York loyalists. "She is trying to persuade him to make war on us," Henry says wearily. I have stepped into his privy chamber in the great castle, and found him with two clerks at either end of a great table and a salt-stained paper before him. I recognize my aunt's great red wax seals and the trailing ribbons; she uses the sun in splendor, the great York crest created by my father. "But she won't succeed. We have an alliance, we will have betrothals. James is sworn to be loyal to me. He'll hold fast for Tudor England. He won't turn backwards to York."

But though Henry may be right and James is loyal in his heart, he can't persuade his countrymen to support England. His country, his lords, even his heir are all against Tudor

England, whatever the opinions of the king, and it is the country that wins. They turn against him rather than stomach an alliance with the Tudor arriviste, and James has to defend his friendship with England and even his throne. I receive a hastily scribbled note from my mother, but I don't understand what she means:

So you see, I am not riding up the Great North Road.

I know that Henry will have seen this, almost as soon as it was written, so I take it at once to him to demonstrate my loyalty; but as I enter the royal privy chamber I stop, for there is a man with him that I think I know, though I cannot put a name to his darkly tanned face. Then as he turns towards me I think I had better forget everything I have ever known about him. This is Sir Edward Brampton, my father's godson, the man that my uncle saw at the court in Portugal with the forward page boy. He turns and bows low to me, his smile quietly confident.

"You know each other?" my husband says flatly, watching my face.

I shake my head. "I am so sorry . . . you are?"

"I am Sir Edward Brampton," he says pleasantly. "And I saw you once when you were a little princess, too young to remember an unimportant old courtier like me."

I nod and turn my entire attention to

Henry, as if I have no interest in Sir Edward at all. "I wanted to tell you that I have a note from Bermondsey Abbey."

He takes it from my hand and reads it in silence. "Ah. She must know that James is dead."

"Is that what she means? She writes only that she won't be riding up the Great North Road. How did the king die? How could such a thing happen?"

"In battle," Henry says shortly. "His country supported his son against him. It seems that some of us cannot even trust blood kin. You cannot be sure of your own heir, never mind another."

Carefully I do not look towards Sir Edward. "I am sorry if this causes us trouble," I say evenly.

Henry nods. "At any rate, we have a new friend in Sir Edward."

I smile slightly, Sir Edward bows.

"Sir Edward is to come home to England next year," Henry says. "He was a loyal servant of your father's and now he is going to serve me."

Sir Edward looks cheerful at this prospect and bows again.

"So when you reply to your mother, you can tell her that you have seen her old friend," Henry suggests.

I nod and go towards the door. "And tell her that Sir Edward had a forward page boy, who made much of himself, but that he has now left his service and gone to work for a silk merchant. Nobody knows where he is now. He may have gone trading to Afric, perhaps to China, no one knows."

"I'll tell her that, if you wish," I say.

"She'll know who I mean," Henry smiles. "Tell her that the page boy was an insolent little lad who liked to dress in borrowed silks but now he has a new master — a silk merchant as it happens, so he will be well suited in his work, and the boy has gone with him, and is quite disappeared."

Greenwich Palace, London, Christmas 1488

The anxious Tudor scrutiny of the unreliable world around them ceases for the Christmas feast, as if it is finally possible that days can go by and small events happen, notes be written and received, without Henry having to see everything and know everything. With the disappearance of the invisible boy into the unknown it seems that there is nothing left to watch for, and the spies at the ports and the guardians on the roads can rest. Even My Lady the King's Mother loses her frown and regards the arrival of the yule log, the jesters, the players, the mummers, and the choir with a small smile. Margaret is allowed to visit her brother in the Tower and comes back to Greenwich happier than she has been for some time.

"The king is allowing him a schoolmaster and some books," she says. "And he has a lute. He's playing music and composing songs, he sang one to me."

Henry comes to my room every night after

dinner and sits by the fire and talks about the day; sometimes he lies with me, sometimes he sleeps with me till morning. We are comfortable together, even affectionate. When the servants come and turn down the bed and take off my robe, he puts them to one side with his hand. "Leave us," he says, and when they go out and close the door, he slips my robe from my shoulders himself. He puts a kiss on my naked shoulder and helps me into the high bed. Still dressed, he lies on the bed beside me and strokes my hair away from my face. "You're very beautiful," he says. "And this is our third Christmas together. I feel like a man well married, long married and to a beautiful wife."

I lie still and let him pull the ribbon from the end of my plait and run his fingers through the sleek golden hanks of hair. "And you always smell so delicious," he says quietly.

He gets up from the bed and unties the belt on his robe, takes it off, and lays it carefully on a chair. He is the sort of man who always keeps his things tidy. Then he lifts the bedding and slides in beside me. He is desirous and I am glad of it, for I want another child. Of course, we need another son to make the succession secure; but on my own account, I want that wonderful feeling of a baby in my belly and the sense of growing life within. So I smile at him and lift the hem of my robe and help him to move on me. I reach for him and feel the warm strength of his flesh. He is quick and gentle, shuddering with his own easy pleasure; but I feel nothing more than warmth and willingness. I don't expect more, I am glad to at least feel willing, and grateful to him that he is gentle. He lies on me for a little while, his face buried in my hair, his lips at my neck, then he lifts himself away from me and says, surprisingly: "But it's not like love, is it?"

"What?" I am shocked that he should say such a bald truth.

"It's not like love," he says. "There was a girl when I was a young man, in exile in Brittany, and she would creep out from her father's house, risking everything to be with me. I'd be hiding in the barn, I used to burn up to see her. And when I touched her she would shiver, and when I kissed her she would melt, and once she held me and wrapped her arms and legs around me and cried out in her pleasure. She could not stop and I felt her sobs shake her whole body with joy."

"Where is she now?" I ask. Despite my indifference to him I find I am curious about her, and irritated at the thought of her.

"Still there," he says. "She had a child by me. Her family got her married off to a farmer. She'll probably be a fat little farmer's wife by now with three children." He laughs.

"One of them a redhead. What d'you think? Henri?"

"But no one calls you a whore," I observe.

His head turns at that and he laughs out loud, as if I have said something extraordinary and funny. "Ah, dear heart, no. Nobody calls me a whore for I am King of England and a man. Whatever else you might like to change in the world, a York king on the throne, the battle reversed, Richard arising from the grave, you cannot hope to change the way that the world sees women. Any woman who feels desire and acts on it will always be called a whore. That will never change. Your reputation was ruined by your folly with Richard, for all that you thought it was love, your first love. You have only regained your reputation by a loveless marriage. You have gained a name but lost pleasure."

At his casual naming of the man I love, I pull the covers up to my chin and gather my hair and plait it again. He does not stop me, but watches me in silence. Irritated, I realize that he is going to stay the night.

"Would you like your mother to come to court for Christmas?" he asks casually, turning to blow out the candle beside the bed. The room is lit only by the dying fire, his shoulder bronzed by the light of the embers. If we were lovers this would be my favorite time of the day.

"May I?" I almost stammer, I am so surprised.

"I don't see why not," he says casually. "If you would like her here."

"I would like it above anything else," I say. "I would like it very much. I would be so happy to have her with me again, and for Christmas, and my sisters, especially my little sisters . . . they'll be so happy." Impulsively I lean over and kiss his shoulder.

At once, he turns and catches my face and takes the kiss on his mouth. Gently, he kisses me again, and then again, and my distress at his mentioning Richard, and my jealousy of the girl he once loved, somehow prompt me to take his mouth against mine, and put my arms around his neck, then I feel his weight come on me and his body press against the length of me, as my lips open and I taste him and my eyes close as he holds me, and feel him gently, sweetly enter me again, and for the first time ever between the two of us, it does feel a little like love.

WESTMINSTER PALACE, LONDON, SPRING 1489

It is a joyous Christmas with my mother at court, and then a long, cold winter in London. We command a special Mass to be sung for my uncle Edward, who died last year in his expedition against the French.

"He didn't have to go," I say, lighting a candle for him on the altar of the chapel.

My mother smiles, though I know that she misses him. "Oh, he did," she says. "He was never a man who could stay quietly at home."

"You will have to go quietly to your home," I point out. "The feast of Christmas is over and Henry says you have to go back to the abbey."

She turns towards the door and pulls the hood forwards over her silvery hair. "I don't mind, as long as you and the girls are well, and I see that you are happy and at peace in yourself."

I walk beside her and she takes my hand. "And you? Are you coming to love him, as I hoped you would do?" she says.

"It's odd," I confess. "I don't find him heroic, I don't think he is the most marvelous man in the world. I know he's not very brave, he's often bad-tempered. I don't love him as I did Richard . . ."

"There are many sorts of love," she counsels me. "And when you love a man who is less than you dreamed, you have to make allowances for the difference between a real man and a dream. Sometimes you have to forgive him. Perhaps you even have to forgive him often. But forgiveness often comes with love."

In April, when the birds are singing in the fields south of the river, I tell Henry that I will not ride out hawking with him. He is mounting up in the stable yard and my horse, that has been kept inside for days, is curvetting and dancing on the spot, held tightly with his reins by a groom.

"He's just fresh," Henry says, looking from the eager gelding to me. "You can manage him, surely? It's not like you to miss a day's hawking. As soon as you're on him he'll be all right."

I shake my head.

"Have another horse," Henry suggests. I smile at his determination that I should ride with him. "Uncle Jasper will let you have his. He's steady as a rock."

"Not today," I persist.

"Are you not well?" He throws his reins to

his groom and jumps down to come to my side. "You look a little pale. Are you well, my love?"

At that endearment, I lean towards him and his arm comes around my waist. I turn my head so my lips are at his ear. "I have just been sick," I whisper.

"But you're not hot?" He flinches a little. The terror of the sweating sickness that came with his army is still a strong one. "Tell me you're not hot!"

"It's not the sweat," I assure him. "And it's not a fever. It's not something I ate, nor unripe fruit." I smile at him, but still he does not understand. "I was sick this morning, and yesterday morning, and I expect to be sick tomorrow too."

He looks at me with dawning hope. "Elizabeth?"

I nod. "I'm with child."

His arm tightens around my waist. "Oh, my darling. Oh, my sweetheart. Oh, this is the best news!"

In front of the whole court he kisses me warmly on the mouth and when he looks up, everyone must surely know what I have told him, for his face is radiant.

"The queen is not riding with us!" he shouts, as if it is the best news in the world.

I pinch his arm. "It's too soon to tell anyone yet," I caution him.

"Oh, of course, of course," he says. He

kisses my mouth and my hand. Everyone is looking with puzzled smiles at his joy. One or two nudge each other, guessing at once. "The queen is going to rest today!" he bellows. "There's no need for concern. She is well. But she is going to rest. She is not going to ride. I don't want her to ride. She is a little unwell."

This confirms it; even the slowest young man whispers with his neighbor. Everyone guesses at once why Henry has me held tightly to his side and why he is beaming.

"You go and rest." He turns to me, oblivious to the knowing smiles of his court. "I want you to make sure that you rest."

"Yes," I say, near to laughter myself. "I understand that. I think everyone understands that."

He grins, sheepish as a shy boy. "I can't hide how happy I am. Look, I'll catch you the sweetest pheasant for your dinner." He swings himself into the saddle. "The queen is unwell," he tells the groom holding my mount. "You had better exercise her horse yourself. Today, and every day. I don't know when she'll be well enough to ride again."

The groom bows to his knees. "I will, Your Grace," he says. He turns to me: "I'll keep him quiet for you so you can just walk out on him when you have a mind to it."

"The queen is unwell," Henry says to his companions, who are mounting up and beaming at him. "I shan't say more." He is grinning from ear to ear, like a boy. "I don't say more. There's no more to say." He stands in his stirrups and raises his cap from his head and waves it in the air. "God save the queen!"

"God save the queen!" everyone shouts back at him and smiles at me, and I laugh up at Henry. "Very discreet," I say to him. "Very courtly, very reticent, most discreet."

GREENWICH PALACE, LONDON, AUTUMN 1489

This time it is my decision when I go into confinement, and though My Lady the King's Mother chooses the tapestries for my rooms and orders the day bed and the cradle, I have the room set out as I wish, and I tell her that I will go into confinement at the end of October.

"And I shall send for my mother to be with me," I say.

At once her gaze sharpens. "Have you asked Henry?"

"Yes," I lie to her face.

"And he has agreed?"

Clearly, she does not believe me for a moment.

"Yes," I say. "Why would he not? My mother has chosen to live in retirement, a life of prayer and contemplation. She has always been a thoughtful and devout woman." I look at the fixed expression on My Lady's face — she has always prized herself as being formidably holy. "Everyone knows my mother has longed for the religious life," I claim, feeling the lie grow more and more ambitious, and feeling myself tremble with the desire to giggle. "But I am sure she will consent to return to the world to stay with me when I am in confinement."

Then, it is just a question of getting to Henry before his mother does so. I go to his rooms and though the door is shut to his presence chamber, I nod to the guard to let me in.

Henry is seated at a table in the center of the room with his most trusted advisors around him. He looks up as I come in and I see that he is scowling with worry.

"I'm sorry." I hesitate in the doorway. "I didn't realize . . ."

They all rise and bow and Henry comes quickly to my side and takes my hand. "It can wait," he says. "Of course it can wait. Are you well? Nothing wrong?"

"Nothing wrong. I wanted to ask you a favor."

"You know I can refuse you nothing," he says. "What would you like? To bathe in pearls?"

"Just if my mother could be with me when I go into confinement." As I say the words I see the shadow cross his face. "She was such a comfort to me last time, Henry, and she is so experienced, she has had so many children, and I need her."

He hesitates. "She's my mother," I insist, my voice catching a little. "And it's her grand-child."

He thinks for a moment. "Do you have any idea what we are talking about here? Right now?"

I look past his shoulder at the grave-faced men, his uncle Jasper looking gloomily at a map. I shake my head.

"We keep getting reports from all over the country of little incidents of trouble. People planning to overthrow us, people plotting my death. In Northumberland a mob attacked the Earl of Northumberland, as he was collecting taxes for me. Not just a bit of rough play — d'you know, they pulled him off his horse and killed him?"

I gasp. "Henry Percy?"

He nods. "In Abingdon there's a highly regarded abbot plotting against us."

"Who?" I ask.

His face darkens. "It doesn't matter who. In the northeast, Sir Robert Chamberlain and his sons were captured trying to set sail for your aunt in Flanders from the port of Hartlepool. Half a dozen little incidents, none of them connected, as far as we can see, but all of them signs."

"Signs?"

"Of a discontented people."

"Henry Percy?" I repeat. "How was his death a sign? I thought people were objecting to paying tax?"

The king's face is grim. "The people of the North never forgave him for failing Richard at Bosworth," he says, watching me. "So I daresay you too think it serves him right."

I don't reply to this, it is still too raw for me. Henry Percy told Richard that his troops were too tired to fight, having marched from the North — as if a commander brings troops to a battle who are too tired to fight! He put himself at the rear of Richard's army and never moved forwards. When Richard charged off the hill to his death, Percy watched him go without stirring himself. I won't grieve for him in his dirty little death. He's no loss to me. "But none of this has anything to do with my mother," I hazard.

Uncle Jasper gives me a long, cool look from his blue eyes as if he disagrees.

"Not directly," Henry concedes. "She shot her last bolt with the kitchen boy's rebellion. I've got nothing that identifies her with these scattered troubles."

"So she could come into confinement with me."

"Very well," he decides. "She's as safe inside with you as she is inside the abbey. And it shows that she is a member of our family, to anyone who still dreams that she represents York."

"May I write to her today?"

He nods, takes my hand, and kisses it. "I

can refuse you nothing," he says. "Not when you are about to give me another son."

"What if it's a girl?" I ask, smiling at him. "Will you send me a bill for all these favors if I have a girl?"

He shakes his head. "It's a boy. I am certain of it."

Westminster Palace, London, November 1489

My mother promises to come from Bermondsey but there is so much illness in London that she will not come into confinement with me straightaway but waits in her rooms for a few days to make sure that she is not carrying the pox, which comes with a painfully hot fever and terrible red spots all over the body.

"I wouldn't bring it in on you," she says when she finally comes in through the door, padded for silence, which opens so rarely on the outside world.

In a moment I am in her arms and she is hugging me and then stepping back to look at my face, and my big belly, and my swollen hands.

"You've taken all your rings off," she remarks.

"They were too tight," I say. "And my ankles are as fat as my calves."

She laughs at that. "That will all be better when the baby comes," she says, and presses me down to the day bed, sits at the end of it, takes my feet into her lap, and rubs them firmly with her strong hands. She strokes the soles, pulling gently at the toes until I almost purr with pleasure and she laughs at me again.

"You will be hoping for a boy," she says.

"Not really." I open my eyes and meet her gray gaze. "I am hoping that the baby is well and strong. And I would love a little girl. Of course we need a boy . . ."

"Perhaps a girl now, and a boy next," she suggests. "King Henry is still kind to you? At Christmas he looked like a man in love."

I nod. "He's been most tender."

"And My Lady?"

I make a face. "Most attentive."

"Ah well, I'm here now," my mother says, acknowledging that no one can outmatch My Lady the King's Mother but herself. "Does she come in here for her meals?"

I shake my head. "She dines with her son. When I am in confinement she takes my place at the high table in the court."

"Let her have her moment of glory," my mother counsels. "And we'll eat better in here without her. Who do you have as your ladies-in-waiting?"

"Cecily, Anne, and my cousin Margaret," I say. "Though Cecily will do nothing for anyone as she is with child herself. And of course I have the king's kinswomen, and those his mother insists that I keep about me." I lower my voice. "I am sure that they report to her everything I do and say."

"Bound to. And how is Maggie? And her poor little brother?"

"She's allowed to visit him," I say. "And she says that he is well enough. He has tutors now and a musician. But it's no life for a boy."

"Perhaps if Henry gets a second heir he'll let poor Teddy out," my mother says. "I pray for that poor boy, every night of his life."

"Henry can't let him out while he fears that the people might rise up for a duke of York," I say. "And even now there are constant uprisings in the country."

She does not ask me who is rising, or what they are saying. She does not ask me which counties. She goes to the window and draws back a corner of the thick tapestry and looks out as if she has no interest, and from this, I know that Henry is wrong and that my mother has not shot her last bolt of rebellion. On the contrary, she is in the thick of it again. She knows more than I do, she probably knows more than Henry does.

"What's the point of it?" I ask impatiently. "What's the point of going on and on caus-ing trouble, while men risk their lives and have to run away to Flanders with a price on their heads? Families are ruined and mothers lose their sons just as you did, women like my aunt Elizabeth, bereft of her son John, her next boy under suspicion. What d'you hope to achieve?"

She turns and her expression is as tender and as steadfast as ever. "I?" she says with her limpid smile. "I achieve nothing. I am just an old grandmother living in Bermondsey Abbey, glad of a chance to visit my darling daughter. I think of nothing but my soul and my next dinner. Causing no trouble at all."

WESTMINSTER PALACE, LONDON, 28 NOVEMBER 1489

The pains start in the early hours of the morning, waking me with a deep stir in my belly. My mother is with me the moment that I groan, and she holds my hands while the midwives mull some ale and set up the icon so that I can see it while I labor. It is my mother's cool hand on my head when I am sweating and exhausted, and it is her gaze, locked on mine, quietly persuading me that there is no pain, that there is nothing but a divine cool floating on a constant river, that takes me through the long hours until I hear a cry and realize that it is over and that I have a baby and they put my little girl into my arms.

"My son commands that you honor me with naming Her Grace the Princess for me." The sudden appearance of Lady Margaret jolts me back to the real world and behind her I see my mother folding linen and bowing her head and trying not to laugh.

"What?" I ask. I am still hazy with the

birthing ale and with the magic that my mother manages to weave, so that pain recedes and the time passes.

"I shall be very glad to be her name-giver." Lady Margaret pursues her own thought. "And it is so like my son to honor me. I only hope that your boy Arthur is as good and as loving a son to you, as mine is to me."

My mother, who had two royal sons who adored her, turns away and puts the linen into a chest.

"Princess Margaret of the House of Tudor," My Lady says, savoring the sound of her own name.

"Is it not vanity, to name a child after yourself?" my mother inquires, dulcet from the corner of the room.

"She is named for my saint," Lady Margaret replies, not at all disconcerted. "It is not for my own glory. And besides, it is your own daughter who chooses the name. Is it not, Elizabeth?"

"Oh yes," I say obediently, too tired to argue with her. "And the main thing is that she is well."

"And beautiful," my beautiful mother remarks.

Because so many have the pox in London, we don't hold a big christening, and I am churched privately and return to my rooms and to the life of the court without a great feast. I know also that Henry is not going to waste money on celebrating the birth of a princess. He would have had a public holiday and wine flowing in the public fountains for another boy.

"I'm not disappointed in a girl," he assures me as he meets me in the nursery and I find him with the precious baby in his arms. "We need another boy, of course, but she is the prettiest, daintiest little girl that was ever born."

I stand at his shoulder and look into her face. She is like a little rosebud, like a petal, hands like little starfish and fingernails like the tiniest shells ever washed up by a tide.

"Margaret for my mother," Henry says, kissing her white-capped little head.

My cousin Maggie steps forwards to take the baby from us. "Margaret for you," I whisper to her.

GREENWICH PALACE, LONDON, JUNE 1491

Two years pass before we conceive another child, and then at last it is the boy that my husband needed. He greets him with a sort of passion, as if this boy was a fortune. Henry is coming to have a reputation as a king who loves gold in his treasury; this boy is like a new-minted sovereign coin, another Tudor creation.

"We'll call him Henry," he declares, as the boy is put into his arms when he visits me, a week after the birth.

"Henry for you?" I ask him, smiling from the bed.

"Henry for the sainted king," he says sternly, reminding me that just when I think we are most happy and most easy, Henry is still looking over his shoulder, justifying his crown. He looks from me to my cousin Margaret as if we were responsible for the old king's imprisonment in the Tower and then his death. Margaret and I exchange one guilty look. It was probably our fathers working together with our uncle Richard who held a pillow over the poor innocent king's sleeping face. At any rate, we are close enough to the murder to feel guilt when Henry calls the old king a saint and names his newborn son for him.

"As you wish," I say lightly. "But he does look so like you. A copper-head, a proper Tudor."

He laughs at that. "A redhead, like my uncle Jasper," he says with pleasure. "Pray God gives him my uncle's luck."

He is smiling, but I can see the strain around his eyes, with the look I have come to dread, as if he is a man haunted. This is how he looks when he bursts out in sudden complaints. This is the look that I think he wore for all those years when he was in exile and he could trust no one and feared everybody, and every message that he had from home warned him of my father, and every messenger who brought it could be a murderer.

I nod to Maggie, who is as sensitive as I am to Henry's uncertain temper, and she takes the baby and gives him to his wet nurse, and then sits beside the two of them, as if she would disappear behind the woman's warm bulk.

"Is something the matter?" I ask quietly.

He glares at me for a moment, as if I have caused the problem, and then I see him soften, and shake his head. "Odd news," he says. "Bad news."

"From Flanders?" I ask quietly. It is always my aunt who causes this deep line between his brows. Year after year she goes on sending spies into England, money to rebels, speaks against Henry and our family, accuses me of disloyalty to our house.

"Not this time," he says. "Perhaps something worse than the duchess . . . if you can imagine anything worse than her."

I wait.

"Has your mother said anything to you?" he asks. "This is important, Elizabeth. You must tell me if she has said anything."

"No, nothing," I say. My conscience is clear. She did not come into confinement with me this time, she said she was unwell and feared bringing illness into the room with her. At the time I was disappointed, but now I have a clutch of apprehension that she stayed outside to weave treasonous plots. "I have not seen her. She has written nothing to me. She is ill."

"She's said nothing to your sisters?" he asks. He tips his head to where Maggie sits beside the wet nurse, petting my son's little feet as he sleeps. "*She's* said nothing? Your cousin of Warwick? Margaret? Nothing about her brother?"

"She asks me if he can be released," I remark. "And I ask it of you, of course. He is doing nothing wrong —"

"He's doing nothing wrong in the Tower because he is powerless to do anything as my prisoner," Henry says abruptly. "If he were free, God knows where he would turn up. Ireland, I suppose."

"Why Ireland?"

"Because Charles of France has put an invasion force into Ireland." He speaks in a suppressed angry mutter. "Half a dozen ships, a couple of hundred men wearing the cross of St. George as if they were an English army. He has armed and fitted out an army marching under the flag of St. George! A French army in Ireland! Why d'you think he would do that?"

I shake my head. "I don't know." I find I am whispering like him, as if we are conspirators, planning to overthrow a country, as if it is we who have no rights, who should not be here.

"D'you think he is expecting something?"

I shake my head. Truly, I am baffled. "Henry, really, I don't know. What would the King of France be expecting to come out of Ireland?"

"A new ghost?"

I feel a shiver crawl slowly down my spine like a cold wind, though it is a summer day, and I gather my shawl around my shoulders. "What ghost?"

At that single potent word, I have lowered

my voice like him, and the two of us sound as if we are calling up spirits as he leans towards me and says, "There's a boy."

"A boy?"

"Another boy. A boy who is trying to pass himself off as your dead brother."

"Edward?"

"Richard."

My old pain, at the name of the man I loved, given to the brother that I lost, taps on my heart like a familiar friend. I tighten my shawl again and find that I am hugging myself, as if for comfort.

"A boy pretending to be Richard? Who is he? Another false boy, another imposter?"

"I can't trace this one," Henry says, his eyes dark with fear. "I can't find who's backing him, I can't discover where he comes from. They say he speaks several languages, carries himself like a prince. They say he is convincing — well, Simnel was a convincing child, that's what they're trained up to be."

"They?"

"All these boys. All these ghosts."

I am silent for a moment, thinking of my husband surrounded in his mind by many boys, nameless boys, ghost boys. I close my eyes.

"You're tired, I shouldn't have troubled you with this."

"No. Not tired. Only weary at the thought of another pretender."

"Yes," he says, suddenly emphatic. "That's what he is. You are right to name him so. Another pretender. Another liar, another false boy. I shall have to hunt him down, find out who he is and where he comes from, attack his story, split his lies like kindling, disgrace his sponsors, and ruin him and them together."

I say the worst thing that I could say. "What d'you mean — that it is *I* who name him as a pretender? Who could he be if not a pretender?"

He stands at once and looks down on me, as if we were newly married and he still hated me. "Exactly. Who would he be if not a pretender? Sometimes, Elizabeth, you are so stupid that I find you quite brilliant."

He walks out of the room, pale with resentment, and Maggie glances across at me and she looks afraid.

I come out of my confinement to dazzlingly hot summer weather and find the court anxious despite the birth of a second son. Every day brings a new message from Ireland, and the worst of it is that nobody dares to speak of it. Sweating horses stand in the stable yard, men caked in dust are taken straight in to see the king, his lords sit with him to hear their report, but nobody remarks upon it. It is as if we are at war but nobody will say anything; we are under siege in silence.

To me it is clear that the King of France is taking revenge on us for our long, loyal support of Brittany against him. My uncle died to keep Brittany independent from France; Henry never forgets that he found a safe exile in the little dukedom. He is honor-bound to support his former hosts. There is every reason for us to see France as our enemy. But for some reason, though the privy council is all but a council of war, nobody speaks openly against France. They say nothing, as if they are ashamed. France has put an army into our kingdom of Ireland and yet nobody rages against them. It is as if the lords feel that it is our fault, the failure of Henry to be a convincing king, that is the real problem, and that the French invasion is just another sign of this.

"The French don't care about me," Henry says to me tersely. "France is the enemy of the King of England, whoever he may be, whatever the color of his jacket. They want Brittany for themselves, and they want to cause trouble for England. The shame that they bring on me, of two rebellions in four years, means nothing to them. If the House of York were on the throne, then it would be you that they were conspiring against."

We are standing in the stable yard, and around us is the usual buzz of conversation, the horses led out of their stalls by the grooms, the ladies lifted into the saddles, the gentlemen standing by their stirrups, passing up a glass of wine, holding a glove, talking, courting, enjoying the sunshine. We should be happy, with three children in the nursery and a loyal court around us.

"Of course, France is always our enemy," I reply comfortingly. "As you say. And we have always resisted an invasion, and we have always won. Perhaps because you were in Brittany for all that long time, you learned to fear them overmuch? For look — you have your spies and your reporters, your posts to bring you news, and your lords who are ready to arm in an instant. We must be the greater power. We have the narrow seas between them and us. Even if they are in Ireland they cannot be a serious danger to us. You can feel safe now, can't you, my lord?"

"Don't ask me, ask your mother!" he exclaims, gripped with one of his sudden furies. "You ask your mother if I can feel safe now. And tell me what she says."

PALACE OF SHEEN, RICHMOND, SEPTEMBER 1491

Henry comes to my rooms with his court before dinner and takes me to a window bay, out of the way of everyone. Cecily, my sister, newly returned to court after the birth of her second daughter, raises an eyebrow at Henry's warm embrace of me and his publicly seeking to be alone with me. I smile at her taking notice.

"I want to talk to you," he says.

I incline my head towards him and feel him draw me closer.

"We think it is time that your cousin Margaret was married."

I cannot stop myself glancing over towards her. She is hand in hand with My Lady the King's Mother, who is speaking earnestly to her. "It looks like more than a thought, it looks like a decision," I observe.

His smile is boyish, guilty. "It *is* my mother's idea," he admits. "But I think it is a good match for her, and truly — sweetheart — she has to be settled with a man we can trust.

Her name, and the presence of her brother, mean that she will always live uneasily under our rule. But we can change her name at least."

"Who have you picked out for her?" I ask. "For Henry, I warn you, I love her like a sister, I don't want her sent away to Scotland or" — I am suddenly suspicious — "bundled off to Brittany, or to France to make a treaty."

He laughs. "No, no, everyone knows that she's not a princess of York like you or your sisters. Everyone knows that her husband must keep her safe and out of the way. She can't be powerful, she can't be visible, she must be kept quietly inside our house so that no one thinks she will support another."

"And when she is married and quiet and safe, as you say — can her brother come out of the Tower then? Could he live with her and her safe husband?"

He shakes his head, taking my hand. "Truly, my love, if you knew how many men whisper about him, if you knew how many people plot for him, if you knew how our enemies send money for weapons for him — you would not ask it."

"Even now?" I whisper. "Six years after Bosworth?"

"Even now," he says. He swallows as if he can taste fear. "Sometimes I think that they will never give up."

My Lady the King's Mother comes towards

us, leading Maggie by the hand. I can see that Maggie is not unhappy, she looks flattered and pleased by the attention, and I realize that this proposed marriage might give her a husband and a home and children of her own and free her from her constant vigil for her brother, and her endless anxious attendance on me. More than that, she might be lucky enough to be given a husband who loves her, she might have lands that she can watch grow and become fertile, she might have children who — though they can never have a claim to the throne — might be happy in England as children of England.

I step towards her, and look at My Lady. "You have a proposal for my dear cousin?"

"Sir Richard Pole." She names the son of her half sister, a man so reliable and steady in my husband's cause that he might as well be his warhorse. "Sir Richard has asked me for permission to address Lady Margaret and I have said yes."

I overlook for a moment the fact that she has no right to say yes to a marriage to my cousin. I overlook that Sir Richard is nearly thirty to my cousin's eighteen years, I even overlook that Sir Richard has nothing more than a respectable name, virtually no fortune, and my cousin is an heir to the York throne of England and the Warwick fortune, because I can see Maggie is bright with excitement, her cheeks blushing, her eyes bright.

"You want to marry him?" I ask her quickly in Latin, which neither My Lady nor my husband can easily understand.

She nods.

"But why?"

"To be free of our name," she says bluntly. "To be no longer a suspect. To be one of the Tudors and not one of their enemies."

"Nobody thinks you are an enemy."

"In this court you are either Tudor or enemy," she says shrewdly. "I am sick of being under suspicion."

WESTMINSTER PALACE, LONDON, AUTUMN 1491

We celebrate their wedding as soon as we return to Westminster for the autumn, but their happiness is overshadowed by more bad news from Ireland.

"They have raised up their boy," my husband says to me briefly. We are about to ride out, down to the riverside, and see if we can put up some duck for the hawks. The sunshine is bright in the yard, the court in a bustle calling for their horses. From the doorway of the mews the falconers bring out their birds, each one hooded with a brightly colored bonnet of leather, a little plume at the top. I notice one of the spit boys peering out of the kitchen door, looking longingly at the birds. Good-naturedly, one of the falconers beckons the boy over and lets him slip his hand in a gauntlet and try the weight of the bird on his fist. The boy's smile reminds me of my brother — then I see that it is the spit boy, the little pretender, Lambert Simnel, changed and settled into his new life.

Henry whistles to his man and he comes over with a beautiful peregrine falcon, his breast like royal ermine, his back as dark as sable fur. Henry pulls on the gauntlet and takes the bird on his fist, looping the jesses around his fingers.

"They have raised up their boy," he repeats. "Another one."

I see the darkness in his face and I realize that this hawking trip, and the clatter of the court at play, and Henry's new cape, and even the caress of his falcon are all part of a pretense. He is showing to the world that he is unconcerned. He is trying to look as if everything is all right. In reality, he is, as so often, embattled and afraid.

"This time, they are calling him 'prince.' "

"Who is he?" I ask very quietly.

"This time I don't know, though I have had my men up and down every corner of England and in and out of every schoolroom. I don't think there is one missing child that I haven't identified. But this boy . . ." He breaks off.

"How old is he?"

"Eighteen," he says simply.

My brother Richard would be eighteen, if he were alive. I don't remark on it. "And who is he?"

"Who does he say he is?" he corrects me, irritably. "Why, he says he is Richard, your missing brother Richard."

"And what do people say he is?" I ask.

He sighs. "The traitorous lords, the Irish lords who would run after anything in silk . . . they say he is Prince Richard, Duke of York. And they are arming for him, and rising for him, and I shall have the whole battle of Stoke to fight all over again, with another boy at the head of another army, with French mercenaries behind him and Irish lords sworn to his service, as if ghosts never lie down but come again and again against me."

The sun is still bright and warm but I am cold with horror.

"Not again? Not another invasion?"

Someone shouts from the far side of the yard and a little cheer goes up at some joke. Henry glances over, a bright smile at once on his face, and he laughs as if he knows what the joke was, like a child will laugh, trying to join in.

"Don't!" I say suddenly. It hurts me to see him, even now, trying to play at being a carefree king before a court that he cannot trust.

"I have to smile," he says. "There is a boy in Ireland very free with his smiles. They say he is all smiles, all charm."

I think what this new threat will mean to us — to Maggie, newly married and hoping that her brother might be released to live with her and her husband, to my mother enclosed at Bermondsey Abbey. Neither my mother nor my cousin will ever be free if there is someone pretending to be our Prince Richard, mustering troops in Ireland. Henry will never trust any of us if someone from the House of York is leading a French army against him. "May I write and tell my mother of this false boy?" I ask him. "It's distressing to have Richard's name taken once again."

His eyes grow cold at the mere mention of her name. His face slowly freezes, until he looks as if nothing will ever disturb him: a king of stone, a king of ice. "You can write and tell her whatever you wish," he says. "But I think you'll find your daughterly tenderness is misplaced."

"What d'you mean?" I have a sense of dread. "Oh, Henry, don't be like this! What d'you mean?"

"She knows all about this boy already."

I can say nothing. His suspicion of my mother is one of the troubles that runs through our marriage like a poisoned stream bleaching a meadow which might otherwise grow green. "I am sure she does not."

"Are you? For I am quite sure she does. I am sure that what funds I pay her, and what gifts you have given her, are invested in the silk jacket which is on his back, and in the velvet bonnet which is on his head," he says harshly. "Pinned with a ruby pin, if you please. With three pendant pearls. On his golden curls."

For a moment I can see my brother's curls, twisted around my mother's fingers as he sits with his head in her lap. I can see him so vividly, it is as if I have conjured him, as Henry says the foolish people of Ireland have conjured this prince from death, from the unknown.

"He is a handsome boy?" I whisper.

"Like all your family," Henry says grimly. "Handsome and charming and with the trick of making people love him. I will have to find him and throw him down before he climbs up, don't you think? This boy who calls himself Richard Duke of York?"

"I can't help but wish he was alive," I say weakly. I look over at my adorable brown-headed son, jumping up to the mounting block to his pony, bright with excitement, and I remember my golden-haired little brother who was as brave and as joyous as Arthur, raised in a court filled with confidence.

"Then you do yourself and your line a disservice. I can't help but wish him dead."

I excuse myself from the day's hawking and instead I take the royal barge and go down the river to Bermondsey Abbey. Someone sees the barge coming in, and runs for my Mother to tell her that her daughter the queen is on her way, so she is on the little pier as we land, and comes to meet me, walking through the rowers, who stand at attention, their oars raised in salute, as if she still commanded them, a little nod to one side and the other, a little smile, easy in her authority. She curtseys to me at the gangplank and I kneel for her blessing and bob up.

"I have to talk with you," I say tersely.

"Of course," she says. She leads the way into the abbey's central garden, sheltered by the high warm walls, and gestures to a seat built into a corner, overhung with an old plum tree. Awkwardly I stand, but I nod that she should sit down. The autumn sun is warm; she has a light shawl around her shoulders as she sits before me, her hands clasped lightly in her lap, and listens.

"The king says that you will know all about it already; but there is a boy calling himself by the name of my brother, landed in Ireland," I say in a rush.

"I don't know *all* about it," she says.

"You know something about it?"

"I know that much."

"Is he my brother?" I ask her. "Please, Lady Mother, don't put me off with one of your lies. Please tell me. Is it my brother Richard in Ireland? Alive? Coming for his throne? For my throne?"

For a moment she looks as if she is going to prevaricate, turn the question aside with a clever word, as she always does. But she looks up at my white, strained face, and she puts out her hand to draw me down to sit beside her. "Is your husband afraid again?"

"Yes," I breathe. "Worse than before. Because he thought it was over after the battle at Stoke. He thought he had won then. Now he thinks he will never win. He is afraid, and he is afraid of being afraid. He thinks he will always be afraid."

She nods. "You know, words, once spoken, cannot be recalled. If I answer your question you will know things that you should tell your husband and his mother at once. And they will ask you these things explicitly. And once they know that you know them, they will think of you as an enemy. As they think me. Perhaps they would imprison you, as they have imprisoned me. Perhaps they would not allow you to see your children. Perhaps they are so hard-hearted that they would send you far away."

I sink to my knees before her, and I put my face in her lap, as if I were still her little girl and we were still in sanctuary and certain to fail. "Am I not to ask?" I whisper. "He is my little brother. I love him too. I miss him too. Shall I not even ask if he is alive?"

"Don't ask," she advises me.

I look up at her face, still beautiful in this afternoon golden light, and I see that she is smiling. She is a happy woman. She does not look at all like a woman who has lost two beloved sons to an enemy, and knows that she will never see either of them again.

"But you hope to see him?" I whisper.

The smile she turns to me is filled with joy. "I know I will see him," she says with absolute serene conviction.

"In Westminster?" I whisper.

"Or in heaven."

Henry comes to my rooms after dinner. He does not sit with his mother this evening, but comes directly to me and listens to the musicians play and watches the women dance, takes a hand at cards and rolls some dice. Only when the evening ends and the people make their bows and their curtseys and withdraw does he pull up his chair before the great fire in my presence chamber, snap his fingers for another chair to be placed beside him, and gesture that I shall sit with him, and that everyone but a servant, standing at the servery, shall leave us.

"I know that you went to see her," he says without preamble.

The man pours a tankard of mulled ale and puts a small glass of red wine on a table beside me, and then makes himself scarce.

"I took the royal barge," I say. "It was no secret."

"And you told her of the boy?"

"I did."

"And did she know already?"

I hesitate. "I think so. But she could have

learned it from gossip. People are starting to talk, even in London, about the boy in Ireland. I heard about it in my own rooms tonight; everyone is talking, again."

"And does she believe that this is her son, returned from the dead?"

Again I pause. "I think that she may do. But she is never clear with me."

"She is unclear because she is engaged in treason against us? And does not dare to confess?"

"She is unclear because she has a habit of discretion."

He laughs abruptly. "A lifetime of discretion. She killed the sainted King Henry in his sleep, she killed Warwick on the battlefield shrouded in a witch's mist, she killed George in the Tower of London drowned in a barrel of sweet wine, she killed Isabel his wife and Anne, the wife of Richard, with poison. She has never been accused of any of these crimes, they are still secret. She is indeed discreet, as you say. She's murderous and discreet."

"None of that is true," I say steadily, disregarding the things that I think may be true.

"Well, at any rate . . ." He stretches his boots towards the fire. "She did not tell you anything that would help us? Where the boy comes from? What are his plans?"

I shake my head.

"Elizabeth . . ." His voice is almost plaintive. "What am I to do? I can't keep fighting for England. The men who came out for me at Bosworth didn't all turn out for me at the battle of Stoke. The men who risked their lives at Stoke won't come out for me again. I can't go on fighting for my life, for our lives, year after year. There is only one of me, and there are legions of them."

"Legions of who?" I ask.

"Princes," he says, as if my mother had given birth to a monstrous dark army. "There are always more princes."

Westminster Palace, London, December 1491

As the court sets about the task of the twelve days of merrymaking for Christmas, Henry sends out a force to Ireland, in ships that sail for him from the loyal port of Bristol. They land the soldiers and bring back his spies, who ride to London and tell him that the boy is beloved of everyone who meets him. The moment that he set foot on the quayside the people caught him up and carried him round the town at shoulder height, greeting him like a hero. He has the charm of a young god, he is irresistible.

He is spending the Christmas celebrations as the guest of the Irish lords in one of their faraway castles. There will be feasting and dancing, they will toast to their victory. He will feel invincible as they drink to his health and swear that they cannot fail.

I think of a golden-haired boy with a ready smile and I pray for him, that he does not come against us, that he enjoys his fame and glory, that he decides on a quieter life and returns to wherever he came from. And as Henry escorts me back from the chapel, I take a moment while we are walking alone together to tell him that I think I am with child again.

I see the shadow lift from his face. He is glad for me, at once ordering that I must rest, that I must not think of riding out with the court, that when we move to Sheen or Greenwich I must go by barge and by litter, but I can see he is partly distracted. "What are you thinking?" I ask, hoping that he will tell me he is planning a new bedroom for me in Westminster, better rooms now, since I will be spending more time indoors.

"I am thinking that I have to make us safe on the throne," he says quietly. "I want this baby, I want all our children, to have a secure inheritance."

As my cousin Maggie dances with her new husband, denying her name and gladly answering to "Lady Pole," my husband the king slips away from the court and goes down to the stable yard for an earnest conversation with a man who rides in from Greenwich, with news from France. The French king, who was already arming Ireland against Henry, is now known to be taking an interest in the boy who wears silks in that country. The French king has said that though Henry came to the throne with an army paid by France, anyone now can see that there was a

York prince who should have had the throne all along. Most ominously, the French king is said to be gathering ships for an invasion force to bring the boy in the silk coat to his home: England.

My husband comes back from his secret meeting in the shadowy stable yard and his face is grim. I see his mother glance at him, and her quiet word to Jasper Tudor. Then they both look across the dancing court at me. Unsmiling, they both look at me.

PALACE OF SHEEN, RICHMOND, FEBRUARY 1492

We move to Sheen to see in the spring, but the season is a long time coming and the wind seems to howl up the Thames valley, bringing wintry rain and sometimes hard chips of hail. The snowdrops are out in the garden but they get beaten down into the frozen earth, their little white faces mud-splashed. I order big fires to be built in my rooms and I wear my new Christmas gown of red velvet. My Lady the King's Mother comes in to sit with me and looks at the fire, piled high with logs, and says, "I wonder you can afford such wood in your rooms," as if it is not she who sets the allowance that the king pays me, as if she does not know that I am paid far less than my mother was given when she was Queen of England, as if everyone does not know that I cannot afford great fires in my rooms but will have to scrimp and save for this luxury when the summer weather comes.

I'm too proud to complain. I say, "You are

welcome to come and warm yourself in here whenever you like, My Lady," and I smile inwardly at turning her complaint of my extravagance into my generosity. And I don't stoop to say anything about her years in the coldness of Wales, when she was far from my father's extravagant court, far from our lovely rooms, and never warmed by a good fire.

She looks at the blaze and then at my robe. "I am surprised Henry does not order that you ride out," she says. "It cannot be healthy cooped up indoors. Henry rides out every day and I always walk, whatever the weather."

I turn to where the rain is running in gray drops down the thick panes of the window. "On the contrary, he wants me to rest," I say.

At once her look sharpens, and her gaze goes to my belly. "Are you with child?" she whispers.

I smile and nod.

"He didn't tell me."

"I asked him not to, until I was sure," I say.

Clearly, she expects him to tell her everything, whether I want to share the news or not.

"Well, you shall have all the firewood you need," she says with a sudden burst of generosity. "And I shall send you logs from my own woods. You shall have applewood from my orchards, the scent is so pleasant." She smiles. "Nothing is too good for the mother of my next grandson."

Or granddaughter, I think, but I don't say the words out loud.

My cousin Maggie is with child too, and we compare our widening bellies and claim to have extraordinary fancies for foods, tormenting the cooks by saying that we want coal with marchpane, and mutton and jam.

And then we have news that makes the king happy too. The ship that carried the boy to Cork is captured, returning empty, by one of Henry's fleet that has been cruising constantly off Ireland. The master of the ship, the silk merchant, is questioned, and though he swears that he has no idea where the boy is now, they make him confess to everything else.

Henry comes to my room carrying a mug of mulled ale and a spiced tisane for me. "My Lady Mother said you should have this," he says, smelling at it. "I don't know if you will like it."

"I can assure you that I will not," I say lazily from the bed. "She gave it to me yesterday evening and it tasted so vile that I poured it out of the window. Not even Margaret would drink it and she is as humble as your mother's serf."

Cheerfully, he opens the latch on the window. *"Gardez l'eau!"* he shouts cheerfully, and tips the tisane out into the wet night.

"You seem happy," I say. I slide off the bed and come to sit with him at the fireside.

411

He grins. "I have a plan, which I want to share with you. I want to send Arthur to Wales, to have his own court at Ludlow Castle."

At once I hesitate. "Oh, Henry! He's so young."

"No, he's not. He's six this year. He is Prince of Wales. He must rule his principality."

I hesitate. My brother Edward went to Wales to serve as its prince, and was captured on the road as he came home for his father's funeral. I can't help but dread the thought of Arthur going there too, of the road running east from Wales through Stony Stratford, the village where they took our uncle Anthony and we never saw him again.

"He'll be safe," my husband promises. "He'll be safe in Wales. He'll have his own court and his own guard. And — even better than this — he'll be safe from any pretender. I have made a little progress in this difficult matter with the capture of the silk merchant. But a little progress is better than none at all."

"You have made progress with the silk merchant?"

"The silk merchant is proving most helpful. My advisor has seen him, and spoken with him. He has reasoned with him, and the man has changed his mind, his side, and his loyalty."

I nod. This means that Henry's spy has beaten, coerced, and bribed the silk merchant to say all that he knows about the boy, and now will pay him to spy for us, and the boy — whoever he is — will be betrayed. He has lost a friend and probably does not even know it. "Does he say who the boy is?"

"Nobody can say who he is. He says the name that the boy likes to use."

"He calls himself my brother Richard?"

"Yes."

"And did the silk merchant see any proofs?"

"Merchant Meno met the boy at the Portuguese court, where he was widely known as your brother, popular among all the lads, beautifully dressed, well educated. He told everyone he had escaped, as by a miracle, from the Tower."

"Did he say how?" I ask. If my husband learns that it was my mother and me who put a little page boy into the Tower in place of my brother, then she will face a charge of treason and execution and my life will be ruined for he will never trust me again.

"He never says how," my husband replies irritably. "He says that he promised not to say, until he is restored to his throne. Imagine that! Imagine a boy with the nerve to say such a thing!"

I nod. I can imagine a boy like this only too well. He used to always win at hide-and-seek because he had the patience and the cunning to hide longer than anyone else. He would wait until we were called for dinner before he came out laughing. And he loved his mother and would never put her at risk, not even to prove his claim.

"Pregent Meno now says that the boy wanted to see the world and it so happened that they sailed to Ireland. If you believed him you would think that the boy invented himself, all alone, with no backers and no money and no support. If you believed him you would have to think that Ireland, a country filled with savages wearing little more than animal skins, was an excellent market for silk, and that any clever silk merchant was likely to go there, and most likely to show his wares by dressing his page boy up like a prince."

"But really?"

"Really, the boy must have backers and money and support. Really there must have been a plan, for Pregent Meno chose to sail with him to Ireland — of all places — and he was greeted as a hero on the quayside and borne aloft by half a dozen of the most faithless Irish lords who all happened to be there, waiting on the quay at the same time, and now lives like a king in one of their castles, guarded by an army of Frenchmen who just happen to be there too."

"And shall you capture him?"

"I have sent Meno back to him with gold

in a chest and his mouth full of lies. He will promise friendship, take him on his ship again, guarantee him a safe voyage to his friends in France; but he will bring the boy straight to me."

I keep my face very still. I can hear the beating of my own heart. It is so loud that I think my husband will hear it in our quiet room, over the gentle flickering of the fire. "And what will you do with him then, Henry?"

He puts his hand over mine. "I am sorry, Elizabeth; but whoever he really is, whoever he says he is, I cannot have him wandering around using your name. I'll have him hanged for treason."

"Hanged?"

Grimly, he nods.

"What if he's not an English boy?" I ask. "What if you can't accuse him of treason, because he's something else: Portuguese perhaps or Spanish?"

Henry shrugs, looking at the flames. "Then I'll have him secretly killed," he says flatly. "Just as your father tried to kill me. It's the only way with pretenders to the throne. And the boy knows this as well as I do. And you know it too. So don't look so innocent and so shocked. Don't lie."

BERMONDSEY ABBEY, LONDON, SUMMER 1492

Henry goes on progress to the West Country, and finds himself riding into the little town of Abingdon just as the townsmen are up in arms challenging his rule. To everyone's surprise he is merciful. Generously he halts the trial of the townsmen, graciously he orders their release. To me he writes:

> Faithless and disloyal — but there was nothing I could do but forgive them in the hope that others see me as a kind king, and that they turn away from the treasonous counsels of the Abbot Sant, who — I would swear — inspired all this. I have had every blade of grass he owns off him, and every penny from his treasure box. I have made him a miserable pauper without bringing him to trial. I don't see what else I can do to hurt him.

While Henry is away I go to visit my mother. I ask the prior of Bermondsey Abbey if I might come to stay. I suggest that I need a retreat to consult the health of my soul, and he advises me to bring my chaplain with me on a visit also. I write to my mother to tell her I am coming, and I get a brief, warm note in reply, welcoming my visit and urging me to bring my little sisters with me. I'm not going to take them as she asks. I need to speak to my mother alone.

The first night we dine together in the hall of the abbey and listen to the reading of the sacred text. As it happens, it is that of Ruth and Naomi, a story of a daughter who loves her mother so much that she chooses to be with her rather than making her own life in her own land. I think about loyalty to one's family and love for one's mother as I pray that night and go to bed. Maggie, who has come with me, my most faithful and loving companion, prays beside me and climbs heavily into the other side of the broad bed.

"I hope you sleep," I say warmingly. "For I can't stop my mind whirling."

"Sleep," she says comfortably. "I shall wake twice to use the pot anyway. Every time I lie down the baby turns over and kicks in my belly, and I have to get up to piss. Besides, in the morning you will have your questions answered or . . ."

"Or what?"

She giggles. "Or your mother will be as unhelpful as she always is," she says. "Truly, she's a queen, the greatest queen that England ever had. Whoever stepped up so high? Whoever has been braver? There has never been a more intractable Queen of England than her."

"It's true," I say. "Let's both try and sleep."

Margaret is breathing deeply within moments, but I lie beside her and listen to her peaceful sleep. I watch the slats of the shutters gradually lighten with the autumn dawn, then I rise and wait for the bell for Prime. Today, I will ask my mother what she knows. Today I will not be satisfied with anything less than the truth.

"I know nothing for sure," she says to me quietly. We are seated on the benches at the back of the chapel of Bermondsey Abbey. She has walked with me beside the river, we have attended Prime together and prayed side by side, our penitent heads on our hands. Now she sinks down and puts her hand to her heart.

"I'm weary," she says to explain her pallor.

"You're not ill?" I ask, suddenly fearful.

"Something . . ." she volunteers. "Something that catches my breath and makes my heart race so that I can hear it pounding. Ah, Elizabeth, don't look like that. I am old, my dear, and I have lost all my brothers and four of my sisters. The man I married for passion is dead and the crown I wore is on your head. My work is done. I don't mind sleeping every afternoon, and when I lie down I compose myself in case I don't wake up again. I close my eyes and I am content."

"But you're not ill," I insist. "Shouldn't you see a physician?"

"No, no," she says, patting my hand. "I'm not ill. But I am a woman of fifty-five. I'm not a girl anymore."

Fifty-five is a great age; but my mother does not seem old to me. And I am very far from being ready for her death. "Won't you see a physician?"

She shakes her head. "He could tell me nothing that I don't already know, my dear."

I pause, realizing that I can do nothing against her stubbornness. "What do you know?"

"I know I am ready."

"*I'm* not ready!" I exclaim.

She nods. "You are where I wanted you to be. Your children, my grandsons, are where I hoped that they would be. I am content. Now — never mind my death, which is bound to happen one day whether we like it or not — why have you come to see me?"

"I want to talk to you," I start.

"I know you do," she says gently, and takes my hand.

"It's about Ireland."

"I guessed as much."

I put my hand on hers. "Mother, do you know why the French have a small army in

419

Ireland, and why they are sending more ships?"

She meets my troubled eyes with her straight gray gaze. A nod tells me that she knows all that is happening.

"Are they going to invade England?"

She shrugs. "You don't need me to tell you that a commander who has mustered ships and an army is planning an invasion."

"But when?"

"When they think that the time is right."

"Do they have a leader from the House of York?"

Her joy blooms in a smile that warms her whole face. She looks so filled with happiness that despite myself, I find I am smiling back at her radiance. "Ah, Elizabeth," she whispers. "You know I have always thought it better that you should know nothing."

"Mother, I have to know. Tell me what makes you look so happy."

She looks like a girl again, she is so rosy and joyful, and her eyes are so bright. "I know that I did not send my son to his death," she says. "In the end, that's all I care about. That, loving my husband more than the world itself, I did not fail him in that one great act. I did not foolishly betray both his sons to his enemy. I didn't trust like a fool when I should have been careful. My greatest joy as I face the last of my days is that I did not fail my sons, my husband, or my house.

"I couldn't save Edward, my beloved son, the Prince of Wales, as I should have done. I told them to come quickly, and I warned them to come armed; but they weren't prepared to fight. I couldn't save Edward, as I should have done. It's weighed on my heart that I did not warn him to come to me without stopping for anything. But, thank God, I could save Richard. And I did save Richard."

I give a little gasp and my hand goes to my belly, as if to hold the unborn Tudor safe. "He's alive?"

She nods. That's all she will do. She won't even trust me with a word.

"He's in Ireland? And sailing from there, to England?"

Now she shrugs, as if she knows she did not send him to his death but what he did after, and where he is now, she will not say.

"But Mother, what shall I do?"

She looks at me steadily, waiting for more.

"Mother, think of me for a moment! What should I do if my brother is alive and he comes at the head of an army, to fight my husband for the throne? The throne that should go to my son? What should I do? When my brother comes to my door with his sword in his hand? Am I Tudor or York?"

Gently, she takes both my hands in hers. "Dearest, don't distress yourself. It's bad for you and for the baby."

"But what am I to do?"

She smiles. "You know you can do nothing. What will be, will be. If there is a battle" — I gasp but her smile is steady — "if there is a battle, then either your husband will win, and your son will take the throne; or your brother will win and you will be sister to the king."

"My brother, the king," I say flatly.

"Better that you and I never speak such words," she says. "But I am glad to have seen the day that you could tell me that England is waiting for the boy that I sent out into the darkness — not knowing what might become of him, not even knowing if the little boat would go safely downriver. My heart has ached for him, Elizabeth, and I have spent many, many nights on my knees for him, hoping for his safety, knowing nothing for sure. I pray that your boy never leaves you and you never have to watch him go, not knowing if he will come back again." She sees my anxious face and her beautiful smile gleams out at me. "Ah, Elizabeth! Here you are, well and happy, two boys in your nursery and a new baby in your belly, and you tell me that my son is coming home — how can I be anything but filled with joy?"

"If this boy is your son," I remind her.

"Of course."

GREENWICH PALACE, LONDON, JUNE 1492

Maggie goes into her confinement and gives birth to a baby boy. Tactfully, they call him Henry in tribute to her husband's beloved king. I visit her and hold her adorable little boy before I have to prepare for my own withdrawal from court.

Henry arrives home just before I enter my confinement, and presides over the great dinner that celebrates my departure from court for the long six weeks before the birth and then the month before I am churched and can come back.

"May I send for my mother?" I ask him as we walk together towards the confinement chamber.

"You can ask her," he concedes. "But she's not well."

"The abbot wrote to you? And not to me? Why did he not write at once to me?"

His quick grimace tells me that he has learned this not in a letter but as a secret from his spy network. "Oh," I say, realizing.

"You are watching her? Even now?"

"I have every reason to think that she is at the very center of the plotting of the Irish and the French," he says quietly. "And it won't be the first time she's called the doctor just to send a secret message."

"And the boy?" I ask.

Henry makes a small grimace; I can see him swallow down his apprehension. "Slipped away. Again. He didn't trust Pregent Meno, his former friend; he didn't take the bait I sent him. He's gone somewhere. I don't even know where. Probably France. He's somewhere out there." He shakes his head. "Don't be afraid. I'll find him. And I won't talk of this with you when you are about to go into confinement. Go in with a quiet heart, Elizabeth, and give me a handsome son. Nothing keeps the boy more firmly from our door than our own princes. You can send for your mother if you wish, and she can stay with you till after the birth."

"Thank you," I say. He takes my hand and kisses it, then, with the whole court watching, he kisses me gently on the mouth. "I love you," he says quietly into my ear. I can feel his warm breath on my cheek. "I wish for both of us that we could be at peace."

For a moment I almost hesitate, wanting to tell him what I know, wanting to warn him that my mother is radiant with hope, certain that she will see her son again. For a moment

I want to confess to him that I sent a page boy into the Tower in place of my brother, that among the princes who rise against him, the legion of princes, there may be one who is a true prince — the little boy who set out from sanctuary in a cloak too big for him, who had to sail away from his mother in a little boat on the dark water, who will come back to England and take the throne from our son if he can, whose claims we will have to face together someday.

Almost I speak; but then I see the pale guarded face of his mother among the smiling court, and I think that I dare not tell this suspicious family that the thing they fear most in the world is indeed true, and that I played a part in it.

"God bless you," he says, and whispers again: "I love you."

"And I you," I say, surprising myself. And I turn and go into the shadowy room.

I write to my mother that evening and I receive a brief reply to say that she will come when she is well, but that just now the pain in her heart is a little worse and she is too weary to travel. She asks if Bridget can join her in the convent, and I send my little sister at once, telling her to bring my mother to court as soon as she is well enough. I pass my days in the shaded rooms of my confinement apartment, sewing and reading and listening to calming music from the lutenists who are kept on the other side of the screen, for the benefit of my modesty and of theirs. I am bored in the darkened rooms and it is hot and stuffy. I sleep lightly at night and doze during the day so that I think I am dreaming, floating between wakefulness and sleep, when one night I am awakened by a clear sweet sound, like a flute, or like a chorister singing one note very softly outside my window.

I slip from my bed and lift the tapestry to look out, almost expecting to see carolers outside my window, the sound is so pure, echoing against the stone walls; but all there is to see is a waning moon, curved like a horseshoe floating in a sea of stormy dark-headed clouds which blow past it and over it, though the thick heads of the trees are still and there is no wind. The river gleams like silver in the moonlight, and still I hear the sweet clear noise like plainsong, soaring into the vault of the sky like a choir in a church.

For a moment only I am bewildered, then I recognize the sound, I remember the song. This is the noise that we heard when we were in sanctuary and my brothers disappeared from the Tower. My mother told me then that this is the song the women of our family hear when there is to be a death of one they love very dearly, one of the family. It is the banshee calling her child home, it is the goddess Melusina, the founder of our family, singing a lament for one of her children. As soon as I hear it, as soon as I understand it, I know that my mother, my beloved, beautiful, mischievous mother, is dead. And only she knew, when she told me that she was certain that she would see Richard, whether she meant she would see him on earth or whether she was certain they would meet in heaven.

Henry breaks his own mother's rules about the confinement of the queen, and comes himself to the screen in my chamber to tell me of her death. He is inarticulate, struggling with his duty to tell me and his fear of causing me grief. His face is fixed, expressionless, he is so anxious that I shall see no trace of the huge relief that he feels that such a dangerous opponent is out of his way. Of course, it is only natural for him to rejoice that if a new pretender emerges from the darkness of the past, at least my mother is not here to recognize him. But for me this is nothing but loss.

"I know," I say as Henry stumbles on false words of regret, and I put my finger through the grille to touch his fist as he grips on the metal. "You need not be distressed, Henry. You don't have to tell me. I knew last night that she had died."

"How? Nobody came from the abbey till my servant this morning."

"I just knew it," I say. There is no point telling Henry or his mother about something that would frighten them, seeming like witchcraft. "You know how your mother hears God speak to her in prayer? I had something like that, and I knew."

"A godly vision?" he confirms.

"Yes," I lie.

"I am so sorry for your loss, Elizabeth, I truly am. I know how much you loved her."

"Thank you," I say quietly, and then I leave him at the grille and go into the confinement chamber and sit down. I know that he will be thinking her death makes him safer; he cannot help but be glad that she has died. Even as he puts on mourning his heart will be singing with relief. Alive, my mother was a figurehead for the York rebels, and any endorsement from her of a pretend boy would make him as good as a real prince. Her recognition of any pretender as her son would invalidate Henry's claim to the throne. She could always have destroyed his claim with one word. He could never be sure that she would not say that word. Her death is the best thing that could have happened for Henry and his hard-hearted mother.

But not for me.

As I wait in the quiet confinement room for my baby to come, I cannot imagine what my life will be without her. I understand that her death is the best thing that could have happened for Henry.

But not for me.

I have to give birth without her, knowing that she is not even in this world thinking of me. I try to comfort myself with the knowledge that wherever she is, she will be thinking of me; I try to comfort myself with the memory of the other births when she was with me, when she held my hands and whispered to me so soothingly that it was almost as if the pains floated away on her words; but I am aware all the time that my mother has gone and these pains, and all the other trials of my life, even the triumphs, will come to me without her, and I shall have to bear them without her to comfort me.

And when the baby is born, after long hours of hard struggle, it grieves me all over again that my mother will never see her. She is such a beautiful baby, with dark, dark blue eyes and beautifully fair hair. But she will never be held by my mother, or rocked by her. She will never hear my mother sing. When they take her away to be washed and swaddled, I feel terribly bereft.

They hold my mother's funeral without me, while I am still confined, and read her will. They bury her, as she asked, beside the man she adored, her husband King Edward IV. She leaves nothing — my husband Henry paid her so small a pension, and she paid it out so readily, that she died as a poor woman, asking me and my half brother Thomas Grey to settle her debts and to pay for Masses to be said for her soul. She had none of the fortune that my father heaped on her, no treasures of England, not even personal jewels. The people who called her acquisitive, and said that she amassed a fortune with her wiles, should have seen her modest room and her empty wardrobe chests. When they brought her little box of papers and books to my confinement rooms I could not help but smile. Everything she had owned as Queen of England had been sold to finance the rebellions, first against Richard, and then against Henry. The empty jewelry box tells its own story of an unremitting battle to restore the House of York, and I am very sure that the missing boy is indeed wearing a silk shirt that was bought by my mother, and the pearls on the gold brooch in his hat are her gift too.

Lady Margaret, the King's Mother, comes in state to visit her new grandchild and finds her in my lap, rosy from washing, warm in a towel, unswaddled and beautifully naked.

"She looks well," she says, her pride in another Tudor baby overcoming her belief that the child should be strapped down on her board to ensure that her legs and arms grow straight.

"She is a beauty," I say. "A real beauty."

The baby looks at me with the unswerving questioning gaze of the newborn, as if she is trying to learn the nature of the world, and what it will be like for her. "I think she is the most beautiful baby we have ever had."

It is true, her hair is silver gilt, a white gold like my mother's, and her eyes are a dark blue, almost indigo, like a deep sea. "Look at her coloring!"

"That'll change," Lady Margaret says.

"Perhaps she'll be copper-brown like her father. She'll be exquisite," I say.

"For a name, I thought we would call her —"

"Elizabeth," I say, interrupting rudely.

"No, I had thought —"

"She's going to be Elizabeth," I say again.

My Lady the King's Mother hesitates at my determination. "For St. Elizabeth?" she confirms. "It's an odd choice for a second girl but —"

"For my mother," I say. "She would have come to me if she could, she would have blessed this baby as she blessed all the others. I had a hard confinement without her here and I expect to miss her for the rest of my life. This baby came into the world just as my mother left it, and so I am naming her for my mother. And I can tell you this — I am absolutely sure that a Tudor Elizabeth is going to be one of the greatest monarchs that

England has ever seen."

She smiles at my certainty. "Princess Elizabeth? A girl as a great monarch?"

"I know it," I say flatly. "A copper-headed girl is going to be the greatest Tudor we ever make: our Elizabeth."

GREENWICH PALACE, LONDON, SUMMER 1492

I come out of confinement to find that the court is filled with news of the boy who wears my mother's silk shirts. The boy has written a beautiful letter to all the crowned heads of Christendom, explaining that he is my brother Richard, rescued from the Tower and kept in hiding for many years.

> I myself, at the age of about nine, was also delivered up to a certain lord to be killed. It pleased divine clemency that this lord, pitying my innocence, should preserve me alive and unharmed. However, he forced me first to swear upon the sacred body of Our Lord that I would not reveal name, lineage, or family to anyone at all until a certain number of years. Then he sent me abroad.

"What d'you think?" Henry says grimly, dropping this smooth account into my lap as I sit in the nursery, admiring the new baby, who is feeding greedily from the sleepy wet nurse, one little hand patting the plump blue-veined breast, one little foot waving with pleasure.

I read the letter. "Did he write this to you?" I put my hand on the cradle, as if I would protect her. "He didn't write to me?"

"He didn't write this to me. But God knows, he's written to everyone but us."

I can feel my heart thud. "He hasn't written to us?"

"No," Henry says, suddenly eager. "That counts against him, doesn't it? He should have written to you? To your mother? Wouldn't a lost son, wanting to come home, have written to his mother?"

I shake my head. "I don't know."

Carefully neither of us remark that this boy almost certainly wrote to her, and she certainly replied.

"Will anyone have told him that his —" I break off "— that my mother is dead?"

"For sure," Henry says grimly. "I don't doubt he has many faithful correspondents from our court."

"Many?"

He nods. I cannot tell if he is speaking from his darkest fears or from terrible knowledge of traitors who live with us and daily curtsey or bow and yet secretly write to the boy. In any case, the boy should know that my mother is dead, and I am glad that someone has told him.

"No, this is his letter to the Spanish king and queen, Ferdinand and Isabella," Henry goes on. "My men picked it up on the way to them and copied it and sent it on."

"You didn't destroy it? To prevent them seeing it?"

He grimaces. "He has sent out so many letters that destroying just one would make no difference. He tells a sad tale. He spins a good yarn. People seem to believe it."

"People?"

"Charles VIII of France. He's a boy himself, and all but a madman. But he believes this shadow, this ghost. He's taken the boy in."

"In where?"

"Into his court, into France, into his protection." Henry bites off his answer and looks angrily at me. I gesture to the wet nurse, commanding her to take the baby from the room, as I don't want our little Princess Elizabeth to hear of danger, I don't want her to hear the fear in our voices when she should be feeding peacefully.

"I thought you had ships off Ireland to prevent him leaving?"

"I had Pregent Meno offer him a safe voyage. I had ships off Ireland to capture him if he took another vessel. But he saw through the trap of Pregent Meno, and the French sent ships of their own and they smuggled him out."

"To where?"

"Honfleur — does it make any difference?"

"No," I say. But it makes a difference to my imagining. It is as if I can see the dark sea, dark as my Elizabeth's eyes, the swirling mist, the failing light, and the little boats slipping into an unknown Irish port and then the boy — the handsome young boy in his fine clothes — stepping lightly on the gangplank, turning his face into the wind, heading for France with his hopes high. In my imagining, I see his golden hair lift off his young forehead and I see his bright smile: my mother's indomitable smile.

GREENWICH PALACE, LONDON, SUMMER–AUTUMN 1492

England is arming for war. The men are mustering at Greenwich in the fields around the palace, all of the lords are calling up their men, finding pikes and axes, clothing them in the livery of their house. Every day brings ships from the weapon-masters of London with loads of pikes, lances, and spears. When the wind blows from the west I can smell the hot arid scent of the forges at work, hammering blades, casting cannonballs. Ships laden with the carcasses of slaughtered beasts come downstream from Smithfield market, to be packed into salt or smoked, and the brewery at the palace and every alehouse within a radius of twenty miles is hard at work every day, and the warm powdery scent of yeast is heavy in the evening air.

Brittany — the little independent dukedom that housed and hid Henry during his years when he was a penniless pretender to the throne — is at war with its mighty neighbor of France and has called on Henry for help. I cannot help but smile to see my husband in this quandary. He wants to be a great warrior king as my father was — but he has a great disinclination to go to war. He owes a debt of honor to Brittany — but war is the most costly undertaking and he cannot bear to waste money. He would be glad to defeat France in a battle — but Henry would hate to lose such a battle, and he cannot tolerate risk. I do not blame him for his caution. I saw our family destroyed by the outcome of a battle, I have seen England at war for most of my childhood. Henry is wise to be cautious; he knows that there is no glory on the battle-field.

Even as he is arming and planning the invasion of France he is puzzling how to avoid it, but at the end of the summer he makes up his mind that it has to be done, and in September we leave the palace in a great procession, Henry in his armor on his great warhorse, the circlet of England fixed on his helmet as if it has never been anywhere else. It is the crown that Sir William Stanley wrenched from Richard's helmet, when he dragged it from his battered head. I look at it now, and I fear for Henry, going to war wearing this unlucky crown.

We leave the younger children with their nurses and teachers in Greenwich, but Arthur, who is nearly six years old, is allowed to ride out with us on his pony and watch his father set off for war. I leave the new baby, little Elizabeth, reluctantly. She is not thriving, not on the wet nurse's milk nor on the sops of bread dipped in the juice of meat that the doctors say will strengthen her. She does not smile when she sees me, as I am sure Arthur did at her age, she does not kick and rage as Henry did. She is quiet, too quiet I think, and I don't want to leave her.

I say none of these thoughts to Henry and he will not speak of fear. Instead, we go as if we are traveling on a wonderful progress through the county of Kent where the apples are thick in the orchards and the oasthouses are free with ale. We travel with musicians who play for us when we stop to dine in exquisite embroidered tents set up beside rivers, on beautiful hillsides or deep in the greenwood. Behind us comes an enormous cavalry — sixteen hundred horses and knights, and after them come the footsoldiers, twenty-five thousand of them, and all of them well shod and sworn to Henry's service.

It reminds me of when my father was King of England and he would lead the court on a great progress around the grand houses and priories. For this short time we look like my parents' heirs: we are young and blessed with good luck and wealth. In the eyes of everyone we are as beautiful as angels, dressed in cloth of gold, riding behind waving standards. Beside us is the flower of England; all the greatest men are Henry's commanders, and their wives and daughters are in my train. Behind them is a great army, mustered for Henry against an enemy they all hate. The summer weather smiles on us, the long sunny days invite us to ride out early and rest in the midday heat beside the glorious rivers or in the shade of the greenwood. We look like the king and queen that we should be, the center of beauty and power in this beautiful and powerful land.

I see Henry's head rise up with dawning pride as he leads this mighty army through the heart of England; I see him start to ride like a king going to war. When we go through the little towns on the way and people call out for him, he lifts his gauntleted hand and waves, smiling back in greeting. At last he has found his pride in himself, at last he has found his confidence. With a greater army behind him than this part of England has ever seen, he smiles like a king who is firm on his throne, and I ride beside him and feel that I am where I should be: the beloved queen of a powerful king, a woman as richly blessed as my own lucky mother.

At night he comes to my room in an abbey or in a great house on the way, and he wraps his arms around me as if he is sure of his welcome. For the first time in our marriage I turn my head towards him, not away, and when he kisses me I put my arms on his broad shoulders and hold him close, offering him my mouth, my kiss. Gently, he puts me down on the bed and I don't turn my face to the wall but I wrap my arms around him, my legs around him, and when he enters me, I ripple with the sensation of pleasure and welcome his touch for the first time in our marriage. In Sandwich Castle, for the first time ever, he comes naked to me and I move with him, consenting, and then inviting, and then finally begging him for more and he feels me melt beneath him as I hold him and cry out in pleasure.

We make love all night, as if we were newly married and newly discovering the beauty of each other's body. He holds me as if he will never leave me, and in the morning he carries me over to the window, wrapped in a fur, and kisses my neck, my shoulders, and finally my smiling lips, as we watch the Venetian galleys slicing their oars through the harbor water as they come in, to take his troops to France.

"Not so soon, not today! I can't bear to let you go," I whisper.

"That you should love me like this now!" he exclaims. "I have been waiting for this ever since I first met you. I have dreamed that you might want me, I have come to your bed night after night longing for your smile, hoping that there would come a night when you would not turn away."

"I'll never turn away again," I swear.

The joy in his face is unmistakable, he looks like a man in love for the first time.

"Come back safely to me, you must come back safe," I whisper urgently.

"Promise me that you won't change. Promise me that I will come back and find you like this? Loving like this?"

I laugh. "Shall we swear an oath? You shall swear to come home safe, and I will promise that you will find me loving?"

"Yes," he says. "I so swear," and he puts one hand on his heart and the other in mine, and though I am laughing at the two of us, flushed from bed, handclasped, swearing to be true to each other like new lovers, I hold his hand and I promise to welcome him home as warmly as now when I see him set out.

"Because you love me at last," he says, wrapping me in his arms, his lips to my hair.

"Because I love you at last," I confirm. "I did not think that I ever would, I did not think that I ever could. But I do."

"And you are glad of it," he presses.

I smile and let him draw me back to the bed though the bugles outside are calling. "And I am glad of it," I say.

Henry appoints our son Arthur as Regent of England in his father's absence: a solemn ceremony on the deck of his ship the *Swan*. Arthur is only six years old, but he will not hold my hand, he stands alone, as a prince must, while his father reads out the Latin proclamation of regency, and the lords all around him go down on one knee and swear that they will accept Arthur's rule until Henry comes home safe again.

Arthur's little face is grave, his hazel eyes serious. He is bareheaded, his brown hair with just a glint of copper lifting a little from his face in the breeze from the sea. He replies to his father in perfect Latin; he has learned the speech from his schoolmaster, and practiced it every day with me, and there are no mistakes. I can see that the lords are impressed with him, with his learning and with the set of his shoulders and the proud stance. He has been raised to be Prince of Wales and one day King of England, and he will be a good prince and a compelling king.

Behind him I see Henry's uncle Jasper, filled with pride, seeing his own long-lost brother in this boy's chestnut hair and grave face. Beside him is My Lady the King's Mother, the linen of her wimple flapping slightly in the wind, her eyes fixed on her son's face, not even looking at her grandson Arthur. For her, Henry going to war with France is as terrifying as if she were going defenseless into battle herself. She will be in an agony of anxiety until he comes home again.

She and I stand side by side on the harbor

wall, demonstrating the unity of the houses of Lancaster and York as the sailors loose the ropes on the quayside and the barges either side of the great ship take the strain, and then we hear the roll of the drum and the rowers lean into the work and the barges and the ship move slowly away from the quay. Henry holds out his hand in a salute, taking care to look determined and kingly as the ship slides from the quayside out into the water of the harbor, and then into the channel, where we can hear the waves slap against the sides, and the sails ripple as they are unfurled and fill with wind. The Venetian galleys, heavily loaded with his men, follow behind, their oars cleaving swiftly through the water.

"He's going like a hero," My Lady says passionately. "To defend Brittany and all of Christendom against the greed and wickedness of France."

I nod as Arthur's little hand creeps into mine, and I smile down into his grave face. "He will come home, won't he?" he whispers.

"Oh yes," I say. "See what a great army he has to lead? They're certain to win."

"He'll be in terrible danger," My Lady corrects me at once. "He will be at the forefront, I know it, and France is strong and a dangerous enemy."

I don't say that if that is the case it will be the first battle of his life where he has been anywhere near the front of the fighting, but I squeeze Arthur's hand and say, "There's no need for you to worry, anyway."

There is no need for any of us to worry. Not me, not Maggie, whose husband rides with Henry, not Cecily, whose husband goes too; before they even land in France they are greeted by an envoy to negotiate a peace, and though Henry marches to Boulogne and sets a siege against the mighty walls, he never really expects to recapture the city for England, nor any of the old English lands in France. It was more of a gesture of chivalry towards his old ally of Brittany, and of warning to the King of France, than the first step of an invasion; but it frightens the French into a serious treaty and a promise of lasting peace.

GREENWICH PALACE, LONDON, WINTER 1492

Henry comes home to a triumph of his own ordering. He is welcomed as a hero into London and then sails down to Greenwich as a victor. There are many who think that he should have fought at least one pitched battle, since he went all that way with such a mighty army. The common soldiers were spoiling for a fight and wanted the profits of a victorious campaign. The lords were dreaming of regaining their lost lands in France. There are many to say that nothing was achieved but a handsome payment from France into the king's growing treasury — a fortune for the king but nothing at all for the people of England.

I expect him to be angered by charges of cowardice or money-grubbing. But the man who comes home to me at Greenwich is suddenly careless about his reputation. He has won what he wanted, and it is not the safety of Brittany. He does not seem to care that he did not save Brittany from the French; surprisingly, he does not even care about the cost of taking out the army and bringing them home again. He is filled with a secret joy that I cannot understand.

The royal barge comes alongside the pier that stretches out into the green waters of the river, as smartly as ever. The rowers ship their oars and raise them high in salute. There is a roll of the drum on the barge and a shout from the trumpets on land. Henry nods to the commander of the vessel and steps onshore. He smiles at the salutes from his court, puts a fatherly hand in blessing on Arthur's little head, and kisses me on both cheeks and then on the lips. I can taste his triumph in his wine-sweet mouth.

"I have the boy," he says in my ear. He is almost laughing with glee. "That's what I wanted. That's what I've achieved, that's all that matters. I have the boy."

I feel my smile of welcome dying on my face. Henry looks exultant, like a man who has won a great battle. But he did not fight a great battle, he fought nothing at all. He waves at the crowds who have gathered to see him, at the bobbing boats on the water, the cheering boatmen and waving fishermen. He takes my hand in his arm and we walk together down the pier and along the path through the garden, where his mother waits to greet him. He even walks with a new swagger, like a commander returned in triumph.

"The boy!" he repeats.

I look at our own boys, Arthur walking solemnly ahead in black velvet and Harry, just starting to toddle with his nursemaid holding his hand and veering around the path as he goes to left or right or stops abruptly for a leaf or a piece of gravel. If he takes too long she will scoop him up; the king wants to walk unimpeded. The king must stride along, his two boys going ahead of him to show that he has an heir, two heirs, and his house is established.

"Elizabeth is not very well," I tell him. "She lies too quietly, and she does not kick or cry."

"She will," he says. "She'll grow strong. Dear God, you have no idea what it means to me, that I have the boy."

"The boy," I say quietly. I know that he is not speaking of either of our boys. He means the boy who haunts him.

"He's at the French court, treated like a lord," Henry says bitterly. "He has his own court around him, half of your mother's friends and many of the old York household have joined him. He's housed with honor, good God! He sleeps in the same room as Charles, the King of France, bedfellow to a king — why not, since he is known everywhere as Prince Richard? He rides out with the king, dressed in velvets, they hunt together, they are said to be the greatest of friends. He wears a red velvet cap with a ruby badge and three pendant pearls. Charles makes no secret of his belief that the boy is Richard. The boy carries himself like a royal duke."

"Richard." I repeat the name.

"Your brother. The King of France calls him Richard Duke of York."

"And now?" I ask.

"As part of the peace treaty which I have won for us — it's a great peace treaty, better value for me than any French town, far better than Boulogne — Charles has agreed to hand over to me any English rebel, anyone conspiring against me. And I to him, of course. But we both know what we mean. We both know who we mean. We both only mean one person, one boy."

"What will happen?" I ask quietly, but my face is chilled in the cold November weather and I feel that I want to go inside, out of the wind, away from my husband's hard, exultant face. "What will happen now?"

I begin to wonder if the whole war, the siege of Boulogne, the sailing of so many ships, the mustering of so many men, was just for this? Has Henry become so fearful that he would launch an armada to capture just one boy? And if so, is this not a form of madness? All this, for one boy?

My Lady the King's Mother and the whole court are waiting in rows according to their rank, before the great double door of the palace. Henry goes forwards and kneels before her for her blessing. I see the triumphant beam on her pale face as she puts her hand on his head, and then raises him up to kiss him. The court cheers and comes forwards to bow and congratulate him. Henry turns from one to another, accepting their praise and thanks for his great victory. I wait with Arthur until the excitement has died down and Henry comes back to my side, flushed with pleasure.

"King Charles of France is going to send him to me," Henry continues in an undertone, beaming as people walk past us, going into the palace, pausing to sweep a curtsey or make a deep bow. Everyone is celebrating as if Henry has triumphed in a mighty victory. My Lady is alight with joy, accepting congratulations for the military skill and courage of her son. "This is my prize of victory, this is what I have won. People talk about Boulogne; it was never about Boulogne. I don't care that it didn't fall under the siege. It was not to win Boulogne that I went all that way. It was to frighten King Charles into agreeing to this: the boy as a prisoner, sent to me in chains."

"In chains?"

"Like a triumph, I shall have him come in, chained in a litter. Pulled by white mules. I shall have the curtains pinned back so that everyone can see him."

"A triumph?"

"Charles has promised to send the boy to

me chained."

"To his death?" I ask quietly.

He nods. "Of course. I am sorry, Elizabeth. But you must have known it has to end like this. And anyway, you thought he was dead, for years you had given him up for dead — and now he will be."

I take my hand from the warm crook of his arm. "I'm not well," I say pitifully. "I'm going in."

I am not even pretending to illness to avoid him in this mood; truly, I am nauseated. I sent a beloved husband out into danger and I have prayed every day for his safe return. I promised him that when he came home I would love him faithfully and passionately as we had just learned to do. But now, at the moment of his return, there is something about him that I think no woman could love. He is gloating in the defeat of a boy, he is reveling at the thought of his humiliation, he is hungrily imagining his death. He has taken an entire army over the narrow seas to win nothing but the torture and execution of one young orphan. I cannot see how I can admire such a man. I cannot see how to love such a man, how to forgive him for this single-minded hatred of a vulnerable boy. I shall have to think how to avoid naming this — even privately to myself — as a sort of madness.

He lets me go. His mother steps up beside

him and takes my place as if she were only waiting for me to leave; and the two of them look after me as I go quickly into our favorite palace, which was built for happiness and dancing and celebration. I walk through the great hall where the servants are preparing huge trestle tables for Henry's welcome victory banquet, and I think that it is a poor victory, if they only knew it. One of the greatest kings in Christendom has just taken out a mighty army and invaded another country for nothing but to entrap a lost boy, an orphan boy, into a shameful death.

We prepare for Christmas at Greenwich, the happiest, most secure Christmas that Henry has ever had. Knowing that the King of France has the boy in his keeping, knowing that his treaty with the King of France is strong and holding firm, Henry sends his envoys to Paris to bring the boy home for his execution and burial, watches the yule log dragged into the hall, pays the choirmaster extra for a new Christmas carol, and demands feasts and pageants, special dances and new clothes for everyone.

Me, he drapes me in swathes of silks and velvets and watches while the seamstresses pin and tuck the material around me. He urges them to trim the gowns with cloth of gold, with silver thread, with fur. He wants me shining with jewels, encrusted with gold lace. Nothing is too good for me this season, and my dresses are copied for my sisters and for my cousin Maggie, so that the women of the House of York glitter at court under the Tudor gilding.

It is like living with a different man. The terrible anxiety of the early years has melted away from Henry, and whether he is in the schoolroom interrupting lessons to teach Arthur to play dice, tossing Harry up in the air, dancing little Margaret around till she screams with laughter, petting Elizabeth in her cradle, or wasting his time in my rooms, teasing my ladies and singing with the musicians, he does not stop smiling, calling for entertainment, laughing at some foolish joke.

When he greets me at chapel in the morning he kisses my hand and then draws me to him and kisses me on the mouth, and then walks beside me with his arm around my waist. When he comes to my room at night he no longer sits and broods at the fireside, trying to see his future in the fading embers, but enters laughing, carrying a bottle of wine, persuades me to drink with him, and then carries me to my bed, where he makes love to me as if he would devour me, kissing every inch of my skin, nibbling my ear, my shoulder, my belly, and only finally sliding deep into me and sighing with pleasure as if my bed is his favorite place in all the world, and my touch is his greatest pleasure.

He is free at last to be a young man, to be a happy man. The long years of hiding, of fear, of danger seem to slide away from him and he begins to think that he has come to his own, that he can enjoy his throne, his country, his wife, that these goods are his by right. He has won them, and nobody can take them from him.

The children learn to approach him, confident of their welcome. I start to joke with him, play games of cards and dice with him, win money from him and put my earrings down as a pledge when I up the stakes, making him laugh. His mother does not cease her constant attendance at chapel but she stops praying so fearfully for his safety and starts to thank God for many blessings. Even his uncle Jasper sits back in his great wooden chair, laughs at the Fool and stops raking the hall with his hard gaze, ceases staring into dark corners for a shadowy figure with a naked blade.

And then, just two nights before Christmas, the door to my bedchamber opens and it is as if we had fallen back to the early years of our marriage and all the happiness and easiness is gone in a moment. A frost has fallen; the habitual darkness comes in with him. He enters with a quick cross word to his servant, who was following with glasses and a bottle of wine. "I don't want that!" he spits, as if it is madness even to suggest it, he has never wanted such a thing, he would never want such a thing; and the man flinches and goes out, closing the door, without another word.

Henry drops into the chair at my fireside and I take a step towards him, feeling the old familiar sense of apprehension. "Is something wrong?" I ask.

"Evidently."

In his sulky silence, I take the seat opposite him and wait, in case he wants to speak with me. I scan his face. It is as if his joy has shut down, before it had fully flowered. The sparkle has gone from his dark eyes, the color has even drained from his face. He looks exhausted, his skin is almost gray. He sits as if he were a much older man, plagued with pain, his shoulders strained, his head set forwards as if he were pulling against a heavy load, a tired horse, cruelly harnessed. As I watch him he puts his hand over his eyes as if the glow from the fire is too bright against the darkness within, and I am moved with sudden deep pity. "Husband, what is wrong? Tell me, what has happened?"

He looks up at me as if he is surprised to find that I am still there, and I realize that his reverie was so deep that he was far away from my quiet warm chamber, straining to see a room somewhere else. Perhaps he was even trying to see back into the darkness of the past, to the room in the Tower and the two little boys sitting up in their bed in their nightshirts as their door creaked open and a stranger stood in the entrance. As if he is longing to know what happens next, as if he fears to see a rescue, and hopes to see a murder.

"What?" he asks irritably. "What did you say?"

"I can see that you are troubled. Has something happened?"

His face darkens and for a moment I think he will break out and shout at me, but then the energy drains from him as if he were a sick man. "It's the boy," he says wearily. "That damned boy. He's disappeared from the French court."

"But you sent . . ."

"Of course I sent. I have had half a dozen men watching him the moment he arrived in the French court from Ireland. I have had a dozen men following him since King Charles promised him to me. Do you think I am an idiot?"

I shake my head.

"I should have ordered them to kill him then and there. But I thought it would be better if they brought him back to England for execution. I thought we would hold a trial where I would prove him to be an imposter. I thought I would create a story for him, a shameful story about poor ignorant parents, a drunk father, a dirty occupation somewhere on a river near a tannery, anything to take the shine off him. I thought he would be sentenced to execution and I would have everyone watch him die. So that they would all know, once and for all, that he is dead. So that everyone would stop mustering for him, plotting for him, dreaming of him . . ."

"But he's gone? Run away?" I can't help it; whoever he is, I hope that the boy has got away.

"I said so, didn't I?"

I wait for a few moments as his ill-tempered snarl dies away and then I try again. "Gone where?"

"If I knew that, I would send someone to kill him on the road," my husband says bitterly. "Drown him in the sea, drop a tree on his head, lame his horse, and cut him down. He could have gone anywhere, couldn't he? He's quite the little adventurer. Back to Portugal? They believe he is Richard there, they refer to him as your father's son, the Duke of York. To Spain? He has written to the king and queen as an equal and they have not contradicted him. To Scotland? If he goes to the King of Scots and together they raise an army and come against me, then I am a dead man in the North of England; I don't have a single friend in those damned bleak hills. I know the Northerners; they are just waiting for him to lead them before they rise against me.

"Or has he gone back to Ireland to rouse

the Irish against me again? Or has he gone to your aunt, your aunt Margaret in Flanders? Will she greet her nephew with joy and set him up against me, d'you think? She sent a whole army for a kitchen boy, what will she do for the real thing? Will she give him a couple of thousand mercenaries and send him to Stoke to finish off the job that her first pretender started?"

"I don't know," I say.

He leaps to his feet and his chair crashes back on the floor. "You never know!" he yells in my face, spittle flying from his mouth, beside himself with anger. "You never know! It's your motto! Never mind 'humble and penitent,' your motto is 'I don't know! I don't know! I never know!' Whatever I ask you, you always never know!"

The door behind me opens a crack, and my cousin Maggie puts her fair head into the room. "Your Grace?"

"Get out!" he yells at her. "You York bitch! All of you York traitors. Get out of my sight before I put you in the Tower along with your brother!"

She flinches back from his rage but she will not leave me to his anger. "Is everything all right, Your Grace?" she asks me, forcing herself to ignore him. I see she is clinging to the door to hold herself up, her knees weak with fear, but she looks past my furious husband to see if I need her help. I look at

458

her white face and know that I must look far worse, ashen with shock.

"Yes, Lady Pole," I say. "I am quite all right. There is nothing for you to do here. You can leave us. I am quite all right."

"Don't bother on my account, I'm going!" Henry corrects me. "I'm damned if I'll spend the night here. Why would I?" He rushes to the door and jerks it away from Maggie, who staggers for a moment but still holds her ground, visibly trembling. "I'm going to my own rooms," he says. "The best rooms. There's no comfort for me here, in this York nest, in this foul traitors' nest."

He storms out. I hear the bang in the outer presence chamber as they ground their pikes as he tears open the door, and then the scuffle as his guard hastily fall in behind him to follow him. By tomorrow, the whole court will know that he called Margaret a York bitch and me a York traitor, that he said my rooms were a foul traitors' nest. And in the morning everyone will know why: the boy who calls himself my brother has disappeared again.

WESTMINSTER PALACE, LONDON, SPRING 1493

We stay in London for the spring, so that Henry can be at the center of his spy network, receiving reports first from Antwerp and then from the city of Malines of the miracle at my aunt's court in Flanders. Everyone is talking of the moment when her nephew came to her from France, escaped by the intervention of angels, knelt at her feet, and looked up into her face and she recognized, with an outburst of joy, her lost nephew Richard.

She writes to everyone, in an explosion of gladness, telling them that the age of miracles is not over, for here is her nephew who was given up for dead, walking among us like an Arthur awakened from sleep and returned to Camelot.

The monarchs of Christendom reply to her. It is extraordinary, but if she recognizes her nephew, then who can deny him? Who could know better than his own aunt? Who would dare to tell the Dowager Duchess of Burgundy that she is mistaken? Anyway, why should she be mistaken? She sees in this boy the certain features of her nephew, and she tells everyone that she knows him for her brother's son. None of her dear friends, the Holy Roman Emperor, the King of France, the King of Scotland, the King of Portugal, and the monarchs of Spain, deny him for a moment. And the boy himself: everyone reports that he is princely, handsome, smiling, composed. Dressed in the best clothes that his wealthy aunt can have made for him, creating his own court from the increasing numbers of men who join him, he speaks sometimes of his childhood and refers to events that only a child at my father's court could know. My father's servants, my mother's old friends escape from England as if it is now an enemy country. They make their way to Malines to see him for themselves. They put to him the questions they have composed to test him. They scan his face for any resemblance to the pretty little prince that my mother adored, they try to entrap him with false memories, with chimeras. But he answers them confidently, they believe him too, and they stay with him. They all are satisfied with their own tests. Every single one of them, even those who set out to disprove him, even those who were paid by Henry to embarrass him, are convinced. They fall to their knees, some of them weep, they bow to him, as to their prince. It is Richard, back from the dead, they write back to England in delight. It is Richard, snatched from the very jaws of death, the rightful King of England restored to us once more, returned to us once more, the son of York shining again.

More and more people start to slip away from the households of England. William, the king's favorite farrier, is missing from the forge. Nobody can understand why he would leave the favor of the court, the shoeing of the finest horses in the kingdom, the patronage of the king himself — but the fire is out and the forge is dark and the whisper is that William has gone to shoe the horses of the true King of England, and won't stay with a Tudor pretender any longer. A group of neighbors who live near to my grandmother Duchess Cecily disappear from their handsome homes in Hertfordshire, and travel in secret to Flanders, almost certainly with her blessing. Priests go missing from their chapels, their clerks forward letters to known sympathizers, couriers take money from houses in England to the boy. Then, worst of all, Sir Robert Clifford, a lifelong courtier for York, a man trusted by Henry to be his envoy to Brittany, packs his bags with Tudor treasures and goes. His place is empty in our chapel, his table is not prepared for dinner in our hall. Shockingly, unbelievably, our friend Sir Robert with his entire household has disappeared; and everyone knows he has gone to the boy.

Then it is we who look like a court of pretenders. The boy looks and sounds like the real thing while we pretend to confidence; but I see the strain in the face of My Lady the King's Mother and the way that Jasper Tudor stalks the halls like an old warhorse, nervously, his hand drifting towards his belt where his sword should be, always watching the hall when he eats, always alert to the opening of a door. Henry himself is gray with fatigue and fear. He starts his working day at dawn, and all day men come into the small room in the center of the palace where he meets his advisors and his spies with a double guard on the door.

The court is hushed; even in the nursery where there should be spring sunshine and laughter, the nurses are quiet and they forbid the children to shout or run around. Elizabeth is sleepy and still in her cradle. Arthur is all but silent; he does not know what is happening but he senses that he is living in a palace under siege, he knows that his place is threatened, but he has been told nothing about the young man whose nursery this was, who did his lessons at this very table. He does not know of a Prince of Wales who preceded him, who was studious and thoughtful and the darling of his mother, too.

His sister Margaret is guarded. She is quiet as they order her to be as if she knows that something is wrong, but does not know what to do.

Their little brother Harry is starting to insist on having his own way, a stout little boy with a shouting laugh and a love of games and music; but even he is quietened by the haste and anxiety of the palace. Nobody has time to play with him anymore, nobody will pause to talk with him as they move swiftly through the great hall, busy with secret business. He looks around in bewilderment at the people who only a few months ago would always stop and swing him up to the ceiling, or toss a ball for him, or take him down to the stable to see a horse, but who now frown and hurry past.

"S' William!" he calls to Thomas Stanley's brother as he walks by. "Harry too!"

"You can't," Sir William says shortly, and he looks at Harry coldly, and goes on to the stables, so the child stops short and looks around for his nurse.

"It's all right," I say, smiling at him. "Sir William is just in a hurry."

But he frowns. "Why no play Harry?" he asks simply, and I have no answer that I can give him. "Why no play Harry?"

The king deploys the whole court against the news from Malines; there is nothing more important. Lords and councillors go to Ireland at his command and speak to the Irish lords and beg them to remember their true loyalty, and not to run after a false prince again. Traitors are forgiven in a rush of generosity, and released from prison, sworn anew to loyalty with us. Old forgotten alliances are reforged. Ireland must be made secure, the people of that country must turn their hearts away from a darling boy of York and cleave only to Tudor. One of Henry's small trusted circle goes to Bristol and starts to muster ships for a fleet to patrol the narrow seas. They have to look for ships coming from France, from Flanders, from Ireland, even from Scotland. The boy seems to have friends and allies everywhere.

"You are expecting an invasion?" I ask him incredulously.

There is a new line on his face, a deep groove between his eyebrows. "Of course," he says shortly. "The only thing I don't know is when. Of course the other thing I don't know is where, nor how many they will be. Those are, of course, the only important things. And I don't know them."

"Your spies don't tell you?" Despite myself, my voice has a touch of scorn as I speak of his spies.

"Not yet, no," he says defensively. "There are secrets being well kept by my enemies."

I turn to go to the nursery, where a physician is coming to see Elizabeth.

"Don't go," he says. "I need . . ."

I turn back, my hand on the latch; I want

to ask the physician if the better weather will make Elizabeth stronger. "What?"

He looks helpless. "No one has tried to speak to you? You would tell me if anyone had spoken to you?"

My mind is on my sick child, I genuinely don't understand him. "Speak to me of what? What d'you mean?"

"Of the boy . . ." he says. "Nobody has spoken to you of him?"

"Who would do so?"

His dark look is suddenly intent, suspicious. "Why, who do you think might speak of him?"

I spread my hands. "My lord. I really don't know. Nobody has spoken to me of him. I cannot think why anyone *would* speak to me. Your unhappiness is clear enough for everyone to see. Nobody is going to talk to me about the thing that is driving my husband . . ." I bite off the rest of the phrase.

"Driving me mad?" he asks.

I don't respond.

"Somebody in my court is receiving orders from him," he says as if the words are wrenched from him. "Somebody is planning to overthrow me and put him in my place."

"Who?" I whisper. His fears are so powerful that I glance over my shoulder to see that the door behind me is shut tight and step towards him, so that nobody can hear us.

"Who is plotting against us in our own court?"

He shakes his head. "One of my men picked up a letter but it had no names."

"Picked it up?"

"Stole it. I know there are a few men, come together for love of the House of York, hoping to restore the boy. Maybe more than a few. They worked with your mother as their secret leader, they even work with your grandmother. But there are more than these — men who pass daily as friends or comrades or servants of mine. Someone who is as close to me as a brother. I don't know who to trust — I don't know who is my true friend."

I have a sudden chilling sense, Henry's daily experience, that outside the closed door, beyond the carved panels of thick polished wood, there are people, perhaps hundreds of people, who smile at us as we go into dinner but write secret letters, store up secret weapons, and have a plan to kill us. We have a large busy court, what if a quarter of them are against us? What if half of them are against us? What if they turn against my boys? What if they are poisoning my little daughter? What if they turn against me?

"We have enemies in the very heart of this very court," he whispers. "They may be the ones who turn down our beds, they may be the ones who serve our food. They may be the ones who taste our food and assure us that it is safe to eat. Or they may ride along-side us, play cards with us, dance holding your hand, see us to bed at night. We may call them cousin, we may call them dearest. I don't know who to trust."

I don't promise him my loyalty, since there is no comfort to be had in words anymore. My name and my house are his enemies, my affinity may be massing against him; mere words will not overcome that. "You do have people you can trust," I assure him. I list them for him, as if I am singing hymns against darkness. "Your mother, your uncle, the Earl of Oxford, your stepfather and all his kin, the Stanleys, the Courtenays, my half brother Thomas Grey — all the people who stood by you at Stoke will stand by you again."

He shakes his head. "No, because they *weren't* all beside me at Stoke. Some of them found an excuse to stay away. Some of them said they would come but delayed and were not there in time. Some of them promised their love and loyalty but flatly refused to come. Some of them pretended to illness, or could not leave their homes. Some were even there, but on the other side, and begged for my forgiveness afterwards. And anyway, even of those who were there — they won't stand by me again, not again and again. They won't stand by me against a boy under the white rose, not one who they believe is a true prince."

He goes back to the table where his letters and his secret ciphers and his seals are carefully laid out. He never writes a letter now, he always composes code. He hardly ever writes so much as a note, it is always a secret instruction. It is not the writing table of a king but of a spymaster. "I won't detain you," he says shortly. "But if someone says so much as one word to you — I expect you to tell me. I want to hear anything, everything — the slightest whisper. I expect this of you."

I am about to say of course I would tell him, what else does he think I would do? I am his wife, his heirs are my beloved sons, there are no beings in the world that I love more tenderly than his own daughters — how can he doubt that I would come to him at once? But then I see his dark scowl and I realize that he is not asking for my help; he is threatening me. He is not asking for reassurance but warning me of his expectation that must not be disappointed. He does not trust me, and, worse than that, he wants me to know that he does not trust me.

"I am your wife," I say quietly. "I promised to love you on our wedding day and since then I have come to love you. Once we were glad that such love had come to us; I am still glad of it. I am your wife and I love you, Henry."

"But before that, you were his sister," he says.

Kenilworth Castle, Warwickshire, Summer 1493

Once again Henry moves the court to Kenilworth Castle, the safest in England, centrally placed so that he can march out to any coast to meet an invasion, easily defended if everything goes wrong and an invasion sweeps inland to him. This time there is not even the pretence of being a carefree court in summertime; everyone is afraid, certain that they are attached to a king who is facing invasion for the second time in only eight years, convinced that a better claimant to the throne is gathering his forces against Henry Tudor: a pretender now as he always has been.

Jasper Tudor, grim-faced, rides out to the West Country and Wales to uncover the dozens of local conspiracies that are joining together to welcome an invasion. None of the people of the west is for Tudor, they are all looking for the prince over the water. Henry himself opens other inquiries, riding from one place to another, chasing whispers, trying to find those who are behind the constant flow of men and funds to Flanders. Everywhere from Yorkshire to Oxfordshire, from the east to the central counties, Henry's appointed men hold inquiries trying to root out rebels. And still the reports of treasonous groups, hidden meetings, and musters after dark come in every day.

Henry closes the ports. No one shall set sail to any destination for fear that they are going to join the boy; even merchants have to apply for a license before they can send out their ships. Not even trade is trusted. Then Henry passes another law: no one is to travel any great distance inland either. People may go to their market towns and back home again, but there is to be no mustering and marching. There are to be no summer gatherings, no haymaking parties, no shearing days, no dancing or beating of the parish bounds, no midsummer revels. The people are not to come together for fear that they make a crowd and raise an army, they are not to raise a glass for fear that they drink a toast to the prince whose family's court was a byword for merrymaking.

My Lady the King's Mother is bleached with fear. When she whispers the prayers of the rosary her lips are as pale as the starched wimple around her face. She spends all her time with me, leaving the best rooms, the queen's apartments, empty all day. She brings her ladies and the members of her immediate family as the only people that she can trust, and she brings her books and her studies, and she sits in my rooms as if she is seeking warmth or comfort or some sort of safety.

I can offer her nothing. Cecily, Anne, and I barely speak to one another, we are so conscious that everything we say is being noted, that everyone is wondering if our brother will come to rescue us from this Tudor court. Maggie, my cousin, goes everywhere with her head down and her eyes on her feet, desperate that no one will say if one York boy is on the loose, then at least the other one could be put to death and so secure the Tudor line from his threat. The guards on Teddy have been doubled and doubled again, and Maggie is sure that he does not get his letters from her. She never hears from him and now she is too afraid to ask after him. We all fear that one day they will get the order to go into his room while he is asleep and strangle him in his bed. Who would countermand the order? Who would stop them?

The ladies in my rooms read and sew, play music and games, but everything is muted and nobody speaks quickly or laughs or makes a joke. Everyone examines everything they say before they let one word out of their mouths. Everyone is watching their own words for fear of saying something that could be reported against them, everyone is listening to everyone else, in case there is something that they should report. Everyone is silently attentive to me, and whenever there is a loud knock at my door, there is an indrawn breath of terror.

I hide from these terrible afternoons in the children's nursery, taking Elizabeth onto my lap and stretching out her little hands and feet, singing softly to her, trying to persuade her to show me her faint, enchanting smile.

Arthur, who has to stay with us until we can be certain of the safety of Wales, is torn between his studies and the view from the high window, where he can see his father's army growing in numbers, drilling every day. Every day too he sees messengers coming from the west, bringing news from Ireland or from Wales, or from the south — from London, where the streets are buzzing with gossip and the apprentices are openly wearing white roses.

In the afternoons I take him riding with me but after a few days Henry forbids us to go out without a fully armed guard. "If they were to snatch Arthur then my life wouldn't be worth a groat," he says bitterly. "The day that he and Harry die is the day of my death sentence and the end of everything."

"Don't say that!" I put out my hand. "Don't ill-wish them!"

"You're tenderhearted," he says grudgingly, as if it is a fault. "But foolish. You don't think, you don't realize what danger you are in. You cannot take the children out of the castle walls without a guard. I am beginning to think that they should be housed separately — so that anyone coming for Arthur couldn't get Henry."

"But my lord husband," I say. I can hear the quaver in my voice, I can hear the whine of reasonableness against the clarity of a madman.

"I think I'll keep Arthur in the Tower."

"No!" I scream. I cannot contain my shock. "No, Henry. No! No! No!"

"To keep him safe."

"No. I won't consent. I can't consent. He's not to go into the Tower. Not like . . ."

"Not like your brothers?" he asks, quick as a striking snake. "Not like Edward of Warwick? Because you think they are all the same? All boys who might hope to be king?"

"He is not to go into the Tower like them. He is the proclaimed prince. He must live freely. I must be allowed to ride out with him. We cannot be in such danger in our own country that we are prisoners in our own castles."

His head is turned away from me so I cannot see his expression as he listens. But when he turns back I see his handsome face is twisted up with suspicion. He looks at me as if he would flay the skin from my face to see my thoughts.

"Why are you so determined upon this?"

he asks slowly. Almost, I can see his suspicions gathering. "Why are you so determined to keep your sons here? Are you riding out with Arthur to meet with them? Are you hoodwinking me with this talk of safety and riding out? Are you planning to take my son out to hand him over? Are you are working with the Yorks to steal my son from me? Have you made an agreement? Forged a deal? Your brother as king, Arthur as his heir? Will you put Arthur in his keeping now, and tell him to invade as soon as the wind turns against me and he can sail?"

There is a long silence as I realize what he has said. Slowly, the horror of his mistrust opens like a chasm below my feet. "Henry, you cannot think that I am your enemy?"

"I am watching you," he says, not answering. "My mother is watching you. And you will not have my son and heir in your keeping. If you want to go anywhere with him, you will go with men that I can trust."

My rage leaps up and I round on him, shaking. "Men you can trust? Name one!" I spit. "Can you? Can you name even one?"

He puts his hand to his heart as if I have rammed him in the chest. "What do you know?" he whispers.

"I know that you can trust no one. I know that you are in a lonely hell of your own making."

Northampton, Autumn 1493

We move to Northampton and Henry receives the courtiers that he had sent to negotiate with my aunt, the dowager duchess. All trade is to be banned between England and Flanders, nobody can come and go, and Flanders shall have no English wool while the boy, the one boy, holds his little court, and the determined woman who claims he is her nephew writes urgently to other kings and queens, pressing his claims.

Henry's representatives gleefully report that they have insulted my aunt. At her very court, in her presence, they suggested that she scrapes the countryside of bastard boys to send against Henry Tudor. They made a scurrilous joke suggesting that the boy is her love child. They say she is like many older women: mad for sex, or maddened by sex, or simply mad because she is a woman and everyone knows that women's grasp of reason is a weak one. They say that she is a mad woman from a mad family and so my grandmother Cecily

Duchess of York, nearly eighty years old, and my dead mother and I, and all my sisters and my cousin Margaret are insulted too. Henry lets all these things be said by his ambassadors, and repeated in my hearing, as if he does not care what filth is thrown at York, as long as something sticks which besmirches the boy.

I hear this gossip flinty-faced, I don't demean myself to complain. Henry is stooping very low, he has lost all judgment. To insult the boy, to insult my aunt, he will say anything. I see his mother watching me, bright-eyed with her own delirious fears, and I turn my head away as if I do not want to see her, nor hear the abuse her son commands.

But the ambassador William Warham did not waste his time in Flanders in slandering my aunt; he had his clerks and his men search the country for families who are missing a boy. Hundreds of people responded, people who now say that twenty years ago they lost a newborn from the cradle; could this be the boy? People who say that their child wandered off and never returned; did the duchess steal him? People whose beloved child fell into the river and was swept downstream and the body never found — is he alive and pretending to be Richard Duke of York? One applicant after another comes forwards to tell their sad stories of missing children; but there is nothing to link even one of them to the boy who behaves so courteously in his little palace, who speaks so warmly of his father, and who visits his aunt Margaret so comfortably.

"You don't know who he is," I say flatly to Henry. "You have spent a small fortune and had Sir William pay half the mourning mothers in Christendom for their stories, and you still don't know who he is. You have no idea who he is."

"I will have his history," he says simply. "I will have his history even if I have to write it myself. I can tell you some of it already. He turns up somewhere, into some family somewhere, ten years ago. He's with them for something like four years. Then Sir Edward Brampton happens by, and takes him to Portugal — Sir Edward admits that himself. In Portugal they call the boy Richard Duke of York, and he's known in the Portuguese court as the missing prince. Then, he's dismissed by Sir Edward, it doesn't matter why, and the boy travels with Pregent Meno — Meno admits that too, I have it in writing. Meno takes him to Ireland, the Irish rise up for him, they call him Richard Duke of York — I have their confessions — and he escapes to France. King Charles of France accepts him as the York prince, but just when he is to be handed over to me, he escapes to your aunt."

"You have all this written down?" I ask.

"I have signed reports from witnesses. I can trace him every moment of every day from Portugal," Henry says.

"But nothing before then. Nothing to show that he is born and bred into the family somewhere," I point out. "You say yourself that he turns up there. He himself will say that he turns up there from England, rescued from the Tower. Everything that you have written down, sworn to for certain, does nothing to disprove his claim. Everything you have collected as evidence only confirms him as a son of York."

He crosses the room in one swift stride and snatches up my hand, holding it so tightly that the bones are crushed together. I flinch but I won't cry out.

"That's all I have for now," he says through gritted teeth. "As I said. What I don't have I will write myself. I will write this boy's parentage into his story, I will create it: common people, nasty people. The father a bit of a drunk, the mother a bit of a fool, the boy a bit of a runaway, a wastrel, a good-for-nothing. D'you think I can't write this and get someone — a drunk married to a fool — to swear to it? Do you think I can't set up as historian? As storyteller? D'you think I can't write a history which years from now, everyone will believe as the truth? I am the king.

Who shall write the record of my reign if not me?"

"You can say anything you like," I say levelly. "Of course you can. You're the King of England. But it doesn't make it true."

A few days later Maggie, my cousin, comes to me. Her husband has been made Arthur's Lord Chamberlain, but they cannot take up residence in Wales while the west is threatened by a rival prince. "My husband, Sir Richard, tells me that the king has found a name for the boy."

"Found a name? What do you mean, found a name?"

She makes a little face, acknowledging the oddness of the phrase. "I should have said, that the king now says he knows who the boy is."

"And?"

"The king says he is to be called Perkin Warbeck, the son of a boatman. From Tournai, in Picardy."

"Does he say that the boatman is a drunk, married to a fool?"

She does not understand me. She shakes her head. "He has nothing else but this name. He says nothing else."

"And is he sending the boatman and his wife to Duchess Margaret? So that the boy can be faced by his parents and forced to confess? Is he taking the boatman and his wife to the kings and queens of Christendom so that they can show who he truly is, and claim their son back from these royal courts which have kept him for so long?"

Margaret looks puzzled. "Sir Richard didn't say."

"It's what I'd do."

"It's what anyone would do," she agrees. "So why is the king not doing it?"

Our eyes meet, and we say nothing more.

Westminster Palace, London, Winter 1493

The Holy Roman Emperor has died and Henry sends ambassadors to pay the respects of England at his funeral. But when they get there, they find that they are not the only noblemen representing their country. For the Holy Roman Emperor's son and heir, Maximilian, goes everywhere arm in arm with his new and dearest friend: Richard, son of Edward, King of England.

"They said what?" Henry demands. He has ordered me into his presence chamber to hear this report from the returning ambassadors, but he does not greet me nor set a chair for me. I doubt he even sees me: he is blinded with rage. I sink down into my seat as he strides about, shaking with anger. The ambassadors throw a quick glance at me to see if I am going to intervene. I sit like a cold statue. I am going to say nothing.

"The heralds called him 'Richard, son of Edward, King of England,' " the man repeats.

Henry rounds on me. "Do you hear this?

Do you hear this?"

I incline my head. On the other side of the king I notice My Lady, his mother, lean forwards so that she can see me, as if she expects me to weep.

"Your dead brother's name," she reminds me. "Abused by this forger."

"Yes," I say.

"The new emperor, Maximilian, loves the ki— the boy," the ambassador offers, flushing over the terrible slip. "They are together all the time. The boy represents the emperor when he meets with his bankers, speaks for him with his betrothed. He is the emperor's principal friend and confidant. He is his only advisor."

"Oh, and what did you call him?" Henry asks, as if it does not much matter.

"The boy."

"What d'you call him when you see him at the emperor's court? When he's at the emperor's side? When he is, as you describe, so central to the emperor's happiness, at the heart of his court? His only friend and advisor? When you greet this youth of such great importance? What do you call him at court?"

The man shuffles, passes his hat from one hand to another. "It was important not to insult the emperor. He is young, and hot-headed, and he is the emperor, after all. He loves and respects the boy. He tells everyone of his miraculous escape from death, he constantly speaks of his high birth, of his rights."

"So what did you call him?" Henry asks quietly. "When you were all in the emperor's hearing?"

"Mostly I didn't speak to him. We all avoided him."

"But when you did? On those rare occasions. Those very rare occasions. When you had to?"

"I called him 'my lord.' I thought it was the safest thing to say."

"As if he was a duke?"

"Yes, a duke."

"As if he was Richard, Earl of Shrewsbury and Duke of York?"

"I never said Duke of York."

"Oh, who do you think he is?"

This question is a mistake. Nobody knows who he is. The ambassador is silent, twisting the brim of his hat. He has not yet been primed with the story which we have learned by rote.

"He is Warbeck, the son of a Tournai boatman," Henry says bitterly. "A nobody. His father is a drunk, his mother is a fool. And yet you humbled yourself and bowed to him? Did you call him 'Your Grace'?"

The ambassador, uncomfortably aware that he will have been spied on in his turn, that the reports piled facedown on Henry's table will include accounts of his meetings and conversations, flushes slightly. "I may have done. It's how I would address a foreign duke. It wouldn't mean that I respect his title. It wouldn't indicate that I accept his title."

"Or a king. Because you would call a king 'Your Grace'?"

"I did not address him as a king, Sire," the man says with steady dignity. "I never forgot that he is a pretender."

"But he's a pretender now with a powerful backer," Henry breaks out, suddenly furious. "A pretender living with an emperor and announced to the world as Richard, son of Edward, King of England."

For a moment everyone is too frightened to speak. Henry's bulging gaze holds his frightened ambassador. "Yes," the man concurs into the long silence. "That's what everybody calls him."

"And you did not deny him!" Henry bellows.

The ambassador is frozen like a statue of fear.

Henry exhales a shuddering sigh, and stalks back to his seat, pauses with his hand on the high carved back, stands under the cloth of estate as if to indicate to everyone his greatness. "So if he is King of England," Henry says with slow menace, "what do they call me?"

Again the ambassador looks at me for help. I keep my eyes down. There is nothing I can do to divert Henry's rage from him; it is all I can do to avoid being its target myself.

The silence lasts, then Henry's ambassador finds the courage to tell him the truth. "They call you Henry Tudor," he says simply. "Henry Tudor, the pretender."

I am in my rooms, Elizabeth is quiet in the cradle beside me and my sewing is in my hand, but little work is being done. One of My Lady's endless kinswomen is reading to us from a book of psalms, My Lady the King's Mother nodding along to the well-known words as if they are somehow in her ownership, the rest of us silent, listening, our faces composed into expressions of pious reflection, our thoughts anywhere. The door opens and the commander of the yeomen of the guard stands there, his face grave.

My ladies gasp, and someone gives a little frightened scream. I rise slowly to my feet and look to my cousin Maggie. I see her lips working, as if she is about to speak, but she has lost her voice.

Slowly, I rise to my feet and find that I am trembling so that I can barely stand. Maggie takes two steps towards me, putting her hand under my elbow, holding me up. Together we face the man responsible for my safety who looms in my doorway, neither coming in nor announcing a visitor. He is silent as if he cannot bear to speak either. I feel Maggie shudder and I know she is thinking, as I am, that he has come to take us to the Tower.

"What is it?" I ask. I am glad that my voice is quiet and steady. "What is it, Commander?"

"I have to make a report to you, Your Grace," he says. He looks awkwardly around the room as if he is uncomfortable at speaking in front of all the ladies.

The relief that he is not here to arrest me almost overwhelms me. Cecily, my sister, drops into her seat and gives a little sob. Maggie steps back and leans against my chair. My Lady the King's Mother is unmoved. She beckons him in. "Enter. What is your report?" she says briskly.

He hesitates. I step towards him so he can speak to me quietly. "What is it?"

"It's Yeoman Edwards," he says. His face suddenly flushes as if he is ashamed. "I beg your pardon, Your Grace. It's very bad."

"Is he sick?" My first fear is of plague.

But My Lady has joined us and she is quicker than me. "Has he gone?"

The captain nods.

"To Malines?"

He nods again. "He told no one he was going, nor where his loyalties lay; I'd have arrested him at once if I'd had so much as a whisper. He's been under my command, guarding your door for half a year. I never dreamed . . . Forgive me, Your Grace. But I had no way of knowing. He left a note for his girl, and that's how we know. We opened it." Hesitantly, he proffers a scrap of paper.

I have gone to serve Richard of York, true King of England. When I march in behind the white rose of York I will claim you for my bride.

"Let me see that!" Lady Margaret exclaims, and snatches it from my hand.

"You can keep it," I say dryly. "You can take it to your son. But he won't thank you for it."

The look she turns on me is quite horrified. "Your own yeoman of the guard," she whispers. "Gone to the boy. And Henry's own groom has gone."

"He has? I didn't know."

She nods. "Sir Ralph Hastings's steward has gone and taken all the family's silver to Malines. And Sir Edward Poynings's own tenants . . . Sir Edward, who was our ambassador in Flanders, can't keep his own men here. There are dozens of men, slipping away — hundreds."

I glance back at my ladies. The reading has stopped and everyone is leaning forwards trying to hear what is being said; there is no mistaking the avidity on their faces, Maggie and Cecily among them.

The commander of my guard dips his head in a bow and steps backwards and closes the door behind him. But My Lady the King's Mother rounds on me in a fury, flinging a pointing finger to my kinswomen.

"We married those girls — your sister and your cousin — to men we could trust, so that their interests would lie with us, to make them Tudors," she hisses at me, as if it is my fault that they are eager for news. "Now we can't be sure that their husbands aren't hoping to rise as Yorks, and their interests go quite the other way. We married them to loyal nobodies, we gave men who had almost nothing a princess of York so that they would be true to us, so that they would be grateful. Now perhaps they think that they can take their makeshift wives and reach for greatness."

"My family is faithful to the king," I say staunchly.

"Your brother . . ." She swallows her accusation. "Your sister and your cousin have been established and enriched by us. Can we trust them? While everyone is running away? Or will they too use their fortune and their husbands against us?"

"You chose their husbands," I say dryly into her white anxious face. "There's no point complaining to me if you fear that your handpicked men are faithless."

The court takes no joy in the coming of summer, and though I buy Arthur his first horse and his first proper saddle, and then have to comfort Henry, who demands a full-size horse of his own, as good as his brother's, I cannot pretend that it is a summer as it should be, or that the court is a happy one. The king goes everywhere shrouded in silence, his mother spends most of her time in the chapel, and every time someone is missing from dinner or from prayers, everyone looks around and whispers, "Has he gone too? Dear God, has he gone as well? To the boy?"

It is as if we are players on a small tawdry stage, like players who pretend that all is well, that they are comfortable on their stools in their ill-fitting crowns. But anyone looking to the left or to the right can see that this false court is just a few people perched on a wagon, trying to create an illusion of grandeur.

491

Margaret visits her brother in the Tower before the court leaves London, and comes back to my rooms looking grave. His lessons have been stopped, his guard has been changed, he has become so silent and so sad that she fears that even if he were to be released tomorrow, he would never recover the spirits of the excited little boy that we brought to the capital. He is nineteen years old now but he is not allowed out into the garden; he is allowed only to walk around the roof of the Tower every afternoon. He says he cannot remember what it is like to run, he thinks he has forgotten how to ride a horse. He is innocent of anything but bearing a great name, and he cannot put that name aside, as Margaret has done, as I and my sisters have done, burying our identities in marriage. It is as if his name as a duke of the House of York will drag him, like a millstone around his neck, down into deep water, and never release him.

"Do you think the king will ever let Edward go?" she asks me. "I don't dare to ask him, this summer. Not even as a favor. I don't dare to speak to him. And anyway, Sir Richard has ordered me not to. He says we can say nothing and do nothing that might cause the king to doubt our loyalty."

"Henry can't doubt Sir Richard," I protest. "He has made him chamberlain to Arthur. He'll send him to govern Wales as soon as it is safe for him to leave court. He trusts him more than anyone else in the world."

Her quick shake of the head reminds me that the king doubts everybody.

"Is Henry doubting Sir Richard?" I whisper.

"He has set a man to watch us," she says in an undertone. "But if he can't trust Sir Richard . . . ?"

"Then I don't think Teddy will ever be released," I finish grimly. "I don't think Henry will ever let him go."

"No, King Henry won't . . ." she concedes. "But . . ."

In the silence between us, I can see the unspoken words as clearly as if she had traced them on the wood of the table and then polished them away: "King Henry will never release him: but King Richard would."

"Who knows what will happen?" I say shortly. "Certainly, even in an empty room, you and I should never, ever speculate."

We get constant news from Malines. I start to dread seeing the door of the king's privy chamber close and the guard stand across it with his pike barring the way, for then I know that another messenger or spy has come to see Henry. The king tries to ensure that no news escapes from his constant meetings but quickly word gets out that the Emperor Maximilian has visited his lands in Flanders and the boy, the boy who may not be named, is traveling with him as his dearly beloved fellow monarch. The court in Malines is no longer grand enough for him. Maximilian gives him a great palace in the city of Antwerp, a palace hung with his own standard and decorated with white roses. His name, Richard, Prince of Wales and Duke of York, is emblazoned at the front of the building, his retainers wear the York colors of murrey — a deep berry crimson — and blue, and he is served on bended knee.

Henry comes to me as I am stepping into my barge for an evening on the water. "May I join you?"

It is so rare for him to speak pleasantly these days that I fail to answer him at all, I just gawp at him like a peasant girl. He laughs as if he is carefree. "You seem amazed, that I should want to come for a sail with you."

"I am amazed," I say. "But I am very pleased. I thought you were locked in your privy chamber with reports."

"I was, but then I saw from my window that they were getting your barge ready, and I thought: what a lovely evening it is to be on the water."

I gesture to my court and a young man bounds out of his seat; everyone else moves along and Henry sits beside me, nodding that the boatmen can cast off.

It is a beautiful evening; the swallows are twisting and turning low over the silvery river, dipping down to snatch a beakful of water and then swirling away. A curlew lifts up from the riverbank and calls low and sweet, its wings wide. Softly, the musicians on the following barge set a note and start to play.

"I am so glad you came with us," I say quietly.

He takes my hand and kisses it. It is the first gesture of affection between us for many weeks, and it warms me like the evening sunlight. "I am glad too," he says.

I glance at him and take in the weariness in his face and the tension in his shoulders. For a moment I wonder if I can speak to him as a wife should speak to her husband, scolding him for not taking care of himself, urging him to rest, caring for his health. "I think you have been working too hard," I say.

"I have many worries," he says quietly, as if he has not been on the very brink of madness. "But this evening I should like to be at peace with you."

I glow towards him, and I can feel my smile broaden. "Oh, Henry!"

"My love," he says. "You are always — whatever troubles I have — you are always my love."

He takes my hand, he carries it to his lips, he kisses it gently, and I cup my other hand to his cheek. "I feel as if you have suddenly come back to me, from a long dangerous journey," I say wonderingly.

"I wanted to come on the water," he explains. "Where in the world is more beautiful than the river and a summer evening in England? And where is there better company?"

"The best company in England, now that you're here."

He smiles at the compliment and his face is warm, happy. He looks years younger than the frantic man who waits for messengers from Flanders. "And I have plans," he promises.

"Good plans?"

"Very. I have decided that it's time to proclaim Henry as Duke of York. Now that he's four."

"He's not yet four," I correct him.

"Near enough. He should have his title."

I wait, my smile fading from my face. I know my husband well enough to realize that there will be more.

"And I'll make him Lieutenant of Ireland."

"At three and a half?"

"He's nearly four. Don't you worry! He won't have to go anywhere or do anything. I'll make Sir Edward Poynings his deputy in Ireland and send him over there with a force."

"A force?"

"To make sure that they accept Henry's rule. To establish our son's name in Ireland."

I look away from my husband's intent face to the green banks where the swish of our oars barely stirs the reeds. An oystercatcher calls its sudden piping warning, and I can just see the little chick, pied brilliant white and glossy black like its parents, crouch down low as we go past.

"You are not honoring our little son Henry," I say quietly. "You are using him."

"This is to show them in Malines, in Antwerp, in Flanders, to show them even in London, in Ireland, that they don't have the Duke of York. *We* have him, and his name is Henry Duke of York. He is Lieutenant of Ireland and the Irish will bow the knee to him and I will have the head of anyone who mentions any other duke."

"You mean the boy," I say flatly. It is almost as if the color is draining away from the golden sunset. The joy is going from the evening as the rose is going from the light.

"They call him Richard Duke of York. We will show them that we have Henry Duke of York. And his claim is stronger."

"I don't like our boy being used to claim a name," I say cautiously.

"It's his own name," my husband insists. "He's the second son of the King of England, so he's the Duke of York. Certainly he must claim his name and prevent anyone else from using it. We show the world that we claim the name. There is only one Duke of York and he's a Tudor."

"Don't we show the world that we are frightened that someone else is using the name?" I ask. "By making Henry a duke now? While he is still in the nursery? Doesn't it look as if we are laying claim to a name that someone else is using? Doesn't it make us look weak, rather than strong?"

There is a cold silence, and I turn to look at him and I am shocked to see that suddenly Henry is white-faced, and shaking with fury. By commenting on his plan I have triggered his rage, and he is beside himself.

"You can turn back," he bellows over his shoulder to the steersman, ignoring me. "Turn back and put me ashore. I am tired of this, I am sick of this."

"Henry . . ."

"I am sick of all of you," he says bitterly.

WESTMINSTER PALACE, LONDON, AUTUMN 1494

Two weeks of celebration follow the creation of Harry as Duke of York, two weeks in which he eats ridiculous food at great banquets, is dressed like a little king, stays up too late until he is dizzy with fatigue, then cries himself to sleep for tiredness to wake in the morning in a state of unbearable excitement to another glorious day.

Even I, critical of the mummery of this ennobling, can see how my boy Harry rises to it and relishes it. He is a most joyously vain boy; there is nothing he likes more than being the center of admiration and the focus of attention and for these days everyone praises his schooling, his strength, and his beauty, and little Harry blushes like the red rose of Lancaster under the excessive admiration.

Arthur, always quieter and more sober than his boisterous brother and noisy sister Margaret, sits beside me during the great church service when Thomas Langton, Bishop of Winchester, assists the archbishop to institute

Harry as Duke of York. During the banquet, when Henry lifts Harry onto a table so that everyone can see him, Arthur only says quietly: "I hope he doesn't sing. He's been longing to sing for everyone."

I laugh. "I won't let him sing," I assure him. "Though he does have a beautiful voice."

I break off because Margaret, already wild with jealousy at the attention being paid to her brother, slips down from her chair and pulls at the king's cape. Horrified, her nurse-maid runs after her and curtseys low to the king and begs his pardon. But we are in public, celebrating our power. This is not the king whose heart pounds at the sudden noise of a gun salute, who falls into white-faced rage in a moment; this is Henry as he wants people to see him. This Henry does not mind his children out of their chairs, ill-mannered. This is the Henry who has learned what he must do to appear kingly in public. I taught him myself. He roars with laughter as if he is genuinely amused, and he lifts Margaret up so she stands side by side with her brother and waves at the court. He beckons to Elizabeth's nursemaid and she holds the baby out so that everyone can see the three children side by side.

"The children of England!" my husband shouts exultantly, and everyone cheers. He throws out a hand for Arthur and me to join them. Reluctantly, Arthur stands up and pulls back my chair so that we can both go to the king where he stands, his arms wrapped around his younger children, and all six of us can take the applause as if we were play-actors indeed.

Harry turns to his father and whispers. His father bends down to hear and then claps his hands for attention and everyone falls silent. "My son, the Duke of York, is going to sing!" he announces.

Arthur gives me one long inscrutable look and we all stand in silence and listen as Harry, in a sweet light soprano voice, sings "A Very Merry Welcome to Spring" and everyone taps the table or hums the chorus, and when he is done they burst into completely spontaneous applause. Arthur and I smile as if we are quite delighted.

At the end of the two weeks of celebration there is a joust, and Princess Margaret is to award the prizes. I have to order Harry from the royal box, as he cannot bear the disappointment that I will not allow him to ride in the joust on his pony, nor even parade in the arena.

"You can stand here and wave at the crowd, or you can go to the nursery," I say firmly.

"He has to stay," my husband overrules me. "He has to be seen by the crowd. And he has to be seen smiling."

I turn to my sulky little son. "You heard the

king," I say. "You must wave and you must smile. Sometimes we have to do things that we don't want. Sometimes we have to look happy even when we are sad or angry. We are the royal family of England, we have to be seen in our power and our joy. And we have to look glad."

Harry always listens to an appeal to his vanity. Sulkily, he bows his copper head only for a moment, and then he steps to the front of the royal box and lifts his hand to wave at the crowd who bellow their approval. The cheers excite him, he beams and waves again, then he bounces like a young lamb. Beyond him, my son Arthur lifts his hand to wave as well, and smiles. Gently, unseen by the crowd, I get a firm grip of the back of Harry's jacket and hold him still before he shames all of us by jumping over the low wall altogether.

As the jousters come into the arena I catch my breath. I had expected them to be wearing Tudor green, the eternal Tudor green, the compulsory springtime of my husband's reign. But he and his mother have ordered them into the colors of York to honor the new little Duke of York, and to remind everyone that the rose of York is here, not in Malines. They are all wearing blue and the deep scarlet murrey of my house, the livery I have not seen since Richard, the last king of York, rode out to his death at Bosworth.

Henry catches the look on my face. "It

looks well," he says indifferently.

"It does," I agree.

The Tudor presence is stated in the roses which stud the arena, white for York overlaid by the red for Lancaster, and sometimes the new rose which they are growing in greater and greater numbers for occasions like this: the Tudor rose, a red marking inside a white flower, as if every York is actually a Lancaster at heart.

Everyone is invited to the tournament and everyone in England comes: loyalist, traitor, and those very many who have not yet made up their minds. London is filled with people, every lord from every county in England has come with his household, every squire has come with his family, everyone has been commanded to come to celebrate the ennobling of Henry. The palace is filled, there is not a spare inch of floor in the great hall, everyone beds down where they can find a space. The inns for two miles in every direction are bursting at the seams, with four to a bed. All the private houses take in guests, the very stables host men sleeping in the hay barns above the horses. And it is this concentration of so many lords and gentry, citizens, and commoners, this gathering of all the people of England, that makes it so easy, so horribly easy for Henry to arrest everyone he suspects of treason or disloyalty, or even a word out of place.

The moment the joust is over and before anyone can go home, Henry sends out his yeomen of the guard, and men — guilty and innocent alike — are snatched from their lodgings, from their houses, some even from their beds. It is a magnificent attack on everyone whose names Henry has compiled from the time that the boy was first mentioned till now, at the moment that they were most unsuspecting, when they had stepped into Henry's trap. It is brilliant. It is ruthless. It is cruel.

The lawyers are not alert, most of them have come to the joust as guests, the clerks are still taking their holidays. The accused men can find no one to represent them, they cannot even find their friends to post the massive fines that Henry sets for them. Henry snatches them up quickly, dozens at a time, in a city that has been lulled into carelessness by days of merrymaking into forgetting that they are ruled by a king who is never careless, and hardly ever merry.

THE TOWER OF LONDON, JANUARY 1495

We move the court to the Tower as if we are under siege, and I take up residence in my least favorite rooms, in the worst season of the year. Henry finds me, seated on the stone windowsill under a narrow arrow-slit window, looking out at the dark clouds and the constant cold rain on the river beneath the Tower.

"This is cozy," he says, warming his hands at the fire.

When I say nothing, he nods at my ladies to leave us and they skitter out of the room, their leather shoes slapping on the stone floors, their skirts sweeping the rushes aside.

"The children are next door," he says. "I ordered them to be housed there, myself. I know you like them to be near you."

"And where is Edward of Warwick? My cousin?"

"In his usual rooms," Henry says with a little grimace at his own embarrassment. "Safe and sound, of course. Safe in our keeping."

"Why did we not stay at Greenwich? Is there some danger that you're not telling me about?"

"Oh no, no danger." He rubs his hands before the fire again and speaks so airily that I am now certain something is badly wrong.

"Then why have we come here?"

He glances to make sure that the door is locked. "One of the boy's greatest adherents, Sir Robert Clifford, is coming back home to England. He betrayed me, but now he's coming back to me. He can come here and report to me, thinking to win my favor, and I can arrest him without further trouble. He can go from privy chamber to prison — just down a flight of steps!" He smiles as if it is a great advantage to live in a prison for traitors.

"Sir Robert?" I repeat. "I thought he had betrayed you without possibility of return when he left England? I thought he had run away to be with the boy?"

"He was with the boy!" Henry is exultant. "He was with the boy and the foolish boy trusted him with all his treasure and his plans. But he has brought them all to me. And a sack."

"A sack?"

Henry nods. He is watching me carefully. "A sack of seals. Everyone who is plotting for the boy in England, everyone who ever sent him a letter closed it under their seal. The

506

boy received the letter and cut the seal from it, he kept the seals, by way of a pledge. And now, Sir Robert brings me the sack of seals. I have every seal. A complete collection, Elizabeth, that identifies everyone who is plotting for the boy against me."

His face is jubilant, like a rat catcher with a hundred rat tails.

"Do you know how many? Can you guess how many?" I can tell by the tone of his voice that he thinks he is setting a trap for me.

"How many?"

"Hundreds."

"Hundreds? He has hundreds of supporters?"

"But now I know them all. Do you know the names on the list?"

I have to bite my tongue on my impatience. "Of course I don't know who wrote to the boy. I don't know how many seals and I don't know who they are. I don't even know if it is a true collection," I say. "What if it is false? What if there are names on it of men who are faithful to you, who perhaps wrote long ago to Duchess Margaret? What if the boy has sent you this sack on purpose, and Sir Robert is working for him, to fill you with doubt? What if the boy is sowing fear among us?"

I see him catch his breath at a possibility that he had not considered. "Clifford has returned to me — the only one who has returned to me! — and brought me information as good as gold," he says flatly.

"Or false gold, fool's gold, that people mistake for the real thing," I say stoutly. I find my courage and I face him. "Are you saying that any of my kinsmen or -women, or ladies, are on the list?" Not Margaret! I am thinking desperately. Not Margaret. God send that she has had the patience not to rebel against Henry in the hopes of freeing her brother. Please God none of my kinswomen have played their husbands false for love of a boy that they secretly think is my brother? Not my grandmother, not my aunts, not my sisters! Please God that my mother always refused to speak with them, just as she never spoke to me. Please God that no one I love is on Henry's list and that I shall not see my own kinsmen and -women on the scaffold.

"Come," he says suddenly.

Obediently, I rise to me feet. "Where?"

"To my presence chamber," he says, as if it is the most ordinary thing in the world that he should come to my room to fetch me.

"I?"

"Yes."

"What for?" Suddenly my rooms seem very empty, the door to the children's schoolroom is shut, my ladies sent away. Suddenly I realize that the Tower is very quiet and the prisons for traitors are just a half a dozen steps away, as Henry reminded me just a moment ago. "What for?"

"You can come and see Clifford brought before me. Since you are so astute about whose name might or might not be in his bag of seals, since you are casting doubt on it, you can see it for yourself."

"It's a matter for you and your lords," I say, hanging back.

He puts out his hand, his face quite determined. "You had better come," he says. "I don't want people observing your absence and thinking anything of it."

I put my hand in his, feeling how cold he is as he grips me, and I wonder if it is fear that makes his fingers so icy. "Whatever you wish," I say steadily, wondering if I can get a message to Margaret, if anyone in the presence chamber will be close enough for me to whisper a request that she bring me something, a shawl or a cape against the cold of the room. "My ladies must come with me."

"Some of them are there already," he says. "I particularly wanted them to be there. Some of them have to be there, some of them have questions to answer. You will be surprised at how many people are waiting for us. For you."

We enter the presence chamber of the Tower hand in hand as if we are in a procession. It is a long room that runs the length of the

Tower, dark as it is lit only by narrow windows at either end, crowded this afternoon with people pressing themselves back against the cold walls to leave a space before the banked fire for the table, the great chair, the cloth of estate hung high over the chair. My Lady the King's Mother stands on one side of the empty throne, her husband Lord Thomas Stanley beside her, his brother Sir William beside him. She has my sisters Cecily and Anne beside her, and Margaret my cousin is there too. Maggie shoots me one frightened look, her eyes dark, and then drops her gaze to the ground.

Sir Robert Clifford, Richard's friend and loyal companion at the Battle of Bosworth and long before that day, bows as we come in. He looks strained, a leather sack like a pedlar's pack in one hand, a sheet of paper in the other, as if he were coming to market to deal with a difficult trader. Henry takes the great chair under the cloth of gold, and looks him up and down, as if taking the measure of the man who has turned his coat twice.

"You may tell me what you know," Henry says quietly.

My Lady steps a little closer to her son's chair and puts her hand on the carved back, as if she would show them as inseparable, conjoined. In contrast, I find myself shrinking away. Margaret looks at me quickly as if she is afraid that I might faint. The room is stuffy; I can smell the nervous sweat of the waiting lords. I wonder who has good reason to be fearful. I look from Cecily to Anne to Margaret and wonder if they are about to be entrapped. Sir Robert Clifford dabs his damp upper lip.

"I have come straight from the court . . ." he starts.

"It's not a court," Henry corrects him.

"From . . ."

"From the feigned lad Warbeck." Henry speaks for him.

"Warbeck?" Sir Robert hesitates as if to confirm the name, as if he has never heard it before.

Irritated, my husband raises his voice. "Warbeck! Of course! Warbeck! That's his name, for God's sake!"

"With this." Sir Robert holds out the sack.

"The seals of the traitors," Henry prompts him.

Sir Robert is pale. He nods. "The proof of their treachery."

"Cut from their treasonous letters to the boy."

Sir Robert nods nervously.

"You may show me. Show me one at a time."

Sir Robert steps up to the table, within reach of the king, and I see Jasper Tudor raise himself up on his toes, as if he is ready to spring forwards and defend his nephew against some trick. They are afraid, even now, even in the heart of the Tower, that Henry may be attacked.

It is like a children's game as Sir Robert plunges his hand in the bag and hands over the first seal. Henry takes it, turns it around in his hand. "Cressener," he says shortly.

There is a little murmur from one corner of the court, where the absent young man's kinsmen are standing. They look utterly shocked. A man drops to his knees. "Before God, I knew nothing of it," he says.

Henry just looks at him, as the clerk behind him makes a note on a sheet of paper. Henry holds out his hand for another seal. "Astwood," he says.

"Never!" a woman exclaims, and then bites back the denial, realizing that she does not want to be seen defending a traitor.

Henry holds out his hand, disregarding the gasp from the lords. I see the seal as it comes from the bag, almost as if by magic, as if I suddenly have the eyes of a hawk that can see far, far below the crouching mouse, the dash of a pheasant chick. As Sir Robert hands over the small red seal, I recognize the imprint of my mother's ring.

Sir Robert knows it too. He hands it over without saying a name, and Henry takes it without comment, turns and looks at me, his gaze absolutely expressionless, his dark eyes as flat and unloving as Welsh slate. Silently, he puts it on the table, beside the seals of the other traitors. Uncle Jasper glares at me, and his mother turns her face away. I meet my sister Cecily's frightened gaze but I dare not signal to her to say nothing. I keep my face perfectly still; the most important thing is that we none of us confess to anything.

Another seal comes from the bag. I find I am holding my breath as if preparing for something yet more terrible. Henry puts it on the table without saying the name, and the whole of the court cranes forwards as if they would read it, despite him.

"Dorlay," he says bitterly. There is a low moan from one of my ladies as he names her brother.

Sir Robert passes another seal from the bag, and I hear My Lady gasp in horror. She reels back, grips the chair to steady herself as Henry rises to his feet. His hand is on the seal, I can't see the inscription, and for a moment, in my terror, I think he will turn to me, I think he will name me as a traitor. I think it is my seal in his hand. The court is breathless, looking from the king's shocked face to the pallor of his mother. Whatever Henry was planning in this ordeal, it was not that he should find this seal in the bag. His hand shakes as he holds out the seal with the familiar crest.

"Sir William?" he asks, and his voice falters as he looks past his mother to her brother-in-law, the trusted beloved brother of her husband, whose army saved Henry's life at Bosworth, who handed him the crown of England and was made Lord Chamberlain, the highest position in the kingdom, and given a fortune as a mere part of his reward. "Sir William Stanley?" he repeats, disbelievingly. "This is your seal?"

"It's not possible," Thomas, Lord Stanley, says hastily.

Terribly, at that moment, a laugh forces its way out of my mouth. I am so horrified and so shocked and so startled that I laugh like a fool and bury my face in my hands and find I cannot catch my breath for wanting to laugh, laugh out loud at the madness of this moment. I choke and peal after peal of laughter escapes me.

It is because I see, so blindingly clearly, that yet again the Stanleys have put a man on either side, as they always do, as my mother herself warned me they always do. There is always a Stanley on either side of the battle, or one who has sworn he is on his way, or one promising an army but unfortunately failing to deliver. Whenever there is a moment that a family must choose a side, the Stanleys are always to be found on both sides at once.

Even at Bosworth, though they were to be found on the winning side at the very end, they had promised their loyalty and their army to Richard. At the start of the day they were sworn to be his allies. Richard even had Thomas Stanley's son as a hostage, to prove their goodwill. He was certain they would ride to his aid even as they waited on the hill to see which way the battle was going, and then thundered down to support Henry.

And now, they have done it again. *"Sans changer!"* I choke. *"Sans changer!"*

It is the Stanley motto: never changing. But they are only unchanging in the pursuit of their own safety and success, and then I feel Maggie at my side and her fingers pinching the inside of my arm as she whispers urgently, "Stop it! Stop it!" and I bite the back of my hand and choke into silence.

But as my laughter drains away, I realize how powerful "the boy" has become. If the Stanleys have divided — one to Henry's side, one to the boy's — then they must know that he will invade and they must think that he might win. To have a Stanley on your side is like a pedigree — it shows that your claim is a good one. They only ever join a winning side. If Sir William is backing the boy it is only because he thinks he will triumph. If Lord Thomas has allowed it, it is because he thinks the boy has a good chance and a better claim.

Henry glances at me as I struggle to compose myself. He turns back to Sir William and his face is blank. "I gave you everything you asked for," he says flatly, as though loyalty should be bought.

Sir William inclines his head.

"You yourself handed the crown of England to me on the battlefield."

It is terrible how the people have fallen away from Sir William as if they have suddenly seen on him the pockmarks of the plague. Without seeming to move, everyone has receded from him by a clear pace and he stands alone, facing the king's horrified gaze.

"You are my stepfather's brother, I have treated you as an uncle." Henry looks at his mother. She is swallowing convulsively as if bile is rising in her throat and she is going to vomit. "My mother assured me that you were her kinsman, you were a man we could trust."

"A mistake," Thomas, Lord Stanley, says. "Sir William can explain, I know . . ."

"There are forty important men promised with him," Sir Robert prompts unasked. "He has recruited supporters. Between them they have sent the boy a fortune."

"You are of the royal family of England and yet you side with a pretender?" Henry struggles with the words as if he cannot believe that he is saying this to his uncle. He had thought to shame me with the proof of my mother's disloyalty, he had thought to shock the court with half a dozen names that he would send to the hangman to teach the others to be loyal in future. He did not think that in this theater of asserting his power he would find a traitor in his own family. I look at his mother, who is clinging to the back of his chair as her knees give way beneath her, looking with staring eyes from her husband to his brother as if they are equally faithless. At that horror-stricken glance from her I realize that they probably are. The brothers never act without each other. Perhaps they decided that Sir William would back the pretender and Thomas, Lord Stanley, maintain his fatherhood of the king. Both of them waiting to see who would win. Both of them determined to be on the winning side. Both of them judging that Henry Tudor was likely to lose.

"Why?" he asks brokenly. "Why would you betray me? Me! After you supported me? Me! Who gave you everything?"

Then I see him snap off the questions, as he hears in his own voice the weakness in his tone. It is the whine of a boy who was never loved, who was always in exile hoping one day to come home. The boy who could never understand why he should be far from his mother, why he should have no friends, why he should live in a foreign land and have only enemies at home. Henry remembers that there are some questions which should never be asked.

The last thing he wants his court to hear is why Sir William was ready to risk everything for the boy, to throw away everything he had gained from the king. Why Sir William would take that choice could only be for a residual love and loyalty for the House of York, and his belief that the boy is the true heir. Henry doesn't want to hear this. The last thing he should invite is a justification from the Stanleys. Who knows how many people would agree with them? He slams his hand flat on the table. "I won't hear a word from you."

Sir William shows no intention of speaking. His face is pale and proud. I can't look at him without thinking that he knows his cause is a good one. He is following a true king.

"Take him away," Henry says to the guards at the door and they step forwards and Sir William goes with them without a word. He does not ask for mercy and he does not try to explain. He goes with his head held high, as if he knows he will have to pay the price for doing the right thing. I have never seen him, in all my life before, walk like a proud man. I have always thought of him as a turncoat, one who would go from one side to the other for the winnings. But today, as they take him out as a traitor, when he is going to his death, when he is utterly lost for supporting the boy who says he is my brother — Sir William goes gladly, his head held high.

Sir Robert, whose family lands were confiscated by Sir William and who has borne him a grudge since then, watches him go with a broad smile, and reaches into the sack of seals as if to give us all another surprise.

"Enough," Henry says, looking as sick as his mother. "I will inspect them on my own, in my rooms. You can go. You can all go. I want no one —" He breaks off and looks past me as if I am the last person who might give him comfort in this moment of betrayal. "I want none of you."

WESTMINSTER PALACE, LONDON, FEBRUARY 1495

Henry's suspicion of me and all Yorks drives him onwards to find a husband that he can trust who can marry my sister Anne and thus eliminate her as a center for rebellion. His choice falls on Thomas Howard, Earl of Surrey, who has been punished long enough for being loyal to the House of York and is released from the Tower. He was Richard's man; but made it clear to Henry that his loyalty was always only to the crown. Once the crown was on Henry's head he followed it. Henry has doubted this, and suspected him, but his faithful waiting in the Tower, like a dog for the return of his master, has convinced Henry to take the risk. So Thomas is betrothed to my sister Anne, takes his title back into his hand, and has every reason to think that the Howard dynasty will rise under the Tudors as it was set to do under the Yorks.

"Do you mind?" I ask Anne.

She gives me one level look. She is nineteen, and has been proposed as a bride all around

Christendom.

"It's time," she says shortly. "And it could be worse. Thomas Howard is a coming man, he will rise in the king's favor. You'll see. He'll do anything for him."

Henry wastes little time on the wedding that he has ordered; he can think of nothing but the sack of seals and the names of the men who have been betraying him ever since he took the crown on his head.

Jasper Tudor, the only man in the world that Henry can trust, heads a commission to try the traitors and with eleven lords and eight judges, drags into court anyone who has ever spoken of the boy or whispered the name Prince Richard. Before Jasper come priests, clerks, officials, lords, their families, servants, sons, a terrible parade of men who had taken the Tudor shilling, sworn the Tudor oaths of loyalty, but then decided that the boy was the true king. Despite their position, despite the wealth that Henry had given them, these lords have gone against their own interests, drawn to the boy as if they could not help themselves, following a brighter star than their own selfish good. They are like martyrs for the House of York, pledging their faith, gambling their own safety, sending words of love and loyalty in their own hands sealed with their family crests.

They pay a heavy price. The lords are publicly beheaded, the common men hanged, gutted while they are still alive, their bellies and their lungs dragged out of their sliced bodies and burned before their glaring eyes, then finally they die as they are cut into pieces, quartered like a carcass, their mangled bodies sent around the kingdom to be displayed at city gates, at crossroads, at village squares.

From this, Henry hopes that his country will learn loyalty. But I recognize — knowing this country as I do, and he does not — that all the people will learn is that good men, wise men, wealthy men, men as privileged as Sir William Stanley, men as knowing and as cunning as the king's own uncle, are ready to die for the boy. All they will judge from the many deaths and the festering body parts is that many, many good men believed in the boy, and were ready to die for him.

Stanley goes to the scaffold in silence neither begging for mercy nor offering to unmask other traitors. There is no way that he could declare more loudly that he thinks the boy is the true king and that Tudor is a pretender, that Tudor was always a pretender, today as on the day of the battle of Bosworth Field. Nothing could ring out more clearly than Stanley's silence, nothing publishes the boy's claims more strongly than the grinning skulls of his adherents on the gates of every town of England, making everyone wonder at the cause for which these men died so terribly.

Henry sends out commissions to seek for traitors in every county of England. He thinks they will root out treason. I think that all they will do, wherever they go, is prove to the people that the king thinks there is treason everywhere. All Henry tells the market towns when his yeomen of the guard march in and set up a hearing for the local gossips is that their king is afraid of everyone, even the tongue-waggers in the alehouses. All he demonstrates is that their king is afraid of almost everything, like a child dreading the darkness at bedtime who imagines threats everywhere.

Jasper Tudor comes back to Westminster after scouring the country for treason, looking exhausted, gray with fatigue. He is a man of sixty-three, who thought he had brought his beloved nephew to the throne in a blaze of courage nearly a decade ago, and that the great task of his life was done. Now he finds that for every man who died on the battlefield fighting against them, there are ten enemies in hiding, twenty, a hundred. York was never defeated, it just stepped back into the shadows. For Jasper, who fought all his life against York, who suffered exile from his own beloved country for nearly twenty-five years, it is as if his great victory over the House of York has never happened. York is stepping forwards again and Jasper has to find his courage, find his power, and ready himself for another battle. But now he is an old man.

His wife, my aunt Katherine, sends him out on his mission with an obedient curtsey and a hard face. Half the people he will arrest and see hanged are loyal servants of our house and personal friends to her. But My Lady the King's Mother, who has loved him, I believe, ever since she was a young widow and he was her only friend, looks at him with hollow eyes, as if she would drop to her knees before him and beg him to save her boy again, as he has saved him so often before. They shrink into themselves, the king, his mother and his uncle, trusting no one else now.

Thomas, Lord Stanley, whose loveless marriage to My Lady the King's Mother brought him to greatness and brought an army to her son, is excluded from their councils, as if he shares a taint of treason with his dead brother. If they cannot trust the brother-in-law of My Lady the King's Mother, if they cannot trust her husband, if they cannot trust their own kinsmen that they have loaded with honor and money, then who can they trust?

They can trust no one, they fear everyone.

Henry never comes to my rooms in the evenings anymore. Terrified of a boy, he cannot think of making another child. We have the heirs that he needs: our own boy and his little brother. Henry looks at me as if he cannot contemplate making another child on me, one that would be half York, one that would be half traitor by birth. All the warmth, all the tenderness that was growing between us is frozen out by his terror and mistrust. As his mother looks at me askance, as the king puts out his hand to lead me in to dinner but hardly touches my fingers, I walk like the traitor Sir William: with my head up, as if I refuse to feel shame.

I see the eyes of the court upon me all the time, but I dare not meet their eyes and smile. I cannot judge who might smile at me, thinking that I am the cruelly treated wife of a husband who has lost once again his new habit of kindness, a man who has been told all his life that he should be king and now doubts it more than ever before. Or perhaps they are smiling at me because they are undetected, and think I am hidden too. Perhaps they are plotting treason and think I am with them. Perhaps they are smiling at me because they saw my mother's seal in the traitor's sack, and believe that my own seal was hidden away, lower down in the bag.

I think of the boy in Malines, the boy with golden-brown hair and hazel eyes, and imagine him walking like me, with his head up, as we children of York were taught to do. I think of him learning of the loss of the treasure, of the sack of seals; a crushing blow to his plans, the betrayal of his allies. They say that he expressed regret that Sir Robert had betrayed him, but that he did not curse or swear. He did not gulp as if he might be sick, and order everyone from the room. He behaved like a boy who was taught by a loving mother that the wheel of fortune may well turn against you, and there is no point in railing against it, or wishing it otherwise. He took the bad news like a prince of York, not like a Tudor.

Worcester Castle, Summer 1495

Nobody will tell me what is happening. I walk in a circle of silence, as if I am held like a leech in a jar of thick glass. Henry comes to my rooms but hardly speaks to me. He gets into my bed and does his duty as if he were visiting a brothel, a stewhouse; we have lost all the love that was growing between us. Now he wants to make another Tudor to have as a reserve against the boy. He has consulted astronomers and they think that a third Tudor prince would make his throne more secure. It seems that two heirs and one of them proclaimed as the Duke of York is not enough for him. We need to hide behind a wall of babies, and Henry will get them on me for necessity but not for love.

In July I tell him that I have missed my course and am with child again, and he nods silently; even this news cannot bring him joy. He stops coming to my room as a man released from a duty and I am glad to sleep with the companionship of one of my sisters, or with Margaret, who is at court while her husband scours the east of England for hidden traitors. I have lost the desire to lie with my husband, his touch is cold and his hands are bloody. His mother looks at me as if she would call the yeomen of the guard to arrest me for nothing more than my name.

Jasper Tudor is never here at court anymore, but is always riding to get reports from the east coast, where they are certain that the boy will land, from the North, where they think the Scots will invade with the white rose on their banners, or from the west, where Henry's attempts to crush the Irish has rebounded on him and the people are angrier and more rebellious than ever before.

I spend most of my time in the nursery with my children. Arthur studies with his schoolmasters and every afternoon is ordered out into the tilt yard to master his horse and to learn his skills with lance and sword. Margaret is quick with her lessons and quick in her temper; she will snatch a book from her brothers and run and lock herself in a room before they can shout and chase after her. Elizabeth is as light as a feather, a little baby as pale as snow. They tell me she will fatten up soon, she will be as strong as her brothers and sister, but I don't believe them. Henry is preparing a betrothal for her, he is desperate to make an alliance with France and will use this little treasure, this child of porcelain, to make a treaty. He will use her as fresh bait to catch the boy. I don't argue with him. I cannot worry now about her wedding in twelve years' time, I can only think that this day she has eaten nothing but a little bread and some milk, some fish at dinnertime, no meat at all.

My little boy Henry is bright and willing, quick to learn but easily distracted, a child born for play. He is to go into the Church, and I seem to be the only one who thinks this is ridiculous. My Lady the King's Mother plans he will be a cardinal like her great friend and ally John Morton. She prays that he will rise through the Church and become a pope, a Tudor pope. It is pointless to tell her that he is a worldly child who loves sport and play and music and food with a most unclerical relish. It does not matter to her. With Arthur as King of England and Henry as Pope in Rome she will have this world and the next in the hands of Tudors and God will have fulfilled the promise he made her when she was a frightened little girl who feared that her son would never rule anything but a couple of castles in Wales and would shortly be driven, by my father, from them.

Her great friend John Morton stays in the south of England, as we spend our summer here in the center of the country, far from the dangerous coast, close to Coventry Castle. Morton is guarding the south coast for My Lady's fearful son, who goes to and from the court without warning, as if he is riding his own patrols, as if he cannot even trust his spies anymore, but has to see everything for himself. We never know if he will attend dinner, we never know if he will sleep in his own bed; and when his throne is empty the courtiers look around as if for another king who could be seated there. Now the Tudors trust no one but the handful of people who fled with them into exile long ago. Their world has shrunk to the tiny court that hid with them in Brittany; it is as if all the allies and the friends they made, and all the guards and soldiers they recruited after the battle of Bosworth, had never joined them, as if they have no support at all.

It is the court of a frightened pretender and there is no majesty or pride or confidence about it. Working alone, I can do nothing, when I process on my own to dinner with my head held high, smiling around at friends and suspects alike, trying on my own to overcome the impression that the king is afraid and his court are uncertain.

Then, one evening, John Kendal, the Bishop of Worcester, stops me on my way to my rooms with a kindly smile, and asks me, as a man offering to show a rainbow or a pretty sunset: "Have you seen the light from the beacons, Your Grace?"

I hesitate. "Beacons?"

"The sky is quite red."

I turn to the arrow-slit window in the castle and look out. To the south the sky is quite rosy, and as far as I can see there is a light on a hill, and then another, and then another behind and behind one after another all the way until I can see nothing more.

"What is it?"

"The king commanded beacons to warn him of the landing of Richard of York," John Kendal says.

"You mean the pretender," I remind him. "The boy."

In the glow of the lights I catch his hidden smile and I hear his low laugh. "Of course. I forgot his name. These are the beacons. He must have landed."

"Landed?"

"These are his beacons. The boy is coming home."

"The boy is coming home?" I repeat like a fool. It cannot be that I have mistaken the bishop's delight in the rosy light of the beacons. He is illuminated with joy as if the beacons were welcoming flares to guide ships safely into port. He smiles at me to share his delight that the Plantagenet boy is homeward bound.

"Yes," he says. "They are lighting his way home at last."

Next day Henry thunders out of the castle surrounded by his guard, without a word of farewell to me, riding west to raise troops, visiting castles in the Stanley areas, desperate to keep them loyal, uncertain of them all. He does not even say good-bye to the children in the nursery or go to his mother for her blessing. She is horrified by his sudden departure and spends all her time on her knees on the stone floor of the chapel at Worcester, not even coming to breakfast, for she is fasting, starving herself to draw down a blessing on her son. Her thin neck at the top of her gown is red and raw, as she is wearing a hair shirt against her skin to mortify her paper-thin flesh. Jasper Tudor rides beside Henry, like a tired old warhorse that does not know how to stop and rest.

Confused rumors come back to us. The boy has landed in the east of the country, coming into England through Hull and York, as my father did when he returned in triumph from his exile. The boy is following in King Edward's footsteps as his true son and heir.

Then we hear that the winds blew the boy off course and he has landed in the south of England and there is nobody there to defend the coast but the archbishop and some local bands. What shall prevent the boy from marching on London? There is no one to block the road, there is no one who will deny him.

Henry's guard rides into the stable yard without warning, and the grooms brush down the exhausted horses and the men stained with mud from the road take the back stairs to their rooms in silence. They don't shout for ale or boast of their journey, they return to the court like men silent with grim determination, afraid of defeat. Henry dines with the court for two nights, hard-faced, as if he has forgotten all his lessons about being a smiling king. He comes to my rooms to lead me in to dinner and greets me curtly.

"He landed." He spits out the words as he leads me to the top table. "He got a few men onshore. But he saw the defense and sheered off like a coward. My men killed a few hundred of them, but like fools they let his ship get away. He fled like a boy and they let him go."

I don't remind my husband that once he too came to the coast and saw that there was a trap and sailed away without landing. We called him a coward then, too. "So where is he now?"

He looks at me coldly, as if measuring whether it is safe to tell me. "Who knows? Perhaps he's gone to Ireland? The winds were blowing west, so I doubt he'll have landed in Wales. Wales at least should be faithful to a Tudor. He'll know that."

I say nothing. We both know that he can trust nowhere to be faithful to a Tudor. I hold out my hands and the groom of the ewery pours warm water on my fingers and holds out a scented towel.

Henry rubs his hands and throws the towel at a page boy. "I captured some of his men," he says with sudden energy. "I have about a hundred and sixty of them, Englishmen and foreigners, all traitors and rebels."

I don't need to ask what will happen to the men who sailed with the boy for England. We take our seats and face our court.

"I shall send them round the country and have them hanged in groups in every market town," Henry says with sudden cold energy. "I shall show people what happens to anyone who turns against me. And I shall try them for piracy — not treason. If I name them as pirates I can kill the foreigners as well. Frenchman and Englishman can hang side by side and everyone will look at their rotting bodies and know that they dare not question my rule no matter where they were born."

"You won't forgive them?" I ask, as they pour a glass of wine. "Not any of them? You won't show mercy? You always say that it is politic to show mercy."

"Why in hell's name should I forgive them? They were coming against me, against the King of England. Armed and hoping to overthrow me."

I bow my head under his fury and know that the court is watching Henry's rage.

"But the ones that I execute in London will die as pirates do," he says with sudden harsh relish. His temper vanishes, he beams at me.

I shake my head. "I don't know what you mean," I say wearily. "What have you advisors been telling you now?"

"They've been telling me how pirates are punished," he says with a cruel joy. "And this is how I will have these men killed. I will have them tied down by St. Katherine's Wharf at Wapping. They are traitors and they came against me by sea. I shall find them guilty of piracy and they will be tied down and the tide will come in and slowly, slowly, creep over them, lapping up their feet and their legs till it splashes into their mouths and they will drown inch by inch in a foot of water. D'you think *that* will teach the people of England what happens to rebels? Do you think that will teach the people of England not to defy me? Never to come against a Tudor?"

"I don't know," I say. I am trying to catch my breath as if it is me staked out on the beach with the rising tide splashing against my closed lips, wetting my face, slowly rising. "I hope so."

Days later, when Henry is gone again on his restless patrolling of the Midlands, we hear that the boy has landed in Ireland and set siege to Waterford Castle. The Irish are flocking to his standard and Henry's rule in Ireland is utterly overthrown.

I rest in the afternoons; this baby is sitting

heavily on my belly and makes me too weary to walk. Margaret sits with me, sewing at my side, and whispers to me that Ireland has become ungovernable, the rule of the English is overthrown, everyone is declaring for the boy. Her husband, Sir Richard, will have to go to that most dangerous island; Henry has commanded him to take troops to fight the boy and his adoring allies. But before Sir Richard has even ordered the ships to transport his troops, the siege is lifted without warning, and the elusive boy is gone.

"Where is he now?" I ask Henry as he prepares to ride out, his yeomen of the guard behind him, armed and helmeted as if they are on campaign, as if he expects an attack on the highways of his own country.

His face is dark. "I don't know," he says shortly. "Ireland is a bog of treachery. He is hiding in the wetlands, he is hiding in the mountains. My man in Ireland, Poynings, has no command, he has lost all control, he knows nothing. The boy is like a ghost, we hear of him but we never see him. We know they are hiding him but we don't know where."

WESTMINSTER PALACE, LONDON, AUTUMN 1495

The king does not come to my bedroom at night, not even to sit and talk with me; he has not come for months. The days when we were friends and lovers seem very far away now. I do not let myself grieve for the loss of his love, I sense that he is fighting a battle in his own heart as well as constantly patrolling the roads of England. His fear and hatred consume him, he cannot even take pleasure at the thought of another child in my belly. He cannot sit beside my fire and talk quietly with me, he is too restless, hagridden by his constant fear. Out in the darkness, somewhere in England, in Ireland, or in Wales, the boy is awake, and Henry cannot sleep quietly at my side.

Sir Richard Pole has finally sailed for Ireland to try to find Irish chieftains who can be persuaded to hold to their alliance against the boy, and Maggie comes to my rooms every night after dinner and we spend the evening together. We always make sure to keep one of My Lady's women with us, in earshot, and we always speak of nothing but banalities; but it is a comfort for me to have her by my side. If the lady-in-waiting reports to My Lady, and of course we must assume that she does, she can say that we spent the evening talking of the children, of their education, and of the weather, which is too damp and cold for us to walk with any pleasure.

Maggie is the only one of my ladies that I can talk to without fear. Only to her can I say quietly, "Baby Elizabeth is no stronger. Actually, I think she is weaker today."

"The new herbs did no good?"

"No good."

"Perhaps when the spring comes and you can take her into the country?"

"Maggie, I don't even know that she will see the spring. I look at her, and I look at your little Henry, and though they are so near in age, they look like different beings. She's like a little faerie child, she is so small and so frail, and he is such a strong stocky boy."

She puts her hand over mine. "Ah, my dear. Sometimes God takes the most precious children to his own."

"I named her for my mother, and I fear she will go to her."

"Then her grandmother will look after her in heaven, if we cannot keep her here on earth. We have to believe that."

I nod at the words of comfort, but the thought of losing Elizabeth is almost unbearable. Maggie puts her hand on mine.

"We do know that she will live in glory with her grandmother in heaven," she repeats. "We know this, Elizabeth."

"But I had such a picture of her as a princess," I say wonderingly. "I could almost see her. A proud girl, with her father's copper hair and my mother's fair skin, and our love of reading. I could almost see her, as if standing for a portrait, with her hand on a book. I could almost see her as a young woman, proud as a queen. And I told My Lady the King's Mother that Elizabeth would be the greatest Tudor of them all."

"Perhaps she will be," Maggie suggests. "Perhaps she will survive. Babies are unpredictable, perhaps she will grow stronger."

I shake my head on my doubts, and that night, at about midnight, when I am wakened by a deep yellow autumn moon shining through the slats of the shutters, my thoughts go at once to my sick baby. I get up and put on my robe. At once Maggie, sleeping in my bed, is awake. "Are you ill?"

"No. Just troubled. I want to see Elizabeth. You go to sleep."

"I'll come with you," she says, and slips out of bed and throws a shawl over her nightgown.

Together we open the door and the dozing

sentry gives a jolt of surprise as if we are a pair of ghosts, white-faced with our hair plaited under our nightcaps. "It's all right," Maggie says. "Her Grace is going to the nursery."

He and his fellow guard follow us as we walk in our bare feet down the cold stone corridor, and then Maggie pauses. "What is it?" she asks.

"I thought I heard something," I say quietly. "Can you hear it? Like singing?"

She shakes her head. "Nothing. I can't hear anything."

I know what the sound is then, and I turn to the nursery in sudden urgency. I quicken my stride, I start to run, I push my way past the guard and race up the stone steps to the tower, where the nursery is warm and safe at the top. As I open the door the nurse starts up from where she is bending over the little crib, her face aghast, saying: "Your Grace! I was just going to send for you!"

I snatch up Elizabeth into my arms and she is warm and breathing quietly but white, fatally white, and her eyelids and her lips as blue as cornflowers. I kiss her for the last time and I see her fleeting tiny smile, for she knows I am here, and then I hold her, I don't move at all, I just stand and hold her to my heart as I feel the little chest rise and fall, rise and fall, and then become still.

"Is she asleep?" Maggie asks hopefully.

I shake my head and I feel the tears running down my face. "No. She's not asleep. She's not asleep."

In the morning, after I have washed her little body and dressed her in her nightgown, I send a short message to her father to tell him that our little daughter is dead. He comes home so quickly that I guess he had the news ahead of my letter. He has a spy set on me, as he has on everyone else in England, and that they have already told him that I ran from my bedchamber in the middle of the night to hold my daughter in my arms as she died.

He comes into my rooms in a rush and kneels before me, as I am seated, dressed in dark blue, in my chair by my fireside. His head is bowed as he reaches blindly for me. "My love," he says quietly.

I take his hands and I can hear, but I don't see, my ladies skitter out of the room to leave us alone. "I am so sorry I was not here," he says. "God forgive me that I was not with you."

"You're never here," I say softly. "Nothing matters to you anymore but the boy."

"I am trying to defend the inheritance for all our children." He raises his head but speaks without any anger. "I was trying to make her safe in her own country. Oh, dear child, poor little child. I didn't realize she

541

was so ill, I should have listened to you. God forgive me that I did not."

"She wasn't really ill," I say. "She just never thrived. When she died it wasn't a struggle at all, it was as if she just sighed, and then she was gone."

He bows his head and puts his face against my hands in my lap. I can feel a hot tear on my fingers, and I bend over him and hold him tightly, I grip him as if I would feel his strength and have him feel mine.

"God bless her," he says. "And forgive me for being away. I feel her loss more than you know, more than I can tell you. I know it seems that I'm not a good father to our children, and I'm not a good husband to you — but I care for them and for you more than you know, Elizabeth. I swear that at least I will be a good king for them. I will keep the kingdom for my children and your throne for you, and you will see your son Arthur inherit."

"Hush," I say. With the memory of Elizabeth, warm and limp in my arms, I don't want to tempt fate by foretelling the future of our other children.

He gets up and I stand with him as he wraps his arms around me and holds me tightly, his face against my neck as if he would inhale comfort from the scent of my skin.

"Forgive me," he breathes. "I can hardly ask it of you; but I do. Forgive me, Elizabeth."

"You are a good husband, Henry," I re-assure him. "And a good father. I know that you love us in your heart, I know that you wouldn't have gone away if you had thought we might lose her, and see, here you are — home almost before I had sent for you."

He tips his head back to look at me, but he does not deny that it was his spies who told me that his daughter was dead. He did not hear it first from me. "I have to know every-thing," is all he says. "That's how I keep us safe."

My Lady the King's Mother plans and ex-ecutes a great funeral for our little girl. She is buried as a princess in the chapel of Edward the Confessor in Westminster Abbey. Arch-bishop Morton performs the funeral service, the Bishop of Worcester, who told me that the boy was coming home, serves the Mass with quiet dignity. I cannot tell Henry that the bishop was smiling the night that the beacons were lit for the landing of the boy. I cannot report on the priest who is burying my child. I fold my hands before me and I rest my head against them and I pray for her precious soul and I know without doubt that she is in heaven; and that I am left to the bit-terness of a loss on earth.

Arthur, my firstborn and always the most thoughtful of my children, puts his hand in mine, though he is now a big boy of just nine.

"Don't cry, Lady Mother," he whispers. "You know she's with our lady grandmother, you know she has gone to God."

"I know," I say, blinking.

"And you've still got me."

I swallow my tears. "I still have you," I agree.

"You'll always have me."

"I'm glad of that." I smile down at him. "I am so glad of that, Arthur."

"And perhaps the next baby will be a girl."

I hold him close to me. "Whether she is a girl or a boy, she can't take the place of Elizabeth. Do you think if I lost you, I wouldn't mind because I still had Harry?"

His own eyes are bright with tears but he laughs at that. "No, though Harry would think so. Harry would think it a very good exchange."

WESTMINSTER PALACE, LONDON, NOVEMBER 1495

My cousin Maggie comes to my privy chamber in Westminster, carrying my box of jewels by way of excusing her arrival. In these suspicious times we always make sure that when we are together we are clearly doing something; she fetches things for me, I send her on errands. We never look as if we have met only to put our heads together, whispering secrets. By the way she carries the box, in front of her, for all to see, demonstrating that we are going to look at my jewels, I guess at once that she wants to speak to me in private.

I turn to my maid-in-waiting. "Please fetch the dark purple ribbon from the wardrobe rooms," I say.

She curtseys. "I'm sorry, Your Grace, I thought you wanted the blue."

"I did, but I have changed my mind. And Claire — go with her and bring the matching purple cloak."

The two of them leave as Margaret opens the box of jewels and holds up my amethysts as if to show me. The other women are closer to the fireside, and can see us but not hear what we are saying. Margaret holds the jewels to the light to make them sparkle with a deep purple fire.

"What?" I ask tersely as I seat myself before my looking-glass.

"He's in Scotland."

A little bubble of laughter, or perhaps it is a sob of fear, forms in my throat. "In Scotland? He's left Ireland? You are sure?"

"Honored guest of King James. The king acknowledges him, is holding a great meeting of the lords, calls him by his title: Richard Duke of York." She stands behind me, lifting up the amethyst coronal to show me.

"How d'you know?"

"My husband, God bless him, told me. He got it from the Spanish ambassador, who got it from the Spain dispatches — everything that they write to Spain they send a copy to us, the alliance between the king and the Spanish has grown so strong." She checks that the women at the fire are engaged in their own conversation, puts the amethysts around my neck, and goes on. "The Spanish ambassador to Scotland was called in by King James of Scotland, who raged at him and said that our King Henry was a cat's-paw in the hands of the Spanish king and queen. But he — James — would see the rightful king of England take his throne."

"Is he going to invade?"

Margaret puts the coronal on my head. I see my wondering face in the looking-glass before me, my eyes wide, my face pale. For a moment I seem like my mother, for a moment I am a beauty as she was. I pat my white cheeks. "I look like I have seen a ghost."

"We all look like that," Margaret says, a weak reflected smile over my head as she fastens the amethysts around my neck. "We are all going around as if a ghost is on his way to us. They are singing in the streets about the Duke of York, who dances in Ireland and plays in Scotland and will walk in an English garden and everyone will be merry again. They say he is a ghost come to dance, a duke brought back from the dead."

"They say it is my brother," I say flatly.

"The King of Scotland says that he will put his life on it."

"And what does your husband say?"

"He says there will be war," she replies, the smile fading from her face. "The Scots will invade to support Richard, they will invade England, and there will be war."

WESTMINSTER PALACE, LONDON, CHRISTMAS 1495

Henry's uncle Jasper comes home from one of his long hard rides as pale as the men that he has tried and sent to the gallows, with deep lines of weariness grooved into his face. He is old, much more than sixty, and he has worked this year like a man desperate to see his nephew safe on his throne, terribly aware that time is running out for them both. Old age is dogging him, disaster is walking at Henry's heels.

My aunt Katherine, always a dutiful wife, puts him to bed in their rich and comfortable rooms, calls physicians, apothecaries, and nurses to care for him, but she is elbowed aside by My Lady the King's Mother, who prides herself on her knowledge of medicine and herbs and says that Jasper's constitution is so strong that all he needs is good food, rest, and some tinctures of her own creation to get well. My husband Henry visits the sickroom three times a day, in the morning to see how his uncle has slept, before dinner to make sure that he has the very best that the kitchen can offer and that it is served to him first, hot and fresh, on bended knee, and then last thing at night, before he and his mother go to the chapel and pray for the health of the man who has been the keystone of their lives for so very long. Jasper has been like a father to Henry, and his only constant companion. He has been his protector and his mentor. Henry would have died without his uncle's constant loving care. To My Lady, I think he has been the most potent of influences a woman can know: the love she never named, the life she never led, the man she should have married.

Both Henry and his mother share a confident assumption that Jasper, who has always ridden hard and fought hard, who has always escaped danger and thrived in exile, will once again slide through the claws of death and dance at the Christmas feast. But after a few days they look more and more grave, and after a few more they are calling on the physicians to come and see him. A few days more, and Jasper insists on seeing a lawyer and making his will.

"His will?" I repeat to Henry.

"Of course," he snaps. "He is a man of sixty-three. And devout, and responsible. Of course he is making his will."

"He is very ill then?"

"What do you think?" He rounds on me.

"Did you think that he had taken to his bed for the pleasure of a rest? He has never rested in his life; he has never been away from my side when I needed him; he has never spared himself, not for one day, not for one moment . . ." He breaks off and turns away from me so that I cannot see the tears in his eyes.

Gently, I go behind him, as he is seated in his chair, and put my arm around his back to hold him tightly; I lean down and rest my cheek against his for comfort. "I know how much you love him," I say. "He has been like a father and more for you."

"He has been my protector, and my teacher, my mentor and my friend," he says brokenly. "He took me from England to safety and endured exile for my sake when I was only a boy. Then he brought me back to claim the throne. I wouldn't even have made it to the battlefield without him. I couldn't have found my way across England, I wouldn't have dared to trust the Stanleys, God knows I wouldn't have won the battle but for his teaching. I owe him everything."

"Is there anything I can do?" I ask helplessly, for I know there will be nothing.

"My mother is doing everything," Henry says proudly. "In your condition you can do nothing to help her. You can pray if you like."

Ostentatiously, I take my ladies to chapel and we pray and command a sung Mass for the health of Jasper Tudor, uncle to the King of England, old irrepressible rebel that he is. Christmas comes to court but Henry commands that it be celebrated quietly; there is to be no loud music and no shouts of laughter to disturb the sickroom where Jasper lies sleeping, and the king and his mother keep their constant vigil.

Arthur is taken in to see his dying uncle, Harry goes in after him. Little Princess Margaret is spared the ordeal but My Lady insists that the boys kneel at the bedside of the greatest Englishman the world has ever known.

"Welshman," I say quietly.

On Christmas Day we go to church and celebrate the birth of Jesus Christ and pray for the health of his most beloved son and soldier Jasper Tudor. But on the day after, Henry comes to my room unannounced early in the morning and sits on the foot of my bed as I sleepily rise up, and Cecily, who is sleeping with me, jumps up, curtseys, and scuttles out of the room.

"He's gone," Henry says. He does not sound grieved so much as amazed. "My Lady Mother and I were sitting with him and he stretched out his hand to her and he smiled at me, and then he lay back on his pillows and breathed out a long sigh — and then he was gone."

There is a silence. The depth of his loss is

so great that I know I can say nothing to comfort him. Henry has lost the only father he ever knew; he is as bereft as an orphan child. Clumsily, I get to my knees, my big belly making me awkward, and I stretch my arms out towards him to hold him. He has his back to me and he does not turn, he does not realize I am reaching out to him in pity. He is all alone.

For a moment I think he is absorbed in grief, but then I realize that the loss of Jasper only adds to his perennial fears.

"So who is going to lead my army against the boy and the Scots?" Henry asks, speaking to himself, cold with fear. "I am going to have to face the boy in battle, in the North of England, where they hate me. Who is going to command if Jasper has left me? Who will be at my side, who can I trust, now that my uncle is dead?"

PALACE OF SHEEN, RICHMOND, WINTER 1496

Maggie comes into my room with so rapid a step and with so fierce a glance towards me that I can tell, knowing her as I do, that she is desperate to speak with me. I am sitting with My Lady the King's Mother, with sewing in my hands, listening to one of her women reading one of her eternal homilies on religion, reading aloud from a hand-copied manuscript, for God knows no one would bother to print such a dirge, and Maggie curtseys to us both and sinks to a stool and takes up some sewing and tries to look composed.

I wait till the end of a chapter and for the girl to turn the manuscript page, and I say, "I will walk in the garden."

My Lady looks out of the window where a gray full-bellied sky promises snow and says, "You had much better wait until the sun comes out."

"I'll wear my cloak, and my muff and my hat," I say, and my ladies, after a little hesitating glance at My Lady the King's Mother in case she is going to overrule me, fetch my things and wrap me as if I were a bulky parcel.

My Lady lets them do their work, as she has no appetite for countermanding me in my own rooms anymore. Since the death of Jasper she has aged a dozen years. I look at her now and sometimes I no longer see the powerful woman who dominated me and my husband, but instead a woman who spent all her life on a cause, sacrificed the love of her life for her son, and now waits to hear if the cause is lost and her son is on the run again.

"Margaret, will you give me your arm?" I ask.

Maggie rises with careful lack of interest, as if she had planned to stay indoors, and puts on her own cloak.

"You must have a guard," My Lady rules. "And you three —" she points to the nearest women, barely looking to see who they are "— you three shall walk with Her Grace."

They do not look very pleased at the thought of a cold walk with snow coming, but they rise and fetch their capes from their rooms and with a guard before and behind us, and ladies around us, finally Maggie and I are alone together and we can talk without being overhead.

"What?" I say tersely as soon as the guards are ahead and the women lagging behind. Maggie takes my arm to save me from slipping on the frosty ground. Beside us the gray, cold river is rimmed with white on the banks, while a seagull, no whiter than the frost, calls once overhead and then wheels away.

"He's married," she says shortly.

She never needs to say his name. Indeed, we maintain the convention that we have no name for him.

"Married!" At once I have a clutch of fear that he has married beneath himself, some sympathetic serving girl, some opportunistic widow who has loaned him money. If he has married badly, then Henry will crow with joy and scorn him, calling him Peterkin and Perkin all the more, the son of a drunkard and a drudge, now wedded to a slut. Everyone will say that it proves he is no prince, but a lowly pretender. Or they will say that he has learned common ways, vulgar ways, to be dazzled by the widow of some minor grandee and marry her for her dower money. If his bride is unchaste, some slattern in a hovel, he might as well give up and go home.

I stop still. "Oh, dear God, Maggie. Who is she?"

She is beaming. "A good marriage, even a great marriage. He has married Katherine Huntly, kinswoman to the King of Scotland himself, daughter of the Earl of Huntly, the greatest lord of Scotland."

"The Earl of Huntly's daughter?"

"And they say she is a beauty. She was given

in marriage by King James himself. They were betrothed before Christmas, they are married now, and they are already saying that she is with child."

"My little bro . . . Ri . . . he is married? The boy is married?"

"And his wife with child."

I take her arm and we walk on. "Oh, if only my mother could have seen this."

Maggie nods. "She would be so glad. So glad."

I laugh aloud. "She would be delighted, especially if the girl is beautiful and has a fortune. But Maggie, do you know where they married? And how they looked?"

"She wore a gown of deepest red, and your bro . . . he wore a white shirt and black hose and a black velvet jacket. They held a great tournament to celebrate."

"A tournament!"

"King James paid for everything, it was all done very well. They are saying it was as grand as our court, some say better. And now the king and the new couple have gone to his hunting palace at Falkland in Fife."

"My husband knows all this." I state the obvious.

"Yes. I know it from Sir Richard, who has to go to Lincoln to muster an army for war with Scotland. He had it from one of the king's spies. The king is in his council right now, commanding the repair of the castles in the North of England and preparing for an invasion from Scotland."

"An invasion led by the King of Scotland?"

"They say it is a certainty this spring, now that he is married into the royal family of Scotland. The King of Scotland is certain to put him on the throne of England."

I think of my brother as I last saw him, a handsome little boy of ten with fair hair and bright hazel eyes and an impish smile. I think of the tremble of his lower lip when we kissed him goodbye and wrapped him up warmly and sent him out of sanctuary, all on his own, into the boat to go downriver, praying that the plan would work and that he would get overseas to our aunt Margaret the duchess and that she would save him. I think of him now, fully grown, a man on his wedding day dressed in black and white. I imagine him smiling his impish smile, and his bride beautiful at his side.

I put my hand to my belly, where I am growing a little Tudor, my brother's enemy, the son of the man who usurped my brother's throne.

"There's nothing you can do," Maggie says, seeing the smile die away from my face. "There is nothing either of us can do but hope to survive and pray that nobody puts the blame on us. And see what happens."

In February I prepare for my confinement,

leaving a court still subdued by mourning for Jasper, and still uneasy at the news from the youthful joyful court in Scotland where we hear that they spend their time hunting in the snow, and planning to invade our northern lands as soon as the weather is better.

Henry holds a grand dinner before I go into the darkened room, and the Spanish ambassador, Roderigo Gonzalva de Puebla, attends as an honored guest. He is a small man, dark and good-looking, and he bows low towards me and kisses my hand and then rises up to beam at me as if he is confident that I shall find him very handsome.

"The ambassador is proposing a marriage for Prince Arthur," Henry tells me quietly. "The youngest Spanish princess, the Infanta Katherine of Aragon."

I look from Henry's smiling face to the smug ambassador and understand that I am to be pleased. "What a good idea," I say. "But they are still so young!"

"A betrothal, to indicate the friendship between our countries," Henry says smoothly. He nods to the ambassadors and leads me to the top table out of earshot. "It's not just to link Spain to our interests, a constant ally against France, it's to get the boy. They have promised me if Arthur is betrothed, that they'll tempt the boy to visit them with the promise of an alliance. They'll get him to Granada and hand him over to us."

"He won't go," I say certainly. "Why would he leave his wife in Scotland and go to Spain?"

"Because he wants the support of Spain for his invasion," Henry says shortly. "But they will stand as our ally. They will give us their infanta in marriage, and they will capture our traitor to make sure that she marries the only heir to the throne. Their interests become our interests. And they are newly come to their thrones themselves. They know what it is like to fight for their kingdom. When they betroth their princess to our prince they sign a death warrant for the boy. They will want him dead just as we do."

The court rise to their feet and acknowledge us, bowing low to me, and the server of the ewery comes to me with the golden bowl filled with warm water. I dip my fingers in the scented water and wipe them on the napkin. "But, husband —"

"Never mind," Henry says shortly. "When you have had our new baby and come back to court we will talk of these things. Now you must receive the good wishes of the court, go to your confinement, and think about nothing but a good birth. I am hoping for another boy from you, Elizabeth."

I smile, as if I am reassured, and I glance down the court where the ambassador de Puebla is seated, above the saltcellar, an honored guest, and I wonder if he could be a man so two-faced, so inveterate in his own ambition, that he would promise friendship to a boy of twenty-two and betray him to his death. He feels my gaze upon him and looks up to smile at me, and I think, Yes, yes, he is.

PALACE OF SHEEN, RICHMOND, MARCH 1496

I enter my confinement with a heavy heart, still missing my little girl Elizabeth, and this labor is long and hard. My sister Anne laughs and says she will study how it is done as she is with child, but what she sees makes her fearful. They give me strong birthing ale after some hours, and I wish I had my mother with me to fix me with her cool gray gaze, and to whisper to me of the river and rest, and help me through the pain. At about midnight I can feel the urgency of the baby and I squat like a peasant woman and bear down and then I hear the little faint cry and I cry too, for joy that I have had another child, for sheer exhaustion, and I find I am sobbing as if heartbroken, missing the brother that I fear I will never see, and his wife that I will never meet, and their baby, a cousin to this child, who will never play with her.

Even with the new baby girl in my arms, even wrapped up in my great bed with my ladies praising my courage and bringing me warmed ale and sweetmeats, I feel haunted by loneliness.

Maggie is the only one who sees my tears and she wipes them from my face with a scrap of linen. "What's wrong?"

"I feel like the last of my line, I feel as if I am utterly alone."

She does not rush to comfort me, nor even disagree with me and point to my sisters, exclaiming over the baby as she is swaddled and bound and put to the wet nurse's breast. She looks grim, tired as I am from staying up all the night, her cheeks wet with tears like mine. She does not disagree with me. She makes the pillows comfortable behind me and then she speaks.

"We are the last," she says quietly. "I cannot give you false words of comfort. We are the last of the Yorks. You, your sisters, me and my brother, and perhaps England will never see the white rose again."

"Have you heard anything from Teddy?" I ask.

She shakes her head. "I write, but he doesn't reply. I am not allowed to visit. He is lost to me."

We call the new baby Mary, in honor of Our Lady, and she is a dainty pretty little girl, with eyes of the darkest blue and hair of jet black. She feeds well and she grows strong and though I don't forget her pale, golden-headed sister, I find I am comforted by this new baby in the cradle, this new Tudor for England.

I emerge from confinement to find the country mustering for war. Henry comes to the nursery to see the new baby, but he does no more than glance at her in my arms. He does not even hold her. "There's no doubt that the King of Scotland will invade, and at the head of his army will be the boy," Henry says bitterly. "I have to recruit troops in the North and half of them are saying that though they'll fight against the Scots, they will lay down their arms if they see the white rose. They will defend against the Scots, but they will join a son of York. This is a kingdom of traitors."

I am holding Mary in my arms, and I feel as if I am offering her as a sop to his temper. There may be a son of York in Scotland, arming and readying his men, but here at our favorite palace of Sheen I have given Henry a Tudor princess, and he will not even look at her.

"Is there nothing we can do to persuade King James not to ally himself with . . . with the boy?"

Henry shoots me a secretive glance. "I have offered him an alliance," he confesses. "It doesn't matter if you don't like it. I doubt that it will stick. We'll probably never have to send her."

"Send who?"

He looks furtive. "Margaret. Our daughter Margaret."

I look at him as if he is mad. "Our daughter is six years old." I state the obvious. "Do you think to marry her to the King of Scotland, who is — what? — more than twenty?"

"I think to offer her," he says. "When she is of marriageable age he will only be in his thirties, it's not a bad match."

"But my lord — this is to chose all our children's marriages with your eyes only on the one boy. You have already promised Arthur to Spain in return for them kidnapping him?"

"He won't go. He's too cunning."

"And so, you would give up our little daughter to your enemy to buy the boy?"

"You would rather he was roaming free?" he snaps.

"No, of course not! But . . ."

Already, I have said too much and alerted Henry's fears.

"I shall propose her as a wife for the King of Scotland, and in return he will give me the boy in chains," Henry says flatly. "And whether you are thinking of sparing our little girl or of the boy when you say you don't want such a marriage, it makes no difference. She is a Tudor princess, she must be married where she can serve our interests. She has to do her duty, as I have to do mine — every day. As every one of us has to do."

I tighten my grip on our new baby. "And this child too? You've hardly looked at her. Is every one of our children only of value as a card for you to play? In this one game? In this single unstoppable disproportionate war against a boy?"

He is not even angry; his face is bitter as if his duty is hard for him, harder than anything he would propose for anyone else. "Of course," he says flatly. "And if Margaret is the price for the death of the boy, then it is a good bargain for me."

This summer, two new lines are graven on Henry's face, which run from nose to mouth and mark how his lips are habitually down-turned. An habitual scowl grooves his face as one report after another comes to him of the Scottish preparation for war and the weakness of the defenses of northern England. Half of the northern gentry have already crossed over the border of Scotland to be with the boy, and the families they have left behind are not stirring themselves to fight for Henry against their kinsmen.

Every evening after dinner Henry goes to his mother's rooms and the two of them count, again and again, the names of those that they can trust in the North of England. My Lady has drawn up a list of those that they can be sure of and those that they doubt.

I see both lists when I enter the rooms to bid her good night. The scroll of those they trust and that they judge to be able is weighted with an ink pot, a quill beside it, as if they are hoping to write more names, to add loyalists. The scroll of those they mistrust lolls over the table and unrolls itself towards the floor. Name after name is written with a query beside it. Nothing could exhibit more vividly that the king and his mother are afraid of their own countrymen and -women, that the king and his mother are counting their friends and finding the list too short, that the king and his mother are counting their enemies and seeing the numbers grow every day.

"What do you want?" Henry snaps at me.

I raise my eyebrows at his rudeness in front of his mother, but I curtsey to her, saying very low: "I come to bid you good night, Lady Mother."

"Good night," she says. She barely looks up, she is as distracted as her son.

"A woman stopped me on the way to chapel today, and she asked me if her debt to the king could be excused, or if she could be given longer to pay," I say. "It seems that her husband was charged with a minor offense but he was given no choice of punishment. He has to pay a fine, a very heavy fine. She says they will lose their house and their land and be ruined. She says that he would have preferred to serve time in prison than see everything he has worked for broken up. His name is George Whitehouse."

They both look at me as if I am speaking Greek. Both of them are utterly uncomprehending. "He is a loyal subject," I say. "He just got into a brawl. It is hard that he should lose his family home for an alehouse brawl, because the fine is greater than he can pay. The fines were never so heavy before."

"Do you understand nothing?" My Lady demands, and her tone is quietly furious. "Do you not see that we have to get every penny, every groat that we can, from everyone in the kingdom, so that we can raise armies and pay for them? Do you think we would excuse some alehouse drunkard his fine when it will buy us a soldier? Even if it buys us an arrow?"

Henry is poring over his list, not even looking up, but I am certain that he is listening. "But this man is a loyal subject," I protest. "If he loses his house and his family, if he is ruined because the king's men sell it over his head to collect an impossible fine, then we lose his love and his loyalty. Then we have lost a soldier. The safety of the throne is built on those that love us — only on those that love us. We rule by the consent of the governed — we have to make sure that those who are loyal to us continue as loyal. That list . . ."
I point to the names of those whose loyalty is

in doubt. "That list will grow if you fine good men into bankruptcy."

"It's all very well for you to say such a thing — you who are loved, who have always been loved!" My Lady the King's Mother suddenly bursts out. "You who come from a family who prided themselves on being so unendingly, so showily . . ." I am horrified, waiting for what she is going to say ". . . so unceasingly endearing!" she spits as if it were the gravest fault. "Endearing! D'you know what they say about the boy?"

I shake my head.

"They say that everywhere he goes he makes friends!" She is shouting, her voice raised, her face flushed, her anger quite out of control at the mere mention of the boy and his York charm. "They say that the emperor himself, the King of France, the King of Scotland simply fell in love with him. And so we see his alliances: with the emperor, with the King of France, with the King of Scotland, easy alliances that cost him nothing. Nothing! Though we have to pledge peace, or the marriage of our children, or a fortune in gold to earn their friendship! And now we hear that the Irish are mustering for him again. Though they get nothing for it. Not money — for we pay them a fortune to stay loyal — but him they serve for love. They run to his standard because they love him!"

I look past her at my husband, who keeps

his head turned away. "You could be be-loved," I say to him.

For the first time he looks up, and meets my eyes. "Not like the boy," he says bitterly. "Apparently I don't have the knack of it. No one is beloved like the boy."

The woman who stopped me on my way to chapel and begged me to tell my husband the king that his subjects could not pay their fines, could not pay their taxes, is one of very many. Again and again people ask me to intercede for them to get a debt forgiven, and again and again I have to tell them that I can-not. Everyone has to pay their fines, everyone has to pay their taxes, and the tax collectors now go armed and ride with a guard. When we go on progress, this summer to the west, and ride over the green hills of Salisbury Plain, we take Henry's privy purse officers with us, and everywhere we go they make a new valuation of the properties, lands, and businesses, and present a new bill for taxes.

Now I am sorry that I told Henry how my father used to look over the heads of the people reading the loyal address and calculate how much they could pay. My father's system of loans and fines and borrowings has become Henry's hated tax system and everywhere we go, we are followed by clerks who count the glass windows in the houses, or the flocks of sheep in the meadows, or the crops in the fields, and present the people who come to see us with a demand for payment.

Instead of being greeted by people cheering in the streets, crowding to wave at the royal children and blow kisses to me, the people are out of sight, bundling their goods into warehouses, smuggling away their account books, denying their prosperity. Our hosts serve the meanest of feasts and hide away their best tapestries and silverware. Nobody dares show the king hospitality and generosity, for either he or his mother will claim it as evidence that they are richer than they pretend, and accuse them of failing to declare their wealth. We go from one great house and abbey to another like grasping tinkers who visit only to steal, and I dread the apprehensive faces that greet us and their looks of relief when we leave.

And everywhere we go, at every stop, there are hooded men, following us like the figure of Death itself, on foundering horses, who speak to my husband in secret and sleep the night and then ride out the next day on the best mounts in the stables. They head west, where the Cornishmen, landowners, miners, sailors, and fishermen are declaring that they will not pay another penny of the Tudor tax, or they ride east, where the coast lies dangerously open to an invasion, or they go north to Scotland, where we hear that the king is building an army and casting guns the like of which have never been seen before, for his beloved cousin: the boy who would be King of England.

"At last I have him." Henry walks into my room, ignoring my ladies, who leap to their feet and drop into low curtseys, ignoring the musicians, who trail into silence and wait for an order. "I have him. Look at that."

Obediently I look at the page he shows me. It is a mass of symbols and numbers, saying nothing that I can understand.

"I can't read this," I tell him quietly. "This is the language you use: spies' language."

He tuts with impatience and draws another sheet of paper from under the first. It is a translation of the code from the Portuguese herald, sealed by the King of France himself to prove that it is true. *The so-called Duke of York is the son of a barber in Tournai and I have found his parents and can send them to you . . .*

"What do you think of that?" Henry demands of me. "I can prove that the boy is an imposter. I can bring his mother and father to England and they can declare him the son of a barber in Tournai. What do you think?"

I sense Margaret, my cousin, taking a few steps closer to me, as if she would defend me from the rising volume of Henry's voice. The more uncertain he is, the more he blusters. I rise to my feet and I take his hand in my own.

"I think that it proves your case completely," I say, just as I would soothe my son Harry, if he were arguing with his brother, near to tears with frustration. "I am sure that this will make your case completely."

"It does!" he asserts furiously. "It is as I said — he is a poor boy from nowhere."

"It is just as you said," I repeat. I look up at his flushed angry face and I feel nothing but pity for him. "This proves that you are completely right."

A little shudder goes through him. "I shall send for them, then," he says. "These low-born parents. I shall bring them to England and everyone can see the lowly parentage of this false boy."

But Henry does not send for the Tournai barber and his wife. He sends yet another spy to Tournai, who cannot find them. I have a brief amusing picture in my mind of Tournai filled with men wrapped in their cloaks with their hoods pulled forwards to hide their faces, looking for someone — anyone — who will say that they had a boy who disappeared from home and who took it upon himself to pretend to be King of England, and who is now married into the royal family of Scotland and personal friend and well beloved of most of the rulers of Christendom.

It is such a ludicrous proposal that when Henry goes on looking for a bereft mother, for a missing boy, for anything — a name if nothing else — that I see it as the measure not of his determination to unravel a mystery, but of his increasing desperation to create an identity for the boy and pin a name on him. When I suggest that really anyone would do, it does not have to be a Tournai barber — he might as well seek anyone who is prepared to say that the boy was born and raised by them, and then went missing — Henry scowls at me and says: "Exactly, exactly. I could have half a dozen parents and still no one would believe that I have found the right ones."

One evening in autumn I am invited into the queen's rooms — they are still called the queen's rooms — by My Lady the King's Mother, who tells me that she needs to talk with me before dinner. I go with Cecily my sister, as Anne is in her confinement, expecting her first child; but when the great double doors are thrown open I see that My Lady's presence chamber is empty, and I leave Cecily to wait for me there, beside the economical fire of small off-cut timbers, and I go into My Lady's privy chamber alone.

She is kneeling before a prie-dieu; but when I come in, she glances over her shoulder, whispers "Amen," and then rises to her feet. We both curtsey, she to me as I am queen, I to her as she is my mother-in-law; we press cool cheeks against each other as if we were exchanging a kiss, but our lips never touch the other's face.

She gestures towards a chair that is the same height as hers, on the other side of the fireplace, and we sit simultaneously, neither one of us taking precedence. I am beginning to wonder what all this is about.

"I wish to speak to you in confidence," she

begins. "In absolute confidence. What you tell me will not go beyond the walls of this room. You can trust me with anything. I give you my sacred word of honor."

I wait. I very much doubt that I am going to tell her anything, so she need not assure me that she will not repeat it. Besides, anything that might be of use to her son, she would repeat to him in the next moment. Her sacred word of honor would not even cause a second's delay. Her sacred word of honor is worth nothing against her devotion to her son.

"I want to speak of long-ago days," she says. "You were just a little girl and none of it was your fault. No blame is attached to you by me or anyone. Not by my son. Your mother commanded everything, and you were obedient to her then." She pauses. "You do not have to be obedient to her now."

I bow my head.

My Lady seems to have trouble in starting her question. She pauses, she taps her fingers on the carved arm of her chair. She closes her eyes as if in brief prayer. "When you were a young woman in sanctuary, your brother the king was in the Tower, but your little brother Richard was still with you in hiding. Your mother had kept him by her side. When they promised her that your brother Edward was to be crowned they demanded that she send Prince Richard into the Tower, to join his brother, to keep him company. Do you remember?"

"I remember," I say. Despite myself I glance towards the heaped logs in the fireplace as if I could see in the glowing embers the arched roof of the sanctuary, my mother's white desperate face, the dark blue of her mourning gown, and the little boy that we bought from his parents, took hold of, washed, commanded to say nothing, and dressed up as my little brother, hat pulled low on his head, a muffler across his mouth. We handed him over to the archbishop, who swore he would be safe, though we did not trust him, we did not trust any of them. We sent that little boy into danger, to save Richard. We thought it would buy us a night, perhaps a night and a day. We could not believe our luck when no one challenged him, when the two boys together, my brother Edward and the pauper child, kept up the deception.

"The lords of the privy council came and demanded that you hand your little brother over to them," My Lady says, her voice a lilting murmur. "But now, I wonder if you did?"

I look at her, meeting her gaze with an honest frank stare. "Of course we did," I say bluntly. "Everyone knows that we did. The whole privy council witnessed it. Your own husband Thomas, Lord Stanley, was there. Everyone knows that they took my little brother Richard to live with my brother the king, in the Tower, to keep him company before his coronation. You were at court yourself, you must have seen them take him to the Tower. You must remember, everybody knew, that my mother wept as she said good-bye to him, but the archbishop himself swore that Richard would be safe."

She nods. "Ah, but then . . . then, did your mother lay a little plot to get them out?" My lady draws closer, her hand reaching out like a claw clasping my hands in my lap. "She was a clever woman, and always alert to danger. I wonder if she was ready for them to come for Prince Richard? Remember, I joined my men with hers in an attack on the Tower to rescue them. I tried to save them too. But after that, after it failed, did she save them — or perhaps just save Richard? Her youngest boy? Did she have a plot that she did not tell me about? I was punished for helping her, I was imprisoned in my husband's house and forbidden from speaking or writing to anyone. Did your mother, loyal and clever woman that she was, did she get Richard out? Did she get your brother Richard out of the Tower?"

"You know that she was plotting all the time," I say. "She was writing to you, she was writing to your son. You would know more than I do about that time. Did she tell you she had him safe? Have you kept that secret, all this long time?"

She whips back her hand as if I were as hot

as the embers in the hearth. "What d'you mean? No! She never told me such a thing!"

"You were plotting with her to free us, weren't you?" I ask, as sweet as sugared milk. "You were plotting with her to bring in your son to save us? That was why Henry came to England? To free us all? Not to take the throne, but to restore it to my brother and to free us?"

"But she didn't tell me anything," Lady Margaret bursts out. "She never told me anything. And though everyone said that the boys were dead, she never held a Requiem Mass for them, and we never found their bodies, we never found their murderers nor any trace or whisper of a plot to kill them. She never named their killers and no one ever confessed."

"You hoped that people would think it was their uncle Richard," I observed quietly. "But you didn't have the courage to accuse him. Not even when he was dead in an unmarked grave. Not even when you publicly listed his crimes. You never accused him of that. Not even Henry, not even *you* had the gall to say that he murdered his nephews."

"Were they murdered?" she hisses at me. "If it was not Richard? It doesn't matter who did it! Were they murdered? Were they both killed? Do you know that?"

I shake my head.

"Where are the boys?" she whispers, her

voice barely louder than the flicker of flame in the hearth. "Where are they? Where is Prince Richard now?"

"I think you know better than me. I think you know exactly where he is." I turn back to her, and I let her see my smile. "Don't you think it is him, in Scotland? Don't you think he is free, and leading an army against us? Against your own son — calling him a usurper?"

The anguish in her face is genuine. "They've crossed the border," she whispers. "They've mustered a massive force, the King of Scotland rides with the boy at the head of thousands of men, he's cast cannon, bombards, he's organized them — no one has seen such an army in the North before. And the boy has sent a proclamation . . ." She breaks off, and from inside her gown she draws it out. I cannot deny my curiosity; I put out my hand and she passes it over. It is a proclamation by the boy, he must have had hundreds made, but at the bottom is his signature, RR — Ricardus Rex, King Richard IV of England.

I cannot take my eyes from the confident swirl of the initial. I put my finger on the dry ink; perhaps this is my brother's signature. I cannot believe that my fingertip will not sense his touch, that the ink will not grow warm under my hand. He signed this, and now my finger is on it. "Richard," I say wonderingly, and I can hear the love in my voice. "Richard."

"He calls upon the people of England to capture Henry as he flees," Henry's mother says, her voice quavering. I hardly hear her, I am thinking of my little brother, signing hundreds of proclamations Ricardus Rex: Richard the King. I find I am smiling, thinking of the little boy that my mother loved so much, that we all loved for his sunny good nature. I think of him signing this flourish and smiling his smile, certain that he will win England back for the House of York.

"He has crossed the Scottish border, he is marching on Berwick," she moans.

At last I realize what she is saying. "They have invaded?"

She nods.

"The king is going to go? He has his troops ready?"

"We've sent money," she says. "A fortune. He is pouring money and arms into the North."

"He is riding out? Henry will lead his army against the boy?"

She shakes her head. "We won't put an army in the field. Not yet, not in the North."

I am bewildered. I look from the bold proclamation in black ink to her old, frightened face. "Why not? He must defend the North. I thought you were ready for this?"

"We can't!" she bursts out. "We dare not

march an army north to face the boy. What if the troops turn on us as soon as we get there? If they change sides, if the men declare for Richard, then we will have done nothing but give him an army and all our weapons. We dare not take a mustered army anywhere near him. England has to be defended by the men of the North, fighting under their own leaders, defending their own lands against the Scots, and we will hire mercenaries to bolster their ranks — men from Lorraine and from Germany."

I look at her incredulously. "You are hiring foreign soldiers because you can't trust Englishmen?"

She wrings her hands. "People are so bitter about the taxation and the fines, they speak against the king. People are so untrustworthy, and we can't be sure . . ."

"You can't trust an English army not to change sides and fight against the king?"

She hides her face in her hands; she sinks into her chair, almost sinking to her knees as if in prayer. I look at her blankly, unable to conjure an expression of sympathy. I have never in my life heard of such a thing as this: a country invaded and the king afraid to march out to defend his borders, a king who cannot trust the army he has mustered, equipped, and paid. A king who looks like a usurper and calls on foreign troops even as a boy, an unblooded boy, demands his throne.

"Who will lead this northern army if the king won't go?" I ask.

This alone gives her some joy. "Thomas Howard, Earl of Surrey," she says. "We are trusting him with this. Your sister is bearing his child in our keeping, I am certain he won't betray us. And we have her and his first child as a hostage. The Courtenays will stand by us, and we will marry your sister Catherine to William Courtenay, to make them hold firm. And to have a man who was known to be loyal to the House of York riding against the boy will look good, don't you think? It must make people stop and think, won't it? They must see that we kept Thomas Howard in the Tower and he came out safely."

"Unlike the boy," I remark.

Her eyes snap towards me and I see terror in her face. "Which boy?" she asks. "Which boy?"

"My cousin, Edward," I say smoothly. "You still hold him for no reason, without charge, unjustly. He should be released now, so that people cannot say that you take boys of York and hold them in the Tower."

"We don't." She answers by rote as if it is the murmured response to a prayer that she has learned by heart. "He is there for his own safety."

"I ask for his release," I say. "The country thinks he should be freed. I, as queen, request it. At this moment, where we should show that we are confident."

She shakes her head and sits back in her chair, firm in her determination. "Not until it is safe for him to come out."

I rise to my feet, the proclamation still in my hand that calls for the people to rise against Henry, refuse his taxation, capture him as he flees back to Brittany where he came from. "I can't comfort you," I say coldly. "You have encouraged your son to tax people to the point of their ruin, you have allowed him to hide himself away and not go out and show himself and make friends, you have encouraged him to pursue and persecute this boy who now invades us, and you have urged him to recruit an army that he cannot trust, and now to bring in foreign soldiers. Last time he brought in foreign soldiers they brought the sweat, which nearly killed us all. The King of England should be beloved by his people, not an enemy to their peace. He should not be afraid of his own army."

"But is the boy your brother?" she demands hoarsely. "That's what I called you here to answer. You know. You must know what your mother did to save him. Is your mother's favorite boy coming against mine?"

"It doesn't matter," I say, suddenly seeing my way clear and away from this haunting question. I have a sudden lift of my spirits as I understand, at last, what I should answer. "It doesn't matter who Henry is facing.

Whether it is my mother's favorite boy or another mother's son. What matters is that you have not made *your* boy the beloved of England. You should have made him beloved and you have not done so. His only safety lies in the love of his people, and you have not secured that for him."

"How could I?" she demands. "How could such a thing ever be done? These are faithless people, these are a heartless people, they run after will-o'-the-wisps, they don't value true worth."

I look at her and I almost pity her, as she sits twisted in her chair, her glorious prie-dieu with its huge Bible and the richly enameled cover behind her, the best rooms in the palace draped with the finest tapestries and a fortune in her strongbox. "You could not make a beloved king, for your boy was not a beloved child," I say, and it is as if I am condemning her. I feel as hardhearted, as hard-faced, as the recording angel at the end of days. "You have tried for him, but you have failed him. He was never loved as a child, and he has grown into a man who cannot inspire love nor give love. You have spoiled him utterly."

"I loved him!" She leaps up suddenly furious, her dark eyes blazing with rage. "Nobody can deny that I loved him! I have given my life for him! I only ever thought of him! I nearly died giving birth to him and I have sacrificed everything — love, safety, a husband of my choice — just for him."

"He was raised by another woman, Lady Herbert, the wife of his guardian, and he loved her," I say relentlessly. "You called her your enemy, and you took him from her and put him in the care of his uncle. When you were defeated by my father, Jasper took him away from everything he knew, into exile, and you let them go without you. You sent him away, and he knew that. It was for your ambition; he knows that. He knows no lullabies, he knows no bedtime stories, he knows no little games that a mother plays with her sons. He has no trust, he has no tenderness. You worked for him, yes, and you plotted for him and you strove for him — but I doubt that you ever, in all his baby years, held him on your knees and tickled his toes, and made him giggle."

She shrinks back from me as if I am cursing her. "I am his mother, not his wet nurse. Why would I caress him? I taught him to be a leader, not a baby."

"You are his commander," I say. "His ally. But there is no true love in it — none at all. And now you see the price you pay for that. There is no true love in him, neither to give nor receive — none at all."

Horrifying stories come from the North, of the Scots army coming in like an army of wolves, destroying everything they find. The defenders of the North of England march bravely against them, but before they can join battle, the Scots have melted away, back to their own high hills. It is not a defeat, it is something far worse than that: it is a disappearance. It is a warning which only tells us that they will come again. So Henry is not reassured, and demands money from Parliament — hundreds of thousands of pounds — and raises more in reluctant loans from all his lords and from the merchants of London to pay for men to be armed and stand ready against this invisible threat. Nobody knows what the Scots are planning, if they will raid constantly, destroying our pride and our confidence in the North of England, coming out of the blizzards at the worst time of year; or if they will wait for spring and launch a full invasion.

"He has a child," Maggie whispers to me. The court is busy with preparations for Christmas. Maggie and her husband have been at Ludlow Castle with my son Arthur, introducing him to his principality of Wales, but they have come home to Westminster Palace in time to celebrate the Christmas feast. On the way Maggie listens to the gossip in the inns and great houses and abbeys where they stop for hospitality. "They all say that he has a child."

At once I think how glad my mother would

be, how she would have wanted to see her grandchild. "Girl or boy?" I ask eagerly.

"A boy. He's had a boy. The House of York has a new heir."

Foolishly, wrongly, I clasp her hands and know that my bright joy is mirrored in her smile. "A boy?"

"A new white rose, a white rosebud. A new son of York."

"Where is he? In Edinburgh?"

"They say that he's living with his wife in Falkland, at a royal hunting lodge. They live quietly together with their baby. They say she is very, very beautiful and that he is happy to stay with her, they are so much in love."

"He won't invade?"

She shrugs. "It's not the season, but perhaps he wants to live quietly. Newly married, with a beautiful wife and a baby in her arms? Perhaps he thinks this is the best that he can get."

"If I could write to him . . . if I could just tell him . . . oh, if I could tell him that this is the best."

Slowly, she shakes her head. "Nothing goes across the border but the king knows of it," she says. "If you sent so much as one word to the boy, the king would see it as the greatest betrayal in the world. He would never forgive you, he would doubt you forever, and he would think you have been his hidden enemy all along."

"If only someone could tell the boy to stay where he is, to find joy and keep it, that the throne won't bring him the happiness he has now."

"I can't tell him," Maggie says. "I've found that truth for myself: a good husband and a place that I can call my home at Ludlow Castle."

"Have you really?"

Smilingly, she nods. "He's a good man, and I am glad to be married to him. He's calm and he's quiet and he is loyal to the king and faithful to me. I've seen enough excitement and disloyalty; I can think of nothing better to do in my life than to raise my own son and to help yours to become a prince, to run Ludlow Castle as you would wish, and to welcome your son's bride into our home, when she comes."

"And Arthur?" I ask her.

She smiles at me. "He is a prince to be proud of," she says. "He is generous, and fair. When Sir Richard takes him to watch the judges at their work his desire is to be merciful. He rides well and when he goes out he greets people as his friend. He is everything that you would want him to be. And Richard is teaching him all that he knows. He's a good guardian for your boy. Arthur will make a good king, perhaps even a great king."

"If the boy does not claim his throne."

"Perhaps the boy will think that loving a

woman and loving his child is enough," Maggie says. "Perhaps he will understand that a prince does not have to become a king. Perhaps he will think that it is more important to be a man, a loving man. Perhaps when he sees his wife with the child in her arms he will know that this is the greatest kingdom a man can wish for."

"If I could tell him that!"

"I can't get a letter to my own brother, just down the river in the Tower of London. How could we ever get a letter to yours?"

THE TOWER OF LONDON,
SUMMER 1497

The Cornishmen start by grumbling that the king is taxing them too hard, and then that he has stolen their rights to the tin that they mine. They are a hardworking, bitter set of men who face danger daily, in the tiny cramped conditions underground, speaking their own strange language, living more like barbarians than Christian men. Far away from London, in the utmost west of the country, they are easily persuaded by dreams or rumors. They believe in kings and angels, in appearances and miracles. My father always said that they were Englishmen like no others, Cornishmen, not of English stock at all, and that they had to be ruled with kindness, as if they were the mischievous elves that live alongside them.

In days, in moments, they are agreed and furious; they go through the west like a summer fire, blazing up, jumping a field or two, raging on faster than a galloping horse. Soon they have the whole of Cornwall up in arms, and then the other western counties join with them, equally angry. They form separate armies led by men from Somerset, Wiltshire, and Cornwall under the command of a Cornish blacksmith, Michael Joseph, An Gof, a man said to be ten feet high who has sworn that he will not be ruined by a king whose father was no king, who is trying new ways, Tudor ways, Welsh ways against good Cornishmen.

But it is not just a rebellion of ignorant men: yeomen turn out for them, fishermen, farmers, miners, and then, worst of all, a nobleman, Lord Audley, offers to lead them.

"I'll leave you and my mother and the children here," Henry says tersely to me, his horse waiting at the head of his yeomen of the guard, who are arrayed in battle order outside the White Tower, the gates closed, the cannons rolled up to the walls, everything ready for a war. "You'll be safe here, you can hold out against a siege for weeks."

"A siege?" I hold Mary on my hip, as if I were a peasant woman seeing a husband off to battle, her own future desperately uncertain. "Why, how close are they going to get to London? They're coming all the way from Cornwall! They should have been contained in the West Country! Are you leaving us with enough troops? Is London going to stay loyal?"

"Woodstock, I'm going to Woodstock. I can

muster troops there and cut off the rebels as they come up the Great West Way. I have to get my troops back from Scotland, as soon as I can. I sent them all north to face the boy and the Scots, I wasn't expecting this from the southwest. I'm recalling Lord Daubney and his force, I've sent orders for them to turn back south at once. I'll get them back here, if the messenger finds them in time."

"Lord Daubney is a Somerset man," I observe.

"What d'you mean by that?" Henry shouts at me in his desperation, and Mary flinches at his raised voice and wails pitifully. I tighten my grip on her little plump body and rock her, stepping from one foot to the other.

I keep my voice low so as not to disturb her, and not to unsettle Henry's bodyguard, who are lining up grim-faced. "I mean only that it will be hard for his lordship to attack his fellow countrymen," I say. "He will have to fire on his neighbors. The whole county of Somerset has joined with the Cornishmen, and he will have known Lord Audley from boyhood. I don't suggest that he will fail you, I just mean that he is a man from the west and he is bound to sympathize with his people. You should put other men round him. Where are your other lords? His kinsmen and peers that would keep him to your side?"

Henry makes a sound, almost a moan of distress, and puts his hand on his horse's neck as if he needs the support. "Scotland," he whispers. "I have sent almost everyone north, the whole army and all my cannon and all my money."

For a moment I am silent, seeing the danger that we are in. All my children including Arthur are in the Tower as the rebels march on London, the army is too distant to recall; if Henry's small force cannot stop them on the road we will be besieged. "Be brave," I say, though I am sick with fear myself. "Be brave, Henry. My father was captured once and driven from his kingdom once and he still was a great king of England and died in the royal bed."

He looks at me bleakly. "I've sent Thomas Howard the Earl of Surrey to Scotland. He was against me at Bosworth and I kept him in the Tower for more than three years. Do you think that will have made a friend of him? I have to gamble that marriage to your sister makes him a safe ally for me. You tell me that Daubney is a Somerset man and will sympathize with his neighbors as they march against me. I didn't even know that. I don't know any of these men. None of them knows me or loves me. Your father was never alone like me, in a strange land. He married for love, he was followed by men with a passion. He always had people that he could trust."

We take up battle stations in the Tower, with

cannon rolled out, the fires kept burning and the cannonballs stacked beside the guns. We hear that there is a mighty rebel army, perhaps as many as twenty thousand men, marching on London from Cornwall and gathering strength as it marches. That is an army big enough to take the kingdom. Lord Daubney gets south in time to block the Great West Way and we expect that he will turn them back, but he does not even delay them. Some say that he orders his troops to clear the road, and lets them go by.

The rebels come on, nearing London, growing in numbers. They are led by Lord Audley, and we know that other lords must be sending them arms, money, and men. I hear nothing from Henry, I have to trust that he is mustering his men, preparing a force and readying himself to march against them. I have no word from him and he does not write to his mother either, though she spends her days on her knees in the chapel that blazes, night and day, with the light of the votive candles that she has lit for him.

My son Arthur, in the Tower for safety with us, comes to me. "Is my father blocking the rebels' march?" he asks me.

"I am sure," I say, though I am not sure.

In his rooms Edward, my cousin, must hear the marching feet, the shouted orders, the changing of the guard at four-hourly intervals. Maggie, who joins me as her husband rides out with mine, is the only one of us who is allowed to see him. She comes to me with her face grave.

"He's very quiet," is all she says. "He asked me why we were all here, he knows we are all here in the Tower, and why there was so much noise. When I said that there were rebels marching on London all the way from Cornwall he said —" She breaks off and puts her hand over her mouth.

"What?" I ask. "What did he say?"

"He said that there was not much to come to London for, it is a very dull place. He said someone should tell them that there is no company in London at all, and it is lonely. It's very, very lonely."

I am horrified. "Maggie, has he lost his wits?"

She shakes her head. "No, I'm sure not. It's just that he has been kept alone for so very long, he has almost forgotten how to speak. He is like a child who has had no childhood. Elizabeth — I have failed him. I have failed him so badly."

I go to embrace her, but she turns away from me and drops a curtsey. "Let me go to my room and wash my face," she says. "I can't speak of him. I can't bear to think of him. I have changed my name and denied my family and left him behind. I have snatched my own freedom and left him in here, like a little bird in a cage, like a blinded songbird."

"When this is over . . ."

"When this is over it will be even worse!" she exclaims passionately. "All this time we have been waiting for the king to feel safe on his throne; but he never feels safe. When this is over, even if we triumph, the king will still have to face the Scots. He may have to face the boy. The king's enemies come one after another, he makes no friends and he has new enemies every year. It is never safe enough for him to release my brother. He will never be safe on the throne."

I clap my hand over her trembling mouth. "Hush, Maggie. Hush. You know better than to talk like this."

She drops a curtsey and goes from my rooms and I don't detain her. I know she speaks nothing but the truth and that these battles, between these ill-armed desperate men from the west, the war in the North between the Scots and the English, the mustering rebels in Ireland, and the conflict to come between the boy and the king, will give us a summer of bloodshed and an autumn of reckoning, and nobody can tell what the count will be, or who will be the judge or the victor.

The panic starts at dawn. I can hear the shouted commands and the noise of running feet as the commander of the watch calls out the troops. The tocsin starts to sound a warning and then all the bells through the City of London and beyond, all the bells of England, start to sound as the alarm is given that the Cornishmen have come and now they are not demanding that taxes be forgiven and the king's false advisors dismissed, now they are demanding that the king be thrown down.

Lady Margaret, the king's mother, comes out of the chapel, blinking like a frightened owl at the dawn light, and at the uproar inside the Tower. She sees me at the entrance to the White Tower and hurries across the green towards me. "You stay here," she says harshly. "You're commanded to stay here for your own safety. Henry said that you were not to leave. You and the children are to stay here."

She turns towards one of the commanders of the guard, and I realize that she will give the order for my arrest if she thinks for a moment that I am hoping to escape.

"Are you mad?" I suddenly demand bitterly. "I am Queen of England, I am the king's wife and mother of the Prince of Wales! Of course I am staying here in this, my home city, among my people. Whatever happens I would not leave. Where do you think I would go? *I* am not the one that spent my life in exile! I did not come in at the head of an army, speaking a foreign language! I am English born and English bred. Of course I am going to stay in London. These are my people, this is my country. Even if they carry arms against me they are still my people and this is still where I belong!"

She wavers in the face of my unexpected fury. "I don't know, I don't know," she says. "Don't be angry, Elizabeth. I am only trying to keep us all safe. I don't know anything, anymore. Where are the rebels?"

"Blackheath," I say shortly. "But they have lost a lot of men. They went into Kent and there was a skirmish."

"Are they opening the city gates to them?" she asks. We can both hear the uproar in the streets. She clutches hold of my arm. "Are the citizens and their militia going to let them into London? Are they going to betray us?"

"I don't know," I say. "Let's go up on the walls where we can see what's happening."

My Lady, my sisters, Maggie, Arthur and the younger children, and I all go up the narrow stone steps to the perimeter walls of the Tower. We look south and east, to where the river winds out of sight, and we know that, not far away, only seven miles, the Cornish rebels are triumphantly occupying Blackheath, outside our palace of Greenwich, and setting up camp.

"My mother once stood here," I tell my children. "She was here under siege, just like this, and I was with her, just a little girl."

"Were you frightened?" six-year-old Henry asks me.

I hug him, and smile to feel him pull away from me. He is eager to stand on his own two feet, he wants to look independent, ready for battle. "No," I say. "I wasn't frightened. For I knew that my uncle Anthony would protect us, and I knew that the people of England would never hurt us."

"I will protect you now," Arthur promises. "If they come, they will find us ready. I am not afraid."

At my side, I feel My Lady shrink back. She has no such certainties.

We walk around the walls to the north side, so that we can look down into the streets of the City. The young apprentices are running from house to house, banging on doors and holloaing to summon men to defend the city gates, borrowing weapons from dusty old cupboards, calling for old pikes to be brought out of the cellars. The trained military bands are running down the streets, ready to defend the walls.

"See?" Arthur points them out.

"They're for us," I observe to My Lady the King's Mother. "They're arming against the rebels. They're running to the city gates to close them."

She looks doubtful. I know that she fears that they will throw open the gates as soon as they hear the rebels cry that they will abolish taxes. "Well, anyway, we're safe in here," I say. "The Tower gates are shut, the portcullis is down, and we have cannon."

"And Henry will be coming with his army to rescue us," My Lady asserts.

Margaret, my cousin, exchanges a quick skeptical look with me. "I am sure he will," I reply.

In the end it is Lord Daubney, not Henry, who falls on the exhausted Cornishmen as they are resting after their long march from the west. The cavalry go through the sleeping men slashing and hacking as if they were practicing sword thrusts in a hayfield. Some of them carry a mace — a great swinging ball that can knock a man's head clean from his shoulders, or smash his face into a pulp, even inside a metal helmet. Some of them carry lances and stab and thrust as they go, or battle-axes with a terrible spike at one end that can punch through metal. Henry has planned the battle and put cavalry and archers on the other side of the rebel army so there is no escape for them. The Cornishmen, armed with little more than staves and pitchforks, are like the sheep of their own thin-earth moorland, herded this way and that, rushing in terror trying to get out of the way, hearing the whistle of thousands of arrows, running from the cavalry only to find the infantry, armed with pikes and handguns, stolidly advancing towards them, deaf to all calls of brotherhood.

They beat the Cornishmen to their knees, they go facedown in the mud before they drop their weapons, raise their hands, and offer their surrender. An Gof, their leader, breaks away from the battle and runs for his life, but is ridden down like a leggy broken-winded stag after a long chase. Lord Audley the rebel leader offers his sword to his friend Lord Daubney, who accepts it grim-faced. Neither lord is quite sure if he has been fighting on the right side; it is a most uncertain surrender, in a most ignoble victory.

"We're safe," I tell the children, when the scouts come to the Tower to tell us that it is all over. "Your father's army has beaten the bad men and they are going back to their homes."

"I wish I had led the army!" Henry says. "I should have fought with a mace. Bash! Swing and bash!" He dances around the room miming holding the reins of a galloping horse with one hand and swinging a mace with his other little fist.

"Perhaps when you are older," I say to him. "But I hope that we will be at peace now. They will go back to their homes and we can go back to ours."

Arthur waits for the younger children to be distracted and then he comes to my side. "They're building gallows at Smithfield," he says quietly. "An awful lot of them won't be going back to their homes."

"It has to be done." I defend his father to my grave-faced son. "A king cannot tolerate rebels."

"But he's selling some of the Cornishmen into slavery," Arthur tells me flatly.

"Slavery?" I am so shocked that I look at his serious face. "Slavery? Who said so? They must be mistaken?"

"My Lady the King's Mother told me herself. He's selling them to barbarian galleys and they'll be chained to the oars till they die. He's selling them to be slaves in Ireland. We'll have no friends in Cornwall for a generation. How can a king sell his people into slavery?"

I look at my son, I see the inheritance we are preparing for him, and I have no answer.

It is a victory, but one so reluctantly won that there is little joy. Henry gives out knighthoods grudgingly, and those who are so honored dread the charges that will come with their new titles. Massive punitive taxes are laid on anyone who sympathized with the rebels, and lords and gentry have to pay huge fines to the Exchequer to guarantee their future good behavior. The leaders of the Cornishmen are briskly tried and hanged, their entrails drawn out of them and then they are quartered, hacked alive as they die in agony. Lord Audley loses his head in a prompt execution when the crowd laugh at his grave face as he puts his head on the block for defending his tenants against his king. Henry's army pursues the Cornishmen all the way back to Cornwall and they disappear into the lanes which are so shielded with hedges that they are like green tunnels in a green land, and nobody can tell where the traitors have gone, nor what they are doing.

"They're waiting," Henry tells me.

"What are they waiting for?" I ask, as if I don't know.

"For the boy."

"Where is he now?"

For the first time in many months Henry smiles. "He thinks he is setting out on campaign, financed by the King of Scotland, supported by him."

I wait in silence, knowing that triumphant beam well enough by now.

"But he is not."

"No?"

"He is being tricked on board a ship. He is to be handed over to me. James of Scotland has finally agreed that I shall have the boy."

"You know where he is?"

"I know where he is and I know the name of the ship that he will set sail in: him and his wife and his son. James of Scotland has utterly betrayed him to me, and my allies the Spanish will pick him up at sea, pretending friendship, and bring him to me. And at last, we will make an end of him."

Woodstock Palace, Oxfordshire, Summer 1497

Then, we lose him again.

The court behaves as if we are on a summer progress, but really we are trapped in the middle of England, afraid to move in one direction or another, waiting for trouble but not knowing where the boy may land. Henry hardly ever leaves his room. At every place where we stay he creates a headquarters ready for a siege, receiving messages, sending out orders, commanding more arms, mustering soldiers, even getting his own armor fitted new, and he readies himself to wear it on the field of battle. But he does not know where the battle will be, as he has no idea where the boy has gone.

Arthur cannot return to Ludlow Castle. "I should be in my principality!" he says to me. "I should be with my people."

"I know. But your guardian Sir Richard has to command his men in the king's armies. And while your father does not know where the boy might land, it is safer if we are all together."

He looks at me, his brown eyes dark with concern. "Mother, when are we going to be at peace?"

I can't answer him.

One moment the boy was said to be in his love nest with his new bride, beloved of the Scots king, confidently planning another venture; but then we hear that the boy has sailed from Scotland, and disappeared once again, as this boy so skillfully seems to do.

"D'you think he has gone to your aunt?" Henry asks me. Every day he asks me where I think the boy has gone. I have Mary on my knee, and am sitting in a sunny spot in her nursery in a high tower of the beautiful palace. I hold her a little tighter as her father stamps up and down before us, too loud, too big, too furious for a nursery, a man spoiling for a fight and on the edge of losing control. Mary regards him gravely, not at all afraid of him. She watches him as a baby might watch a bearbaiting: a curious spectacle but not one that threatens her.

"Of course I don't know where he's gone," I say. "I can't imagine. I thought you told me that the Holy Roman Emperor himself had ordered the duchess not to support or succor him?"

"Why would she ever do as she is told?" Henry rounds on me. "Faithless as she is to anything but the House of York? Faithless as she is to anything but ruining my life and destroying my rightful hold on my own kingdom!"

This is too loud for Mary and her lower lip turns down, her face trembles. I turn her towards me and show her a smile. "There," I say. "Hush. Nothing's wrong."

"Nothing's wrong?" Henry repeats incredulously.

"Nothing for Mary," I say. "Don't distress her."

His angry glance falls on her as if he would shout to warn her that she is in danger, her house on the brink of collapse, thanks to an enemy like a will-o'-the-wisp. "Where is he?" he asks again.

"Surely, you have all the ports watched?"

"Costs me a fortune, but there is not an inch of the coast that is not patrolled."

"Then if he comes, you will know. Perhaps he has gone back to Ireland."

"Ireland? What d'you know about Ireland?" he demands, swift as a snake.

"I don't know!" I protest. "How should I know? It's just that he was there before. He has friends there."

"Who? What friends?"

I stand up to face him, holding Mary close. "My lord, I don't know. If I knew anything, I would tell you. But I know nothing. All I ever hear is what you tell me, yourself. No one else speaks to me of him, and anyway, I would not listen if they did."

"The Spanish may yet take him," Henry says, more to himself than to me. "They have promised him their friendship and they will capture him for me. They have promised me that they have ships waiting off the coast for him and he has agreed to meet with them. Perhaps they will —"

There is a sudden loud hammering on the door, Mary cries out, and I clutch her tighter to me and stride across the room, away from the door, towards the bedroom, as if I am running away, suddenly afraid. Henry spins on his heel, his face white. I pause on the threshold of the bedroom door, Henry just a step before me so that when the messenger walks in, dirty from the road, he sees the two of us, pale with fear, as if we are expecting attack. He drops to his knee. "Your Grace."

"What is it?" Henry demands roughly. "You frightened Her Grace, coming in so loudly."

"It's an invasion," he says.

Henry sways and clutches at the back of the chair. "The boy?"

"No. The Scots. The King of Scots is marching."

We have to trust Thomas Howard, Earl of Surrey, my sister Anne's husband, to save England for Henry. We, who trust nothing and fear everything, have to trust to him; but it is the rain that serves us best. Both the English and the Scots set sieges and are all but destroyed by the unceasing rain. The English troops, camped on wet ground before stoical castles, fall ill, and melt away in the driving mist to their own homes, to warm fires and dry clothes. Thomas Howard cannot keep them loyal, cannot even keep them in their ranks. They don't want to fight, they don't care that Henry is defending his kingdom against England's oldest enemy. They don't care about him at all.

Thomas Howard stands before Henry in the privy chamber. I am at one side of Henry's great chair, his mother at the other, as Henry rages at him, accusing him of dishonesty, treachery, faithlessness.

"I could not make the men stay," Thomas says miserably. "I could not even make their leaders stay. They had no appetite for the fight and there were scant rewards. You don't know what it was like."

"Are you saying I don't go to war?" Henry bursts out.

Thomas shoots a quick horrified glance at me, his sister-in-law. "No, Your Grace, of course not. I only meant that I cannot describe to you how hard this campaign is. It's very wet and very cold in this part of your country. The food is scanty and it's hard to get firewood in some places. Some nights the men had to sleep without anything to eat in the cold rain, and wake without breakfast. It's hard to supply an army and the men had no passion for the fight. Nobody doubts Your Grace's courage. That has been shown. But it is hard to make the men stand firm in this country in this weather."

"Enough of this. Can you take the field again?" Henry is biting his lips, his face dark and furious.

"If you command me, Sire," Surrey says miserably. He knows, as we all do, that any hint of refusal will see him back in the Tower, named as a traitor, his marriage to Anne not enough to save him. Again he glances quickly at me, and sees at once, from my impassive expression, that I cannot help him. "I should be proud to lead your men. I will do my best. But they have gone home. We will have to muster them all over again."

"I can't keep hiring men," Henry decides abruptly. "They won't serve, and I have no funds to pay them. I shall have to make peace with Scotland. I hear that James is down to the last coin in his treasury too. I shall make peace. And I shall move what men I have left away from the borders. They must come south to be ready."

"Ready for what?" his mother asks.

I don't know why she asks, except to hear her own fears in words.

"Ready for the boy."

WOODSTOCK PALACE, OXFORDSHIRE, AUTUMN 1497

A team of dirty, exhausted messengers rides post, passing the message from one station to another, changing horses as they tire and fall lame, one man pantingly passing a scroll sealed in sheepskin to another. "For the king, at Woodstock Palace!" is all they say, and a new horse and a new man plunges on along the dusty autumn roads, little more than dirt tracks, to ride from dawn till it grows too dark for him to tell the deep sloughs of mud on the road from the overgrown grass of the verge, until he has to sleep, sometimes wrapped in his cloak, under a tree, restlessly waiting for the first light of dawn to thunder to the next post with the precious packet: "For the king, at Woodstock Palace!"

The court is preparing to go out hawking, the riders mounting, the hawk carts with the rows of hooded hawks rolling out of the mews, the falconers running alongside the carts speaking soothingly to the blind birds, promising them sport and feeding if they will be good birds, be steady and patient now, stand proudly on their perches: don't bate, don't flap.

Henry is dressed handsomely in dark green velvet with dark green leather riding boots and green leather gloves. He is trying so hard to look like a king living on his own fortune, comfortable with his court, happy in his kingdom, beloved of his people. Only the new lines around his pinched mouth betray him as a man living with gritted teeth.

We are near the open gate of Woodstock Palace when I hear hooves on the road and turn to see a hard-ridden horse and the rider bowed over his neck urging him on. The yeomen of the guard at once gather before the king and six of them turn and stand in a line before me, and I observe, amazed, that they are shouldering their arms and then grounding their pikes. They have seen a single man riding as fast as he can towards our palace and they are readying for an attack. They actually think that a man might ride up to our court as we prepare to go hawking, and cut down Henry, King of England, where he stands. They actually think that they have to stand between me and any subject of this kingdom. I see their fear and I realize that they know nothing of what it is to be a queen of the House of York.

They hold their pikes firm, in a line of defense, as the man hauls on his reins and his weary horse skids almost to a halt and then walks towards us. "Message for the king," he says, hoarse with the dust in his throat, as Henry recognizes his messenger, puts a hand on one of his beefeaters' shoulders, turns him away, and approaches the shivering horse and the exhausted rider.

The man jumps from the saddle, but he is so weary that his legs buckle beneath him and he has to grab on the stirrup leather to keep himself up. He puts a hand inside his jacket and pulls out a battered sealed packet.

"Where from?" Henry asks quietly.

"Cornwall. The very far west of Cornwall."

Henry nods and turns to the court. "I must stay and read this," he calls. His voice is determinedly light, the smile he is straining to show them all is a grimace, like a man in pain. "A little business, nothing but a little business must detain me. You go on, I'll ride after!"

People murmur and mount up, and I gesture to my groom to hold my horse as I stand beside Henry and watch them go by. As the hawk cart goes past us, one of the falconers is tying the leather curtains to keep the birds cool and clean till they get to the fields where the hunt will start; then they will take the hoods off and the hawks will mantle their wings and look about them with bright eyes. One of the lads is running behind, carrying spare jesses and leashes. I glimpse his face when he ducks his head in a bow as he goes past the king: Lambert Simnel, promoted from his place as scullery boy, now a royal falconer, loyal in the king's service — a pretender who has found happiness.

Henry does not even see him. He does not see anybody as he turns and goes into the east door that leads up the great stairs to his presence chamber. I follow, and there is his mother, waiting in his rooms, watching from the window. "I saw the messenger coming from far away," she says to him quietly, like a woman waiting for the worst news in the world. "I have been praying since the moment I saw the dust on the road. I knew it was the boy. Where has he landed?"

"Cornwall," he answers. "And I have no friends in Cornwall now."

It is pointless to tell him that he has no friends in Cornwall now since he broke their pride, and broke their hearts, and hanged the men that they loved and followed. I wait in silence as Henry rips open the wrapping of the letter and takes out the paper. I see the seal of the Earl of Devon, William Courtenay, my sister Catherine's husband, and the father of her adored son.

"The boy has landed," Henry says, reading rapidly. "The Sheriff of Devon attacked his camp with a strong force." He pauses; I see him take a breath. "The sheriff's men all deserted and went over to the boy as soon as they saw him."

Lady Margaret presses her hands together as if she is praying but says nothing.

"The Earl of Devon, my brother-in-law." Henry looks at me as if I am responsible for William Courtenay. "The Earl of Devon, William Courtenay, was going to attack himself but thought they were too strong and he could not trust his men. He's fallen back to Exeter." He lifts his head. "The boy has just landed and already he has all of Cornwall and much of Devon; and your brother-in-law has fallen back to Exeter because he cannot trust his men to stay true to him."

"How many?" I ask. "How many men does the boy have?"

"About eight thousand." Henry gives a mirthless bark of a laugh. "More than I had, when I landed. It's enough. It's enough to take the throne."

"You were the rightful heir!" his mother says passionately.

"The Earl of Devon, William Courtenay, is trapped in Exeter," Henry says. "The boy has set a siege." He turns to his writing table and shouts for clerks. His mother and I step back as the men run into the room and Henry gives orders. Lord Daubney is to march towards the boy's forces, and relieve William Courtenay in Exeter. Another army commanded by Lord Willoughby de Broke is to hold the south coast so that the boy cannot get away. Every lord in the country is commanded to raise men and horse and meet Henry to march on the West Country. They must all come, there can be no excuses.

"I want him brought to me alive," Henry says to each of his clerks. "Write that to each commander. He must be taken alive. And tell them to fetch his wife and son too."

"Where are they?" I ask "His wife and his son?" I cannot bear the thought of the young woman with her baby, the young woman who may be my sister-in-law, in the midst of an army setting a siege.

"St. Michael's Mount," Henry says briefly.

My Lady the King's Mother gives an irritated exclamation at the thought of the boy and his son weaving themselves into the story of Arthur, a legend she has tried so hard to attach to our boy.

The clerks hand over the orders, dripping with hot wax, and Henry stamps them with his seal ring and signs with a spiky up-and-down scratch of the pen HR: Henricus Rex. I think of the proclamation that I saw signed with RR: Ricardus Rex, and know that once again there are two men who claim to be king treading the soil of England, once again there are two rival royal families, and this time I am divided between the two.

We wait. Henry cannot bring himself to go hawking, but sends me out to dine in the tents in the woods with the hunters and to play the part of a queen who thinks that all is well. I take the children with me on their little ponies, and Arthur on his hunter rides proudly at my side. When one of the lords asks me if the king is not coming I say that he will come in a while, he was detained by some business, nothing of importance.

I doubt very much that anyone believes me. The whole court knows that the boy is somewhere off our coasts; some of them will know that he has landed. Almost certainly, some of them will be preparing to join him, they may even have his letter of array in their pockets.

"I'm not afraid," Arthur tells me, almost as if he is listening to the words and wondering how they sound. "I am not afraid. Are you?"

I show him an honest face and a genuine smile. "I'm not afraid," I say. "Not at all."

When I get back to the palace there is a desperate message from Courtenay. The rebels have broken in through the gates of Exeter, and he is wounded. With the walls breached, he has made a truce. The rebel army has been merciful, there has been no looting, they have not even taken him prisoner. Honorably, they release him and in return he has allowed them to go on, along the Great West Way, heading for London, and he has promised he will not pursue them.

"He let them go?" I ask disbelievingly. "To march on London? He promised not to pursue them?"

"No, he'll break his word," Henry says. "I will order him to break his word. A promise to rebels like that need not be kept. I'll order him to trail behind them, block their retreat. Lord Daubney will come down on them from the north, Lord Willoughby de Broke will attack from the west. We will crush them."

"But he made a promise," I say uncertainly. "He has given his word."

Henry's face is dark and angry. "No promise given to that boy counts before God."

His servants come in with his hat, his gloves, his riding boots, his cape. Another goes running to the stables to order his horses, the guard is mustering in the yard, a messenger is riding for all the guns and cannon that London has.

"You're going to your army?" I ask. "You're riding out?"

"I'll meet with Daubney and his army," he says. "We'll outnumber them by three to one. I'll fight him with odds like these."

I catch my breath. "You're going now?"

He kisses me perfunctorily, his lips cold, and I can almost smell the scent of his fear. "I think we'll win," he says. "As far as I can be certain, I think we'll win."

"And what will you do then?" I ask. I dare not name the boy and ask what Henry plans for him.

"I will execute everyone who has raised a

hand against me," he says grimly. "I will show no mercy. I will fine everyone who let them march by and did not stop them. When I have finished, there will be no one left in Cornwall and Devon but dead men and debtors."

"And the boy?" I ask quietly.

"I will bring him into London in chains," he says. "Everyone has to see that he is a nobody, I will throw him down into the dust and when everyone understands at last that he is a boy and no prince, I will have him killed."

He looks at my white face. "You will have to see him," he says bitterly, as if all of this is my fault. "I will want you to look him in the face and deny him. And you had better make sure that you say no word, give no look, not a whisper, not even a breath of recognition. Whoever he looks like, whatever he says, whatever nonsense he spouts when he is asked: you had better be sure that you look at him with the gaze of a stranger, and if anyone asks you, you don't know him."

I think of my little brother, the child that my mother loved. I think of him looking at picture books on my lap, or running around the inner courtyard at Sheen with a little wooden sword. I think that it will not be possible for me to see his merry smile and his warm hazel eyes and not reach out to him.

"You will deny him," Henry says flatly. "Or I will deny you. If you ever, by so much as a word, the whisper of a word, the first letter of a word, give anyone, *anyone* to understand that you recognize this imposter, this commoner, this false boy, then I will put you aside and you will live and die in Bermondsey Abbey as your mother did. In disgrace. And you will never see any of your children again. I will tell them — each one of them — that their mother is a whore and a witch. Just like her mother, and her mother before that."

I face him, I rub his kiss from my mouth with the back of my hand. "You need not threaten me," I say icily. "You can spare me your insults. I know my duty to my position and to my son. I'm not going to disinherit my own son. I will do as I think right. I am not afraid of you, I have never been afraid of you. I will serve the Tudors for the sake of my son — not for you, not for your threats. I will serve the Tudors for Arthur — a true-born king of England."

He nods, relieved to see his safety in my unquestionable love for my boy. "If any one of you Yorks speaks of the boy other than as a young fool and a stranger, I will have him beheaded that same day. You will see him on Tower Green with his head on the block. The moment that you or your sisters or your cousin or any of your endless cousins or bastard kinsmen recognize the boy is the moment that you sign the warrant for his execution. If anyone recognizes him then they die and he dies. D'you understand?"

I nod my head and I turn away from him. I turn my back on him as if he were not a king. "Of course I understand," I say contemptuously over my shoulder. "But if you are going to continue to claim that he is the son of a drunken boatman from Tournai, you must remember not to have him beheaded like a prince on Tower Green. You'll have to have him hanged."

I shock him, he chokes on a laugh. "You're right," he says. "His name is to be Pierre Osbeque, and he was born to die on the gallows."

With ironic respect I turn back to him and sweep a curtsey, and in this moment I know that I hate my husband. "Clearly, we will call him whatever you wish. You can name the young man's corpse whatever you wish, that will be your right as his murderer."

We do not reconcile before he rides out and so my husband goes out to war with no warm farewell embrace from me. His mother gives him her blessing, clings to his reins, watches him go while she whispers her prayers, and looks curiously at me, as I stand dry-eyed and watch him ride off at the head of his guard, three hundred of them, to meet with Lord Daubney.

"Are you not afraid for him?" she asks, her eyes moist, her old lips trembling. "Your own husband, going out to war, to battle? You did not kiss him, you did not bless him. Are you not afraid for him riding into danger?"

"Really, I doubt very much that he'll get too close," I say cruelly, and I turn and go inside to the second-best apartment.

East Anglia, Autumn 1497

The king keeps all England informed as the rebellion disappears, and then melts away, before his carefully slow advance. The Cornishmen slip away every night as they realize that not one, not two, but three armies are mustered and slowly marching on them, and one night the boy goes too, taking a wild ride with only two companions, escaping the teeth of the trap that Henry has set for him, gaining the coast, learning of the ships waiting offshore to capture him, and plunging into the sanctuary of Beaulieu Abbey.

But England is not as it was. The king's writ runs up to the high altar now, his mother and her friend the archbishop have made sure of that. There is no sanctuary for the boy though he claims it as a king ordained by God to rule. The abbey breaks its own time-honored traditions, and hands over the boy. Unwillingly, he has to come out to make his surrender to a king who rules England and the Church too.

He came out wearing cloth of gold, and answering to the name of Richard IV — a hastily scribbled note which I guess is from my half brother, Thomas Grey, is tucked under my stirrup when I am taking the children out on their ponies. I did not see the hand that tied it to the stirrup leathers and I can be sure that no one will ever say that I saw it and read it. *But when the king questioned him, he denied himself. So be it. Mark it well. If he himself denies it, we can deny him.*

I scrunch the paper into a tiny ball and tuck it in my pocket to burn later. It is good of Thomas to let me know, and I am glad that the boy saw one friendly face in a room full of enemies, before he denied himself.

The rest of the news I have, as the court has it, as England has it, in long triumphant dispatches from Henry that are written by him personally, to be read aloud, throughout the country. He sends verbose announcements to the kings of Christendom. I imagine Henry's words bawled out at every village marketplace, at every town cross, on the steps of country churches, at the entrance to staple halls. He writes as if he were creating a story, and I read it almost smiling, as if my husband were setting up to be a Chaucer, to give the people of England a tale of their beginnings, an entertainment and an explanation. He becomes the historian of his own triumph, and I cannot be the only person who thinks that he has imagined a victory that he did not experience in the windswept fields of Devon. This is Henry the romancer, not Henry a true king.

Henry's story is that there was once a poor man, a man who kept the watergate at Tournai in Flanders. He was a weak man, a bit of a drunkard, married to a common woman, a bit of a fool, and they had a son, a silly boy who ran away from home and fell into bad company, serving as a page to someone (it doesn't matter much who or why) and went to the court of Portugal and for some reason (for who knows what silly lads will say?) passed himself off as a prince of England and everyone believed him. Then, suddenly he became a servant for a silk merchant. He learned to speak English, French, Spanish, and Portuguese (which is a little surprising but presumably not impossible). Dressed in his master's clothes, showing off the goods for sale, parading himself like a May Day pageant in Ireland, he was again mistaken for a prince (don't pause to ask if such a thing is likely) and was persuaded to take on the pretense all across Christendom — to what end and why is never discussed.

How such a poor ignorant boy from a common home should fool the greatest kings of Christendom, the Duchess of Burgundy, the Holy Roman Emperor, the King of France, the King of Scotland, should delight the court of Portugal and tempt the monarchs of Spain, Henry does not say. It is part of the magic of the fairy tale, like a goose-girl who is really a princess, or a girl who cannot sleep on a pea even when it is covered by twenty feather mattresses. Amazingly, this common, vulgar, ill-educated boy, the son of a drunkard and a fool, engages the richest, most cultured men in Christendom, so that they put their wealth and their armies at his disposal. How he learns to speak four languages and Latin, how he learns to read and write with an elegant hand, how he learns to hunt and joust, hawk and dance so that people admire him as a courageous graceful prince, though he was raised in the backstreets of Tournai, Henry doesn't say. How he learns the royal smile, the casual warm acknowledgment of homage, Henry does not even consider in his long account, though of all the men in the world he would have been the most struck by this. This is a story of magic: a common boy puts on a silk shirt, and everyone falls for the illusion that he has royal blood.

As my half brother wrote to me that one time: *So be it.*

I receive only one private letter from Henry during this busy time as he writes and re-writes explanations of how the boy, John Perkin, Piers Osbeque, Peter Warboys — for Henry offers several different names — made his transformation to prince and back again.

I am sending his wife to join you at court, Henry writes, knowing that there is no need for him to say whose wife is joining me. *You will be surprised at her beauty and elegance. You will oblige me by making her welcome and comforting her in the cruel deceit that has been played on her.*

I hand his letter to his mother, who stands with her hand out, waiting impatiently to read it. Of course, the boy's wife has been cruelly, amazingly deceived. Her husband wore a silk shirt and she was blinded by beautiful tailoring. She could not see that beneath it he was a common little boy from Flanders. Easily deluded, amazingly deluded, she saw the shirt and thought he was a prince, and married him.

PALACE OF SHEEN, RICHMOND, AUTUMN, 1497

I sit in my rooms waiting for the woman that we are to call Lady Katherine Huntly. She is not to be known by her married name; I suspect that no one is yet quite sure of her married name, whether it is Perkin or Osbeque or Warboys.

"She is to be considered as a single woman," My Lady the King's Mother announces to my ladies. "I expect the marriage will be annulled."

"On what grounds?" I ask.

"Deception," she replies.

"In what way was she deceived?" I ask demurely.

"Obviously." My Lady snubs me.

"Not much of a deception, if it was obvious," Maggie whispers tartly.

"And where is her child to be housed, My Lady?" I ask.

"He is to live away from court with his nursemaid," My Lady says. "And we are not to mention him."

"They say that she's very beautiful," my sister Cecily volunteers, sweet as Italian powders.

I smile at Cecily, my face and my eyes quite blank. If I want to save my throne, my freedom, and the life of the baby of the boy who calls himself my brother, I am going to have to endure the arrival of Lady Katherine, a beautiful, single princess, and much, much more.

I can hear the noise of her guard outside the door, the quick exchange of passwords, and then the door is thrown open. "Lady Katherine Huntly!" the man bellows quickly, as if they fear that someone might say: "Queen Katherine of England."

I stay seated, but my Lady the King's Mother surprises me by rising from her chair. My ladies sink down, as low as if they were honoring a woman of full royal blood, as the young woman comes into the room.

She is wearing black, in mourning as if she is a widow, but her cape and gown are beautifully made, beautifully tailored. Who would have thought that Exeter had such seamstresses? She is wearing a black satin dress trimmed with rich black velvet, a black hat on her head, a black riding cloak over her arm, she is wearing gloves of black embroidered leather. Her eyes are dark, hollowed in her pale face, her skin utterly clear, like the finest palest marble. She is a beautiful young woman in her early twenties. She curtseys low to me and I see her scanning my face, as if she is looking for some resemblance to her husband. I give her my hand and I rise to my feet and I kiss one cool cheek and then another for she is cousin to the King of Scotland, whoever she married, whatever the quality of the silk of his shirt. I feel her hand tremble in mine and again I see that wary look as if she would read me, as if she would know where I stand in this unfolding masque which her life has become.

"We welcome you to court," My Lady says. There is no careful reading needed for My Lady. She is doing what her son requested, welcoming Lady Katherine to court with such kindliness that even the most hospitable host would have to wonder why we are making such a fuss of this woman, the disgraced wife of our defeated enemy.

Lady Katherine curtseys again and stands before me as if I am going to interrogate her. "You must be tired," is all I say.

"His Grace the King was most kind," she says. She speaks with such a strong Scots accent that I have to strain to understand her soft voice with the enchanting lilt. "I had good horses and we rested on the way."

"Please be seated," I say. "We will dine in a little while."

Composedly, she takes her seat, folds her hands in her black silk lap, and looks at me. I note her earrings of black and the only other piece of jewelry that she wears, a gold brooch that is pinned to her belt: two gold hearts entwined. I permit myself a small smile, and there is an answering warmth in her eyes. I imagine that we are never going to say more than this.

We line up to prepare to enter the hall for dinner. I go first as queen, My Lady walks at my shoulder, slightly behind me, and Lady Katherine Huntly must come next, my sisters taking one step down the order of precedence. I glance back and see Cecily's pale face, her lower lip pressed tight. She is now fourth behind me, and she does not like it.

"Is Lady Huntly going to return to Scotland?" I ask My Lady the King's Mother, as we proceed into dinner.

"Surely she will," My Lady replies. "What would she stay here for? Once her husband is dead?"

But apparently she is in no hurry to leave. She stays until my husband has completed his slow progress from Exeter to the palace. The outriders come into the stable yard and send a message to my rooms that the king is approaching and expects a formal welcome. I order my ladies to come with me and we go down the broad stone stairs to the double entrance doors, which are held wide open, welcoming the return of the hero. We arrange ourselves at the head of the steps. My Lady the King's Mother's ladies stand beside us, she makes sure she is on the same step as me so that I am not more prominent, and we wait in the bright autumn sunshine, listening for the clatter of the horses' hooves.

"Has he sent the boy directly to the Tower?" Maggie asks me as she bends to pull out the train of my gown.

"He must have done," I say. "What else would he do with him?"

"He hasn't . . ." She hesitates. "He hasn't killed him on the way here?"

I glance at the boy's wife, all in black like a widow. She is wearing her black velvet cape against the cold and the gold brooch of twin hearts is pinned at the neck.

"I haven't heard," I say. I cannot help a little shiver. "Surely he would have sent word if he had done that? To the boy's wife if not to me? Surely I would have known?"

"Surely he wouldn't have executed him without a public announcement," she says uncertainly.

Behind us, in the darkened hall, I hear the constant ripple of noise as the servants come through and run down the stairs to the stable yard so that they can line the road to watch the king come home in triumph.

First we hear the king's trumpets, a victorious bray of sound, and everyone cheers. Then there is another noise — a ridiculous "tootletoot-toot!" from someone on the roadside, and everyone laughs. I feel Maggie stand a little closer, as if we are somehow threatened by the "toot-toot" of a toy trumpet.

Around the corner come the first riders, half a dozen standard bearers carrying the royal standard, the cross of St. George, the Beaufort portcullis, and the Tudor rose. There is a red dragon on a white and green ground, and a red rose for Lancaster. Only the Round Table of Camelot is missing from this ridiculous display. It is as if the king is showing all of his badges, naming all of his antecedents, as if he is trying to demonstrate his claim to the throne that he only won by force of arms, as if he is trying once again to convince everyone that he is the rightful king.

Then he comes, wearing his enameled breastplate but no helmet so that he looks martial and brave, about to fight a battle or a joust. He is beaming, a broad bright confident smile, and when the servants on the roadside and the people from the nearby villages, who have been running alongside the procession and now line the road, cheer and wave their hats, Henry nods to one side and the other as if agreeing with them.

Behind him come his usual companions, the men of his court. No one else is in armor, the rest are all dressed for a day's ride, booted, caped, one or two in quilted jackets, and among them, a young man I don't know, who attracts my attention in the first moment, and then I find that I can't look away from him.

He is dressed like all the others, with good leather boots — his a dark tan color — a good pair of brown breeches, a thick jacket fitted across his broad shoulders, and his riding cape rolled and belted on the saddle behind him. His bonnet is of brown velvet and at the front of it he has a beautiful brooch with three pendant pearls. I know him at once, not by the brooch but by the golden brown of his hair and his merry smile, my mother's merry smile, and the proud set of his head that is just how my father used to ride. It is him. It has to be him. It is the boy. He has not been sent to the Tower, nor brought wrapped in chains, nor tied backwards on his horse with a straw hat crammed on his head to shame him. He rides behind the king like one of his companions, like a friend, almost as if he were a kinsman.

Someone points him out to the people on the roadside and they start to jeer, an ugly noise, and someone shouts, "Traitor!" Someone else makes a mock bow, and a woman screams, "Smiling now! You won't smile for long!"

But he does smile. He lifts his head and he nods in acknowledgment to one side or the other, and when some silly girl, taken by his easy charm, shouts "Hurrah!" instead of an insult, he sweeps his hat from his head with all the charm and easiness of my father, King Edward, who could never ride past a pretty woman on the roadside without throwing her a wink.

Bare-headed in the bright autumn sunshine, I can see how his gold hair shines. This boy's hair is straight, cut long and smooth, falling to his shoulders, but I can see where it curls on his collar at the back. His eyes are brown, his face tanned by the weather, his eyelashes long and dark. He is the most handsome man in the whole court, and beside him, dressed in his shiny new armor, my husband the king looks like a man trying very hard.

The boy is looking anxiously at the ladies of the court as they stand, waiting on the steps, until he sees his wife, and he throws her the cheekiest grin, as if they were not in the most terrible circumstances that anyone could imagine. I glance sideways at her, and see a different young woman altogether. The color has flooded into her pale cheeks, her eyes are bright, she is dancing a little on the spot and gazing at him, blind to the king and the parade of banners, radiant, as if the joy of seeing him is greater than any other worry in the world. As if it does not matter very much what circumstances they are in, as long as they are together.

And then he looks from her to me.

He knows me at once. I see him take in the

elegance of my gown, the deference of my ladies, and that I hold myself like a queen. I see him note my high headdress and my richly embroidered dress. Then he looks into my face and his smile, his roguish laughing smile, just like my mother's irreverent joy, shines through. It is a smile of complete confidence, of recognition, of delight in his return. I have to bite the inside of my cheek to prevent myself from running forwards to greet him with my arms open wide. But I cannot stop my heart lifting and I feel myself glowing as if I want to cheer. He's home. The boy who calls himself my brother Richard is home at last.

Henry holds up his hand for the cavalcade to halt and a page boy flings himself from his horse and rushes to take the king's bridle. Henry dismounts heavily, his armor clattering, and he walks up the shallow steps towards me and kisses me warmly on the mouth, turns to his mother and bows his head for her blessing.

"Welcome home, my lord," I say formally, loudly enough for everyone to hear my greeting. "And blessing on your great victory."

Oddly, he does not make any formal reply, though the clerks are waiting to record his words at this moment of history. He turns a little to one side and then I see him gasp — just a tiny little betraying breath — as he sees her: the boy's wife. I see the color rise in his cheeks, I see how his eyes brighten. He steps towards Lady Katherine and he does not know what to say; like a lovestruck page he is breathless at the sight of her and wordless when he should speak.

She drops him a low, deferential curtsey and when she rises up he takes her hand. I see her lower her eyes modestly, and the little hint of her smile, and finally I understand why she has been sent to be my lady-in-waiting, and why her husband rides freely among the king's men. Henry has fallen in love for the first time in his life, and with the worst choice he could possibly have made.

His mother, who was watching every step of her son's victorious arrival, invites me to her rooms that evening before the grand victorious dinner. She tells me that Henry has appointed two of my ladies-in-waiting and taken two from her court to serve Lady Katherine until he can find suitable ladies to wait on her. Apparently Lady Katherine is to have a little court of her own, and her own rooms; she is to live as a visiting princess of Scotland and be served on bended knee.

Lady Katherine has been invited to go to the royal wardrobe to choose a gown suitable for the feast to celebrate the king's victory. It seems that the king would like to see her wear another color, other than black.

I remember, wryly, that once I was commanded to wear a gown of the same cut and color as Queen Anne, and that everyone remarked how beautiful I was, standing beside her in a matching gown, and her husband could not take his eyes off me. It was the Christmas feast before the queen died, and she and I wore the same red gown, except she wore it as if it were her shroud, poor lady, she was so white and thin. I stood beside her and the color scarlet put a flush in my cheek and brightened the gold of my hair and the sparkle in my eyes. I was young, and in love, and I was heartless. I think of her now, and her calm dignity when she saw me dance with her husband, and I wish I could tell her that I am sorry, and that now I understand far more than I did then.

"Have you asked the king when Lady Katherine is going home?" My Lady demands abruptly. She is standing with her back towards a mean fire, her hands tucked into her sleeves. The rest of the room is cold.

"No," I say. "Will you ask him?"

"I will!" she exclaims. "I certainly will. Have you asked him when Pero Osbeque is to go to the Tower?"

"Is that his name now?"

She flushes, furious. "Whatever he is called. Peter Warboys, whatever they call him."

"I have had very little speech with His Grace," I say. "Of course his lords and the gentlemen from London wanted to ask him about the battle and so he went to his presence chamber with them all."

"Was there a battle?"

"Not really, no."

She takes a breath and looks at me, a sly cautious look as if she is unsure of her ground. "The king seems very taken with Lady Katherine."

"She's a very beautiful woman," I agree.

"You must not mind . . ." she goes on. "You must not object . . ."

"Object to what?" It is hardly a challenge, my voice is so calm and pleasant.

"Nothing." She loses her nerve before my smiling serenity. "Nothing at all."

Lady Katherine comes to my rooms before dinner obediently wearing a new gown from the royal wardrobe but keeping to her chosen color of deepest black. She is wearing the gold brooch of intertwined hearts on a thin chain of gold, lying over a veil of white lace that covers her shoulders. The warm cream of her skin glows under the fabric, veiled and visible at the same time. When the king enters my presence chamber, his eyes rake the room for her, and when he sees her he gives a little start, as if he had forgotten how beautiful she is, and he is shaken by desire all over again. She curtseys as politely as the other ladies, and when she comes up she is smiling at him, a hazy smile like a woman who laughs through her tears.

Henry gives me his arm to lead me in to dinner and the rest of the court take their places behind us, my ladies following me in order of precedence, the gentlemen behind them. Lady Katherine Huntly, her dark eyes fixed modestly on the ground, takes her rightful place behind My Lady the King's Mother. As Henry and I lead the way down the wide stone stairs to the great hall to the blast of trumpets and the murmur of applause from the people who have crowded into the gallery to see the royal family at their dinner, I sense, more than I actually see, that the boy who is to be called Peter Warboys, or perhaps Pero Osbeque or John Perkin, has walked past the woman who was once his wife, bowed his head low to her, and taken his place with the other young noblemen of Henry's court.

The boy seems to be at home at court. He goes from hall to stable to hawking mews to gardens and he is never seen to miss his way, never asks anyone which is the direction of the treasure house, or where would he find the king's tennis court? He will fetch a pair of gloves for the king without asking where they are kept. He is comfortable with his companions, too. There is an elite of handsome young men who lounge in the king's rooms and run errands for him, who like to call at my rooms to listen to the music and chatter with my ladies. When there are cards they are quick to take a hand, if there is archery they will take a bow and excel each other. Gambling, they are free with money; dancing, they are graceful on the floor; flirting is their principal occupation, and every one of my ladies has a favorite among the king's young men and hopes that he sees her half-hidden glance.

The boy falls into this life as if he had been born and bred at a graceful court. He will sing with my lutenist if invited, he will read in French or Latin if someone hands him the storybook. He can ride any horse in the stables with the relaxed, easy confidence of a man who has been in the saddle since he was a boy, he can dance, he can turn a joke, he can compose a poem. When they put on an impromptu play he is quick and witty, when called to recite he has lengthy poems by heart. He has all the skills of a well-educated young nobleman. He is, in every way, like the prince he pretended to be.

Indeed, he stands out from these handsome young men in only one thing. Night and morning he greets Lady Katherine by kneeling at her feet and kissing her outstretched hand. Every morning, first thing, on the way to chapel, he drops down to his knee, pulls his hat from his head, and kisses, very gently, the hand she holds out to him and stays still for the brief moment that she rests her hand on his shoulder. In the evening, when we leave the great hall, or when I say that the music must stop in my rooms, he bows low to me with his odd, familiar smile, and then he turns to her and kneels at her feet.

"He must be ashamed that he brought her so low," Cecily says after we have all observed this for several days. "He must be kneeling for her forgiveness."

"Do you think so?" Maggie asks her. "Don't you think that it is the only way that he can touch her? And she touch him?"

I watch them more closely after that, and I believe Maggie is right. If he can pass something to her, he makes sure that their fingertips brush. If the court is riding he is quickly at the shoulder of her horse to lift her into the saddle, and at the end of the day he is first into the stable yard, his own horse's reins tossed to a groom so that he can lift her down, holding her for one moment before putting her gently on her feet. When they are playing cards their shoulders lean together at the table, when he is standing beside her horse and she is mounted high above him, he steps backwards until his fair head can brush against her saddle and her hand can drop from the reins to touch the nape of his neck.

She never rebuffs him, she does not avoid his touch. Of course, she cannot; while she is his wife she must be obedient to him. But clearly, there is a passion between them that they do not even try to hide. When they pour the wine at dinner he looks from his table over to hers and raises his glass to her and gets a quick half-hidden smile in return. When she walks past the young men playing at cards she pauses, just for a moment, to look at his hand, and sometimes leans down as if to see better, and he leans back and their cheeks brush, like a kiss. Throughout the court they move, two exceptionally beautiful young people, kept apart by the specific order of the king and yet going through the day in parallel; always with one eye on the other, like performers separated by the movement of a dance who are certain to come together again.

Now that it is safe to travel in England again, Arthur my son must go to Ludlow Castle and Maggie and his guardian Sir Richard Pole will attend him. I see them off from the stable yard, my half brother Thomas Grey at my side.

"I can't bear to let him go," I say.

He laughs. "Don't you remember our mother when Edward had to go? Lord save her, she went with him, all that long way, even though she was pregnant with Richard. It is hard for you, and hard on the boy. But it is a sign that things are getting back to normal. You should be glad."

Arthur, bright and excited high on his

horse, waves his hand at me and follows Sir Richard and Maggie out of the stable yard. The guard falls in behind him.

"I don't think I can be glad," I say.

Thomas squeezes my hand. "He'll be back for Christmas."

Next day the king tells me he will take a small company to London to show the crowds Perkin Warbeck, the pretender.

"Who's going with you?" I ask, as if I don't understand.

Henry flushes slightly. "Perkin," he says. "Warbeck."

Finally they have settled on a name for him, and not just for him. They have named and described a whole family Warbeck with uncles and cousins and aunts and grandparents, the Warbecks of Tournai. But though this extensive family is established, at least on paper, all with occupations and addresses, none of them is summoned to see him. None of them writes to him with reproaches, or offers of help. Though there are so many of them, so well recorded, not one offers a ransom for his return. The king weaves them into the story of Perkin Warbeck and we never ask to see them, any more than one might ask to see a black cat or a crystal slipper or a magic spindle.

In London the boy gets a confused reception. The men, who have seen their taxes rise and rise and unlawful fines invade every part of their income, curse him for the expense that his invasions have caused, and groan at him as he rides by. The women, always quick to malice, start by catcalling and throwing dirt; but even they soften, they cannot help but admire his downturned face, his shy smile. He rides through the streets of London with the modest air of a boy who could not help himself, who was called and answered a call, who could not help but be himself. Some people rage against him, but many shout out that he is a fair boy, a rose.

Henry makes him go on foot, leading a broken-down old horse, with one of his followers in chains, mounted up. The man in the saddle, grim-faced, is the sergeant farrier who ran from Henry's service to be with the boy. Now all of London can see him, head bowed, bruised, tied to the saddle like a Fool. Usually people would throw filth, and then laugh to see the rider and the humiliated groom spattered with mud from the gutters, showered with the contents of chamber pots flung from overhead windows. But the boy and his defeated supporter make a strangely silent pair as they go through the narrow streets to the Tower and then someone says, terribly clearly, into a sudden hush: "Look at him! He's the spit of good King Edward."

Henry hears of this the moment the words are out of the man's mouth; but too late to call the words back, too late to deafen the crowd. All he can do is make sure that the crowd never again sees the boy who looks so like a York prince.

So that is to be the first and last time that the boy has to walk the streets of London inviting abuse. "You will confine him to the Tower," My Lady orders her son.

"In time. I wanted the people to see that he was nothing, no threat, an idle foolish boy. Nothing more than a little lad, the boy that I always called him — lighter than air."

"Well, they have seen him now. And they don't call him lighter than air. They don't know what to call him, though we have told them his name over and over again. And the name that they want to give him should never be spoken. Surely, now you will charge him and execute him?"

"I gave him my word that he should not be killed when he surrendered to me."

"That's not binding." Anxiety makes her overrule him. "You've broken your word for less than this. You don't have to keep your word to such as him."

His face is suddenly illuminated. "Yes, but I gave my word to her."

My Lady turns a furious glare on me, accusing me at once. "Her? She never had the nerve to ask for mercy for him?" she suddenly rages, her face filled with hatred. "She never soiled her mouth speaking for such a traitor? For what reason? What did she dare to say?"

Coolly, I show her a mutinous face and silently I shake my head. "No, not me," I say icily. "You are mistaken, again. I have not asked for mercy for him. I have not spoken for or against him. I have no opinion on the matter, and I never have done." I wait while her anger curdles into embarrassment. "I think His Grace must mean another lady."

Horrified, My Lady turns back to her son as if he is betraying her, as if it is she who is suffering infidelity. "Who? What woman has dared to ask you for his life? Who do you listen to — instead of me, your own mother, who has guided every step of your way?"

"Lady Katherine," he says. He has a silly little smile on his face at her very name. "Lady Katherine. I have given my word of honor to the lady."

She sits in my room like a dignified widow, always in black, with her hands always filled with some work or another. We sew shirts for the poor and always she is hemming a sleeve or turning a collar, her head bowed over her work. The chatter and laughter of the women go on around her, all the time, and sometimes she raises her head and smiles at a joke, and sometimes she quietly replies, or adds her own story to the conversation. She speaks of her childhood in Scotland, she speaks of her cousin the King of Scotland and of his court. She is not lively, but she is courteous and pleasant company. She has charm; I sometimes find myself smiling when I look at her. She has poise. She is living in my court and my husband is visibly in love with her and yet she never shows, by so much as a sideways glance to me, that she is aware of this. She could taunt me, she could flaunt herself, she could embarrass me, but she never does.

She never mentions her own husband, she never speaks of this last extraordinary year: the little ship that took them to Ireland, their lucky escape from the Spanish who would have captured them, their triumphant landing and victorious march from Cornwall into Devon, and then their defeat. She never speaks of her husband at all, and so she avoids giving his name. The great question — what is the true name of this young man who never walks past her without a smile — is never answered by her.

He, himself, is like a nameless person. The Spanish ambassador addresses him once, in public, as Perkin Warbeck, and the young man turns his head slowly, like a playactor, like a dancer, and looks away, far away. It is a snub so confident, so graceful, that you would swear that only a prince could do it. The ambassador looks a fool, and the boy looks mildly regretful that he is forced to cause a moment's embarrassment to a man who should have known how to behave.

It is Henry the king who rescues the court from the scandalous sight of a paroled traitor snubbing the ambassador of our greatest ally. We expect him to reprimand the boy and send him out, but instead the king blunders off his throne, down the presence chamber in a hurry, turns towards my ladies, catches Lady Katherine's hand, and says suddenly, "Let's have some dancing!"

The musicians strike up at once, and he takes both her hands and faces her. He is flushed, as if he is the one who has made a blunder, instead of the pretender and his wife. And she is as she always is, as cool as a stream in winter. Henry bows to start the dance, she curtseys, and then she smiles, like the sun coming out from behind a cloud. Radiant, she smiles at my husband and I can see his heart lift at that small, tiny approval.

Palace of Sheen, Richmond, Christmas 1497

The Christmas season brings my children home to me. Henry, Margaret, and Mary return to us from Eltham Palace and Arthur comes from Ludlow with his guardian, Sir Richard Pole, and my darling Maggie. I run down to the stable yard to greet the troop from Ludlow as they come riding in, on an evening when the persistent cold rain of the day is just turning to swirling flakes of snow.

"Thank heaven you are in before it got any colder!" I fall on Arthur as if I would save him from darkness itself. "But you're so warm!" I stop myself exclaiming "and so lovely!" for my oldest boy is, as he always is, a revelation to me. In the few months of his absence he has grown a little taller. I can feel the wiry strength of his arms as he hugs me, he is a prince in every sense. I cannot believe this is the baby I held in my arms and the toddler whose steps I guided, when I see this coltish youth whose head now comes to my chin, and who steps back from my embrace to bow to me with all the elegance of his grandfather, my father, King Edward.

"Of course I'm warm," he says. "Sir Richard had us in a breakneck canter for the last half hour."

"I wanted to get in before nightfall," Sir Richard explains and he dismounts and bows low to me. "He's well," he says shortly. "Healthy, strong, and learning something new every day. He's very good in dealing with the people in Wales. Very fair. We're making a king here. A good king."

Maggie tumbles down from her horse, curtseys to me, and then bounds up to hug me. "You're looking well," she observes, stepping back to scrutinize me. "Are you happy?" she asks doubtfully. "How is everything here? His Grace the King?"

Something makes me turn and look towards the shadow of the doorway, to the open door. The torchlight is behind her, but I can see the silhouette of Katherine Huntly, her velvet dress black against the flickering darkness of the doorway. She is watching me greet my son, though her own baby boy is far away tonight and she is not allowed to see him. She is hearing my son's guardian say that he is a good Prince of Wales though she thought her own son was born for that position, and he was always addressed with that title.

I beckon her forwards. "You remember

Lady Katherine Huntly," I say to Sir Richard.

Maggie curtseys to her and for a moment we three women stand still, as the drifting snow swirls around us as if we were untitled statues in a wintry garden. What should the names be on the bases of the statues? Are we two cousins and a sister-in-law, destined to live together in silence, never speaking the truth? Or are we two unlucky daughters of the defeated House of York and an imposter who has won her place with us by the low means of charming the king? Will we ever know for sure?

His Grace the King appoints six ladies-in-waiting at his own cost to serve Lady Katherine. They will work for her, as my ladies serve me, running errands, writing notes, giving small gifts to the poor, keeping her company, helping her choose her clothes and dressing her, praying with her in chapel, singing and making music with her when she is merry, reading with her when she wants to be quiet. She has her own set of rooms on my side of the great palace: her bedchamber, her privy chamber, her presence chamber. Sometimes she sits with me, sometimes she joins My Lady the King's Mother, where she gets a chilly welcome, and sometimes she retreats with her ladies to her own presence chamber, a little court within a court.

Even the boy is given two servants of his own who go with him everywhere and serve him, fetching his horse, attending him when he rides, preparing his bedchamber, squiring him in to dine. They sleep in his room, one on a pallet bed, one on the floor, so that they are, as it were, his jailers; but when the boy turns to one of them to give him his gloves or ask for his cape, it is clear that they serve him gladly. He lives in the king's side of the building, in the rooms inside the royal wardrobe, guarded like treasure. The doors to the wardrobe and the treasure house are locked at night so that — without being imprisoned in any way — it happens that he is locked inside each night, as if he were a precious jewel himself. But during the day he walks in and out of the palace, nodding casually to the yeomen of the guard as he strolls by, rides out on a fast horse, either with the court or on his own or with his chosen friends, who seem proud to ride with him. He takes a boat out on the river, where he is not watched nor prevented from rowing as far as he likes. He is as free and as lighthearted as any of the young men of this young, lighthearted court, but he seems — without ever claiming pre-eminence — to be a natural leader, finer than his peers, acknowledged by them almost as if he were a prince.

In the evening he is always in my rooms. He comes in and bows to me, says a few words of greeting, smiles that curiously warm and intimate smile, and then seats himself near to Katherine Huntly. Often we see them talking, head to head, low-voiced, but there is no sense of conspiracy. When anyone comes near them they look up and make a place for whoever passes by, they are always courteous and charming and easy. If they are left alone they speak and reply, question and answer, almost as if they were singing together, almost as if they wanted nothing more than to hear each other's voice. They may talk of the weather, of the score in the archery competition, of almost nothing; but everyone senses their irresistible affinity.

Often I see them sitting in the oriel window, side by side, shoulder brushing against shoulder, knees just touching. Sometimes he leans forwards and whispers in her ear and his lips nearly brush her cheek. Sometimes she turns her face towards him and he must feel her warm breath on his neck, as close as a kiss. For hours in the day they will sit like this, quiet as obedient children on a settle, tender as young lovers before their betrothal, never touching, but never more than a hand-span apart, like a pair of cooing doves.

"My God, he adores her," Maggie remarks, watching this restrained, unstoppable court-ship. "Surely he cannot always be at arm's length? Do they never slip away to her rooms?"

"I don't think so," I say. "They seem to have settled for being constant companions, but no longer husband and wife."

"And the king?" Maggie asks delicately.

"Why, what have you heard?" I ask dryly. "You've only been at court a few days, people must have rushed to tell you everything. What have you heard already?"

She makes a grimace. "It's common talk that he can't take his eyes off her, when they ride out he is always near her, when he dances he asks for her as his partner, he sends out the best dishes for her. He is constantly offering gifts which she quietly returns, again and again he sends her to the royal wardrobe, he orders silks for new gowns, but she will only wear black." She looks at me, and finds me impassive. "You've seen all this? You know all this?"

I shrug. "I have seen most of it now, with my husband. I saw it once before with someone else's husband. I was once the girl that everyone watched as they turned their backs on the queen. I was once the girl that got the gowns and the gifts."

"When you were the king's favorite?"

"Just as she is. Worse than she is, for I gloried in it. I was in love with Richard and he was in love with me and we courted right under the nose of his wife, Anne. I wouldn't do that now. I would never do that now. I didn't realize then how painful it is."

"Painful?"

"And demeaning. For the wife. I see the court look at me as they wonder what I am thinking. I see Henry look at me as if he hopes that I don't notice that he stammers like a boy when he talks to her. And she . . ."

Maggie waits.

"She never looks at me at all," I say. "She never looks at me to see how I am taking it, or to see if I notice her triumph. She never looks at me to see if I observe that my husband adores her; and oddly it is only her gaze that I could endure. When she curtseys to me or speaks to me, I think she is the only person who understands how I feel. It is as if she and I are in this together, and we have to manage it somehow together. She cannot help that he has fallen in love with her. She does not seek his favor, she does not entice him. Neither she nor I can help it that he has fallen out of love with me, and in love with her."

"She could leave!"

"She can't leave," I say. "She can't leave her husband, she could not bear to leave him here, and Henry seems determined that he shall live at court, live here like a kinsman almost as if he were . . ."

"As if he were your brother?" Maggie whispers, quiet as a breath.

I nod. "And Henry won't let her go. He looks for her every morning in chapel, he can't close his eyes and say his prayers until he has seen her. It makes me feel . . ." I break off and I blot my eyes with the corner of my sleeve. "I'm such a fool but it makes me feel unwanted. It makes me feel plain. I don't feel like the first lady of the court of England. I don't feel that I am where I should be, in my mother's place. I'm not even in my usual second place to My Lady the King's Mother. I have dropped below that. I am humbled. I am Queen of England but disregarded by the king my husband, and the court." I pause and try to laugh, but it comes out as a sob. "I feel plain, Maggie! For the first time in my life! I feel humbled! And it's hard."

"You are the first lady, you are the queen, nobody and nothing can take that from you," she insists fiercely.

"I know. I know that really," I say sadly. "And I married without love, and now it seems that he loves someone else. It is ridiculous that I should care at all. I married him thinking of him as my enemy. I married him hating him and hoping for his death. It should be nothing to me that he now lights up when another woman enters the room."

"But you do care?"

"Yes. I find that I do."

The court prepares joyfully for Christmas. Arthur is summoned to his father, who tells him that his betrothal to the Spanish princess

Katherine of Aragon is confirmed and will take place. Nothing can delay it, now that the monarchs of Spain are confident that there is no pretender threatening Henry's throne. But they write to their ambassador to ask him why the pretender has not been executed, as they had expected either his death in battle or a prompt beheading on the battlefield. Why has he not been put on trial and swiftly dispatched?

Lamely, the ambassador replies to them that the king is merciful. As merciless usurpers themselves, they do not understand this, but they allow the betrothal to go ahead, stipulating only that the pretender should die before the marriage ceremony. That is mercy enough, they suggest. The ambassador hints to the king that Isabella and Ferdinand, the King and Queen of Spain, would prefer it if there was not a drop of doubtful blood left in the country, not Perkin Warbeck, nor Maggie's brother; they would prefer it if there were no heir of York at all.

"Not Lady Huntly's baby?" I ask. "Shall we be Herods now?"

Arthur comes to walk with me in the garden, where I am huddled in my furs and striding out for warmth, my ladies trailing away behind me. "You look cold."

"I am cold."

"Why don't you go indoors, Lady Mother?"

"I am sick of being indoors. I am sick of

everyone watching me."

He offers me his arm, which I take with such a glow of pleasure to see my boy, my firstborn child, with the manners of a prince.

"Why are they watching you?" he asks gently.

"They want to know how I feel about Lady Katherine Huntly," I say frankly. "They want to know if she troubles me."

"Does she?"

"No."

"His Grace, my father, seems very happy to have captured Mr. Warbeck," he begins carefully.

I cannot help but giggle at my boy Arthur practicing diplomacy. "He is," I say.

"Though I am surprised to find Mr. Warbeck in favor, and at court. I thought that my father was taking him to London and would imprison him in the Tower."

"I think we are all surprised at your father's sudden mercy."

"It's not like Lambert Simnel," he says. "Mr. Warbeck isn't a falconer. What is he doing coming and going so freely? And is my father paying him a wage? He seems to have money to pay for books and to gamble. Certainly my father gives him the best clothes and horses, and his wife, Lady Huntly, lives in state."

"I don't know," I say.

"Does he spare him for your sake?" he asks

very quietly.

My face is quite expressionless. "I don't know," I say again.

"You do know, but you won't say," Arthur asserts.

I hug his arm. "My son, some things are safer left unsaid."

He turns to face me, his innocent face puzzled. "Lady Mother, if Mr. Warbeck is indeed who he said he was, if he is being allowed the run of the court for that reason, then he has a greater right to the throne than my father. He has a greater right to the throne than me."

"And that is exactly why we will never have this conversation," I reply steadily.

"If he is who he says he is, then you must be glad he is alive," he pursues, with all the doggedness of a young man in pursuit of the truth. "You must be glad to see him. It must be as if he were snatched from death, almost as if he were risen from the dead. You must be happy to see him here, even if he never sits on the throne. Even if you pray that he never sits on the throne. Even if you want the throne for me."

I close my eyes so that he does not see the glow of my happiness. "I am," I say shortly; and he is a wise young prince, for he does not speak of this again.

We have dancing and celebrating, a joust and

players. We have a choir sing most beautifully in the royal chapel, and we give away sweetmeats and gingerbread to two hundred poor children. The broken meats from the feast feed hundreds of men and women at the kitchen door for the twelve days. Henry and I lead out the dancers on the first day of Christmas, and I look behind me, down the line and see that Lady Katherine is dancing with her husband, and they are handclasped, both flushed, the handsomest couple in the room.

Every day provides a new entertainment. We have a masque hunt led by a great giant of a man playing the Spirit of the Greenwood on a big bay horse, we have mummers and a performance of strange tall men, Egyptians, who eat live coals and are so terrifying that Mary ducks her head into my lap and Margaret cries and even Harry leans back in his little chair to feel my comforting hand on his shoulder. And all through the dancing and masquing and jockeying for position, there is Lady Katherine Huntly, the most beautiful woman at court, in her black velvet. There is my husband, quite unable to take his eyes off her, there is her husband always half a pace to the left or the right of her, always with her, but only rarely her partner, exchanging one swift unreadable glance with her before she goes forwards to the king, in obedience to his beckoning wave, and curtseys to him and waits, composed and lovely, for him to make awkward conversation.

I see that in this season of celebration he prefers to watch entertainers with her, or ride beside her, or dance with her, or listen to music, anything where he does not have to find words to say. He cannot speak to her. For what could he say? He cannot court her: she is the wife of his prisoner, a proclaimed traitor. He cannot flirt with her: there is something very sobering about her dark black gown and her luminously pale face; he cannot fall to his knees and declare his love for her, though truly I think this is what he would most naturally do, because that would be to dishonor her since she is in his keeping, to dishonor me, his faultless wife, and to dishonor his own name and position.

"Shall I take her to one side and simply tell her that she must demand to go back to Scotland?" Maggie asks me directly. "Shall I tell her that she has to free you from this constant insult?"

"No," I say, taking a careful stitch of a plain shirt. "For I am not insulted."

"The whole court sees the king looking hound-eyed at her."

"Then they see a king making a fool of himself; he is not making one of me," I say sharply.

Maggie gasps at my daring to speak against the king.

"It's not her at fault," I continue. We both glance across the sunny chamber to where Lady Katherine is sitting, hemming a collar for a poor man's shirt, her dark head bowed over the task.

"She has the king dancing to her tune like she was a tuppenny fiddle player," Maggie says bluntly.

"She does nothing to encourage him. And it keeps her husband safe. While the king is besotted with her, he will not kill her husband."

"It's a price you're prepared to pay?" Maggie whispers, shocked. "To keep the boy safe?"

I cannot help but smile. "I think it's a price that both she and I are paying. And I would do so much more than this, to keep this young man safe."

Maggie sees me to bed as if she were still my chief lady-in-waiting instead of a beloved visitor, and blows out the candle by my bedside before leaving the room. But I am wakened by the tolling of the chapel bell, and someone hammering on my door and then bursting into the room. My first thought is that despite his passive appearance, the boy has raised a secret army and is coming against Henry, and there is an assassin with a naked blade in the palace. I jump out of bed and grab at my robe and scream: "Where is Arthur? Where is the

Prince of Wales? Guards! To the prince!"

"Safe." Maggie comes running in, her hair down in its nighttime plait, barefooted, wearing only her nightgown. "Richard has him safe. But there is a fire, you must come at once."

I throw a robe over my gown and hurry out of the door with her. There is a babel of noise and confusion, the bell ringing and men shouting and people running from one place to another. Without needing to say a word, Maggie and I dash side by side to the rooms of the royal nursery and there, thanks to God, are Harry, Margaret, and Mary, the two older ones tumbling down the stairs with their nursemaids shrieking to them to go as fast as they can but to be careful, and Mary big-eyed in the arms of her nursemaid. I drop to my knees and hold the oldest two to me, feeling their warm little bodies, feeling my heart thud with relief that they are safe. "There is a fire in the palace," I tell them. "But we are not in danger. Come with me and we will go outside and watch them put it out."

A guard of yeomen go running past me, carrying flails and buckets of water. I tighten my grip on my children's hands. "Come on," I say. "Let's go outside and find your brother and your father."

We are halfway down the gallery to the great hall when the door to Lady Katherine's room flies opens and she dashes out, her black cape flung over her white nightgown, her dark eyes wide, her hair a rich tumble around her face. When she sees me she halts. "Your Grace!" she says and curtseys low and stays down, waiting for me to go past her.

"Never mind that, come at once," I say. "There is a fire, come at once, Lady Katherine."

She hesitates.

"Come!" I command. "And all your household with you."

She pulls her hood over her hair and hurries to walk behind me. As I go on with my children I just glimpse, out of the corner of my eye, the young man that is called Perkin Warbeck, wrapped in a cloak, slide from Lady Katherine's inner private room and fall in behind us, with my household.

I glance back to be sure, and he meets my gaze, his smile warm and confident. He shrugs and spreads his hands, a gesture wholly French, completely charming. "She is my wife," he says simply. "I love her."

"I know," I say, and hurry onwards.

The front doors are wide open and they have made a line of people passing pails of water up the stairs. Henry is in the stable yard, making them hurry, drawing water from the well, urging the lad to work harder at the pump. It is painfully slow, we can smell the acrid hot smoke on the wind and the bell tolls loudly as the men shout for more water and say that the flames are taking hold. Arthur is there with Sir Richard, his guardian, wearing nothing but his breeches and a cape over his bare shoulders.

"You'll freeze to death!" I scold him.

"Go and get a jacket from our traveling carts," Maggie orders him. "They're not unpacked yet."

Arthur ducks his head in obedience to her and goes to the stables.

"It's a terrible fire, in the wardrobe rooms, you'll lose your gowns, and God knows how many jewels!" Henry shouts at me above the noise. I can hear a crack as the expensive window glass shatters in the heat and then there is a noise like a blast as one of the roof beams caves in and the flames shoot upwards like an explosion.

"Is everyone out of the building?" I shout.

"As far as we can tell," Henry says. "Except . . . my love, I am sorry . . ." He steps away from the line of men frantically slopping pails of water one to another. "I am so sorry, Elizabeth, but I am afraid the boy is dead."

I glance behind me. Lady Katherine is there, but the boy has melted into the crowds of people milling around the front doors of the palace, starting back as another roar comes from the fire and flames lick out of an upper window.

"Will you tell her?" Henry asks me. "There

665

is no doubt that he is lost to the blaze. He was sleeping in the wardrobe rooms, of course, and they were locked. It's where the fire started. We must prepare ourselves for his death. It's a tragedy, it's a terrible tragedy."

Something about Henry alerts me. He is strangely like our son Harry, when he looks at me with his blue eyes as honest and as open as a summer sky and tells me some great fib about his homework, or his sister, or his tutor.

"The boy is dead?" I ask. "He has died in the fire?"

Henry looks down, shrugs his shoulders, heaves a sigh, puts his hand over his eyes as if weeping. "He can't have got out of that," he said. "It was raging by the time anyone knew of it, it was like hell." He puts out his hand to me. "He won't have suffered," he says. "Tell her that it would have been merciful and quick. Tell her that we are all so sorry."

"I'll tell her what you say," is all I promise, and I leave my husband to command the men who are bellowing for sand to fling on the flames and "Water! More water!" I walk back to where Lady Katherine is standing with Harry and Margaret beside her.

"Lady Katherine . . ." I beckon her out of their hearing and she drops a quick kiss on my son's copper head and comes to me.

"The king believes that your husband was

in his bed in the wardrobe rooms," I say levelly. There is no intonation in my voice at all, I am as bland as milk.

She nods, expressionless.

"The king fears that he must have died in the blaze," I say.

"It is the wardrobe rooms that are on fire?"

"It's where the fire started, and it has taken hold."

Both of us absorb the curious fact that the fire should start not in the kitchen, nor the bakery, nor even in the hall where there are great fires always burning, but in the wardrobe rooms where the strictest watch is kept, where the only naked flames are the candles, which are lit when the seamstresses are at work and doused when they leave for the evening.

"I suppose," I observe, "that since the king thinks that your husband is dead, he will not look for him."

She is very still as she takes in this thought, then she looks up at me. "Your Grace: the king holds our son, my little boy. I could not leave without him. And my husband will not leave without us. I see that he has a chance to escape, but I don't even have to ask him what he will do; he would never leave without us. He would have to be carried out half-dead to go without us."

"It may be that this chance has come from God," I point out. "A fire, confusion, and the expectation of his death."

She meets my eyes. "He loves his son, and he loves me," she says. "He is as honorable . . . as honorable as any prince. And he has come home now. He will not run away again."

Gently, I touch her hand. "Then he had better reappear soon, with some explanation," I advise her shortly, and I walk away from her to stand with my children, and promise them that their ponies will have been taken from their stables and are safely turned out in the damp winter fields.

In the morning the flames are doused down but the whole palace, even the gardens, smells terribly of wet timbers and dank smoke. The wardrobe rooms are the great storehouse of the palace and priceless treasures have been lost to the flames, not just the costly gowns and ceremonial costumes, but the jewels and the crowns, even the gold and silver plate for the table, some of the best pieces of furniture and stores of linen. Thousands of pounds of goods have been destroyed, and Henry pays men to sift through the embers for jewels and melted metals. They bring up all sorts of rescued objects, even the lead from the windows has melted and twisted out of shape. It is terrible what has been lost; it is amazing what has survived.

"How did Warbeck ever get out of this

alive?" Lady Margaret bluntly demands of Henry, as the three of us stand, looking at the ruin that was the king's apartments, the charred roof beams open to the sky still smoking over our heads. "How could he survive it?"

"He says that his door caught fire and he was able to kick it open," Henry says shortly.

"How could he?" she asks. "How could he not die of the smoke? How could he not be burned? Someone must have let him out."

"At least no one was killed," I say. "It's a miracle."

The two of them look at me, their faces like a mirror of suspicion and fear. "Someone must have let him out." The king repeats his mother's accusation.

I wait.

"I shall make inquiry among the servants," Henry swears. "I will not have a traitor in my palace, in my own wardrobe rooms, I will not be betrayed under my own roof. Whoever is protecting the boy, whoever is defending him, should take warning. Whoever saved him from the fire is a traitor, as he is. I have spared him so far, I will not spare him forever." Suddenly he turns on me. "Do you know where he was?"

I look from his flushed angry face to his mother's white one. "You would do better to discover who set the fire," I say. "For someone has destroyed our most valuable goods to burn the boy out. Who would want him dead? It was no accidental blaze in those rooms, someone must have heaped up clothes and kindling and put a flame to it. It could only be someone trying to kill the boy. Who would that be?"

It is the way that My Lady stammers that gives her away to me, listening for one of them to lie. "H— he h—has dozens of enemies, dozens," she says flatly. "Everyone resents him as a traitor. Half the court would want to see him dead."

"By fire? In his bed?" I say, and my voice is as sharp as an accusation. She drops her glance to the ground, unable to meet my eye.

"He's a traitor," she insists. "He is a lost soul, a brand fit for burning."

Henry glances at his mother, uncertain as to what we are saying. "Nobody can think that I wanted him dead," he says. "All I have ever said is that it would have been better for Lady Katherine if she had never married him. No more than that. Nobody could think that I wanted his death."

His mother shakes her head. "Nobody could accuse you. But perhaps someone thought they were doing you a service. Protecting you from your own generosity. Saving you from yourself."

"If he had died, then Lady Katherine would be a widow," I say slowly. "And free to marry again."

My Lady takes the cross at her belt firmly in her hands and holds it tightly, as if she is warding off temptation. I wait for her to speak but for once she chooses to be silent.

"Enough of this," Henry says suddenly. "We should not be troubled amongst ourselves. We are the royal family, we should always be united. We have been saved from the flames and our household is safe too. It is a sign from God. I shall build a new palace."

"Yes," I agree. "We should rebuild."

"I shall call it Richmond, after my title and my father's title before me. I shall call it the Palace of Richmond."

ON PROGRESS, SUMMER 1498

The boy continues to sleep in the rooms of the wardrobe in the different houses as we go on our summer progress along the coast of Kent following the pilgrim road to Canterbury, the high hills of the Weald spreading out around us. As the warm sunshine makes the hedges green and the apple trees bob with white and pink blossom, Lady Katherine allows the king to buy her new clothes, she stops wearing mourning black like a widow, like a woman who has lost her husband, and instead puts on the king's choice for her, a gown of tawny medley, trimmed with black velvet, which sets off her creamy skin, flushed now with early-summer sunshine, and her dark shining hair that she wears under the bonnet of tawny velvet that he orders for her.

They ride together, quite alone, leading the court, and I and my ladies follow behind, the gentlemen of the court with us, the boy among them, sometimes riding near to me and smiling across.

Henry orders a new riding coat for himself, tawny velvet — like hers — and he and the young woman match perfectly as their horses go side by side down the trim lanes of Kent, cantering when the ground is soft, walking on the stony roads, always a discreet distance ahead of the rest of us, until we come in sight of the sea.

Henry talks to her now, he has found his voice, asking her about her childhood and her early years in Scotland. He never speaks of her husband, it is as if the two and a half years of her marriage never existed. They never speak of the boy, they never refer to him as they ride together. She is courteous, she never pushes herself forwards; but when the king orders a new saddle put on a new horse for her, she is obliged to ride with him and smile her thanks.

I see the boy as he watches this, and I see his brave smile and the set of his head, as if he were not watching the wife he loves being taken away from him. He rides behind them, noting how she leans towards Henry to hear something he says, how Henry puts his hand on her reins, as if to steady her horse. When the boy sees this, his chin comes up and his smile brightens, as if he had sworn to himself that he will be afraid of nothing.

For me, it is a curious pain to watch my husband of more than twelve years ride away from me with another woman, a beautiful young woman, at his side. I have never seen Henry in love before; now I see him shy, charming, eager, and it is like seeing him anew. The court is discreet, forever coming between me and the king and his constant companion, falling back to ensure they are uninterrupted, entertaining me so that I don't watch them. It reminds me of Queen Anne, whose health was failing even then, silently watching her husband seek me out, and how I danced with him before her. I knew I was breaking her heart, I knew that she had lost her son to death and was now losing her husband to me, but I was too dazzled and too entranced to care. Now I know what it is to be a queen and see the young men of the court write poems and send letters to another woman, see someone else be named as the most beautiful woman of the court, the queen of everyone's choice, and see your husband run after her too.

It is a humbling experience, but I don't feel humbled. I feel as if I understand something that I did not know before. I feel that now I have learned that love does not follow merit; I did not love Henry because he impressed me as a conquerer of England, as a victor of battle. I loved him because I first came to understand him, and then I pitied him, and then my love just flowered for him. And now that he does not love me, it makes no differ-ence to how I feel. I love him still for I see him being, as he often is, mistaken, ill-judging, fearful, and this does not make me jealous but, on the contrary, it makes me tender towards him.

And I am not even angry towards Lady Katherine for her part in this. When she dismounts from her expensive new horse at the end of a beautiful day and Henry puts her husband aside with one touch on his shoulder, so that she has to slide from her saddle into Henry's arms, she sometimes looks over at me as if this is no joy but a trouble to her. Then I am not angry with her, but I am sorry for her, and for me. I think that no one could understand how I feel but another woman, no one could understand her dilemma but me.

Lady Katherine comes to my rooms at the end of the day, to sit with my ladies, and finds that I smile at her gently, patiently, just as Queen Anne used to smile at me. I know she cannot prevent what is happening, just as I could not help myself with Richard. If the king honors a woman with his attention, then she is powerless under his admiration. What I don't know is how she feels. I fell in love with Richard, who was King of England and the only man who could rescue me and my family from our descent into obscurity. What she feels for the King of England, married as she is to a declared traitor who is living on borrowed time, I can't imagine.

THE TOWER OF LONDON, SUMMER 1498

We come back to London and Henry rules that we will spend a week in the Tower before going to Westminster. The boy rides in under the portcullis, as taut as a bowstring. His eyes flick across to me just once and meet mine, blank to blank, and then he looks away.

As usual, the lords who have homes in London go to their great houses and only a small court lives with us, the royal household, within the precincts of the Tower. The king, My Lady the King's Mother and I are housed in our usual rooms in the royal apartments. The Lord Chamberlain's office puts the boy in the Lanthorn Tower, with the other young men of the court, and I see him make a little gesture with his hand, as he turns towards the stone arch of the perimeter wall, and his smile grows brighter, the set of his head indomitable, as if he refuses to see ghosts.

Edward of Warwick is in the Garden Tower, where the lost princes were once kept. Sometimes I see his face at the window when we are crossing the green, just as people used to say they saw my little brothers. I am not allowed to visit him; the king rules that it would distress him, and would upset me. I will be allowed to go later — in some unspecified better time. The boy never glances towards the face at the window, never strays towards the dark doorway and the tight spiral stone staircase that leads to the rooms over the archway. He walks around the Tower and the gardens and the chapel as if he were blind to the old buildings, as if he cannot and will not see the place where William Hastings was beheaded on a log of wood for loyalty to his old master my father, the place where the uncrowned King Edward used to play on the green, where the boy they called the little Prince Richard used to shoot arrows at the butts before they went inside to the darkness, and never came out again.

WESTMINSTER PALACE, LONDON, SUMMER 1498

We come back to Westminster Palace early in the summer to celebrate Trinity Sunday in the abbey. In the morning when we go to chapel I look around for Lady Katherine, who is missing from my ladies. Her husband, the boy, is not in his usual place among the king's favored companions. I lean towards Cecily in her dark dress, in double mourning for her husband and daughter, who died this spring, and say tersely: "In God's name, where are they?"

Dumbly, she shakes her head.

Then, while Henry, My Lady, and I are breakfasting in the king's privy chamber after chapel, two servants come in and kneel before the breakfast table, their heads down, saying nothing.

"What is it?" Henry asks, though surely it is obvious to all of us that something has happened to the boy. I drop a piece of bread onto my plate, half rise to my feet, with a sense of sudden dread of what is going to come next.

"Forgive me, Your Grace. But the boy has got away."

"Got away?" Henry repeats the words almost as if they have no meaning. "How do you mean: got away?"

His mother glances at him sharply, as if she hears like me the detachment in his voice like a man repeating words he has prepared.

"The boy?" she demands. "The Warbeck boy?"

"Escaped," one of them says.

"How could he escape? He's not imprisoned?" I ask.

They bow their heads at the incredulity in my voice. "He had a key cut to fit the lock." One of them looks up to tell me. "His companions were asleep, perhaps drugged, they slept so heavily. He opened the door and walked out."

"Walked out?" Henry repeats.

"He had a key."

"Walked out?"

"Perhaps he drugged the guards."

Some strange prescience teaches me to look, not at Henry's well-manifested surprise and growing anger, but at his mother. She is looking at him, not with her usual expression of approbation and approval, but as if she has never seen him before, as if he is doing something which surprises even such a wily old plotter as herself. I sink back down into my chair again.

"How could he have got a key? How could he have got drugs?" Henry demands, loud enough to be heard through the door in the presence chamber where anyone could be waiting to wish him the best of the day, ears pricked for gossip.

Nobody replies that the boy could have got anything he wanted, since Henry himself had given him free run of the court and an allowance of money which would cover the price of some leather trim for his saddle, or a feather for his hat, or indeed cheap sleeping powders and a fee to a locksmith. Nobody points out that if the boy wanted to escape, he could have walked down to the stables and taken his horse and ridden away any day since last October. He did not have to wait till the nighttime, when he would be locked in and then need a key to get himself out. The whole story has a fairy-tale quality to it, like his name, like his history. Now the boy, who once passed as a prince only because someone dressed him in a silk shirt, disappears from a locked room in the dead of night.

"He must be recaptured!" Henry shouts.

He snaps his fingers for one of his clerks and the man bustles in, his tonsure shining, his writing desk around his neck, his quills sharpened at the ready. Henry rattles off a string of orders: the ports to be locked shut, the sheriffs of every county to be on alert to look for the boy, messengers to ride down the main highways to alert all the inns and guesthouses along the way.

"Pay a reward for his recapture, dead or alive," his mother suggests.

I keep my gaze on my plate and I don't say quickly, "Oh, they are not to hurt him!" I am a princess of York and I know that the stakes are always those of life or death. And he will have known this too; he will have known, when he slipped away into the darkness, that he was signing his own death warrant. Once he broke his parole they would be certain to go after him with a sword.

"I think I'll tell them to bring him in alive," Henry says carelessly, as if it does not much matter either way. "I would not want to distress Lady Katherine."

"She will be distressed," I observe.

"Yes, but now she must see that her husband has run away and left her, run like a coward and left her as if he did not regard himself as married anymore," Henry said firmly to me, impressing me with his view. "She must see that he can care nothing for her if he would just go — abandon her completely."

"Faithless." His mother nods.

"You had better go and break the news to her," Henry says. "Tell her that he organized his own escape and he did it quite without honor, drugging a guard and sneaking out like a thief. Leaving her alone, and their son fatherless. She must despise him for this. I expect she will get her marriage annulled."

I rise from my seat and as he pulls back the heavy wooden chair for me I turn and face him, my gray eyes looking into his dark ones. "I shall certainly tell her that you think she should despise him, I shall certainly tell her that you think she should regard herself as a single woman, as you have always done. In addition, shall I assure her that your motives are chivalrous when you call for her marriage to be annulled?" I ask icily, and I walk out and leave him and his mother to call for a map of the kingdom and calculate where the boy might be.

That night, Henry comes to my bedroom, surprising me and Cecily, who was going to be my bedmate for the night. She scuttles from the room, pulling her robe around her as Henry strolls in, bringing a jug of mulled ale, and a glass of wine for me, just as he used to do when we were happy together.

He gives me my glass, sits at the fireside, pours himself a tankard of ale, and drinks a deep draft, like a man who has reached a safe haven and can afford to celebrate.

"He was plotting, you know," he says shortly. "Plotting his escape with Flanders, with France, with Scotland. The usual allies. The friends who never forget him."

I don't ask who "he" is. "They helped him get out?" I ask.

Henry chuckles, puts out his booted foot, and kicks a log that is teetering on the edge of the fire. "Well, someone certainly helped him. Bundled him out and set him free."

I find that I am looking at him coldly, trying to understand what he is saying. "Was he drugged like his guards?" I ask eventually. "Was he drugged and kidnapped and put out of the castle?"

Henry does not meet my eyes. Again, he reminds me of Harry, who will twist his finger in his hair and look at his boots and tell me whatever little lie would best suit his case.

"How would I know?" Henry says. "How ever would I know what these traitors will do?"

"So where is he now?"

He chuckles. This, he is willing to admit. "I know where. I'll give him a few days to know his predicament. He's on his own, he has no supporters. He'll sleep cold and damp. I'll pick him up tomorrow, or the day after, soon."

I curl my feet up in my chair. "And why is this a triumph for us? Since you come to me to celebrate?"

He smiles at me. "Ah, Elizabeth. You know me so well! It is a triumph, though it is a hidden one. I had to break this new habit, this accidental accord that had come about. I never thought he would be like this, at the heart of my own court! There he was, happy as a pig in clover, sneaking into his wife's rooms — don't deny it, I know he was — and dancing with the ladies, writing poems, singing songs, going hunting, all at my expense, dressed like a prince and everywhere greeted like one. That's not what I wanted when I dragged him out of sanctuary and named him as a common pretender. I had him in chains at Exeter. I had him confessing everything I put before him. He signed anything I wanted, he took whatever name I gave him. He was humbled to dirt, the son of a drunk boatman. I didn't expect him to bob up, bob up into her bedroom. I didn't expect him to come to court and charm everyone he met. I didn't expect him to live like a prince when I had made him confess that he was a liar and a cheat. I didn't think she would . . . who would have dreamed that she would . . . a princess?"

"Stand by him?"

"Go on loving him," he says quietly. "When I had made him look a fool."

"What did you want? What did you hope would happen?"

"I thought everyone would see that he was a pretender, like the other feigned lad, Simnel, my falconer. I thought they would cluster to see him and laugh at his impertinence and then forget all about him. I thought he would be humbled by being kept around us, I thought he would sink."

"Sink?"

"I thought he would disappear into the crowd of hangers-on and placemen and toadies and beggars who go with us everywhere. Chased off now and then, reprimanded here and there, but always trailing along behind, living hand to mouth. I thought he would become one of them. I thought he would be the page boy at the back of the procession, the one that no one likes, who gets a kicking when the Master of the Horse is drunk. I thought people would despise him. I didn't expect him to shine."

"I did nothing to recognize him." I make it clear. "I never brought him into my company. He was never invited into my rooms."

"No," Henry says thoughtfully. "But he strolled in as if he belonged there. He made his own place. People liked him, gathered round him. He was just . . ." He pauses and then he says the one betraying word: "Recognized."

I give a little gasp. "Someone recognized him as Prince Richard? My brother?"

"No. No one would be such a fool. Not at my court. Not surrounded by spies. He was recognized for himself. People saw him as a power, as a person, as a Someone."

"People just happen to like him."

"I know. I can't have that. He has that

damned charm that you all have. I can't have him at court being happy, being charming, looking like he belongs here. But — and this was the problem — I had given my word to him when he surrendered to me. His wife went down on her knees to me, and I gave my word to her. And she held me to it. She would never have allowed me to imprison him or put him on trial."

He frowns at the glowing embers of the fire, quite unaware that he is confiding to his wife the commands of his mistress.

"And there's another thing. I established that he is the son of a Flanders boatman — which I thought a very good story at the time — but of course that makes him no subject of mine, so I can't try him for treason. He's not my subject, he's not treasonous. I wish someone had warned me of that when we were going to such trouble to find his parents in Flanders. We should never have found them in Flanders, we should have found them in Ireland, somewhere like that."

I absorb in silence the cynicism of the creation of the boy's story.

"So now I have two bad choices: either I can't try him for treason because he's foreign, or —"

"Or?"

"Or he's not foreign but the rightful king!" Henry bursts out laughing, swigs from his tankard, looks at me bright-eyed over the dull pewter. "You see? If he's who I say he is, then I can't try him for treason. If he's who he says he is, then he should be King of England and I am the traitor. Either way I was stuck with him. And every day he grew more and more happy that I was stuck with him. So I had to get him out, I had to make him betray the sanctuary that I had given him."

"Sanctuary?"

He laughs again. "Wasn't he born in sanctuary?"

I take a breath. "It was my brother Prince Edward who was born in sanctuary," I say. "Not Richard."

"Well, anyway," he says carelessly. "So the main thing is that I've got him out of his comfortably safe billet at my court. Now he's on the run, I can prove that he's plotting against me. He's broken his word that he would stay at court. He's dishonored his promise to his wife too. She thought he would never leave her; well, he has. I can arrest him for breaking his parole. Put him in the Tower."

"Will you execute him?" I ask, keeping my voice light and level. "Do you think you will execute him?"

Henry puts down his tankard and throws off his cloak and then his nightgown. He gets into my bed naked, and I just glimpse that he is aroused. Winning excites him, catching someone out, tricking someone, getting money off them or betraying their interest brings him so much pleasure that it makes him amorous.

"Come to bed," he says.

I show no sign of unwillingness. I don't know what might depend upon my behavior. I untie the ribbons on my nightgown and I drop it to the floor, I slide between the sheets and he grabs me at once, pulls me beneath him. I make sure that I am smiling as I close my eyes.

"I can't execute him," he says quietly, thrusting inside me with the words. I keep my smile on my face as he makes love while speaking of death. "I can't behead him, not unless he does something stupid." Heavily he moves on me. "But the joy of him is that he is certain to do something stupid," he remarks, and his weight bears down on me.

For a manhunt for a known traitor, a claimant to the throne, the ghost that terrorized Henry's life for thirteen years, the pursuit is curiously leisurely. The guards who slept on duty are cautioned and return to their posts, though everyone expected them to be tried and executed for their part in the escape. Henry sends out messengers to the ports but they travel easily, setting out to north and west, south and east, as if riding for pleasure on a sunny day. Inexplicably, Henry sends out his own personal guard, his yeomen, in boats, rowing upstream, as if the boy might have gone deeper into England, and not to the coast to get back to Flanders, to Scotland, to safety.

His wife has to sit with me while we wait for news. She has not gone back into widow's black but she is no longer gorgeous in tawny velvet. She wears a dark blue gown and she sits half behind me, so that I have to turn to speak to her, and so that visitors to my rooms, even the king and his mother, can hardly see her, hidden by my great chair.

She sews — heavens, she sews constantly; little shirts for her son, exquisite nightcaps and nightgowns fit for a prince, little socks for his precious feet, little mittens so that he does not scratch his peerless complexion. She bends her head over her work and she sews as if she would stitch her life together again, as if every small hemming stitch would take them back to Scotland, to the days when it was just her and the boy, in a hunting lodge, and he was full of the stories of what he had done and what he had seen and who he said that he was — and nobody asked him what he might do and what he might claim and who he would have to deny.

They find him within a few days. Henry seems to know exactly where to look for him, almost as if he had been bundled, drugged, thrown out of a boat onto the riverbank, and left to sleep it off. They say that he had gone up the valley of the Thames, on foot, stumbling on the tow path, splashing through marshes, following the course of the river through thick woodland and over hedged fields, to the charterhouse at Sheen, where the former prior had once been a good friend to my mother, and where the current prior took the boy in and gave him sanctuary. Prior Tracy himself rode to Henry, asked for an audience, and begged for the young man's life. The king, bombarded with pleas for clemency, with a holy prior down on his knees refusing to rise until the boy is granted his life, once again decides to be gracious. With his mother seated beside him, as if they are both judges on the Last Day, he rules that the boy should stand on a scaffold of empty wine barrels for two days, to be seen by everyone who passes by, mocked, cursed, scorned, and a target for any urchin with a handful of filth, and then be taken to the Tower of London, and there be imprisoned pending the king's pleasure: that is, forever.

THE TOWER OF LONDON, SUMMER 1498

They keep him in the Garden Tower. I imagine Henry laughing his new overconfident ringing laugh at the irony of the boy who said he was Prince Richard being returned to where Prince Richard was last seen. They put the boy in the very rooms where Prince Richard and Prince Edward were kept.

The window that overlooks the green was where their little faces could sometimes be seen, and sometimes they would wave at people who gathered on the green to see them or, coming out of chapel, call a blessing to them. Now there is one pale face at the window — the boy's — and people who see him closely say that he has lost his looks, he is almost unrecognizable for the bruises on his face. His nose has been broken and is ugly, squashed cross-wise against his handsome face. He has a bloody scar behind his ear where someone kicked him when he was down, and the ear itself is half torn away and has gone sticky and fetid.

No one now would mistake him for a York prince. He looks like an alehouse brawler, injured many times, who has gone down once too often and cannot rise again. No one will fall in love with his smile now that his front teeth have been kicked in. No one ever again will be swayed by his York charm. No one gathers on the green now to wave at him, no one reports that they have seen him, as if seeing him is an event, something to write home to a village: *I have seen the prince! I went to the Tower and I looked towards his window. I saw him wave, I saw his radiant smile.*

Now he is a prisoner, like any other in the Tower. He has been sent there to avoid attention and little by little everyone will forget him.

His wife, Lady Katherine, will not forget him, I think. Sometimes I look at her down-turned face and I think she will never forget him. She has learned a deep fidelity that I do not recognize. She has changed from her eternal hemming of fine linen to working on a thick homespun. She is sewing a warm jacket, as if she knows someone who lives inside damp stone walls and who will never again bask in the sun. I don't ask her why she is making a warm thick jacket lined with silks of deep red and blue — and she does not volunteer a reason. She sits in my rooms, her head bent over her sewing, and sometimes she glances up and smiles at me, and sometimes she puts down her work and gazes out of the window, but she never says one word about the boy she married, and she never ever complains that he broke his parole, broke his word to her, and is paying for it.

Margaret comes to visit court, traveling from my son's court in Ludlow, and of all the places in my rooms, she chooses a seat beside Lady Katherine, saying nothing. Each young woman takes a silent comfort from the other's nearness. It is part of Henry's great joke on the House of York that Margaret's brother, Teddy, is housed in the same tower as Katherine's husband; he lives on the floor below. The two boys, one the son of George Duke of Clarence, and one who claimed to be the son of Edward King of England, are in rooms so close that if the boy stamped on the floor then Teddy would hear him. Both of them are walled up behind the thick cold stones of our oldest castle for the crime of being a son of York, or — worse — claiming to be one. Truly, it is still a cousins' war; for here is a pair of cousins, imprisoned for kinship.

WESTMINSTER PALACE, LONDON, AUTUMN 1498

The child I am carrying sits heavily against my spine and my legs ache as if I have an ague. Sitting, lying, walking, all cause me pain. This is the child that we conceived the night of Henry's deep joy that the boy had run from court and broken his parole. I think he weighs so heavily on my back because his father lay so heavily on me that night, because there was no pleasure in our coupling, there was no love in it, there was Henry bearing down on me, on England, on the boy, aroused by his own triumph.

I miss my mother in this season, when the leaves fall like a blizzard of brown and gold and my windows are hazy with mist in the morning. I miss her when I see the bright shiver of yellow birch leaves reflected in the gray of the river water. Sometimes I can almost hear her voice in the plashing of the water against the stone pilings of the pier, and when a seagull suddenly cries, I almost start up, thinking it is her voice. If it is her son in the Tower, I owe it to her, to him, to my house, to try to get him released.

I approach My Lady the King's Mother first. I speak to her when she is kneeling in the royal chapel; she has finished her prayers but she is resting her chin on her hands, her eyes on the beautifully jeweled glass monstrance, the wafer of the Host gleaming palely within. She is transfixed, as if she is seeing an angel, as if God is speaking to her. I wait for a long time. I don't want to interrupt her instructing God. But then I see her settle on her heels and sigh, and put her hand to her eyes.

"May I speak with you?" I ask quietly.

She does not turn her head to glance at me, but her nod tells me that she is listening. "It will be about your bro . . ." she starts and then presses her lips together and her dark eyes flick towards the crucifix, as if Jesus Himself must take care not to hear such a slip.

"It is about the boy," I correct her. The king and the court have quite given up calling him Mr. Warbeck or Mr. Osbeque. The names, the many names that they pinned on him, never quite stuck. To Henry he was for so long the juvenile threat, the naughty page, "the boy," that now this is the name that signifies him: a boy. I think this is a mistake, there have been so many boys, Henry has feared a legion of boys. But still Henry likes to insult him with his youth. He is "the boy" for Henry, and the rest of the court follows suit.

"I can do nothing for him," she says regretfully. "It would have been better for him, for all of us, if he had died when everyone said that he was dead."

"You mean, after the coronation?" I whisper, thinking of the little princes and the grief in London, while everyone wondered where the children had gone, and my mother was sick with heartbreak in the darkness of sanctuary.

She shakes her head, her eyes on the cross, as if that one great statement of truth can protect her from her constant lies. "After Exeter, they reported him dead."

I take a breath to recover from my mistake. "So, Lady Mother, since he did not die at Exeter . . . what if he were to agree to go quietly back to Scotland and live with his wife?"

For the first time she looks at me. "You know how it is. If your destiny puts you near to the throne you cannot take yourself away from it. He could go to Ethiop and there would still be someone to run after him and promise him greatness. There will always be wicked people who will want to trouble or unseat my son, there will always be evil snapping at the heels of a Tudor. We have to hold our enemies down. We always have to be ready to hold them down. We have to hold their faces down into the mud. That is our destiny."

"But the boy *is* down," I urge her. "They say that he has been beaten, his beauty is gone, his health is broken. He claims nothing anymore, he agrees to whatever they put to him, he will take any name you choose for him, his spirit is destroyed, he is no longer claiming to be a prince, he no longer looks like a prince. You have defeated him, he is down in the mud."

She turns her head away from me. "He could be diminished, he could be dirty, he could be starved, and yet he would still shine," she says. "He always looks the part that he chooses to play. I heard it from someone who had gone to stare at him, they had gone to laugh at him, but they said that he looked like Jesus: battered and wounded and pained but still the Son of God. They said he looked like a saint. They said he looked like a broken prince, a damaged lamb, a dimmed light. Of course, he can't be freed. He can never be freed."

This vengeful old harridan is Henry's chief and only councillor, so if she refuses me there is no point in approaching Henry. All the same, I wait until he has dined well and drunk deeply and we are seated in his mother's comfortable private rooms. When she steps out for a moment, I take my chance.

"I want to ask for mercy for the boy," I say. "And for my cousin Edward. While I am carrying a new child, a new heir for the Tudors, our line must be safe. Surely we can release these two young men? They can be no threat to us now. In our nursery already we have Prince Arthur and Henry, the two girls, and another child is on the way. I would be at peace in my mind, I would be at peace carrying our child, if I know that those two young men were released, into exile, wherever you wish. I would be able to give birth to my child if I could be easy in my mind." It's my trump card and I expect Henry to at least listen to me.

"It's not possible," he says at once, without even considering the request. Like his mother, he does not look at me as he tells me that my cousin and the boy who passed as my brother are lost to me.

"Why is it not possible?" I insist.

He extends his thin hands. "One" — he counts on his fingers — "the King and Queen of Spain will not send their daughter to marry Arthur unless they are sure our succession is certain. If you want to see your son married, we have to see the boy and your cousin dead."

I nearly choke. "They can't demand such a thing! They have no right to order us to kill our own kinsmen!"

"They can. They do. It is their condition

for the wedding and the wedding *must* go ahead."

"No!"

He continues listing his reasons. "Two — he's plotting against me."

"No!" It is such a contradiction of what my servants have told me about the boy in the Tower, a boy quite without his own will. "He is not! It's not possible. He does not have the strength!"

"With Warwick."

Now I know that it is a lie. Poor Teddy would plot with no one, all he wants is someone to talk to. He swore loyalty to Henry when he was a little boy; his years in terrible solitude have only made his decision more certain for him. He thinks of Henry now as an all-seeing, all-powerful god. He would not dream of plotting against such a power, he would tremble with fear at the thought of it. "That can't be so," I say simply. "Whatever they have told you about the boy, I know that it can't be said of Teddy. He is loyal to you and your spies are lying."

"I say it is so," he insists. "They are plotting and if their plots are treasonous, they will have to die as traitors."

"But how can they?" I ask. "How can they even plot together? Are they not kept apart?"

"Spies and traitors always find ways to plot together," Henry rules. "They are probably sending messages."

"You must be able to keep them apart!" I protest. Then I feel a chill as I realize what is, more probably, happening. "Ah, husband, don't tell me that you are letting them plot together so that you can entrap them? Say you wouldn't do that? Tell me that you would not do such a thing? Not now, not now that the boy is in your power, and broken on your orders. Tell me that you wouldn't do such a thing to poor Teddy, not to poor little Teddy, who will die if you entrap him?"

He does not look triumphant, he looks anxious. "Why would they not refuse each other company?" he asks me. "Why should I not test them and find them true? Why would they not stay silent to each other, turn away from men who come to tempt them with stories of freedom? I have been merciful to them. You can see that! They should be loyal to me. I can test them, can't I? It is nothing but reasonable. I can offer them each other's company. I can expect that they shrink from each other as a terrible sinner? I am doing nothing wrong!"

I feel a wave of pity for him, as he leans forwards to the little fire, and I am shaken by nausea at what I fear he is planning. "You are King of England," I remind him. "Be a king. No one has the power to take that from you. You don't have to test their loyalty. You can afford to be generous. Be kingly. Release them to exile and send them away."

He shakes his head. "I don't feel generous," he says meanly. "When is anyone ever generous to me?"

GREENWICH PALACE, LONDON, WINTER-SPRING 1499

I go to our most beautiful palace for my confinement and Henry and My Lady the King's Mother prepare a celebration dinner in the great hall in January. Everyone is there to celebrate my confinement but my sister Cecily. She is staying away. She has lost her second child, her daughter Elizabeth, and having made a loveless marriage to further her rise in the Tudor world, finds that she is a childless widow; she has gained nothing.

This is bitter for any woman, and especially hard on Cecily. She will stay away from court until she has put off her black gown. I am sorry for her, but there is nothing that I can do, so I say farewell to the court and step into my beautiful rooms for my first confinement without her.

My Lady the King's Mother has the best rooms adjoining Henry's as usual, but I like my own set of rooms that I have prepared for my confinement. They face the river and I order my ladies to pin back the dark tapestries showing scenes from the Bible that My Lady has hung for my edification, and instead I watch the boats going by and people, wrapped up against the cold, striding up and down the riverbank, hugging themselves, their breaths making little clouds around their muffled heads.

I am not well with this baby; it was an unlovely conception and I fear a difficult birth. While I am confined I cannot help but think of the two in the Tower, my cousin and the boy who called himself my brother, and I wonder what they can see from their windows and if the winter afternoons and evenings when the sun sets so early and the sky is so dark seem so very long to them. Poor Teddy must be accustomed, it has been nearly thirteen years since he was free; he has grown to manhood in prison, knowing nothing but the cold walls of his chamber and the little square panes of his window. When I think of him I believe that the baby stirs in me, and I know that I have been very wrong not to save him from this life that is more like death. I have failed him, my kinsman, my cousin. I have failed as a cousin and I have failed as a queen.

Now another young man looks out of a small window at a darkening sky and sees the winter day slide away, and I put my hand on my broad belly and whisper, "Never. That will never happen to you," as if I could save my baby though I cannot save my brother.

Lady Katherine Huntly comes into confinement with me for company and stitches an exquisite nightcap in white pin-tucked linen for my child, though she is never allowed to see her own. She is allowed to visit the prisoner in the Tower and she is away for a day and a night and comes back in silence, and bends over her sewing, trying to avoid speaking to anyone of what she has seen or heard.

I wait till the ladies are at the door of my chamber, taking the dishes for dinner from the servants at the threshold and bringing them in to spread on the big table before the fire so that we can feast and be merry during our long time of waiting before Lent reduces the choice. "How is he?" I ask shortly.

At once she glances around to see if they can hear us, but there is no one in earshot. "Broken," she says simply.

"Is he ill?"

"Wasted."

"Does he have books? Letters? Is he very alone?"

"No!" she exclaims. "People are constantly allowed to come in to see him." She shrugs. "I don't understand why. Almost anyone can go and speak to him. He lives in a presence chamber, the door standing open, any fool in London can come in and pledge allegiance. He is hardly guarded at all."

"He doesn't speak to them, does he?"

A little shake of her head shows that he says nothing.

"He must not speak to anyone!" I say with sudden energy. "His safety depends on his not speaking to them, to anyone."

"They speak to him," she tries to explain to me. "His guards don't keep the door shut, they force it open. He is surrounded by people who come and whisper promises to him."

"He must not reply!" I take her hands in my anxiety that she understands. "He will be watched, he is being watched. He must do nothing that could cause suspicion."

She looks up and meets my eyes. "He is himself," she says. "He has caused suspicion all of his life. Even if he does nothing but breathe."

The labor is long and I am faint with pain by the time that I hear a little weak cry. They give me birthing ale and the familiar scent and the taste remind me of when I had Arthur and my mother was there with her strong arms around me and her voice leading me into dreams where I felt no pain. When I wake, hours later, they tell me that I have given birth to a boy, another boy for the Tudor dynasty, and that the king has sent his congratulations and a rich gift, and his Lady Mother is on her knees for me in her chapel even now, giving thanks that God continues to smile on her house.

They take him away to be christened Edmund, which I take to be the morbid choice of My Lady, as he was a martyred king; but when it is time for me to be churched I find that I am unwilling to leave the confinement chamber. The heaviness and the weariness that came with the baby do not leave me, not even when they take him with his wet nurse to the palace at Eltham and Lady Margaret's confessor, John Morton, puts aside his great cope and mitre as Archbishop of Canterbury and comes like a parish priest to the grille in my chamber and invites me to confess my sins, be blessed, and return to the world. I go slowly to the ironwork grille and rest my hands on the twisted Tudor roses, and I feel imprisoned like the boy, and unlikely to be freed.

"I have a sin of fear," I say to him, my voice very low so that he can only just hear me in the empty chamber.

"What do you fear, my daughter?"

"Years ago, a long, long time ago, I cursed a man," I whisper.

He nods. He will have heard worse things than this, I have to remember that he will have heard far worse things than this. I also have to remember that everything I say will almost certainly be reported to My Lady the King's Mother. There is hardly a priest in

England who does not come under her influence, and this is John Morton, whose life has intertwined with hers and who thinks her half a saint already.

"Who was it you cursed, my child?"

"I don't know who it was," I say. "My mother and I swore a curse against the man who killed the princes. We were so heartbroken when we heard they were missing. My mother especially . . ." I break off, not wanting to remember that night when she sank to her knees and put her head to the stone floor.

"What curse was it?"

"We swore that whoever had taken our boys would lose his own," I say, the words barely audible, I am so ashamed now of what we did then. I am so fearful now of the consequences of the curse. "We swore that the murderer would be left with only a girl as his heir, and his line would die out. We said he would lose a son in one generation and a son in the next — he would lose a young son and then a young grandson in their boyhood."

The priest sighs at the magnitude of the curse, even as the politician in him calculates what this means. We kneel together in silence. He puts a hand on his ivory crucifix.

"You regret this now?"

I nod. "Father, I deeply regret it."

"You wish to lift this curse?"

"I do."

He is silent, praying for a moment. "Who is

707

it?" he asks. "Who killed the princes, your brothers? Who d'you think? Where will your curse fall?"

I sigh and lean my forehead against the iron Tudor rose of the grille, feeling the forged petals bite into my skin. "Truly," I say. "Before God, I don't know for sure. I have suspected more than one; but still I don't know. If it was Richard, the King of England, then he died without an heir, and he saw his son die before him."

He nods. "Does that not prove his guilt? Do you think it was him? You knew him well. Did you ask him?"

I shake my head. "I don't know," I say fretfully. "He said it was not him, and I believed him then. That's what I always tell everyone. I don't know."

He pauses as a thought strikes him. "If the princes, or even one of them, had survived, then whoever kills him now will receive the curse."

I can feel him flinch as I glare at him through the screen, as he arrives so slowly at understanding. "Exactly," I say. "That's the very thing. I have to lift the curse. Before anything else happens. I have to do it now."

He is aghast at the prospect that is opening before him. "The curse would light on the man who ordered your brother's death," he says, as rapidly as prayer. "Even if it were a just death. Even if it were a legal execution.

The curse would fall on he who ordered it?"

"Exactly," I say again. "It would take his son and his grandson when they were still children. It would mean that such an executioner would find his line ends after two generations, with a girl. If it were the man who killed my brother Edward he would be doubly cursed."

The archbishop is white. "You must pray," he says fervently. "I will pray for you. We must give alms, set a priest to pray daily. I will give you spiritual exercises, prayers for every day. You must go on pilgrimage and I will tell you alms that you must give to the poor."

"And will that lift the curse?"

He meets my eyes and I see my own terror reflected back at me, the Queen of England, mother to three precious beloved sons. "No one has power to curse," he says staunchly, repeating the official belief of the Church. "No mortal woman. What you and your mother said was meaningless, the ravings of distressed women."

"So nothing will happen?" I ask.

He hesitates and he is honest. "I don't know," he says. "I will pray on it. God may be merciful. But it may be that your curse is an arrow into the dark and you cannot stop its flight."

The Isle of Wight, Summer 1499

I come out of confinement to find a court intent on merrymaking. We are to make a long progress along the south coast, passing through Kent and Sussex and Hampshire as if they had never lifted a blade against the king, as if they had never mustered for the boy. At Portsmouth we are to take ship and go to the Isle of Wight, that dim blue mass on the horizon. We are going to be happy. Most important, we are going to be seen to be happy.

Henry wears a smile like a mask. Lady Katherine is on his arm, everywhere he walks, her beautiful new horse, a black mare, goes shoulder to shoulder with his warhorse. He has taken to riding his warhorse again as if to remind everyone that he is a commander as well as a king. She inclines her head when he talks to her, she smiles as she listens. When he is merry we can hear her laugh, and when he asks her she sings for him, Scots songs, songs from the highlands, filled with melancholy for a land that is lost, until he says: "Lady Katherine, sing us something merry!" and she laughs and starts a round and the whole court joins in.

I watch them as if I were gazing down from far away. I can see them walking together but only dimly hear what they say. I watch them as I know Queen Anne, wife to my Richard, watched me from her high window when we walked in the garden below and he put my hand in his arm and I leaned towards him, longing for his touch. I cannot blame Lady Katherine for ensnaring the King of England, for I did exactly the same. I cannot blame her for being young — she is eight years younger than me — and this summer I am as tired as if I were ninety years old. I cannot blame her for being beautiful — all courts are mad for beauty and she is a delight to watch. But most of all I cannot blame her for turning the king's head away from me, his true wife, for I think she is doing the only thing she can do to save her husband.

I don't think she is taken with him as he — vividly — is taken with her. I think she is holding him just where she wants him to be: at arm's length but within arm's reach, just at the right proximity so that she can influence him, divert him, soothe him, and soften him, in order to keep her husband alive.

She must have heard — who has not? — the rumors that there is to be a rescue of the boy. The Duchess Margaret sent her embassy to see her beloved protégé and nephew and everyone thinks that she had them whisper to him to wait, that help would come. Everyone knows she will try to save him. She has great influence in Europe, and the greatest kings still call themselves friends of the boy even though they are told he was an imposter. Support is gathering for the boy; if his wife can keep him alive for another season, someone will get him out.

Still the king does not act against the boy but keeps him imprisoned, with constant visitors. Lady Katherine is always at Henry's side, always there with a quick smile and a soft question to remind him to be merciful to the boy that she married in error. Quick to show him that she can forgive and perhaps — who knows? — one day she may go on to love another? The boy does not have to die to set her free for she is already considering an annulment. Henry, at her side every day, often suggests that she should write to the Pope to ask to be freed from her marriage. It would be little more than a formality. She was tricked into marriage by a man bearing a false name. She was utterly dazzled by a silk shirt. It can be overturned by a single letter from Rome. She assures him that she is considering it, she takes it to God in her three daily prayers. Sometimes she slides a shy sideways smile at him and says that she is tempted by the thought of being a single woman again: free.

Henry, in love for the first time in his life, mooning like a calf, follows her with his eyes, smiles when she smiles, and believes her when she assures him that she thinks of him as a great prince, a puissant king, who can forgive a nonentity like her husband. She understands his greatness by the quality of his mercy. He invites her into his presence chamber when people come to him with requests, and he glances at her to make sure that she is listening when he is generous in forgiving a fine or overturning a judgment. He has her on his arm when he talks with the ambassador from Spain, who tactfully — when speaking before the woman he would make a widow — does not insist that the boy and Teddy be killed at once, though the monarchs of Spain continue to urge the betrothal between Arthur and their daughter and the death of the two young men.

We stay at Carisbrook Castle, behind the gray stone perimeter walls, and we ride out every day into the lush green meadows around the castle, where the larks rise up into a blue sky quite empty of clouds. Lady Katherine declares she has never known such a bonny summer, and the king says that every English summer is like this and that when she has been in England, when she has been happy in English summers for years, she will forget the cold rain of Scotland.

He comes to my room at least once a week and he sleeps in my bed, though often he falls asleep as soon as he lies back on the pillows, tired from riding all day and dancing in the evening. He knows that I am unhappy, but guiltily he dares not ask me what is the matter, for fear of what I might say. He thinks I might accuse him of infidelity, of preferring another woman, of betraying our marriage vows. He wants to avoid any conversation like that, so he smiles brightly at me, and walks briskly with me, and comes to my bed and says cheerfully, "God bless, my dear, good night!" and closes his eyes on my reply.

I am not such a fool as to complain of a disappointment in love. I am not such a fool as to weep that my husband is looking away from me, away and towards a younger, more beautiful woman. It is not for disappointed love that my feet are heavy, and I don't want to dance or even walk, and my heart aches on waking. It is not for disappointed love for Henry nor the pain of a betrayed wife. It is for the boy in the Tower, and my fear, my increasing fear, that we are far away from London so that the guards Henry has set on him, and their friends in the alleyways and inns, can conspire together, can plot, can send messages, can weave a rope long enough to hang themselves, and hang the boy with them, and that all these tales of the boy in his room and people coming and going are not mistakes, not slackness of the guard, but a part of the story that Henry is weaving that the boy from Tournai, the watergate keeper's son, faithless and craven to the last, plots with other furtive men of the dark alleys, and leads them like fools to their death.

Henry shows no sign of thinking of the boy or my cousin Teddy at all. He is as merry as a king sure of his throne, certain of his inheritance, and confident of his future. When the Spanish ambassador comes and speaks gravely of traitors yet living in confinement, Henry slaps him on the back and tells him to assure their majesties of Spain the kingdom is safe, our troubles are all over, the infanta must come at once, and she and Arthur will be married at once. There is no obstacle.

"There is the boy," the ambassador remarks. "And Warwick."

Henry snaps his fingers.

WESTMINSTER PALACE, LONDON, SUMMER 1499

We return to London and Henry retires into his private rooms with his mother to review all the reports that have gathered in his absence. Within a day there is a stream of men coming and going by the private stair, almost unobserved by the court. Only I watch them and wonder at so many yeomen of the guard coming from their duty at the Tower to speak privately with the king.

That evening, when the young men of the court visit my rooms to dance with my ladies and to flirt in the hour before dinner, Henry is grim and gray-faced.

"You have had some bad news," I say as he glances back at the court lining up behind us.

He shoots a hard look at me. "Do you know what it is?" he demands. "Have you known all this time?"

I shake my head. "Truly, I know nothing. I have seen people reporting to you all the day and now I see you looking ill, you are

716

so weary."

He takes my hand in a painfully tight grip. "You are missing a cousin," he says.

At once my thoughts go to Teddy in the Tower. "My cousin? He's gone?"

"Edmund de la Pole," he says, spitting out the words. "Another false York. Son of your aunt Elizabeth. The one that she swore to me I could trust."

"Edmund?" I repeat.

"He's run away," Henry says shortly. "Did you know?"

"No, of course not."

The court is ready. Henry glances over his shoulder as if he always fears who is behind him. "I am sick," he says. "Sick to my belly."

He sits at the head of the great table and they bring him the best that the kingdom can supply, but I can see as he takes a small portion from one dish and then another that he tastes nothing. The meat has lost its savor and the marchpane its sweetness. He glances down the table to Lady Katherine, seated at the head of my ladies, and she looks back at him and gives him her sweet, promising smile. He looks at her not as if she is a woman that he desires, but a puzzle that he cannot solve, and the smile dies on her lips as she swallows and turns her face down.

After dinner he goes to his privy rooms with his mother, and they send out for sweet wine and biscuits and cheese and talk into the night. It is long after midnight when he comes to my bedroom and sits heavily on the chair before the fire, and looks into the embers.

"What's the matter?" I ask. I was half-asleep but I slide from the bed and take a stool to sit beside him. "What is the matter, husband?"

Slowly, his head drops till he is resting it on his hand and then even lower so that his hands are over his face. "It's the boy," he says, muffled. "It's the damned boy."

The flames flicker quietly in the little room. "The boy?" I repeat.

"I set people about him that were entrusted to lead him into danger," he says, his head still down, his face hidden from me. "I thought I would entrap him into plotting his freedom."

"To kill him," I say steadily.

"To execute him for a crime," he corrects me. "Breaking his word of surrender. I had some villains come to him and promise they would get him free, they would help him escape. He consented. Then I had them go to Warwick . . ."

I clap my hand over my mouth to stop myself crying out. "Not Teddy!"

"Warwick too. It has to be done. And it has to be done now. The two young fools have cut a hole in the vaulting between their rooms and they whisper to each other."

"They talk to each other? Teddy and the boy?" There is something unbearably tender about the thought of those two, whispering hopes and cheer to each other. "He talks to Teddy?"

"I sent them a plan of escape. The boy agreed, Warwick too once they explained it to him. I sent them a plan that they should take England, raise an army, kill me."

"They must have known it was hopeless . . ."

"The boy knows, but he is desperate to be free. And then — all of a sudden — it is not hopeless." He pauses and chokes as if vomit is rising unstoppably in his throat. "Elizabeth, there was my little plot, half a dozen conspirators, a code book, a message to the duchess, plans for an uprising, enough to see a man hanged, all planned and controlled by me, and . . . and . . ." He stops as if he cannot bear to continue. "And then . . ."

I rise from my stool and put my hand on his bowed shoulder. It is like touching the back of the chair, he is rigid with fear. "What then? What happened then, my dear?"

"They have been joined by others. Others that I had not instructed. Others that are supposed to be loyal to me. They are getting messages from all over the country. Men who will risk their lives and their fortunes to get Warwick out of the Tower, men who will put their families and their livelihoods and their property at risk to set the boy free. There is another rebellion brewing, another rebellion after all we have gone through! I have no idea how many men are ready to rise, I have no idea who is faithless and ready to betray me. But it is starting all over again. England wants the boy. They want the boy on the throne, and they are ready to throw me down."

"No," I say. I can't believe what I am hearing as Henry leaps up, shrugging off my hand from his shoulder, gone from despair to sudden rage.

"It's the Yorks!" he shouts at me. "Your family again! Edmund de la Pole missing! Your cousin at the heart of plots! The white rose painted on every street corner! Your family and your retainers and your servants and your damned charm and family loyalty and magic — God knows what it is that works for you. God knows why it works for him. He has lost his looks, he is beaten to ugliness, I saw to that. He has lost his charm — he can't smile with no teeth. He has lost his fortune and his ruby brooch, and his wife is in my keeping, but still they flock to him. Still they would turn out for him, still I am threatened by him. There he is, imprisoned in the Tower, no friends but the ones I allow him, no companions but the scum that I send to him, and still he musters an army against me and I have to defend myself, and defend you and defend our sons."

I sink down before his rage; almost, I could kneel before him. "My lord —"

"Don't speak to me," he says furiously. "This is his death warrant. I can do nothing now but have him killed. Wherever he is, whatever shape he takes, whatever name he goes by, they seek him out, they believe in him, they want him as King of England."

"He was not plotting!" I say urgently. "You say yourself it was your plot. It was not him and Teddy! He was innocent of anything but what you set men to do to him. He did nothing but agree to your plan."

"He threatens me by breathing," Henry says flatly. "His broken smile is my undoing. Even in prison with a smashed face, he is a handsome prince. There is nothing for him but death."

WESTMINSTER PALACE, LONDON, AUTUMN 1499

Henry summons the council of all his lords to listen to the charges of treason against Teddy; they call him "Edward naming himself of Warwick" as if no one has a name that can be trusted anymore. They call the boy Perkin Warbeck and list dozens of named others. Alarmed, frightened into obedience, the council commands the sheriffs to pick out a jury from the citizens of London who will hear the evidence and choose a verdict.

Lady Katherine comes to my rooms, her face whiter than the lace she has in her hand. She is making a trim for a man's collar and the bright beads for the lace making tremble on the cushion.

She kneels on the floor before me; slowly she removes her headdress and her hair tumbles down. She bows low, almost to my feet. "Your Grace, I beg for mercy," she says.

I look at her bowed head, the lustrous dark hair. "I have no power," I say.

"Mercy for my husband!"

I shake my head. I lean forwards and touch her shoulder. "Truly, I have no power in this court. I had hoped that you would speak to the king for them both."

"He promised me," she says, her voice a little whisper of sound. "He promised me this summer. But now my husband is to be tried before a jury."

I don't offer her a lie that perhaps they will not convict, nor suggest that the evidence will not be damning.

"Could you not persuade the king as you did once before?" I ask her. "Could you not find a smile for him, could you not allow him — allow him whatever he wants?"

Her dark eyes flicker up to mine in one long look, as if to acknowledge the irony that I should urge her to seduce my husband to save the boy. We know what the boy means to both of us.

"I paid my side of the bargain this summer, when he said my husband would be safe," she says. "His Grace said that if he stayed quietly in prison he could be released, later. I gave the king what he wanted in return. I have nothing more to bargain with."

I roll back my head and close my eyes for a moment. I am beyond weariness, both of kings and the bargains they make and the women who have to find ways to please them. "You have lost your influence?"

She nods, looking me straight in the eye

and admitting her shame. "I have nothing left to tempt him." She pauses to apologize to me. "I am sorry. I did not know what else I could do this summer when they told me that my husband was in prison and taking a beating. I had nothing else to offer."

I sigh. "I will speak with him," I say. "But I have nothing to offer him either."

I send my chamberlain to request an audience with the king and I am shown into his privy chamber. His mother stands behind the throne and does not move when I enter. The groom of the chamber sets a seat for me and I face Henry across the polished dark table, his mother standing like a sentry against the world, behind him.

"We know why you are here," My Lady says briefly. "But there is nothing that can be done."

I ignore her and look at my husband. "My lord, I don't come to plead for the two of them. I am here because I am afraid that you are putting us in danger," I say softly.

At once he is alert. This is a man always ready to be alert to danger.

"We are in danger every day that the boy lives," he replies.

"Aside from that. There is a danger that you don't know."

"You have come to warn us?" Lady Margaret asks scornfully.

"I have."

Henry looks at me for the first time. "Has someone spoken to you? Has someone tried to recruit you?"

"No, of course not. I am known to be completely faithful to you." I look at his hard-faced mother. "Everyone at court but the two of you knows I am completely faithful."

"What is it then? Speak."

I draw a breath. "Years ago, when my mother and all my sisters and I were in sanctuary, Richard came to us to tell us that the princes were missing. Mother and I swore an oath against the man who had killed them," I say.

"That was Richard himself," My Lady insists quickly.

Henry's hand stirs slightly as if to silence her.

"Richard put them to death," she repeats, as if repetition will make it so.

I ignore her, and go on. "We swore that whoever had taken them and put them to death would himself see his own son die in childhood. And his grandson would die young also. And his line would end with a girl and she would have no heir."

"Richard's son died, as soon as they named him Prince of Wales," My Lady reminds her silent son. "It is proof of his guilt."

He turns and glances at her. "You knew of this curse?"

She blinks like an old reptile, and I know that John Morton reported my words to My Lady as promptly as he prayed to God.

"You did not think you should warn me?" Henry asks.

"Why should anyone warn you?" she asks, knowing that neither of them can answer such a question. "We had nothing to do with their deaths. Richard killed the boys in the Tower," she asserts steadily. "Or it was Henry Stafford, the Duke of Buckingham. Richard's line is ended, the young Duke of Buckingham is not strong. If this curse has any power it will fall on him."

Henry returns his hard gaze to me. "So what is your warning?" he asks me. "What is our danger? What can it possibly be to do with us?"

I slide off my chair and I kneel before him as if he might judge me too. "This boy," I say, "the one who claims to be Prince Richard of York . . . If we put him to death, that curse might fall on us."

"Only if he is the prince," Henry says acutely. "Are you recognizing him? Do you dare to come here and tell me that you recognize him now? After all that we have been through? After claiming to know nothing all the time?"

I shake my head and bow lower. "I don't recognize him, and I never have. But I want us to take care. I want us to take care for our children. Husband, my lord, we might lose our son in his youth. We might lose a grandson in his youth. Our line might end with a girl and then with nothing. Everything that you have done, everything that we have endured might end with a Virgin Queen, a barren girl, and then . . . nothing."

Henry does not sleep that night at all, not in my bed nor in his own. He goes to the chapel and he kneels beside his mother on the chancel steps, and the two of them pray, their faces buried in their hands — but nobody knows what they pray for. That is between them and God.

I know they are there, for I am in the royal gallery in the chapel, on my knees, Lady Katherine beside me. Both of us are praying that the king will be merciful, that he will forgive the boy and release him and Teddy, that this reign which began in blood with the sweat might continue with forgiveness. That the long Cousins' War might end with reconciliation, and not continue to another generation. That the Tudor way might be merciful and the Tudor line not die out in three generations.

As if he fears losing his nerve, Henry will not wait for the jury to take their places in the capital's Guildhall. Impulsively, he summons his Knight Marshall and the Marshall of the

Household to Whitehall in Westminster to give sentence. There is no evidence brought against the boy; oddly, they don't even call him into court by name. Though Henry worked so hard to give the boy the dishonorable name of a poor drunk man on the watergate in Tournai, they do not use it on this one important document. Though they find him guilty, they do not inscribe the name of Perkin Warbeck on the long roll of the treasonous plotters. They leave his name a blank. Now, as they sentence him to death, they give him no name at all, as if nobody knows who he is anymore, or as if they know his name but dare not say it.

They rule that he shall be drawn *on a hurdle through the city of London to the gallows at Tyburn, hanged, cut down while still living, and his innards torn out of his stomach and burned before his face. Then he shall be beheaded and his body divided into four parts, the head and quarters to be placed where the king wishes to put them.*

Three days later they try my cousin Teddy before the Earl of Oxford in the great hall at Westminster. They ask him nothing, he confesses to everything that they put to him, and they find him guilty. He says that he is very sorry.

WESTMINSTER PALACE, LONDON, SATURDAY, 23 NOVEMBER 1499

Lady Katherine comes to my bedroom like a woman heading for refuge. I hear her quick tread approach the outer door, and the slap of her leather slippers running rapidly through my privy chamber, where the conversation of my ladies-in-waiting is suspended as she goes by, then she taps on my door and my maid opens it a crack.

"You can come in," I say shortly. I am alone, seated on a chair at the window, looking outwards to the river that my mother loved, listening to the low buzz of talk from my rooms behind me, and the distant cry of the seagulls over the water as they swoop and wheel, their white wings very bright against the gray of the sky.

She looks around the empty room for a companion and sees that I am solitary, though a queen is never on her own.

"Can I sit with you?" she asks, her pale face like a desolate child's. "Forgive me, I cannot bear to be alone."

She is wearing black again, anticipating widowhood. I feel a swift unfair pang of envy; she can show her grief, but I, about to lose a cousin and the boy who said he was my brother, have to maintain the illusion of normality in a Tudor-green dress with a smiling face. I cannot recognize the boy in death any more than I could in life.

"Come in," I say.

She enters and pulls up a stool to sit beside me. She has her lace making with her, his beautiful white collar is almost complete, but for once her hands are still. The collar is nearly made but the throat that it was going to encircle will wear a rope halter instead. She looks from her work to me and she sighs, and leaves it aside.

"Lady Margaret Pole has arrived," she remarks.

"Maggie?"

She nods. "She went straight to the king to ask for mercy for her brother."

I don't ask her what the king said. We wait until I hear the challenge at the presence chamber door, the opening of the inner doors, the embarrassed silence that falls as Margaret crosses my privy chamber and the women watch her pass by to my bedroom door. No one can find anything to say to a woman whose brother is to be executed for treason. Then she taps on the door, and I rise up and in a moment we are holding each other, clinging together and looking into the other's strained face.

"His Grace says there is nothing he can do," Margaret remarks. "I went down on my knees to him. I laid my face on his shoe."

I put my wet cheek against hers. "I asked him too, Lady Katherine as well. He is decided. I don't see what we can do but wait."

Margaret releases me and sinks to a stool beside me. Nobody says anything, there is nothing to say. The three of us, still hoping like fools, clasp hands and say nothing.

It grows dark, but I don't call for candles; we let the gray light seep into the room and we sit in the twilight. Then I hear a knock on the outer door, and the ring of riding boots on the floor, and one of my ladies peeps around the bedroom door to say: "Will you see the Marquis of Dorset, Your Grace?"

I rise to my feet as my half brother, Thomas Grey, great survivor that he is, comes into the room and looks around at the three of us. "I thought you would want to know at once," he says without introduction.

"We do," I say.

"He's dead," he says, before we have time to build any false hopes. "He died well. He confessed and died in Christ."

Lady Katherine makes a little choking noise and puts her face in her hands. Margaret crosses herself.

"Did he confess the imposture?" I ask.

"He said that he was not the boy that he had pretended to be," Thomas says. "He had been commanded, if he wanted a merciful death, to tell the crowd, to tell everyone that there was no hope of a living York prince. So he told them that: he was not the boy."

I can feel a little scream of laughter growing inside me, bubbling in my throat. "He told them he was not the boy that he had pretended to be?"

Thomas looks at me. "Your Grace, he swore he would leave no one in any doubt. The king allowed him to be hanged and not gutted, but only if he made everything clear."

I can't help myself, my peal of laughter fights its way out of my grim lips and I laugh aloud. Katherine looks shocked. "He admitted he was not the boy that he had said? When earlier, at Exeter, in his written confession, they made him say that he was the boy Perkin!"

"It was clear to everyone what he meant, if you had been there —" my half brother checks for we all know I could not have been there "— but if you *had* been there you would have seen him penitent."

"And what name did they call him?" I ask, recovering myself. "As they led him to the scaffold?"

Thomas shakes his head. "They didn't name him, not that I heard."

"He died without being given or acknowledging a name?"

Thomas nods. "That's how it was."

I rise to my feet and open the shutters to look out over the dark river. A few lights are bobbing, reflected on the water, as I listen to hear any noise, any singing. It is the feast of St. Clement, and I can hear a choir, very faintly in the distance, a sweet sad singing like a lament.

"Was he in pain?" Lady Katherine rises to her feet, white-faced. "Did he suffer?"

Thomas faces her. "He went up to the scaffold with courage," he said. "His hands were tied behind his back and they helped him gently up the ladder. There were hundreds there, thousands, pushing to see, they had built the scaffold very high so that everyone could see him. But there was no one catcalling or shouting. It was as if they were sorry. Or curious. Some people were crying. It wasn't like a traitor's execution at all."

She nods rapidly, swallowing tears.

"He spoke very briefly, saying he was not who he had pretended to be, then he went up the ladder and they put the noose around his neck. He looked around for a moment, just for a moment, as if he thought something might happen . . ."

"Was he hoping for a pardon?" she breathes, her face agonized. "I could not get him a pardon. Did he think he might be pardoned?"

"Perhaps a miracle," Thomas suggests. "He

looked around and then he bent his head and prayed and they took the ladder out from under his feet and he dropped."

"Was it quick?" Margaret whispers.

"It took an hour, or perhaps more," Thomas said. "No one was allowed close to him, so nobody could drag hold of his feet and break his neck to make it quicker. But he hung quietly enough, and then he was gone. He died like a brave man, and the people at the front of the scaffold were praying for him, all the time."

Lady Katherine drops to her knees and bows her head in prayer, Margaret closes her eyes. Thomas looks from one to another of us, three grieving women.

"So it's over," I say. "This whole long joust of fear and playacting and deception and deceit is over."

"Except for Teddy," Margaret says.

Margaret and I go together to the king to try to save Teddy but he will not see us. Margaret's husband, Sir Richard, comes to me in my rooms and begs me not to intercede for his wife's only brother. "Better for us all if he is put to the death than returned to that prison," he says bluntly. "Better for us all if the king does not think of Margaret as a woman of the House of York. Better for us all if the young man dies now, without a rebellion forming around him again. Please, Your

Grace, teach Margaret to see this with patience. Please, teach her to let her brother go. It's been no life for him, not since he was a little boy. Let it end here, and then perhaps people will forget that my son is of the House of York and he, at least, will be safe."

I hesitate.

"The king is hunting Edmund de la Pole," he says. "The king wants all of the House of York sworn to his service or dead. Please, Your Grace, tell Margaret to give up her brother that she may keep her son."

"Like me?" I whisper, too low for him to hear.

WESTMINSTER PALACE, LONDON, 28 NOVEMBER 1499

On the day of Teddy's execution there is a great storm which thunders over the palace, and the fury of lightning makes us close the shutters and gather around the fires. It pours down on Tower Green, making the grass wet and treacherous in the afternoon as Teddy walks unsteadily along the path to the scaffold of wood, where the black-masked headsman waits with his axe. There is a priest with him, and witnesses before the scaffold, but Teddy sees no friendly face though he looks around for someone to wave at. He was always taught to smile and wave when he saw a crowd, he remembers that one of the House of York must always smile and acknowledge their friends.

There is a clap of lightning that makes him stop in his tracks like a nervous colt. He has never been out in a storm. For thirteen years, he has not felt rain on his face.

My half brother Thomas Grey tells me that he thinks that Teddy did not know what was going to happen to him. He confesses his little sins and gives a penny to the headsman when they tell him to do so. He was always obedient, always trying to please. He puts his fair York head down on the block and he stretches out his arms in the gesture of assent. But I don't think he ever knew that he was agreeing to the scything down of the axe and the end of his little life.

Henry will not dine in the great hall of Westminster that night, his mother is at prayer. In their absence, I have to walk in alone, at the head of my ladies, Katherine behind me in deepest black, Margaret wearing a gown of dark blue. The hall is hushed, the people of our own household quiet and surly, as if some joy has been taken from us, and we will never get it back.

There is something different about the hall as I walk through the silent court and when I am seated, and can look around, I see what has changed. It is how they have seated themselves. Every night the men and women of our extensive household come in to dine and sit in order of precedence and importance, men on one side, women on the other of the great hall. Each table seats about twelve diners and they share the common dishes that are placed in the center of the table. But tonight it is different; some tables are overcrowded, some have empty places. I see that they have grouped themselves regardless of tradition or precedent.

Those who befriended the boy, those who were of the House of York, those who served my mother and father or whose fathers served my mother and father, those who love me, those who love my cousin Margaret and remember her brother Teddy — they have chosen to sit together; and there are many, many tables in the great hall where they are seated in utter silence, as if they have sworn a vow never to speak again, and they look around them saying nothing.

The other tables are those that have taken Henry's side. Many of them are old Lancastrian families, some of them were in his mother's household or serve her wider family, some came over with him to fight at Bosworth, some, like my half brother Thomas Grey or my brother-in-law Thomas Howard, spend every day of their lives trying to show their loyalty to the new Tudor house. They are trying to appear as usual, leaning across the half-empty tables, talking unnaturally loudly, finding things to say.

Almost without trying to, the court has sorted itself into those who are in mourning tonight, wearing gray or black or navy ribbons pinned to their jerkins or carrying dark gloves, and those who are trying, loudly and cheerfully, to behave as if nothing has happened.

Henry would be horrified if he saw the numbers that are openly mourning for the House of York. But Henry will not see it. Only I know that he is facedown on his bed, his cape hunched over his shoulders, unable to walk to dinner, unable to eat, barely able to breathe in a spasm of guilt and horror at what he has done, which can never be undone.

Outside the storm is still rumbling, the skies are billowing with dark clouds and there is no moon at all. The court is uneasy too; there is no sense of victory, and no sense of closing a chapter. The death of the two young men was supposed to bring a sense of peace. Instead we are all haunted by the sense that we have done something very wrong.

I look across at the table where Henry's young companions always sit, expecting them at least to be cracking a jest or playing some foolish prank on each other, but they are waiting for dinner to be served in silence, their heads bowed, and when it comes they eat in silence, as if there is nothing to laugh about at the Tudor court anymore.

Then I see something that makes me glance across to the groom of the servery, wondering that he should allow it — certain that he will report it. At the head of the table of the young men, where the boy used to sit, they have put his cup, his knife, his spoon. They have set a plate for him, they have poured wine as if he were coming to dine. In their

own way, defiantly, the young men are showing their loyalty to a ghost, a dream; express-
ing their love for a prince who — if he was
ever there at all — is gone now.

WESTMINSTER PALACE, LONDON, WINTER 1499

Henry is ill, desperately ill. He falls into illness as if he cannot face the brightness of the world after the storm. He keeps to his chamber and only his most trusted servants are allowed in and out and they will not tell anyone what is the matter with him. People whisper that he has taken the sweat, that the illness he brought to England has finally caught up with him. Other people say that he has a growth in his belly and point to the plates that return untouched from his room. He cannot eat, he is as sick as a dog, the cooks say. His mother visits him every day, sitting with him for a couple of hours in the evening. She has her physicians attend him, and once I see an alchemist and an astrologer going quietly up the private staircase to his rooms. Secretly, for it is against the law to consult astrologers or any sort of fortune-tellers, he has his stars drawn up; and they tell him that he will grow stronger, and he was right to kill an enemy, a weak defenseless enemy. His strength depended on the destruction of a youth in his keeping, it is quite all right to destroy the weak. It is quite all right to destroy a dependent helpless prisoner.

But still the king gets no better, and his mother spends all her time in the chapel praying for him, or in his room begging him to sit up, turn his face from the wall, drink a little wine, taste a little meat, eat. The Master of the Revels comes to me to make plans for the Christmas feasts, the dancers must rehearse and the choristers practice new music, but I don't know if we are going to have a silent court in mourning with an empty throne, and I tell him we can plan nothing until the king is well again.

The other men charged with treason in the last plot for the York prince are all hanged or fined or banished. Occasional pardons are issued in the king's name, with his initial weakly scrawled at the foot of the page. Nobody knows if he has locked himself up, sick with remorse, or if he is just too tired to go on fighting. The plot is over, but still the king does not come out of his chamber; he reads nothing and will see no one. The court and the kingdom wait for him to return.

I go to visit My Lady the King's Mother and find her with all the business of the throne on the table before her, as if she were regent. "I have come to ask you if the king is very ill," I say. "There is much gossip, and I am concerned. He will not see me."

She looks at me and I see that the papers are shuffled into piles, but she is not reading them, she is signing nothing. She is at a loss. "It's grief," she says simply. "It is grief. He is sick with grief."

I rest my hand on my heart and feel it thud with anger. "Why? Why should he grieve? What has he lost?" I ask, thinking of Margaret and her brother, Lady Katherine and her husband, of my sisters and myself, who go through our days and show the world nothing but indifference.

She shakes her head as if she cannot understand it herself. "He says he has lost his innocence."

"Henry, innocent?" I exclaim. "He entered his throne through the death of a king! He came into the kingdom as a pretender to the throne!"

"Don't you dare say it!" She rounds on me. "Don't you say such a thing! You of all people!"

"But I don't understand what you mean," I explain. "I don't understand what he is saying. He has lost his innocence? When was he innocent?"

"He was a young man, he spent his life aspiring to the throne," she says, as if the words are forced from her, as if it is a hard confession, choked out of her. "I raised him to be like this, I taught him myself that he must be King of England, that there was nothing else for him but the crown. It was my doing. I said that he should think of nothing but returning to England and claiming his own and holding it."

I wait.

"I told him it was God's will."

I nod.

"And now he has won it," she says. "He is where he was born to be. But to hold it, to be sure of it, he has had to kill a young man, a young man just like him, a boy who aspired to the throne, who was also raised to believe it was his by right. He feels as if he has killed himself. He has killed the boy that he was."

"The boy that he was," I repeat slowly. She is showing me a boy I had not seen before. The boy who was named for the Tournai boatman was also the boy who said he was a prince, but to Henry he was a fellow-pretender, someone raised and trained for only one destiny.

"That was why he liked the boy so much. He wanted to spare him, he was glad to bind himself to forgive him. He hoped to make him look like a nothing, keeping him at court like a Fool, paying for his clothes from the same purse as he paid for his Fool and his other entertainments. That was part of his plan. But then he found that he liked him so much. Then he found that they were both boys, raised abroad, always thinking of England, always taught of England, always told that the time would come when they must sail for home and enter into their kingdom. He once said to me that nobody could understand the boy but him — and that nobody could understand him but the boy."

"Then why kill him?" I burst out. "Why would he put him to death? If the boy was him, a looking-glass king?"

She looks as if she is in pain. "For safety," she said. "While the boy lived they would always be compared, there would always be a looking-glass king, and everyone would always look from one to the other."

She says nothing for a moment and I think of how Henry always knew that he did not seem like a king, not a king like my father, and how the boy that Henry called Perkin always looked like a prince.

"And besides, he could not be safe until the boy was dead," she says. "Even though he tried to keep him close. Even when the boy was in the Tower, enmeshed in lies, entrapped with his own words, there were people all over the country pledging themselves to save him. We hold England now; but Henry feels that we will never keep it. The boy is not like Henry. He had that gift — the gift of being beloved."

"And now you will never be safe." I repeat her words to her and I know that my revenge on them is here, in what I am saying to the woman who has taken my place in the queen's rooms, behind this table, just as her son took the place of my brother. "You don't have England," I tell her. "You don't have England, and you will never be safe, and you will never be beloved."

She bows her head as if it is a life sentence, as if she deserves it.

"I shall see him," I say, going to the door that adjoins his set of rooms, the queen's doorway.

"You can't go in." She steps forwards. "He's too ill to see you."

I walk towards her as if I would stride right through her. "I am his wife," I say levelly. "I am Queen of England. I will see my husband. And you shall not stop me."

For a moment I think I will have to physically push her aside, but at the last moment she sees the determination in my face and she falls back and lets me open the door and go in.

He is not in the antechamber, but the door to his bedroom is open and I tap on it lightly, and step into his room. He is at the window, the shutters open so that he can see the night sky, looking out, though there is nothing but darkness outside and the glimmering of a scatter of stars like spilled sequins across the sky. He glances round as he sees me come in, but he does not speak. Almost I can feel the ache in his heart, his loneliness, his terrible despair.

"You've got to come back to court," I say flatly. "People will talk. You cannot stay hiding in here."

"You call it hiding?" he challenges.

"I do," I say without hesitation.

"They are missing me so much?" he asks scathingly. "They love me so much? They long to see me?"

"They expect to see you," I say. "You are the King of England, you have to be seen on your throne. I cannot carry the burden of the Tudor crown alone."

"I didn't think it would be so hard," he says, almost an aside.

"No," I agree. "I didn't think it would be so hard either."

He rests his head against the stone window arch. "I thought once the battle was won, it would be easy. I thought I would have found my heart's desire. But — d'you know? — it is worse being a king than being a pretender."

He turns and looks at me for the first time in weeks. "Do you think I have done wrong?" he asks. "Was it a sin to kill the two of them?"

"Yes," I say simply. "And I am afraid that we will have to pay the price."

"You think we will see our son die, that our grandson will die and our line end with a Virgin Queen?" he asks bitterly. "Well, I have had a prophecy drawn up, and by a more skilled astrologist than you and your witch mother. They say that we will live long and in triumph. They all tell me that."

"Of course they do," I say honestly. "And I don't pretend to foresee the future. But I do know that there is always a price to be paid."

"I don't think our line will die out," he says, trying to smile. "We have three sons. Three healthy princes: Arthur, Henry, and Edmund. I hear nothing but good of Arthur, Henry is bright and handsome and strong, and Edmund is well and thriving, thank God."

"My mother had three princes," I reply. "And she died without an heir."

He crosses himself. "Dear God, Elizabeth, don't say such a thing. How can you say such things?"

"Someone killed my brothers," I say. "They both died without saying good-bye to their mother."

"They didn't die at my hand!" he shouts. "I was in exile, miles away. I didn't order their deaths! You can't blame me!"

"You benefit from their deaths." I pursue the argument. "You are their heir. And anyway, you killed Teddy, my cousin. Not even your mother can deny that. An innocent boy. And you killed the boy, the charming boy, for being nothing but beloved."

He puts one hand over his face and blindly stretches his other hand out to me. "I did, I did, God forgive me. But I didn't know what else to do. I swear there was nothing else I could do."

His hand finds mine and he grips it tightly, as if I might haul him out from sorrow. "Do you forgive me? Even if no one else ever does. Can you forgive me? Elizabeth? Elizabeth of York — can you forgive me?"

I let him draw me to his side. He turns his head towards me and I feel that his cheeks are wet with tears. He wraps his arms around me and he holds me tightly. "I had to do it," he says into my hair. "You know that we would never have been safe while he was alive. You know that people would have flocked to him even though he was in prison. They loved him as if he was a prince. He had all that charm, all that irresistible York charm. I had to kill him. I had to."

He is holding me as if I can save him from drowning. I can hardly speak for the pain I feel but I say: "I forgive you. I forgive you, Henry."

He gives a hoarse sob and he puts his anguished face against my neck. I feel him tremble as he clings to me. Over his bent head I look at the stained-glass windows of his room, dark against the dark sky, and the Tudor rose, white with a red core, that his mother has inset into every window of his room. Tonight it does not look to me as if the white rose and the red are blooming together as one, tonight it looks as if the white rose of

York has been stabbed in its pure white heart and is bleeding scarlet red.

Tonight, I know that I do indeed have much to forgive.

AUTHOR'S NOTE

This book is written on a number of levels. It is a fiction about a mystery — so two steps from any historically recorded fact; but at the heart of it are some historical facts that you can rely on, or study for yourself. The death of the princes, traditionally blamed on Richard III, was not, I believe, his act, and the suggestion that one prince actually survived has been made by several historians whose books are listed below. I am inclined to believe the version I tell here. However, nobody knows for sure, not even now.

The support that the dowager queen Elizabeth gave to the Simnel rebellion suggests to me that she was fighting Henry VII (and her own daughter) for a preferred candidate. I cannot think she would have risked her daughter's place on the throne for anyone but her son. She died before the young man who claimed to be Richard landed in England, but it seems that her mother-in-law, Duchess Cecily, supported the pretender. Sir

William Stanley's support (for the pretender against his brother's stepson) is also recorded. Stanley went to his death without apologizing for taking the side of the pretender; this suggests to me that he thought that the pretender might win, and that his claim was good.

The treatment of the young man who was eventually so uncertainly named as Perkin Warbeck is also very odd. I suggest that Henry VII plotted to get "the boy" out of his court by setting a fire in the royal wardrobe which blazed out of control and destroyed the Palace of Sheen, subsequently engineered his escape, and then finally entrapped him in a treasonous conspiracy with the Earl of Warwick.

Most historians would agree that the conspiracy with Warwick was allowed if not sponsored by Henry VII to remove the two threats to his throne, and their deaths were indeed requested by the Spanish king and queen before they would allow the marriage of the infanta and Prince Arthur.

It is possible that we will never know the identity of the young man who claimed to be Prince Richard and confessed to being "Perkin Warbeck." What we can be sure of is that the Tudor version of events is not the truth. Anne Wroe's meticulous research shows the construction of the lie.

This book does not claim to reveal the truth

either: it is a fiction based on many studies of these fascinating times and gives, I hope, an insight into the untold stories and the unknown characters with affection and respect.

BIBLIOGRAPHY

Amt, Emilie. *Women's Lives in Medieval Europe*. New York: Routledge, 1993.

Alexander, Michael Van Cleave. *The First of the Tudors: A Study of Henry VII and His Reign*. London: Croom Helm, 1981. First published 1937.

Arthurson, Ian. *The Perkin Warbeck Conspiracy, 1491–1499*. Stroud: Sutton Publishing, 1997.

Bacon, Francis. *The History of the Reign of King Henry VII and Selected Works*. Edited by Brian Vickers. Cambridge: Cambridge University Press, 1998.

Baldwin, David. *Elizabeth Woodville: Mother of the Princes in the Tower*. Stroud: Sutton Publishing, 2002.

————. *The Kingmaker's Sisters*. Stroud: History Press, 2009.

————. *The Lost Prince: The Survival of Richard of York*. Stroud: Sutton Publishing, 2007.

Barnhouse, Rebecca. *The Book of the Knight of the Tower: Manners for Young Medieval Women.* Basingstoke: Palgrave Macmillan, 2006.

Bramley, Peter. *The Wars of the Roses: A Field Guide and Companion.* Stroud: Sutton Publishing, 2007.

Castor, Helen. *Blood and Roses: The Paston Family and the Wars of the Roses.* London: Faber & Faber, 2004.

Cheetham, Anthony. *The Life and Times of Richard III.* London: Weidenfeld & Nicolson, 1972.

Chrimes, S. B. *Henry VII.* London: Eyre Methuen, 1972.

———. *Lancastrians, Yorkists, and Henry VII.* London: Macmillan, 1964.

Cooper, Charles Henry. *Memoir of Margaret: Countess of Richmond and Derby.* Cambridge: Cambridge University Press, 1874.

Cunningham, Sean. *Henry VII.* London: Routledge, 2007. First published 1967.

Duggan, Anne J. *Queens and Queenship in Medieval Europe.* Woodbridge: Boydell Press, 1997.

Fellows, Nicholas. *Disorder and Rebellion in Tudor England.* Bath: Hodder & Stoughton Educational, 2001.

Fields, Bertram. *Royal Blood: King Richard III and the Mystery of the Princes.* New York: Regan Books, 1998.

Fletcher, A., and D. MacCulloch. *Tudor Rebellions.* Revised 5th ed. Harlow: Pearson Education, 2004.

Gairdner, James. "Did Henry VII Murder the Princes?" *English Historical Review,* VI (1891).

Goodman, Anthony. *The Wars of the Roses: Military Activity and English Society, 1452–97.* London: Routledge & Kegan Paul, 1981.

———. *The Wars of the Roses: The Soldiers' Experience.* Stroud: Tempus, 2006.

Gregory, Phillipa, David Baldwin, and Michael Jones. *The Women of the Cousins' War: The Duchess, the Queen and the King's Mother.* London: Simon & Schuster, 2011.

Gristwood, Sarah. *Blood Sisters: The Hidden Lives of the Women Behind the Wars of the Roses.* London: HarperCollins, 2012.

Halsted, Caroline A. *Richard III as Duke of Gloucester and King of England.* Vol 2. London: Elibron Classics, 2006. First published 1844 by Longman, Brown & Green.

Hammond, P. W., and Anne F. Sutton. *Richard III: The Road to Bosworth Field.* London: Constable, 1985.

Harvey, N. L. *Elizabeth of York: Tudor Queen.* London: Arthur Baker, 1973.

Hicks, Michael. *Anne Neville: Queen to Richard III.* Stroud: Tempus, 2007.

———. *False, Fleeting, Perjur'd Clarence:*

George, Duke of Clarence, 1449–78. Stroud: Sutton Publishing, 1980.

————. *The Prince in the Tower: The Short Life and Mysterious Disappearance of Edward V.* Stroud: Tempus, 2007.

————. *Richard III.* Stroud: Tempus, 2003.

————. *Warwick the Kingmaker.* London: Blackwell Publishing, 1998.

Hipshon, David. *Richard III and the Death of Chivalry.* Stroud: History Press, 2009.

Howard, Maurice. *The Tudor Image.* London: Tate Gallery Publishing, 1995.

Hughes, Jonathan. *Arthurian Myths and Alchemy: The Kingship of Edward IV.* Stroud: Sutton Publishing, 2002.

Hutchinson, Robert. *House of Treason: The Rise and Fall of a Tudor Dynasty.* London: Weidenfeld & Nicolson, 2009.

Jones, Michael K. *Bosworth 1485: Psychology of a Battle.* Stroud: History Press, 2002.

Jones, Michael K., and Malcolm G. Underwood. *The King's Mother: Lady Margaret Beaufort, Countess of Richmond and Derby.* Cambridge: Cambridge University Press, 1992.

Karras, Ruth Mazo. *Sexuality in Medieval Europe: Doing unto Others.* New York: Routledge, 2005.

Kendall, Paul Murray. *Richard the Third.* New York: Norton, 1955.

Laynesmith, J. L. *The Last Medieval Queens:*

English Queenship 1445–1503. New York: Oxford University Press, 2004.

Lewis, Katherine J., Noel James Menuge, and Kim M. Phillips, eds. *Young Medieval Women*. Basingstoke: Palgrave Macmillan, 1999.

MacGibbon, David. *Elizabeth Woodville, 1437–1492: Her Life and Times*. London: Arthur Barker, 1938.

Mancini, D., and A. Cato. *The Usurpation of Richard the Third (Dominicus Mancinus ad Angelum Catonem de Occupatione Regni Anglie per Ricardum Tercium Libellus)*. Translated by C. A. J. Armstrong. Oxford: Clarendon Press, 1969.

Markham, Clements R. "Richard III: A Doubtful Verdict Reviewed." *English Historical Review*, VI (1891).

Mortimer, Ian. *The Time Traveller's Guide to Medieval England*. London: Vintage, 2009.

Neillands, Robin. *The Wars of the Roses*. London: Cassell, 1992.

Penn, Thomas. *The Winter King*. London: Allen Lane, 2011.

Phillips, Kim M. *Medieval Maidens: Young Women and Gender in England, 1270–1540*. Manchester: Manchester University Press, 2003.

Pierce, Hazel. *Margaret Pole, Countess of Salisbury, 1473–1541: Loyalty, Lineage and Leadership*. Cardiff: University of Wales

Press, 2009.

Plowden, Alison. *The House of Tudor.* New York: Weidenfeld & Nicolson, 1976.

Pollard, A. J. *Richard III and the Princes in the Tower.* Stroud: Sutton Publishing, 2002.

Prestwich, Michael. *Plantagenet England, 1225–1360.* Oxford: Clarendon Press, 2005.

Read, Conyers. *The Tudors: Personalities and Practical Politics in Sixteenth Century England.* Oxford: Oxford University Press, 1936.

Ross, Charles Derek. *Edward IV.* London: Eyre Methuen, 1974.

———. *Richard III.* London: Eyre Methuen, 1981.

Royle, Trevor. *The Road to Bosworth Field: A New History of the Wars of the Roses.* London: Little, Brown, 2009.

Rubin, Miri. *The Hollow Crown: A History of Britain in the Late Middle Ages.* London: Allen Lane, 2005.

St. Aubyn, Giles. *The Year of Three Kings: 1483.* London: Collins, 1983.

Seward, Desmond. *The Last White Rose.* London: Constable, 2010.

———. *Richard III: England's Black Legend.* London: Country Life Books, 1983.

Sharpe, Kevin. *Selling the Tudor Monarchy: Authority and Image in Sixteenth Century England.* New Haven: Yale University Press, 2009.

Simon, Linda. *Of Virtue Rare: Margaret Beaufort: Matriarch of the House of Tudor.* Boston: Houghton Mifflin Company, 1982.

Simons, Eric N. *Henry VII: The First Tudor King.* New York: Muller, 1968.

Storey, R. L. *The End of the House of Lancaster.* Stroud: Sutton Publishing, 1999.

Vergil, Polydore, and Henry Ellis. *Three Books of Polydore Vergil's English History: Comprising the Reigns of Henry VI, Edward IV and Richard III.* Reprint, Whitefish, MT: Kessinger Publishing, 1971.

Ward, Jennifer. *Women in Medieval Europe, 1200–1500.* Essex: Pearson Education, 2002.

Weightman, Christine. *Margaret of York: The Diabolical Duchess.* Stroud: Amberley, 2009.

Weir, Alison. *Lancaster and York: The Wars of the Roses.* London: Cape, 1995.

———. *The Princes in the Tower.* London: Bodley Head, 1992.

Williams, C. H. "The Rebellion of Humphrey Stafford in 1486." *The English Historical Review* 43:170 (April 1928): 181–89.

Williams, Neville, and Antonia Fraser. *The Life and Times of Henry VII.* London: Weidenfeld & Nicolson, 1973.

Willamson, Audrey. *The Mystery of the Princes.* Stroud: Sutton Publishing, 1978.

Wilson, Derek. *The Plantagenets: The Kings*

That Made Britain. London: Quercus, 2011.
Wroe, Ann. *Perkin: A Story of Deception.* London: Cape, 2003.

GARDENS FOR THE GAMBIA

Philippa Gregory visited The Gambia, one of the driest and poorest countries of sub-Saharan Africa, in 1993 and paid for a well to be hand-dug in a village primary school at Sika. Now, nearly 200 wells later, she continues to raise money and commission wells in village schools, community gardens, and in The Gambia's only agricultural college. She works with her representative in The Gambia, headmaster Ismaila Sisay, and their charity now funds pottery and batik classes, beekeeping, and adult literacy programs. A recent deep well paid for by the Rotary Club of Temecula provides clean water to a clinic.

Gardens for The Gambia is a registered charity in the UK and the United States and a registered NGO in The Gambia. Every donation, however small, goes to The Gambia without any deductions. If you would like to learn more about the work that Philippa calls "the best thing that I do," visit her website, PhilippaGregory.com, and click ON

GARDENS FOR THE GAMBIA, where you can make a donation and join with Philippa in this project.

"Every well we dig provides drinking water for a school of about 600 children and waters the gardens where they grow vegetables for the school dinners. I don't know of a more direct way to feed hungry children and teach them to farm for their future."

Philippa Gregory

ABOUT THE AUTHOR

Philippa Gregory is the author of several bestselling novels, including *The Other Boleyn Girl*. She studied history at the University of Sussex and received a Ph.D. from the University of Edinburgh. Visit her website at PhilippaGregory.com.